US DARK FEW

US DARK FEW

ALEXIS PATTON

DEDICATION

To all the dreamers and misfits.
And those who prefer dancing in the dark.

Us Dark Few is set in a post-apocalyptic world and takes place in a dangerous underground prison. Elements that might be sensitive for readers are depictions of violence, suicidal ideations, graphic language, mass murder, attempted sexual assault, and sexual activities. Please protect your mental health, and if you are ready, prepare to enter the thrilling world of Us Dark Few.

1

Whoever first said, 'there is nowhere to go but up,' lied. Things can always get worse. Always. You can plummet further between those cracks and crevices because no true rock-bottom exists to halt the descent of misfortune.

Khalani Kanes knew that lesson better than most.

Heavy shackles chafed against her wrists and ankles. Every movement invited a stinging pain where cold metal met skin, but it was the towering mantel in the center of the room that drew her attention.

JUSTICE PREVAILS

The Apollo Creed, carved deep into the stone dais, stared back, mocking her with its falsehoods. Justice didn't exist in the surreal hellscape of Apollo. Not for those who needed it most. Its definition had been warped into a weapon long before Khalani was born.

A colossal guard with deep scars carved into his mangled face yanked her to a rough halt in the Sentencing Hall. Torches formed a broad circle along the walls. The flickering shadows against the rocks made the space more ominous and disturbing, which was probably the point.

Dread manifested inside her, so profound that it nearly took a physical presence. She could smell the bitter fragrance, taste it against her dry lips. Her lungs expanded to grasp more oxygen, but even the air was tainted, a thick layer of regret composed of the sins and screams of those who died where her trembling feet held anchored to the ground.

Tap. Tap. Tap. Tap.

The echo of polished shoes drew her gaze.

An overweight man adorned in a black robe approached the stone mantel. His bald head managed to reflect light, even in the dim cavern. The guards stiffened and stood straighter at his presence.

The Master Judge was here.

He assessed the room with a demented scowl, and his gaze descended on her. Khalani's body shrunk, trying to make herself as small a target as possible. Her limbs would've been chopped to pieces and stuffed in a steel blender if looks could kill.

The Master Judge patiently sat, perched high above her. "Do you know what this is, Miss Kanes?" A permanent X was embedded in the pale skin between his brows as the Master Judge held a familiar, black book.

Khalani rubbed her fingers together as the handcuffs shifted against her wrists. Words failed to escape. As if her tongue had already been twisted and cleaved out.

"This is betrayal," the Master Judge continued. "Betrayal of the highest regard against Apollo. Who did you share this information with?"

Her gaze lifted in disbelief. They didn't know...

The feeble muscles in her back shook and bowed at the weight of her choice. But there wasn't a choice.

Khalani already knew what she had to do.

"No one." She swallowed tightly.

"Do you know what Apollo used to do with liars, Miss Kanes?"

Her body visibly trembled, heart jackhammering against her chest, and he smirked.

"We'd leave them on the surface," the Master Judge whispered in a disturbing tone, leaning forward. "Their bodies burned from the immense radiation as they banged on the doors, begging to be let in as they gradually melted away. You have no family to speak of. There's no one alive that loves you. No one would think twice if we left you outside Genesis to burn and rot. So, I will ask one more time. Did you tell anyone about this book?"

There's no one alive that loves you.

The words reverberated off the stone walls and sank into Khalani like jagged, cruel knives. Her hands balled into fists, but nothing would claw back the raw truth of his statement.

She used to believe that love was like the sun. Unseen in the underground. Unwavering. A bright spot within a bleak universe. But love wasn't like the sun.

Love was like gravity. Pulling and tugging you down to the deepest depths, exposing your core vulnerabilities, ripping barriers apart, and leaving you with nothing but space.

Love was what made her open the door that fateful night.

One month ago, when Douglas rushed into her house past curfew as if a pack of rabid rats were chasing him, she didn't turn him away like any sane person would've. When his hands shook as he revealed the black, tattered book that appeared centuries older than her, she didn't leave.

When he opened his mouth and said, "I need you to keep this for a few days," her answer should've been a resounding, "No." But she ignored the obvious red flags and insisted they were a deep shade of orange.

Douglas was her only friend in Apollo, and it didn't matter that he was 69 years old and smelled of old books and watered-down whiskey.

Friendships don't have to make sense to those outside it.

She first noticed him eyeing her peculiarly as she ate on the ground outside her apartment. For a whole year, he walked by, silently studying her while she sat on the dirt. Then, one day, he suddenly spoke.

"Is the road comfier than a chair?" He paused mid-step.

She glanced up, surprised that the old man was talking to her. She even looked over her shoulder as if some other weirdo was eating dried cereal on the cobblestone.

"Probably not." She turned back around. "But my ass likes being closer to the ground. Reminds me where I'm going someday."

"That's morbid."

"No, just changes your perspective. The place you eat should be a comfort zone, so I've decided that eating on the ground might make me comfortable with the shitty parts of life. Should try it someday," she replied, returning to her meal.

A longer pause and Khalani thought he'd left the strange girl eating on the road alone, but her eyebrows rose when he sat next to her, groaning as he stretched his legs out.

"Well?" she asked after a long but comfortable silence.

He snorted. "Well, it's not the most pleasant my bones have ever felt. But maybe you're right and change only comes with pain."

Douglas ate with her on the road every week after that. She learned that he worked in the Archives, the mysterious building that housed artifacts from the Great Collapse, but he never revealed details of his job. Not to her. Not even to his family. That should've been her first warning sign to stay far away from anything he asked to keep hidden.

Douglas insisted he would return soon to take the book back. "Just hold onto it for a few days. Please," he implored.

It was the fevered way he spoke that did her in.

She agreed to keep the book temporarily and waited for him to knock on her door. But he never did. It wasn't until she entered the town square and found his body hanging in the streets with the word THIEF carved into his forehead that she realized what he'd done.

Khalani should've returned the book then.

If she was smart, she might've been able to avoid being murdered too. But she wasn't sane or normal. She was alone. The kind of alone no one desires. The kind where you think you want to drown, but in reality, all you want is to be saved.

The word Poetry scribbled on the cover didn't mean anything to her. But when Khalani found the courage to open the pages, she swiftly realized the contents weren't beautiful, picturesque, or gentle. They were raw. Unrestrained. Every word, laced with passion and vigor, awoke a spirit inside that'd been long laid to rest. A part of her she didn't know existed.

She continued reading because it was the first time her brain and her heart dared to be on the same page. She kept it to escape. To be free. She read to stand on the earth and bellow out her dissent.

When the guards barged into her home days later and arrested her for a theft she didn't make, Khalani stayed silent. Not because she was a martyr. But she no longer found comfort residing on the ground.

"Speak!" The Master Judge's voice snapped against her like a whip, swiftly drawing Khalani to the present.

"I told no one." Her voice was firm and unyielding.

If she revealed the truth, that she shared the book with Douglas' wife, the Master Judge would kill their whole family. She wouldn't allow that to happen. It was her final bit of strength. The only sliver of good left within her body.

They could take the rest of her empty pieces.

The Master Judge shifted forward, studying her ashen face. Despite the fiery dread coursing through her, she held his stare. The Master Judge frowned and leaned back.

"It's no matter," he stated calmly, but his serpentine gaze promised punishment. "If anyone was involved, we'll sniff them out like the vermin they are."

The Master Judge called a guard forward to the dais, passing the book down to him. The guard threw it haphazardly inside a metal bin and proceeded to fill the container with a dark liquid. Khalani's chest rose in rapid breaths as the crude scent of gasoline blanketed the air.

The Master Judge's mouth curved at the panic in her eyes.

"Do it," he ordered.

The guard grabbed a torch and lit the bin on fire.

She wanted to *scream*. To let every ounce of pain screech from her desperate lungs. But no breath or barrage left her lips. The red flames tethered Khalani's focus as her body hypnotically swayed side to side. Liquid pooled in the corner of her eyes. She couldn't tell if it was from the smoke or her own despair. It was hard to know what was up and down. What was real or not.

Fire licked, cracked, and tore through one of the final things on this earth worth saving. And a sick, gruesome part of her wanted to jump into the flames and burn too.

"If it was up to me, all those useless artifacts in the Archives would be destroyed." The Master Judge wiped his hands. "I would love nothing more than to watch your body hang in the streets, so everyone can see the traitor you are. But the Warden has contacted the court recently. Their prisoners keep dying. Too bad for you. Death would have been quicker."

Shock snaked through her mind as his words slowly registered.

No.

"The Court of Apollo sentences you to life in Braderhelm Prison." The gavel struck the stone slab. Sealing her doom.

2

Since the dead can't speak,
I thought I'd sing for them.

"Move." Her brutish escort shoved her with a heavy push to her back.

She stumbled forward, nearly tripping over the worn sneakers they gave her that were one size too big. They burned her clothes and forced her to change into a thin, tattered, and dilapidated jumpsuit. The grey jumpsuit reeked of urine, and she fought the urge to dry-heave as the repulsive scent enveloped her body.

Khalani was led into Braderhelm Prison through a gargantuan gate, protected by armed guards double her size and wearing long-sleeved, black vests as they sneered at her mercilessly. The frigid air beat against her skin, the thin fabric of her uniform offering little warmth as they descended deep into the earth. Her teeth chattered in the dark for what felt like a mile until the long tunnel opened. The bald guard shoved her into a multi-story area of blocked cells.

She lifted her eyes as the ceiling stretched high above her. Bright lights attached along the stone walls, luminous and vivid, revealing hundreds of prisoners. Braderhelm didn't separate men from women. Both sexes peeked out from cells at the sound of their footsteps, and a dull roar crept through the immense cavern. Prisoners hollered and banged against the bars. The pressure of a hundred eyeballs slid across her thin arms, and Khalani wanted a pit to appear under her feet and swallow her whole.

The guard beside her reached for his gun and aimed the barrel at the ceiling. Three consecutive BANGS erupted from the weapon.

"Quiet down!" the guard shouted.

Silence emanated from the cells, and the guard grunted, sheathing his gun. Shallow air pumped out of Khalani's chest. She warily rose from her ducked position, uncovering her head. Her eyes slid to the left and made contact with a young, male prisoner.

Pale hands fisted around the steel bars, and his beady eyes glared at her with blanket disdain, like he envisioned circling his fingers around her throat and squeezing every drop of life out.

Khalani's head shot forward, and she sped up to the guard who led her inside an elevator. The shiny, modern interior lay in contrast to the caved prison. They quickly rose a few levels before the elevator shuddered to a halt. She followed the guard out, and a dusty sign hung overhead.

Cell Block 7.

The guard forged onward, and prisoners peeked out of their cells.

"She's gonna go quick."

"I'll give her a week."

"Less than that."

"Long enough for her mouth to work." Someone chuckled.

"Apollo-rat."

A girl pushed against the bars and spat at her face. Thick saliva slid down Khalani's cheek as the harsh words bombarded her like a spray of bullets from men and women alike.

Khalani tried to keep her facial expression as blank as possible because she couldn't afford to show any signs of weakness, not in Braderhelm.

Inner dread and darkness continued to trail like permanent shadows with each heavy step she took.

The expressionless guard stopped at an empty cell and opened the bars for her. She walked in and found a dirty, twin-sized cot on the floor with what appeared to be vomit stains on it, and a toilet in the corner. That was it. There were no virtual windows, just a dark, decrepit cell and a musky stench that filled the air.

The guard grabbed her arms roughly and unlocked the manacles. Her fragile skin looked worse than it felt. Or maybe her body was completely numb by that point to feel anything.

"Roll call begins promptly in the morning. You'll hear the morning bell and stand outside your cell to wait for the block guard to complete cell count. *Do not* sleep in during roll call, or you will be punished. Any other questions you will ask him, not me," he said just as she was about to open her mouth and ask if there was any toilet paper.

The guard pulled a thin, metallic device from his pocket. She heard light beeping, and the frightening, razor-sharp tip glowed neon red.

"Hold out your left arm," he commanded.

"What is that?" she whispered. The next moment, her head whipped to the side as the guard backhanded her. Her mouth opened in shock as he got right in her face.

"You do as you're told *when* you're told, prisoner. Now, hold out your arm before I break it."

Her chest heaved up and down in rapid breaths. His ring caught the end of her eye with the hit, and a warm sliver of blood pooled down her cheek. Her hands trembled as she slowly lifted her arm. The burly guard gripped her elbow and lowered the device to her wrist. Her skin prickled at the immense heat as the tip neared, and she panicked. In a last bid of desperation, she tried to pull away, but the guard held firm.

Pain.

That was all she could feel as the guard touched the tip to her wrist. No force was able to stop her screams. Her wails bounced around the walls, constricting the air around her, begging in futile agony to stop.

But no one responded to her cries for help.

Her voice grew hoarse by the time the guard backed away, and Khalani's eyes slid down to the bright-red number 317, branded into her skin.

"You are no longer Khalani Kanes. Khalani Kanes disappeared the moment you stepped foot in our walls. She doesn't exist anymore. You are Prisoner 317. Fall in line, or you will be punished."

Merely a number. No better than genetically bred cattle.

The brutal guard swiftly left, slamming the bars shut with a resounding bang and all that remained was the sound of her breath in the frigid cell. Tears streaked down her face, wet trails of pain continuing in an unending downpour. So many tears that her face could soon forget what it was like to not cry.

Was that possible?

Her back bowed as calamity and misfortune greeted and caressed her body like an old friend. They kissed her face and drew the wet passage of tears further down her feeble skin.

They took away everything. Even her name.

She slid to the ground. It was cold. Hard. The only thing that was…real. Everything else was merely a dream. A nightmare from which she couldn't escape. Slowly moving, she reached inside her pant pocket and grabbed the one personal item they let her bring. A picture of her parents.

She had long, dark hair like her mother and the green eyes of her father. She was on her dad's shoulders, and the camera snapped when they were all laughing. The picture was taken the day before Genesis became habitable, a week before their death.

When the immense dome that shielded the lethal radiation on the surface was completed, many rejoiced at the remarkable feat of human engineering. That was, until the bodies returned. Apollo forced Braderhelm prisoners to construct the dome surrounding Genesis, and every last one of them died from radiation poisoning. Their dead carcasses were carried through the streets to the medical ward.

She still remembers the smell. The odor of charred skin, like it'd been melted in a pot, forced grown men to their knees in shock.

Protesters gathered in Apollo Square, crying out their dissent against the Council, but they were swiftly defeated by the armed force. Bodies lay discarded on the streets, her parents among them, brutally murdered by the Apollo regime.

Khalani was only 8 years old.

She didn't eat for a week. She sat in front of her doorway, assuming her parents would walk through any moment and wrap her in their warm embrace. A concerned neighbor came to check on her and found a tiny, emaciated girl collapsed on the floor, still staring at the doorway.

Waiting. Hoping.

Because she didn't understand the concept of her waking up and them not being there. Not kissing her or telling her to clean her room. Wiping her tears when she was afraid, taking care of her when she was sick, and not caring if they got sick too.

Her parents never returned for her, and they never will. Sometimes, she hated them for that.

But maybe it's impossible to hate someone without loving them.

Out of the corner of her eye, a giant cockroach emerged from a miniscule hole in the stone wall. The creature wiggled its antennas and traveled along the floor.

Her forehead puckered as the cockroach skirted by a piece of black chalk on the ground, half the size of her pinky.

Hours may have passed before she moved. Slowly, like her body weighed a thousand pounds, Khalani reached over and grabbed the chalk. Her eyes lifted to the rocky walls of her cell, marked with black dashes all over.

She didn't have to count all the dashes to know that whoever occupied the cell before her didn't last long. Khalani clenched the chalk tighter. She could leave something behind too. The faintest trace of energy to let the next prisoner know that she once was alive. Khalani gazed at her parents once more and flipped it over on the stone floor.

Maybe poetry was never meant to be calamitous. Such broken tragedies shouldn't be breathed into existence, but it was her truth.

Without a name, the only thing she had left was her voice.

Her trembling fingers slithered across the blank space as she bared her soul to no one.

You remember it
Can't you?
The lighted whispers in the dark
When the hope in life
Wasn't built to fall apart

You feel it
Can't you?
The reverberations within
Collapse of dead wishes
Dreams adjourning before they begin

You hear it
Can't you?
That silence once more
Louder than screams
Hearts dying like mine has before

You realize it
Can't you?
Loss starts with your first breath
Either accept defeat with smeared eyes
Or smile when you encounter death

3

Emptiness has the fragility of feathers and bears the weight of mountains.

A high-pitched alarm resounded throughout the prison, and Khalani sat up abruptly. She didn't sleep. There came the point when her face dried up because no tears were left to cry. Devoid of emotion and energy, she lay on the floor the whole night, watching scenes of her old life play out on the stone crevices of the ceiling.

Rubbing her puffy eyes in exhaustion, she glanced at the steel bars sliding open.

"Roll call!" a deep, masculine voice yelled out.

Footsteps from other prisoners exiting their cells drifted to her. Remembering the guard's words yesterday, Khalani shot to her feet and tentatively walked out of her cell. The bright lights were overwhelming, and she held a hand over her eyes.

"Psstt, hey!"

She turned to her left. A short prisoner with bright blue, braided hair and ivory skin eyed her. "You need to stand on that." The blue-haired girl pointed to a yellow strip on the ground. "Motion sensor."

Khalani shuffled to the line hastily. "Thanks," she whispered, but the strange girl abruptly faced forward, not acknowledging her further.

She kept one foot on the yellow line and peeked over the metal railing. A multitude of prisoners stood rigidly in place on each floor. On the other side of her block, a guard dressed in all black walked by each prisoner, giving them the once-over. His face was hidden from view, but his brutally toned physique was evident, like he could snap her neck in an instant.

Her heartbeat thundered in her chest. What if this guard assigned her to the surface? No prisoners were sent to the surface. Not in the last 10 years. But rumors circled of plans to expand the Genesis dome. Khalani prayed she wouldn't be alive when that day arrived. There were few deaths more painful than radiation sickness.

Khalani fidgeted back and forth, rubbing her fingers against the sleeves of her uniform. The sound of heavy footsteps grating against metal made her stiffen. She stared straight ahead as the guard's large body entered her immediate line of vision.

He was well over six feet tall. The long-sleeved black vest held tight across his broad, muscular frame that could've been chiseled from stone. He clutched an electric pad, marking it as he walked by each prisoner. The guard stopped before her, and she found a spec of courage to lift her head.

His eyes were the color of midnight.

She didn't know eyes could be that black, as if the pupil bled out to the whole iris. She assumed all guards shaved their heads, but gossamer, jet-black hair slightly swept over his forehead. The imposing guard looked a few years older than her, with smooth, golden skin and thick lashes framing his all-consuming eyes. But when their stares connected, Khalani abruptly went rigid at the aggression in his gaze.

His sharp jawline ticked as his cold eyes swept up and down her attire, distaste emanating from him as the putrid scent of her jumpsuit suffocated the air.

"Disgusting," he muttered in revulsion, marking the electric pad.

Khalani's mouth twisted, and her gaze flickered to the slim, silver badge below his left shoulder.

Captain.

"Eyes forward, Kanes," he commanded without looking up.

She turned forward with a snap. It barely registered that he didn't refer to her as Prisoner 317. Not that he needed to. The brand beneath her skin burned more than words and titles ever could.

"Everyone to your assignments!" the guard shouted, and the prisoners on her block started moving. Her eyes danced around frantically. Where the hell was she supposed to go?

"Listen carefully."

Her muscles clenched at the dark, sinewy undertone. She shifted slightly, and the guard stepped close. Too close. His body completely dwarfed hers, dominating the space, nearly suffocating the air around her.

The guard watched her intently, a threatening shadow passing between his eyes which were laser-focused on her. No weapons were discernible. That was scarier for some reason. His stoic, detached energy alone made her want to return to her cell.

"Cell Block 7 is your home now. You are facing the consequences of your actions, and if you don't want your life here to be a living hell, then you do everything I tell you. Understand?" His deep voice grated against her skin. He didn't break eye contact or give any space to breathe.

"Y-Yes." She cleared her throat, forcing her terror away to properly function.

"You will report to Marcela in the north-end tunnels every morning. You'll work half a day there and then proceed to the food hall with the other prisoners. This will be the only meal of the day, no loitering around. Afterward, you'll report to George in the South A-Wing. He'll give you your afternoon assignment."

She nodded to herself, mouthing his words, trying to memorize everything he said. The slightest weight lifted from her chest. She wasn't assigned any work on the dome. Not yet.

"Following your afternoon shift," he continued irritably, "you get a one-hour break in the pit. After that, return to your cell for the nightly roll call. If you're in any way late, I will know, and you won't like what happens as punishment." His eyebrows lowered in an unnerving, I eat small children for breakfast type of way.

"You got me, Kanes?"

"Yes," her voice managed to remain steady.

"Good. There is absolutely no fighting with other prisoners. If you have a problem with another inmate, fix it in the pit. Don't come to me with issues because I don't have time to deal with your personal problems."

She frowned, about to ask what the pit was, but he continued speaking,

"You get a shower token once a week if you perform well in your assignments. Fail to do so, and your stench won't be the only thing that covers this prison." His nose wrinkled. "Don't expect sympathy or pity because you won't get it. Not from me or anyone else down here. Are we clear?"

The guard's sharp features twisted in disdain like she was nothing more than a repugnant bug he would pay front-row tickets to see trampled.

Douglas told her once about the five stages of grief. Denial, anger, bargaining, depression, and acceptance. She understood the first four easily. It was acceptance that forever evaded her. It was futile, like trying to clutch air with bare hands.

The Captain's thinly veiled insults and cruel glare sunk into her skin like a dull knife. Twisting back and forth. Gnawing through her thin walls of self-control. Bitter anger was her sole companion in the underground.

"Very clear," she deadpanned. He could be the last person alive, and she'd rather dig up graves and go to skeletons for sympathy. His eyes narrowed, and he leaned forward, an inch separating them.

"If you think I deal with any attitude, you're severely mistaken. Fail to follow any of these rules, and I *will* make you suffer," the threat came out slow and barely above a whisper.

Shivers raced up the back of her neck, but she slowly nodded, more comfortable with thinly veiled threats than lies of survival. His towering frame stood tense, studying her as his warning lingered in the static air.

"Let's go." He turned abruptly.

Khalani struggled to keep up with him as the guard's long legs tore across the walkway, not bothering to see if she was following. Because he knew she had nowhere else to go.

He led her into the elevator, and they slowly glided past the prisoner cells. She stood as far from him as possible, but the Captain's body was so built he made the elevator small. He didn't hold a rifle around his shoulder like the other guards. Weapons were undoubtedly hidden beneath his vest, but he carried himself with quiet confidence. As if he didn't need any.

They walked in silence through the dim tunnels. The only light source came from wires cemented on the ceiling, emitting a white glow. Her legs moved double-time to match his fast pace, but Khalani took the time while they marched through the complex caves to study her enemy.

Despite his immense size, the guard moved with grace, scanning every corner with a calculating gaze. His warm, rich skin was a rarity compared to most who lived underground. But the Captain's dark features and hooded eyes only added to his serious demeanor.

Khalani was of Hispanic descent, but this guard's roots appeared to be linked to East Asia and on any other man, his sharp nose, angular cheekbones, and pronounced jaw would've made him pretty. This guard wasn't pretty or even handsome.

Those were too feeble terms.

He was a disaster you couldn't tear your focus away from. He was the unmoving calm while you lean on the precipice of death.

"Is there a reason you're staring?"

"No." She snapped her head forward. Crazy peripheral vision, also noted.

"The north-end tunnel is that way." The guard pointed down the decrepit hall. "Any questions? Now is the only time to ask," he warned.

"Do you have a name?" Referring to him as scary, uptight muscle man for the rest of her short life didn't seem appealing.

"I'm the Captain of Braderhelm."

"They don't give Captain's names?"

"That's all you need to know. You won't live long enough to put any names to use." His harsh words lingered in the empty space.

Blood rushed to her face, and emotion quickly overrode logic. "I guess down here, humans are numbered, and only monsters are named. My mistake."

She stepped away, but stiff fingers grabbed her arm, right over the sensitive brand. The Captain's brows got real low as he applied biting pressure over the unhealed wound. She noticeably flinched but he didn't relent. His features twisted into something villainous.

Unstable.

As if each layer beneath his skin was slashed and hewed in violence, and he loosely held the reins of control. He twisted her wrist, and she gasped at the sharp pain.

"Say that to me again." The Captain's head tilted.

Khalani's chin trembled as she stared into his shadowed eyes. The guard's disquieting, formidable presence triggered every flight instinct, screaming for her to run. She kept her mouth shut, breaking into a cold sweat.

"Nothing to say now?" His gaze narrowed, sweeping her small frame. "The only reason I'm not breaking your wrist is because you need it for the next shift, and I don't have patience for your pathetic screams. Unless you're prepared for the consequences, keep that smart mouth shut, or I'll ensure a broken bone will be the least of your problems."

The Captain released his painful grip. She clutched her hand, grimacing, but he didn't give her a chance to speak.

"If there's one thing to learn, Kanes, it's this. Braderhelm is unforgiving, and no one cares about your problems. Fall in line, or you'll die painfully."

"Why not just kill me now then?" she rasped, unable to hold back her feelings of desolation.

His icy stare burrowed into her skin, and the Captain bent his head, their noses barely touching. "Nice try," he quipped. "I expect you to finish a few work shifts before dying. But keep it up, and I'll grant your wish. Now, get the hell out of my sight."

Hate rebounded in the frigid air between them. Her palms itched, preparing to test the limits of his anger, but Khalani turned, hastily escaping before acting on those fatal instincts. Something about the Captain made her hairs stand on end but also compelled her to drive themselves into a head-on collision, inviting pain to numb the hollowness.

After a few steps, she glanced over her shoulder, but he was already gone, taking the intimidating cloud of energy with him. She forced herself to exhale, recognizing her precarious balance between life and death.

A dangerous part of her enjoyed toying with destruction. She didn't mind playing deadly games and winning deadlier prizes. In fact, she yearned for it. Because it had to end. Some way or another.

She needed everything to end.

4

We can be nothing together.

She followed the lighted wires embedded in the ceiling, ignoring the blister that popped on her heel. When the tunnel opened to an expansive dusty cavern, the sound of metal grating against stone amplified. Ten-foot-tall lamps were placed around the room, their bright lights illuminating massive boulders of rocks.

She shuffled to a stop against the gravel, locating the source of the pounding. A row of prisoners swung hefty pickaxes against the sheer stone wall, carving a new passageway in the tunnel. A layer of dust hung in the air, and she fought the urge to sneeze.

"Stop slacking!" A burly guard approached an old man in a prisoner uniform, slumped over in exhaustion.

The prisoner said something inaudible to the guard, and the guard bashed the butt of his gun against the prisoner's head. The prisoner fell face down on the gravel, unmoving.

"Back to work!" the guard yelled at the other prisoners, who didn't spare the unconscious man another glance. Their facial expressions were blank as they continued to swing the pickaxes toward the rock wall, like they'd seen far worse.

A girl shuffled by, pushing a wheelbarrow filled with gravel. Her light blonde hair was matted to her forehead in sweat, face sunken in, and a thin line of ribs protruding through the patchy holes of her grey garment. Khalani's eyes widened at the frailness of her body.

The girl couldn't have been more than thirteen years old and looked like she'd keen over at the faintest breeze. The wheelbarrow probably weighed more than she did.

"Hey," Khalani whispered, walking toward her.

The frail girl slowly turned her head, and Khalani froze at the expression on her face. Her eyes were a blank void, as if a ghost had walked through her body and taken over.

"What do you want?" the girl asked in a monotone voice.

Khalani's body felt rooted to the ground. A name. She couldn't remember the name of the woman the guard had told her to meet. Past details paled to the insurmountable now. Would Khalani end up like her, a breathing shell who lost any evidence of a previous life?

Was this what she already looked like?

"Why are you not working, prisoner?" a guard shouted. The bulky guard charged forward, and her muscles froze in place. His pale blue eyes gleamed with anger as he pulled out a steel baton and hit the young girl on her lower back, and she collapsed with a pitiful cry.

"No. Please, stop!" Khalani yelled.

"What did you say?" The guard turned to her with a merciless glare and got right up in her face.

Her hands were shaking. "I'm s-sorry, sir. It's not her fault. I was asking her a question. The Captain sent me here to meet someone." The name finally blared to mind. "Marcela."

The guard's eyes narrowed as he perused her up and down. She gulped and didn't move an inch. Khalani barely recognized that she'd peed herself a little.

"Keep moving," the guard snapped at the little girl, who slowly hobbled to her feet. She grabbed the wheelbarrow and stumbled away, her back hunched over in pain.

"Marcela is down that way." He nodded his head toward the end of the cavern. "Hurry up, prisoner. Unless you want me to give you a real reason to be late."

Her heart drummed so fast, the beats blended together in a singular vibration. The guard's heavy footsteps echoed behind, tracking her like a demon as she headed toward the back of the cave.

Marcela was a heavy-set woman with auburn hair pulled tight into a high bun. She scrutinized the prisoners with a steely gaze, ready to pounce at the slightest err in movement. Like the human embodiment of a vulture, scouring for prey.

"I wish all the animals didn't die in the Great Collapse," 15-year-old *Khalani told her history teacher, Mr. Harroway.*

"Ah, that is where you are wrong," Mr. Harroway said. "Animals are not truly extinct, and I'm not talking about the ones cloned and genetically bred for food. You forget about us. Humans are animals. Of course, we like to think of ourselves as lions, the old king of the land. But I see us as more akin to vultures, working in packs to scrounge our way to the top. The buzzards that don't recognize themselves as one," he remarked, looking away in thought.

"That's a little dark," Khalani said.

Mr. Harroway chuckled.

"That's human history. Darker than midnight. Why do you think we fled underground?"

"Keep moving!" Marcela yelled at several prisoners.

The shrill of her voice made Khalani flinch, clearing the old memory. Marcela wore all black like the guards, but a silver badge on her vest caught the light, identifying her as a prison employee. Marcela's head snapped up from the electric pad in her hand when Khalani approached.

Marcela pursed her lips in disapproval as she eyed her up and down. "I told them to give me more muscle down here. And they gave me...you." Khalani's brows pinched together, and she opened her mouth, but the woman held her finger up.

"No, no. You speak when I ask you a question. What's your number?" Marcela asked with a scowl on her face.

"My number?"

"The one branded on you," Marcela snapped impatiently.

Khalani glared at the scar on her wrist and ground her teeth. "317. I was told to report to you."

Marcela's fingers quickly raced over the touchpad, and she scowled at the screen. "I expected at least a builder or a farmer, but they sent me a scrawny girl who worked as a food distributor. I need to make a trip to the Warden," Marcela muttered.

A brief surge of panic coursed through her. If Marcela transferred her to another job, she could be assigned something way worse, like the surface.

"When I worked as a food distributor, I lifted heavy boxes constantly," the words rushed out of her.

Marcela snorted, unconvinced, and turned away dismissively.

"I might not look like it, but I'm a hard worker and more than capable of pulling my own weight. You won't hear any complaints or troubles from me," she stated in a firm voice, lifting her hands in exclamation.

Marcela cocked her head to the side and studied her. Moments passed and she eventually conceded.

"Alright, we'll see how you do. Go see 189 over there." Marcela pointed to a male prisoner placing hefty rock chunks inside a wheelbarrow. "He'll be your partner in the tunnels every morning. You'll follow his lead."

Khalani nodded and started to head away when Marcela gripped her shoulder tightly. "*Don't* make me regret this. If you let me down, I will send you to the surface for Genesis detail."

The threat hung in the air like a bullet speeding toward her in slow motion. She nodded quickly, detaching herself from Marcela's hold.

Prisoner 189 was tall, dark-skinned, very skinny—a prominent feature among the prisoners—and while he couldn't have been much older than Khalani, he had a soft, boyish face marred by dirt marks.

He held a hand to his lower back and grimaced as he wiped the sweat off his forehead.

"Um, excuse me. Are you Prisoner 189?" she inquired, rubbing her hands together as she approached.

Prisoner 189 turned to her with tired eyes, and his forehead scrunched in confusion. "You new?" He bent down to grab another large rock from the pile.

"Yes. Marcela said you're my partner in the tunnels. I'm Khalani."

She wasn't going to call herself 317. She refused to give them any more power. It was the most diminutive form of rebellion, but to her, it mattered.

He regarded her open hand and gave her a deadpan stare. "You better put those hands to use and start helping with these rocks. Grab the wheelbarrow over there."

Khalani quickly rushed over to the empty wheelbarrow. She struggled to move the clunky wheels in a straight line, even without weight piled in.

"Start piling those rocks in here," he instructed as she zig-zagged her way over.

The rocks were much heavier than they appeared, and her arms ached after several minutes. The prisoner noticed her arms shaking and began to assist with her load. "Thanks," she whispered.

"First day is always the worst," he grumbled in a low voice. "No matter how much it hurts, you keep going. They will make up reasons to hurt you, so don't give them any." He put the last rock into the wheelbarrow and dusted his hands.

His palms were covered in popped blisters, some oozing blood, but he acted as if he didn't notice. When they finished, they rolled both wheelbarrows to the metal disposal unit on the far side of the cavern. The work was challenging and arduous. Hours passed and she repeatedly rubbed her arms to smooth the aches and cramps, but Marcela's warning rang in her mind. Khalani kept her head down and mouth shut as she worked, pushing through the sharp pain. Her eyes caught with Prisoner 189, and he gave her a nod of respect.

"I half expected you to keel over by now, but you're holding your own weight," he said with a slight tone of surprise.

"I don't give up easily," was her only response.

His calculating gaze shot past her warily, where Marcela was on the other side of the cavern, yelling at prisoners. "What did you do?" He lifted his eyes to her.

"What?" She grunted in pain as she plopped a cumbersome rock in the barrel a quarter of her size.

"I mean, what did you do to wind up in here? You don't seem the type to kill, but I've been wrong about worse things."

"I'm not a murderer," she snapped.

"Had to ask." He shrugged without remorse. "Braderhelm is home to many murderers, and there are few you can trust. If you wanna survive here, I would grow eyes in the back of your head."

"Helpful advice." She pursed her lips. "And I suppose you're in the minority I can trust?"

"No. Carrying someone's trust is too much responsibility. But you don't have to fear anything from me if that puts your mind at ease," he answered.

Khalani's brows pinched together. "How long have you been here?"

"I was sentenced here 262 days ago."

"You remember the exact day?"

"Most people don't." He scrubbed a dirty hand across his face. "But I would rather remember my last semblance of freedom. Better than the future bleeding together in a meaningless and unending abyss. It's a small way I can have control."

"We don't have any control." She slammed a hefty rock inside the wheelbarrow. Harder than necessary. The accompanying silence reminded her why people left her alone. She was too broken.

Khalani closed her eyes as the familiar despair crept back and nearly halted her movement. She lost everything that mattered, like an empty corpse wandering with no purpose. What did she have to live for? She couldn't find the answer anymore and that trivial thought terrified her.

"I'm not saying the pain will get easier," his voice rose, as if he could sense the ruin within her. "But you don't realize how tough you are until you need all your strength."

Khalani's lips drew in a hard line, her knuckles turning white as she clasped the wheelbarrow in a tight grip. Images flashed in her mind. Her parent's lifeless eyes staring at her on a cold table. Douglas closing her door with one final look, his words of hope burning to a fiery crisp.

Her last strength flew away like an extinct dove when the steel bars slammed home, locking her in prison. She breathed for the sake of breathing. She continued to push her body because the physical pain served as a temporary distraction from the emptiness that bellowed inside.

"What cell block are you on?" he interrupted the cold silence.

"Seven," Khalani whispered, trying to forget the useless past.

"Not completely horrible. There are worse block placements. Just watch yourself with Steele," he murmured.

"Steele?"

"Don't stop working." He glanced to the left as a guard walked close by. Khalani promptly grabbed bulkier rocks, huffing from the weight.

When the guard strolled away, he continued in a faint voice, "Takeshi Steele. He's the Captain and runs your block. His aggressive temper precedes him. He's even murdered some of his own guards. My best advice would be to keep your head down and stay out of his way."

So, the devil did have a name. No doubt Takeshi Steele already had her on a mental kill list of inmates. What if she tried to talk to him? An attempt to rectify their earlier conversation. Khalani shook her head as soon as the stupid thought entered her stupid brain.

A loud, high-pitched buzz reverberated across the stone walls, startling her. Everyone around her set down their pickaxes and wheelbarrows and began exiting the tunnel.

"That's the end of the morning shift bell." Prisoner 189 strode toward the exit and peered over his shoulder when she didn't follow.

"C'mon, criminals aren't allowed to straggle. Not unless you like being whipped and roaches served with your meals."

Right there. That's when Khalani knew she officially resided in hell.

5

Don't try to fathom me,
I can't even traverse my jagged depths.

"Get your ass in the back of the line!" A man with shaggy brown hair and a few missing teeth pushed a scrawny kid to the ground.

The boy, sporting a black eye and messy hair that hadn't seen a comb in years, stumbled to his feet. The kid didn't say or do anything to defend himself. He lowered his head and slowly shuffled to the back of the food line.

Khalani frowned and peered over her shoulder at the pale boy. Something about his body language and facial expression indicated that this treatment was routine for him. His eyes met hers, and she quickly snapped her head forward. A hint of guilt brushed her heart, and she didn't know why.

The food hall lay in a spacious man-made cave with high ceilings and stone pillars throughout. All the prisoners were lined up for food, shuffling forward with fatigue. A girl in front continuously rubbed her lower back, groaning in pain.

Khalani's back didn't fare much better.

Several guards stood posted throughout the cave, but Takeshi Steele was nowhere to be found. She was thankful for that, fearing the potential repercussions of their earlier interaction.

She slowly approached the front of the line and grabbed a green tray. A bulky woman with hair tied in a messy bun and red scabs of acne scattered on her face scooped up the 'food' and dumped a clump on her tray.

"Next!" the woman shouted, not sparing her another glance.

Khalani paused and leaned down to sniff the wet slab of processed meat. An odor of burnt feces protruded from the meat, and bile immediately crept into the back of her throat. She held her breath, holding back nausea.

A sharp, electric shock suddenly sliced through her back, and she immediately curled in on herself, hunching over in pain.

"Keep moving, prisoner. You're holding up the line!" a bald guard yelled, clutching a taser with no remorse or care in his cruel eyes.

Her back muscles spasmed as if wrapped tight in a coil. She gritted her teeth and continued to push the tray down as her fingers visibly trembled. All she had to do was keep moving. A female worker handed her the same vitamin D supplement every Apollo citizen took daily.

Shaking, she swallowed the orange pill and noticed the guard tapping the taser against his palm in sweet anticipation. She quickly walked away, letting her brown hair fall to the side of her face in a protective curtain.

The thick strands were the only shield she had.

"You, okay?" Prisoner 189 asked, stepping to her side.

"Fine," she muttered.

"C'mon. You can sit with me."

"It's okay. I'd rather be alone," she admitted, reluctant to be close with anyone.

He lowered his head. "The prisoners like to pick on the fresh meat, especially the first day. You don't want to eat alone."

She met his earnest gaze and eventually nodded, not wanting to invite any more trouble into her life. The broad cave had no tables.

All the prisoners sat on the dirty floor. She took a deep breath, trying to ignore the ache shooting through her spine from the taser and the taxing shift. They maneuvered around people, and he led her to the far corner of the room, stomping on a giant cockroach lingering in the area. Why did the ugliest creatures have to be the hardest ones to extinguish?

Not even the nuclear apocalypse did the trick.

"Lunch today is better than most days." He sat down with a greedy gaze.

Khalani gave him an incredulous look and stared down at the questionable meat. She quickly became cross-eyed, fantasizing the food turning into something, *anything* else.

"If you stare at the meat long enough, you can actually see it move," a girl said over Khalani's shoulder. She turned to see the blue-haired girl from the neighboring cell.

"Serene, don't scare her. She's never gonna eat now."

Serene shrugged as she sat down. "That's fine. More for me," she said, picking up a mouthful of the vile food.

Serene had even paler skin than the average person in Apollo. She had a tiny frame and a beautiful face, but her skin was marred with a deep scar running from the top of her nose down to her left jawline.

Serene glanced up in annoyance. "What?"

"Thanks for helping me earlier today. Not knowing where to go," she quickly explained.

Serene waved her hand in dismissal. "Don't worry about it. The first day is the toughest. I'm Serene, by the way. You've met the know-it-all bastard, Derek."

Serene gestured to Prisoner 189, who gave her a one-finger wave, returning to his meal. She nodded in greeting, gaze reluctantly shifting to the grotesque food on her plate. Her mouth twisted, and she tentatively grabbed the slimy food with her bare hands since utensils weren't provided. Khalani tried not to breathe as she bit down, but the bitter flavor washed through her mouth, and goosebumps prickled her arms. She coughed, holding a hand to her lips, forcefully swallowing the food that tasted like vomit.

The dead cockroach might've been a better option.

Serene chuckled. "You'll get used to the taste."

She didn't know if that was possible. Khalani was still coughing and sputtering over her food. She sounded like a dying old woman.

Derek slapped her back to stop her from hurling. "I know it sucks, but there's actually a decent amount of protein in this. Some days they don't give food, so you eat when you can."

Another inmate sat down with them, placing his tray on the ground in a quick movement. He was older, in his late twenties, maybe, and his lips pinched together as he ran a frustrated hand through his ashy brown hair. He had a broader build than most prisoners, and the corded veins in his arms became more defined as he balled his fists, staring down at the plate of food like it was his worst enemy.

"What happened this time?" Serene griped.

A foreboding haze flashed over the newcomer's eyes. He reached into his pocket and pulled out a pair of broken glasses, placing the mangled pieces on the ground with a hostile glare.

"Damn, Adan. Again?" Serene picked up the fractured material. The frame was crushed, and the wires were twisted like a convoluted pretzel.

"It was Guard Harken. Second time this month. He said I was working too slow in my shift today when he knows full well that I'm the fastest one there," Adan growled.

"Can you fix it?" Derek mumbled, eating his food like it was his last meal.

"Of course, I can. But it's a wasted effort. Gonna keep happening. Give stupid people power, and they'll abuse it as they see fit." Adan's expression was seething as he snatched the broken glasses from Serene's hand and shoved them back into his pocket. They all sat in silence because the harsh truth took up the most space.

Khalani put another rancid bite of food in her mouth to distract from the awkwardness. This time she didn't nearly choke to death.

Progress.

Adan finally seemed to notice her presence as she moved. "Who are you?" he asked, glaring at her skeptically.

She opened her mouth, but Serene beat her to the punch. "This is Khalani Kanes. First day in prison, so give her a break. She's had enough trauma for one day. Khalani, this is my older brother, Adan." Serene waved her hand in dismissal.

Khalani scrunched her forehead. "How do you know my name?"

"I stole the new roster sheet." Serene shrugged. "It's virtually impossible to steal from Takeshi Steele, but one of his new backups had his guard down too long."

"Watch yourself, Serene." Derek frowned. "One day, you'll be caught, and the guards won't hesitate to kill you."

"Which is why I'm *always* careful," she emphasized to Derek and turned back to Khalani. "So, what did you take?"

"Excuse me?"

Serene's green eyes burned with curiosity, and she lowered her voice to a whisper. "What did you take from the Archives? All it said in your file was that you stole an artifact from the Archives, but it didn't say what..." her voice trailed off.

At the mention of the Archives, both Derek and Adan froze as if a steel rod was shoved up their spines. "You stole something from the Archives?" Adan forcefully swallowed as he studied her in dismay.

Khalani opened her mouth but hesitated. She was already a prisoner, but Douglas' family would still be harmed if word got out that Khalani had shared any information with them.

"I guess I'm not a very good thief, seeing as I'm down here, and all it took was a surprise inspection for them to..." Khalani paused, her pulse quickening. "I didn't take anything important. It was just a book." She glanced away, attempting to downgrade the interest in her story and not unravel further.

Derek shifted forward, his focus fixated on her.

"What did the book say? Did it talk about Apollo or any plans with Genesis?"

"N-no. It was poetry."

All she received were blank stares. Khalani bit her lip and tried to explain. "Um, it's stories about life but written with passion and emotion. Poetry is…beautiful."

They all frowned like she was speaking a different language.

"As I said, it won't interest you. And it doesn't even matter anymore. It's gone now," her voice hardened.

Derek sat back, disappointed, but something in his calculating gaze caught her attention. She couldn't put her finger on what the shift was.

"A bunch of dead guys wrote a book on the shittiness of humanity, and they threw you in here for taking that?" Serene frowned.

"Look around, sis. Apollo was always crazy. We just became desensitized to it," Adan mumbled in a subdued voice, throwing a piece of slumpy food back on his tray.

Desensitized. That was the perfect word for it.

She'd always been aware of the Council's ruthless actions but never spoke out against it. She held no power or influence. Her focus was on her own survival. Ignoring the bad happening to everyone else just became easier over time. As if her brain was trained to tune out things that didn't directly affect her.

Maybe that was worse.

"Why did they throw you down here?" She gestured to Serene and Adan, gravitating the attention away from her.

"Before Braderhelm, Adan was one of the best mechanical engineers in Apollo's Surface Division," Serene divulged.

Her eyebrows rose, shifting to Adan. The Surface Division created the material and maintained the Genesis dome and the few suits that could withstand the deadly radiation.

"That's…impressive," she admitted.

Adan snorted. "Yeah. What an accomplishment." Sarcasm dripped from his tone. "They loved me until I refused to work at the Weapon's Lab in Genesis."

Khalani's forehead crinkled. Anyone who turned down the chance to live in Genesis was either deranged or asinine.

"I know what you're thinking," Adan said, noting her incredulous gaze. "But it was hard enough knowing I was contributing all my time to the Genesis dome, a structure responsible for killing hundreds."

"You didn't have a choice," Derek reminded him.

"There's always a choice." Regret tinged his voice. "Always. But I refused to be responsible for more deaths by building weapons for them. I turned in my resignation, and the next day, I was sentenced to Braderhelm for insubordination. And my sister couldn't stay home like I begged her to." Adan's lips pressed together in a tight line, but there was no denying the love in his wayward glance toward Serene.

"You're my brother," Serene stated with raw finality. Like it was all the explanation needed.

Serene turned to Khalani. "Our parents weren't really around when we were younger, so I was always good at stealing when we needed food. I tried to break into the Master Judge's office and steal two Genesis passes. The plan was to hide in Genesis before they transferred Adan to Braderhelm, but they caught me and threw me in here with him."

"It was a stupid plan," Adan interrupted.

"At least I had a plan!"

"Why couldn't you just listen to me and stay home?"

"When have you ever known me to listen?" Serene derided.

"You're a part of the female species. So never."

Serene shook her head, turning back to Khalani. "Wouldn't you do the same? Wouldn't you go to the ends of the underground for your family?"

There was that word again. Family. No matter how many failures, fights, or disappointments, they were the solid foundation that was supposed to anchor you to the ground. Family could drive you crazy while restoring your sanity in the same breath.

Khalani admired the lengths Serene went to protect her brother. She was always more comfortable being alone. It was safer that way. But an undeniable part of her longed for that bond. She would move mountains of rock to speak to her parents again, even for a second.

"My family is gone, but if they were here...there is nothing I wouldn't do for them." Khalani let out a rough breath and glanced away, burying her hopes and wishful thinking in the dark abyss where they belonged.

The silence extended, and Serene nodded in understanding. Even Adan studied her with a newfound appraisal.

"I like you, Khalani," Serene broke the tension. "We survive here by sticking together. We'll watch out for you too."

Her brows furrowed. Khalani thought the 'every man for himself' ideology would overrule Braderhelm Prison, but Derek, Serene, and Adan all had something in common. Their lives were forfeit. The interwoven endings of their dismal fates connected them.

It wasn't a connection she wanted, but it was there, nonetheless. If they had survived this far, maybe there was hope for her. The odds were infinitesimal, but they weren't obsolete. Like a still-beating heart clinging to the edge of life, not quite ready to greet the end.

6

I'm a living, breathing disaster.
Just as aching, vast, and terrible.

The size of Braderhelm continued to impress her with its vast network of tunnels. Apollo was a remarkable engineering feat, mixing natural caves with sprawling caverns to support hundreds of thousands of people. Impressive didn't do the city justice. But when she entered the pit with Serene, her mouth hung open.

She wasn't expecting the cavern to be so massive.

Her eyes lifted to the tall ceiling. White lights hung along the stone walls, illuminating the space in a soft glow, a great dichotomy against the rough exterior of Braderhelm. Many prisoners conversed and walked about.

A pervasive heaviness still hung over the atmosphere, but the prisoners seemed more relaxed as they took advantage of the vast space. Khalani's attention shifted to what lay at the center of the cavern. A large crowd surrounded a circular crater. It was a dirt pit that extended a few feet deep into the ground, like a shallow pool with no water. Cheers rose from several prisoners as they stared into the pit, their eyes alight with excitement and adrenaline. Khalani stepped closer to the throng in curiosity, and a series of grunts and punches echoed back. Through the crowd of people, her eyes finally found an opening to peer into the crater.

Two female prisoners were fighting, blood splayed everywhere. One of the pale girls had the sleeves of her uniform rolled up to her shoulders and dark hair pulled tight into a side braid. The other female prisoner had chopped red hair, and the glint in her eyes was deadly as she swung a punch.

Khalani flinched as the dark-haired girl dodged the hit and drove a closed fist into the other prisoner's jaw, knocking her flat. Blood dripped down the girl's face, nearly the same color as her hair. Khalani thought the fight was over when the dark-haired girl leaned down for the knockout punch. But she came crashing down as the other girl side-swiped her leg.

The redhead took advantage and climbed on top, pummeling her in the face. Three punches. Four. Five. The dark-haired girl on the ground no longer moved, and the redhead stood with her arms raised in victory.

Prisoners whistled and clapped, exchanging flimsy passes labeled Shower Token, seemingly the only thing to bet on within Braderhelm. Even a few guards stood outside the ring, grinning at the raw spectacle.

The girl on the ground slowly sat up, flinching. Sweat and blood gleamed off her skin, and her black hair stuck to her forehead. She crawled to the pit's edge—light highlighting her bloodied lips and swollen eyes—but her leg gave out as she tried to ascend the mound, sending her crashing to the bottom.

Khalani glanced around, waiting for someone to help the poor girl, but no one made a move.

Everyone focused on two male prisoners who dropped into the pit, squaring away to fight. Her eyes shifted back to the defeated girl. Khalani preferred to blend in with the background and maintain a low profile, but she couldn't stand there in feigned ignorance.

She left Serene's side and barely heard her say, "Khalani, wait."

Khalani ignored her, making her way closer to the edge of the ring. Once she found an opening to the front, she spotted the broken girl still trying to crawl away.

"Here, let me help you." Khalani bent down and reached her hand.

She vaguely noticed the cheers halting and whispers picking up steam. She felt multiple eyes on her but ignored them. The defeated girl peered up with deep hatred pulsing from her expression, angry tears forming in the one eye that wasn't swollen shut.

"I don't need your fucking help."

Khalani recoiled. The girl pushed on her hands and slowly rose to her feet, wincing in apparent pain. She hobbled shakily on one leg and lifted herself out of the pit. She took a deep breath and grimaced, unable to stand fully upright. After giving Khalani another irate glare, she disappeared into the crowd.

Khalani stood frozen at the top of the crater, holding her hand like an idiot.

What just happened?

Her eyes swept around, and a couple of prisoners gave Khalani a look of sympathy...or was it pity? Most prisoners who witnessed the embarrassing act shook their heads like she'd committed a social faux pas. An older prisoner who stood a foot taller than Khalani, her head half-shaven with several piercings through her nose and eyebrows, slowly clapped.

"Nice going, new girl. Try to help any losers out of the pit, and you'll find yourself taking their place. Doubt you would last 10 seconds." She smirked as the warning cut through.

"She can come with me, and I'll fill her pit up in less than 10 seconds." A burly guy with missing teeth sneered, and everyone laughed around her.

Khalani's fists tightened, and her cheeks flushed with embarrassment. She quickly pushed toward the back of the ring, making her way out of there as quickly as possible. If she could have any superpower at that moment, it would be invisibility.

"Khalani!" Serene's voice pierced through her thoughts.

She finally broke through the throng of people and spotted Serene's characteristic blue hair following behind her. "I'm sorry. Just had to get out of there," the words rapidly left her mouth when Serene approached.

"I should've told you. You can't intervene with fights in the pit or help the losers. It's taboo in Braderhelm," Serene explained.

Khalani shook her head, internally cursing at herself. She should've known better. In Braderhelm, compassion better served as a tumor that needed to be cut out.

"Don't take it too hard," Serene implored when she noticed her expression. "Just make sure not to interfere next time, okay?"

Silence eclipsed the air, but Khalani pursed her lips and nodded. The notion didn't sit well with her, but she couldn't afford a target on her back, not in prison. Having principles was easy, but sticking to one's principles when it required sacrifice…that was another matter entirely.

"I'm gonna walk around a little," she said. "Need some space." The fighting pit appeared to be the primary source of entertainment in Braderhelm, and Khalani lost her appetite to watch the bloody sport any further.

Serene frowned as if she were tempted to argue but ultimately didn't and nodded. Khalani was grateful she didn't have to explain herself. She was better off in solitude.

She walked through the pit, taking in her surroundings, when she spotted Takeshi Steele in the far corner. His muscular arms were folded against his chest as he leaned against the wall. His demeanor was calm, but his face bred controlled aggression. Those watchful eyes cast around the room like a viper waiting to strike.

Suddenly, his gaze landed on her.

She felt caught in a trap as his shadowed eyes held her own, narrowing, as if daring her to move.

Despite her fear and loathing, Khalani made the snap decision to approach him. She needed little convincing from Derek to know that being on Takeshi Steele's shit list was detrimental to her survival.

Mediating the damage she'd done earlier was imperative.

She ventured toward him, fingers fumbling together as anxiety shrouded her like a veil. He scrutinized her carefully, his body imperceptibly shifting against the wall in response.

Approaching him was either a brilliant decision or a seriously miscalculated move. With each step, Khalani fought the urge to turn around but continued her uneasy advance. She stopped a few feet away, not willing to veer any closer. Takeshi stood still and composed, the dangerous threat never receding from his eyes as he assessed her with a scowl.

"Hi." Her voice cracked. She cleared her throat and waited. And waited.

Takeshi didn't respond, only continued to glower in annoyance. Raw tension brushed against every inch of her body as the awkward silence expanded.

"I wanted to apologize for what I said earlier," she started.

"Is that so?"

She cleared her throat, his resonant voice a warning sign. Like a calm surface with a boiling current beneath. "Yes. I've had a rough week. As you can imagine. I know you don't care, but that is why I made some…illogical comments. It was not my intention to provoke or anger you."

He tilted his head and studied her. For a brief, flickering moment of insanity, she thought he would accept her apology.

"Are you done?" he asked in a dispassionate tone.

And with that, her naïve optimism deflated like air being sucked from her body in a vacuum.

Her brows drew together. "Umm, y-yeah. Yes. I guess I'm done."

Takeshi's muscles held rigid in response as he glanced away, dismissing her.

"Okay." She fumbled her hands by her side at the renewed silence, wanting to disappear and never be found again. "I hope that settles it. I'll leave you to your…guarding." Khalani resisted the urge to slap a palm to her forehead.

Next time she should just ask Takeshi Steele to shoot her. That would undoubtedly receive a better response.

"Don't waste your time *hoping* for things down here," his intense voice echoed past her.

She turned back in surprise. Takeshi stood against the wall like an indomitable force. He was still. Too still.

"What, hoping is for the young?" she asked warily.

"No. Hoping is for the foolish. If your plan is to garner my sympathy to help your cause, you'll be severely disappointed." His black eyes skewered her.

"That wasn't—I...I was trying to be nice," she explained.

"And you expected me to be nice in return?"

"Yes. I don't know. Maybe?"

Takeshi shook his head. "Being nice is a useless endeavor that will only bring unwanted attention. Something you appear to excel at."

"What are you talking about?"

"I see everything." His penetrative gaze flickered over her frame, unimpressed. "Sticking your neck out for a prisoner you don't know. Idiotic."

"I didn't realize helping one another was taboo in Braderhelm."

"Then you're even more naïve than you look. Actions like that will only hasten your death." His merciless expression stared back.

Her skin grew hot, and she shot him a cruel glare. "Is that why you've killed some of your guards, because they tried to help us?" It was the only reasonable explanation she could come up with.

That got his attention. He stepped away from the wall and stalked toward her. He was like a menacing storm, chilling the air seconds before destruction. She stepped back, but he invaded her space like he owned it. He put a hand on her shoulder and pushed her against the wall. Takeshi placed his palm against the stone, centimeters from her head, utterly consuming her vision.

"Remember this." He leaned close. "Any punishment I give is punishment deserved. If you die by my hands, it's because you've earned it...and I'm not above making it hurt," Takeshi's voice lowered, caressing her like a blade. Savage temptation etched itself in his black spheres, pulling her in.

"Are you scared now, Kanes?" He cocked his head.

"Yes," she admitted.

He nodded. "Good. Fear is essential to understanding conse-quences. And there are no shortages of those down here. If I didn't know better, I would say you're hoping to die. Is that it, Kanes?" He bent to whisper in her ear like he was sharing a secret. "Do you want to die?"

She stopped breathing. It was like no one else was present in that cavern but the two of them as he challenged her most base instincts.

The thought of ending everything herself crossed Khalani's mind—even before Braderhelm—but something had always stopped her. When she was surrounded by people, the torment was easier. But when she was by herself, the truth screamed into her open mouth and echoed off the hollow caverns.

I am lost.
　　I am forgotten.
　　　　I am alone.

It was like another creature inhabited her body that looked and sounded like her. But it wasn't her. She was drowning in seas that didn't exist and living a life that was no longer hers. She was getting through the day minute by minute, and there were some minutes when she wanted time to cease completely.

The truth is, it's not the hurt you see that's dangerous. It's the hurt you hide that's the real menace.

"I don't know." The ugly admission broke free.

Takeshi's gaze sharpened in interest, and silence abated. "Killing yourself would be taking the easy way out. If you're that weak, do it, and don't waste more oxygen. If not, fight for the life you have and stop feeling sorry for yourself."

"You have no idea what I'm feeling." Her eyes sliced to his.

"Your feelings are meaningless down here. They will feast on your tears and eat you alive when the bars close at night. You have a lot to learn before Braderhelm breaks you."

"And how long did it take for Braderhelm to break you?" The seething question escaped her tongue before she could bottle the words.

Takeshi's eyes darkened, and his expression shifted ominously. She realized her mistake too late.

"You must like pain."

So fast she barely tracked the movement, he whipped out the taser from his back pocket and pushed the metal into her side. The ensuing electric shock hurt like hell, and she yelped as her skin throbbed and trembled. He pushed off the wall, and his brows drew together.

Through her shaking body, she thought she saw a hint of unrest in his eyes, but it was quickly replaced with a detached glare.

"Pit time is over, 317."

A sharp pang rumbled through her chest. Her name stripped away hurt more than the electrical shock. His eyes pierced hers in aversion, and without another word, he walked away. She held her side with one hand and wiped a stray tear with the other. Her chest felt like it was splitting, raw emotion threatening to cut her into a million pieces. She wanted to fall to her knees and cry and also wanted to punch the nearest human, even if they hadn't wronged her.

She hated her life. She hated Takeshi Steele. She hated this place. She hated God. All the enemies were at the gates, and there was nowhere to hide or seek solitude.

Khalani spent most of her life concealing and covering up the tortured layers of her mind, and all it took was one day for the Captain of Braderhelm to crack her down the center and expose her damaged core. The harsh truth didn't need to be roared in the crisp air; it spilled out of her brittle bones and wandering eyes every second.

Stripped of her barriers, she was nothing but a sad, weak, and lonely mess who didn't belong anywhere.

Not even in prison.

7

*Does anyone win the race of life,
or do we all get participation trophies?*

Khalani roughly wiped a bead of sweat trickling down her face. She peered down at her shaking hands and noticed blood all over them. Her blisters had popped. The black dirt mixed with the red blood. It was a misshapen clash. The ugly mixture cascaded down her palms, and she stared at the colors, recognizing herself in the dirty blend. Pain and anger were her kaleidoscopes.

She lowered her hands to wipe the unseemly hues on her clothing but hesitated, realizing it would get blood on her uniform. And that was a peculiar thought.

Who cared what she looked like anymore?

"You alright?" Derek asked, setting the empty wheelbarrow down. She showed him her hands in answer, and he hissed.

"Here." He ripped off a piece of fabric from his arm and wrapped it over her palms.

She ground her teeth together and shut her eyes as he tightened the fabric, covering up her brokenness. The pressure over the wounds was excruciating, but she kept her mouth shut, having dealt with worse.

"Better?"

"Yeah."

"You two, keep working!" Marcela shrieked at them.

Her triceps burned in agony. It was as if her arms begged to be sliced off, so they could walk away in some sick twisted nightmare. If she could cut herself apart and walk away breathing, she would. Weird thoughts of self-mutilation entered her brain as she went into overdrive mode, loading her wheelbarrow with hefty rocks.

Khalani blocked the pain into the far reaches of her mind, a skill she'd mastered long before being sentenced to prison. Two weeks had passed since her first day in Braderhelm. She hadn't spoken to Takeshi Steele since their last encounter. Avoiding him like the plague was a difficult task since he locked her in a cell every night, but it was one she excelled in.

The work in the tunnels never got any easier. Screaming and punishment went hand-in-hand, sometimes for seemingly nothing. Khalani learned to ignore the hunger pains in her stomach and scoffed down water at any opportunity. She must have already lost ten pounds, as evidenced by her protruding ribs.

The worst part was the migraines. It felt like someone was banging against the walls of her brain with a sledgehammer, trying to conduct a never-ending symphony.

Derek, Serene, and Adan helped keep her sane. She didn't feel nearly as alone when she was with them. After all, misery does love company.

But even they couldn't alleviate the endless sadness residing inside her. Going through the motions of her new desolate reality was her daily dose of torment. Wake, pain, eat, pain, sleep, repeat. Over and over. Like a merry-go-round.

They built a merry-go-round once in Apollo. That was the first time she saw a horse. It was a fake horse, of course, but she didn't care. She rode the merry-go-round after school hundreds of times. It was 60 seconds of happiness.

She wanted to make that blissful minute extend forever.

The Apollo Council voted to destroy the merry-go-round after one month of operation. They said it distracted from daily work that needed to be completed for the city. A convenient excuse. They couldn't let anyone be too happy or talkative with their neighbor.

What better way to make someone depend on you than to isolate them?

"Don't slack on me now," Derek instructed, noting her slowed movements as she got lost in her thoughts.

"Do you ever miss it?" she asked, shifting the rocks in the wheelbarrow to make more room.

"Miss what?"

"Your life before all this."

"I miss sleeping in my bed and taking a shit on my own toilet," Derek said.

Despite the pain, she couldn't help the grin that formed. That is why she liked Derek. No matter how severe or grim the circumstances were, he had this carefree attitude. Like everything, and nothing mattered.

Derek was silent as they continued to work. She thought he wouldn't say anything more about it, but he glanced around, ensuring no guards were nearby.

"I didn't have anything to miss," he whispered. "No family. No friends. My life was my work in Apollo's R&R Labs."

Khalani cut her eyes to him, taken aback. The Research and Resource Labs oversaw Apollo's food supply and studied new methods of underground growth. Due to the lab's critical importance for the survival of Apollo, only scientists with top clearance were allowed.

"But you are so young," she exclaimed.

"Age doesn't matter. They are hungry for new talent, and I had top marks on all my testing. That was one of the happiest days of my life when they accepted me. It didn't last," his voice and gaze drifted off. Curiosity burned inside her.

"Why were you sentenced here, Derek?"

Derek slowed his movements, and his eyes sliced to the floor.

She couldn't tell if it was shame or regret, but a haunting look entered his expression, and his whole demeanor changed. As if he had the weight of the world piled on his shoulders, and only he knew that the weight was beginning to topple. He gripped the sides of the wheelbarrow hard. So hard the veins on his hands were protruding.

"I found something they didn't want me to find." The words came out in a guttural whisper, and his brows drew low on his face.

Khalani frowned and tilted her head. "What do you mean?"

He opened his mouth like he was about to say something. She waited, but nothing came out. He heaved a sigh and shook his head, coming out of a trance.

"It doesn't matter. None of this does." He picked up the ends of the wheelbarrow. "You. Me. Everything around us. All a means to an end." He wheeled his load away.

Her mouth parted at his abrupt departure. Apollo held its scientists in high regard. They wouldn't have imprisoned Derek over something trivial.

Her mind wrapped around the many possibilities, like trying to pinpoint a singular speck of dust in the misty air. She could try to ask Derek again, but something about his expression stopped her.

She recognized that look. It was mirrored in her own gaze and every other prisoner. It was hopeless but layered with something unique. Not hopelessness because you don't see a way out but hopelessness because you had already seen the way out, and the way out is worse.

****

"I'm assigning you to work with Winifred today." George, an old prisoner who gave Khalani her afternoon work, sighed after his eyes swept over her bandages that were bleeding through with blood. She barely even noticed.

"Meet her in the library to help with the Ordinances."

She didn't even know Braderhelm had a library. As the prisoners began to leave for their afternoon shifts, a rigid body suddenly bumped into her, knocking her to the ground. She opened her mouth in a silent exclamation of agony, placing all her weight on her bloody palms to break the fall.

She peered up, and a beefy muscular girl with facial piercings and a half-shaved head stood over her. Khalani vaguely recognized her as the girl who threatened her in the pit her first night in Braderhelm.

"Watch where you're going," she spat the words down at Khalani and walked over her.

Anger welled up in her chest. She stumbled to her feet, ready to retaliate, but the girl had already disappeared around the corner.

"You alright?" Serene appeared at her side, helping wipe the dirt off her garments.

"I'm fine," she seethed. "Who was that?"

"Dana. In here for murdering a woman and her husband. She runs with a pretty bad crowd down here. Don't know what you did to get her attention, but I would stay far away. You don't want to be tossed into the pit with her," Serene warned, noting the violence in her eyes.

Malice rumbled inside her, almost as potent as her hate for Takeshi. Almost. But Dana was twice her size. Even Khalani was smart enough to know that fighting her would be a losing battle. The only thing she could do—the smart thing—was maintain a low profile. Something she was apparently bad at.

Khalani had never been assigned to the library, but every day, she was getting better at navigating Braderhelm. Not exactly a happy achievement, but she'll take her victories where she could.

Khalani walked through the maze of tunnels and approached the black spiral staircase George mentioned. She bit her lip in consternation. The stairs were rusted and looked like they'd crumble the second she put weight on them. The staircase had to have been constructed when Braderhelm was first built. She leaned over and peered up. The library was supposed to be at the top.

Her fingers furiously tapped against the black banister.

She was already a few minutes late. Her eyes strayed upward, and she let out a deep sigh. What the hell. If she was going to die in Braderhelm, being defeated by a staircase wouldn't be a bad way to go out. Maybe she'll return as a ghost and haunt others who attempt to climb its depths.

She tentatively placed a foot on the first step. The board creaked loudly but appeared to be stable. Khalani breathed a sigh of relief and continued the steady climb. Higher and higher, spiraling around the steep steps. The sound of rusting metal echoed down the stone hallway.

After several loops, she approached the top and faced a black door with a small white symbol in the corner. She inspected it closer. It was an odd triangle shape with five points. Weird.

Should she knock?

The few libraries in Apollo were open to the public, but she rarely went due to their poor selection. All books from the Great Collapse were restricted. The Council only allowed its citizens to read books for school, training for various jobs, or the Apollo Ordinances. She didn't expect this library to be any different.

She knocked on the dilapidated door a few times. Dust fell around her knuckles as she rasped against the steel. A full minute passed, and no one came to the door.

"Hello? George sent me here for duty," Khalani shouted.

Silence.

Another 30 seconds passed, and Khalani banged the door louder. "Helloooo!"

The door swiftly opened, and her hand knocked against air as an old woman appeared. She wore a large silver monocle on one eye and had short, dark hair so frizzy and thick, like she'd just tangled with an electric socket. A tiny, silver necklace around the woman's neck caught her eye. She didn't wear prisoner garments like Khalani. She wore a long purple dress that grazed against the floor, with a golden sun covering the front. The woman quickly grabbed Khalani by the arm with speed she wasn't expecting and pulled her through the doorway.

"No noise, no noise! You'll mess her concentration," the old lady yelled, slamming the door shut and rushing past Khalani.

Khalani scrunched her forehead and glanced around in silent confusion. She was wedged in between two towering wooden stacks of books that touched the short ceiling. The smell of old leather wafted through the air, and the room was cast in a dark shadow. The only light emitting through the library came from a candelabra placed on a short circular table at the far end of the bookshelves.

The frizzy-haired woman rushed to the table, laboring over an odd metal object. Khalani traced her hand along the bookshelf. Apollo Ordinance Volume 1. Apollo Ordinance Volume 2. Every leather bind read the same title, similar to what she would find in any Apollo library.

Her attention cut back to the old lady mumbling to herself as she tinkered with the weird gizmo.

"Umm, excuse me, are you Winifred?" Khalani asked.

"Shhh!" The old lady waved her hand over. "Come see, come see."

Once she walked past the two long bookcases, the room opened up. To the left of the circular desk lay a wooden desk lined against the stone wall, papers and books riddled on top. She squinted her eyes. Those didn't appear to be Apollo Ordinance volumes. Or any sanctioned book, for that matter.

She stepped forward to get a closer look, but something else caught her eye. It was a medium-sized painting surrounded by a golden frame and placed in the center of the wall. It depicted a man wearing a long white coat in a desert, walking toward a tall metal building that spiraled to the sky. The building had strands of red and blue colors flowing along the sides, intertwining like coils of DNA.

Khalani continued to study the odd picture, her eyes narrowing when the woman tapped her shoulder. "Come sit. You must see." Excitement tinged the woman's voice.

Khalani forgot about the strange painting as the woman pushed her down on a creaking black chair. In the center of the circular table lay a small wooden box. The frizzy-haired lady flipped the box and held some metal tools toward the bottom.

She meticulously worked, leaning her head so close the monocle almost scratched against the wood.

"Okay." The woman set down the tools. "It should work." She placed the wooden box upright and turned a knob on the back.

Khalani heard a light ticking and leaned back warily. Her muscles tensed as the box opened, and a tiny, porcelain girl in a pink ballet costume emerged. The soft sound of music began to filter through the air.

The woman clapped her hands excitedly, her hair bouncing up and down as she gleamed with happiness. "It works!"

The porcelain girl slowly turned, her arms forming a circle over her head, leg bent behind as the soft melody played on.

Khalani's eyes widened, and she leaned forward, completely hypnotized by the inanimate girl spinning round and round. The haunting hymn encompassed the small space as if the very air wanted to hear more and welcome its release into the world.

She lifted her gaze to the mysterious woman with her hands clasped together, the brightest smile shining across her face. "What is it? Where did it come from?"

The woman still bounced up and down, grinning from ear to ear. "It's a music box! Someone on Genesis threw it down the trash chute. Thought it was garbage. Not Winnie, though. She knew this was special." She tapped on her chest proudly.

The ballerina continued to twirl, and Khalani's mouth held agape. Even though the library was small and dark, a delicate warmth filled the space, easing the restlessness in her body as if the music had cast a spell over her. In a way, she was jealous of the tiny dancer who lived on a steady foundation. Unchanging. Safe. Only needing to turn when the dark doors of her life unraveled.

The music box slowly wound down, and the girl stopped moving. A dreamy sigh escaped the old woman, and Khalani stared at her in amazement. "How did you get that down here?"

The woman's smile disappeared, and she paled as if realizing Khalani was there for the first time.

"Wait, who are you? Why did you come here?"

"George told me to meet you in the library for my afternoon shift. My name is Khalani," she quickly explained.

The woman started to visibly relax, exhaling deeply.

"You're Winifred, right?" Khalani asked.

"Winifred is the name of an old woman. No, no. Call me Winnie. Winnie Talbot." Winnie grabbed the music box delicately and walked to the other desk. She gently tucked the box away in one of the drawers, patting the desk in comfort. "It's been a while since they sent a fellow prisoner to help Winnie."

Khalani frowned in confusion. "You're a prisoner?"

Winnie chuckled. "My goodness, dear girl, why would Winnie ever choose to be in this place? There is no color in these walls or liveliness in the air. Winnie loves color." Winnie looked at her like this was the most obvious fact, and she was clearly the idiot for not catching those details.

"But your outfit…." Khalani gestured to her flowing purple dress.

"Oh, you like it?" Winnie twirled. "Winnie made it herself," she said with pride and a sparkle in her eye.

"It's umm…pretty."

Winnie squinted her eyes, noticing Khalani's ugly attire. She touched the monocle as if to examine her better.

It'd been a week since she had taken a shower, and the hard sweat of labor manifested its ugly undertone over the dull fabric. The grey color of her smelly uniform was the antithesis of Winnie's embodiment. Her energy was unusual but vivacious. Strange yet fascinating. Charming, unapologetic, and intriguing. All at the same time.

"Hmmm, that won't do. Won't do at all." Winnie snapped her fingers. "Winnie will see to getting your own, don't worry. But do have patience. It will take some time to make it for you."

Her forehead puckered as she glanced around the perplexing space as if to find answers written on the book covers. "I don't understand. How were you able to get that…music box in Braderhelm? How can you wear those clothes? Aren't you worried about the guards finding out?"

"Whoah, whoah. Slow down before your mind moves so fast that it turns backward. Not good for the body."

Huh?

Winnie gestured for Khalani to sit down and sighed dramatically as she sat across from her.

"Winnie was sentenced to this place a long time ago. So long, it can be hard to remember anything before. But Winnie refuses to forget. Winnie maintains the Apollo Ordinances and ensures they are distributed to the guards and prisoners every few months, lest they forget who holds their leash. You know of the Ordinances, right?"

Of course, she did. Every citizen did. The Apollo Ordinances were the binding set of laws for the city, cast down since humans first went underground during the Great Collapse. Total submission was mandatory.

The Ordinances explained the history of Apollo, the other underground cities, and the events that led to the Great Collapse. It detailed the greed and power that overtook society and why it was necessary to obey the Council in all things; to prevent the extinction of humanity.

She nodded. "Yes. The first Apollo Council wrote the Ordinances to save us from rebellion and radiation above."

"Is that what they're teaching?" Winnie bent over, choking on laughter. "Those fools, thinking they can re-write history to match what best suits them."

"What do you mean?"

"The Apollo Ordinances are nothing but pure propaganda designed to keep you in line. A few professors in the early years protested against the Ordinances. They worked tirelessly to convince people that the Apollo Council would do away with all democracy and descend into a totalitarian regime. They were all executed, of course. Their predictions slowly came to fruition, and we don't even remember their names.

"Every citizen fell in line because they lost their will to fight. All they could remember was the vision of nuclear bombs descending on their beloved cities, dancing across their screens as their loved ones perished and hope burned. The image of the sun scattered from their minds, and the feel of the ocean water dissipated. Animals and plants died along with their souls. Humanity escaped fiery terror above and thought they would find solace below, but it only brought us closer to hell. How far the mighty have fallen," Winnie trailed off in a dismal voice.

"How do you know all this?"

"Winnie worked in the Archives, and the professors wrote a few books about it," she said nonchalantly, still lost in thought.

Khalani's eyes shot up, and she scooted to the edge of her chair, her hands clasped together. "The Archives? Did you know a man who used to work there? His name was Douglas."

"Douglas?" Winnie tapped her fingers against her chin, staring at the ground as if it contained a montage of memory. "Douglas, hmm. I can't say I remember, but the Archive workers don't generally converse with one another. Too many secrets are held within our brains. Charles was my only friend."

Khalani leaned back in disappointment. She wanted to simply share a memory of him with someone who remembered his face. Grief perforated her heart once more.

"It was because of Winnie's work in the Archives that the guards selected her to be the next keeper of the Braderhelm library. The guards never come and force Winnie to stay here all day, preferring she stay with the books. Call her 'Cookie Winnie.' Call her crazy lady." Winnie's lips pursed.

"Winnie doesn't mind, though. Because they don't pay attention to Winnie, she can get items smuggled into the shipments. But they haven't sent any prisoners up here for a long time. You are the first. It's been…lonely." Winnie stared down at her hands, sagging her back.

Khalani's lips turned down at her expression.

It might not be too far off to say that Winnie was not all there in the head, or at least…not completely normal.

But she didn't fear the old woman. It was hard to explain, but a gentleness in her infectious energy drew her in.

"Well, they sent me to help today. Maybe, if you request it, I can be placed with you more often," Khalani offered in a hopeful voice.

Winnie's attention shifted to Khalani, and she nodded emphatically. "Winnie would like that."

Khalani's lips curved up. Working here definitely beat any other assignment she'd been given. And there was something different about the library, like a semblance of life lay wallowed in the space, untouched by the forsaken walls of Braderhelm.

In here…Khalani felt like she could breathe.

"What do you need help with?" She glanced around the disheveled room and cringed as a colossal cockroach crawled under the corner of a bookcase. Winnie's eyes sparkled and gleamed at Khalani's words.

"This is great! Someone to keep me company while I finish my work. Maybe she can help…no, no. That's a foolish dream, Winnie. No trust. But still, company! Wonderful, wonderful," Winnie mused, pacing back and forth.

It was odd that Winnie kept referring to herself in the third person, but that was probably something Khalani had to get used to.

Winnie kept muttering to herself with no end in sight.

"Uh, Winnie?"

Winnie stopped and focused on her. "Yes, dear?"

"Help with anything?" Khalani reminded her.

"Oh, yes, yes!" Winnie threw her hands up emphatically and disappeared behind one of the stacks. She reappeared a few seconds later, rolling a cart with a dozen books entitled 'Apollo Ordinance Volume 1.'

"We must deliver these books to the guard housing blocks every few months. You can help Winnie by delivering these. Use these papers to jot down each room number you complete." Winnie handed her a couple blank white sheets of paper and a pencil.

She drew back in trepidation, not wanting to get anywhere near where the guards slept.

Winnie patted her shoulder in comfort.

"Not to worry, dear. They prefer to kill prisoners out in the open. Don't venture from your path, and make sure not to enter their rooms. There are worse things that can happen than death."

8

Demons no longer rest in the bedlam of sleep.
I can hear their monstrous steps lingering in the deep.

The guard's quarters were located in the lowest level of Braderhelm. The black granite walls and lit torches that failed to emit warmth forced shivers down her spine.

Khalani rolled the cart of books along the dark hallway. Her sweaty palms clutched the metal handle with a death grip. The eerie disquiet, disrupted by the screeching of wheels against the stone floor, made her shallow breaths pump faster.

She was brutally aware of the imminent danger. The hairs on her arms bristled, and her eyes anxiously slid to every corner, crevice, and steel door she passed. A distant scream echoed down the hall from one of the enclosed rooms. Her eyes widened as she whipped her head around. No prisoner stood visible, but the grating bellow sliced the murky air like a deadly hymn. Blood pooled from her face and goose-bumps chilled her entire body.

The screams ground to a sudden halt, and the only sound left was her frantic heartbeat in the still air.

She needed to leave this place. *Now.*

She wasted no time depositing the books at the foot of every door. There were no bars or cells. It appeared that each guard had an actual bedroom. But she wasn't about to knock and ask for a grand tour. Adrenaline pumped through her bloodstream, so prominent that pain no longer registered in her hands as her body moved at record speed.

Each door had an engraved number, and she quickly scribbled the room numbers down as she shoved the papers and pencil into her pocket. As Khalani bent over in front of one of the steel doors, it suddenly swung open.

Black boots entered her vision.

Her muscles froze, eyes slowly lifting. Rising across a wide chest in a black vest, past broad shoulders, to a face that peered down on her with a sinister grin. The man's bald head was so shiny the skin looked waxed. The eerie expression in his gaze made her heart sputter to a halt.

"Are you here to help me, prisoner?" The guard's grin deepened as his cold blue eyes perused her hunched-over frame.

Khalani swiftly stood ramrod straight, icy fear lathering her skin. She held out the book, her hands visibly trembling. "Your yearly review of the Apollo Ordinance, sir." She tilted her head forward, using her hair to partially obscure her face.

The guard stepped closer, and his cold-blooded energy prickled at her senses. Khalani subtly shifted back, ready to bolt out of there. He smirked at her movement and hovered closer. His piercing stare offered no kindness or blanket disregard but rather a cruel interest. Something far worse.

"Prisoners shouldn't be wandering these halls alone."

She bit the inside of her lip and tried to remain calm, but her heart pounded against the confines of her chest. "I was instructed to deliver the Ordinances to each room."

He leaned against the wall and shook his head. "Well, you seem to be moving rather slowly. That will require some punishment. Luckily for you, I'm in a forgiving mood. Come in here, and you can help me forget this happened."

Shallow breaths bumped out of her chest. Winnie's words rang in her ear like an alarm bell.

"I'm sorry. I must leave to finish my work." She swallowed tightly as the words came out in a quick breath. She turned, but her shoulder was quickly captured in a vicelike grasp.

The guard squeezed harder, making her face squint and eyes water. His grip was so impenetrable that his fingertips would soon imprint on her bones. Khalani held her breath, and every single muscle in her body became rigid as a flood of terror shrouded her veins.

"Please, let me go," she pleaded.

The guard ignored her begging, slowly pulling out a silver switchblade with his other hand. Her green eyes nearly popped out of their sockets.

He casually rubbed the blade along her forearm, and she tried to pull back, but as soon as she moved, he pushed the knife into her skin, drawing a thin line of blood down her arm. Her adrenaline went into overdrive as red liquid pooled across her arm.

He was going to kill her. She was going to be murdered in this decrepit dungeon.

She frantically glanced around for help. No one else stood in the hallway. She was alone. What would happen if she were to scream? Would anyone come to her aid? But she already knew the answer to those desperate thoughts.

In Braderhelm, rape might be standard practice.

Despite her best efforts, the guard pulled her closer and slid his other hand around her neck, the blade kissing her skin as she gulped. Khalani flinched at his touch and tried to turn away, but he squeezed her chin harshly and forced her gaze back to him.

"You don't look too bad. Must be new here. If you don't give me any trouble, I won't be too rough with you. Promise," he whispered the last part in her ear.

Heavy pressure prickled against her skin, constricting the air around her. She couldn't breathe.

Her muscles were paralyzed as the guard forced her closer. She wasn't moving.

Why wasn't she moving?

The wet slime of his tongue darted along her earlobe. She closed her eyes, nails scraping against her palms, as her mind began to shut down. His heavy breath sank into her neck, and the hard bulge in his pants pressed against her stomach.

"Get down on your knees and take it," he commanded.

Khalani's eyes flashed open. Without thinking, she leaned into his weight and forcefully shoved her knee between his legs. The guard let out a heavy groan and released her arm. His back bowed, and he clasped his stomach.

"You little bitch," he swore, still bent over.

Khalani didn't waste any time escaping. She left the cart and sprinted full speed up the stairs. Her legs pumped faster and faster, like a ferocious fire raged behind her.

Every prisoner was still finishing their afternoon shift, and no one saw her running for her life. She didn't stop running until she got to her cell block. She put her hands on her knees and coughed in exhaustion as sweat ran over her entire body.

She rubbed her hands over her hair, realizing her limbs were shaking. Her eyes slid down both sides of the hall, frantically looking for signs of the guard, but he was nowhere to be found.

Her heart refused to slow its vicious pace. As the entire predicament replayed in her mind, Khalani finally realized the severity of her actions.

"What did I do? What did I do?" she asked herself.

She just assaulted a guard.

Khalani buried her face in her hands and sank back against the wall. Her mind conjured unthinkable scenarios. Suffering she'd no doubt face from her actions. It might not matter that he assaulted her first. She was a lowly prisoner. The guards could inflict any punishment desired without consequence.

She was already dead.

The bell—signaling the end of the afternoon shift—rang, startling Khalani. She held a hand to her heart and tried to focus on inhaling but struggled to catch a single breath.

She was having a panic attack.

The blood, still streaming from her arm, caught her eye, momentarily distracting her. She slowly wiped the blood on her uniform, and a sizeable cut presented in a cruel line down her forearm. How many markings would she receive in Braderhelm?

How long would she have to live?

One thing Khalani knew, she couldn't hide outside her cell. She had no choice but to go to the pit and hoped that if the guard was there, the number of people around would deter him from killing her on the spot.

She rubbed her fingers together, eyes meticulously sliding to every space of open air in the caves as she walked to the pit. Her muscles were coiled tight like a wire, expecting the guard to emerge from the shadows any moment and wrap his hands around her throat.

As she quickly descended into the pit, the soft, distant echo of cheers emerged from the fighting ring. It all reverberated as a dull ringing in her ears.

Her vision was cloudy and murky. The sound of prisoners talking jumbled into a tumultuous mixture of white noise. Thoughts collided within her brain at a thousand miles an hour. It was hard to concentrate. Think. Feel. Her panic manifested and grew to greater heights as she surveyed the pit.

Where was he?

"Khalani."

Was he waiting to strike when she least expected it?

"Khalani."

Would she meet her demise quickly, or would death come slowly and be filled with pain? If her death was guaranteed, maybe the only way she could gain control was by doing it herself…

"Khalani!"

She flinched as Serene's voice filtered through her raging mind.

"What's wrong?" Serene frowned. "Did you not hear me?"

"Sorry." She rubbed a hand through her hair and tried to catch a shallow breath. "Sorry. I got lost in thought."

"What happened to your arm?"

She quickly pulled her arm back, attempting to hide the ugly cut. She wasn't prepared to talk about what happened. Khalani didn't have any siblings growing up. Dealing with problems on her own was how she'd survived thus far. She didn't know how to operate any other way.

"Happened on shift today." She waved her hand dismissively.

Serene's eyes narrowed. "That happened in the library? The wound looks fresh. Did a guard do that?"

Damnit. Serene noticed way too much. "It's no big deal." She glanced away dismissively, wanting to disappear once more. Forever invisible.

"Khalani," Serene repeated in a soft voice.

She turned back and saw the worry plastered on her face. Khalani felt a strange presence in her chest, like a physical weight as pertinent and real as food swallowed down her throat.

"I'm worried about you. I know you like your space, and we haven't known each other long…but you can talk to me. You don't have to go through everything alone," Serene insisted.

She froze. No one had cared about her well-being or got close enough to worry, not since Douglas died. She drove people away because the pain of losing someone you love was too agonizing to bear. Affection was akin to weakness.

"I'm sorry, Serene. But it's better this way. People who get close to me, they always get hurt. That's what I do. I hurt people. And this time…I'd rather just let it be me." Khalani shook her head, fighting back tears. It was all too much. She wanted to scream and never be heard again. All at the same time.

Serene stepped closer, and Khalani nearly shifted back at the warmth in her expression. "Cruel people don't look back on the pain they inflict," Serene insisted. "And that's not you. I saw it in your eyes the first day you spoke of your family. We are more alike than you think, and if I didn't have my brother…it would be worse than death. That's why I'm here. I told you I would look out for you.

"*I know* why you keep pulling away," Serene emphasized. "I get it. But you don't have to worry about us leaving you. We're in here for life, too. Remember? Deep down, you know that being alone isn't what you want. So, talk to me."

Serene's words impacted her like a chipped knife slicing her open, leaving her exposed. Khalani wanted to run, but another part, a stronger part, ached for someone to hug her and tell her that everything would be okay. Even if it was a lie.

She fidgeted, uncertainty clawing through, but Serene never left her side. "Are you sure you wanna hear this shit?" Khalani tentatively glanced up, her resistance faltering.

"Yeah. I do." No hesitation. Her crystal blue eyes were filled with compassion, like Serene *understood* the trials and toles of loneliness.

Khalani fully let out a breath, like she was about to walk off the edge of a cliff. She wavered but decided to tell Serene everything that happened in the guard's quarters. By the time she finished, Serene's jaw hung open in shock and outrage.

"You should've killed that asshole when you had the chance."

"Shh, keep your voice down."

"Have you seen him in here at all?" Serene cast an incensed look around the room.

Khalani gave another slow perusal of the pit and slowly shook her head. "No. But he *will* find me. I can't escape."

Serene placed a hand on her shoulder. "Don't think this is a death sentence. He's not your block guard, and I don't think he would try anything out in the open, like in the pit. They've been cracking down on guards killing prisoners because there aren't enough of us. We just need to make sure he doesn't get you alone," she stated.

"How?" The skepticism was evident in her tone.

"I'm sure if you tell Winifred what happened, she won't make you go to the guard's quarters again. In the meantime, you stick with us on the way to your assignments. Only the Captain has access to all the cells, and although Steele has a major boulder stuck up his ass, I don't think he would allow a prisoner to be murdered on his block."

Wonderful. Putting her life in Takeshi Steele's hands. She was as good as dead.

The fear and paranoia were evident on her face, and Serene gave her a reassuring squeeze. "You'll get through this. We all will."

"Have you always been so positive?" Khalani asked.

"No. But why worry about something that hasn't happened yet? That's just putting yourself through it twice."

Khalani didn't know how to argue with that logic. She nodded, grateful for Serene talking her down. There was no smiling or hugging. Just an understanding that filtered through the space. An acceptance that whatever came their way, whether it be a short death or a long painful life, it wouldn't have to be experienced alone.

That tiny, singular thought was enough to keep her body moving forward. Serene guided her toward the fighting pit, insisting it would be a necessary distraction. And for once, she agreed.

More people than usual stood around the crater, gazing intently at the fight. Her eyes widened when she saw who was in the pit. It wasn't prisoners. It was two Braderhelm guards.

"They let guards fight each other?" Khalani asked Serene.

She didn't recognize either guard, but they didn't hold back as they rammed their fists into each other's faces. The crowd cheered as the two men started wrestling to the ground, each trying to gain the upper hand. One was trying to go for an armbar while the other was trying to wrap his legs around the guard's neck.

"The guards can't take all their aggression out on the prisoners. They still need some type of slave labor. This is a way to channel it," Serene explained.

Blood sprayed as a fist connected with a nose. The crunch could be heard from here. Prisoners cheered and hollered, and the noises constricted around her as the vision shifted. Khalani imagined blood dripping from her body as a blade sliced her throat, her life ending in a violent affair.

That was her fate if the guard found her. Would there even be a body left behind? Her breaths came heavier as the crowd cramped around her, fighting for a closer look at the brutality.

Claustrophobia mixed in with her fear, a deadly combination. Her palms were sweaty, and it felt like she was being touched all over, crawling beneath her skin. She was having a panic attack again, and bile crept up her throat.

She turned to Serene. "I'm feeling a little sick."

"You want me to come with?"

"No, no." Khalani waved her hand. "I'll be fine. Just need a little air. I won't leave the pit. Promise."

Serene assessed her with a frown but eventually said, "Okay." Khalani didn't waste another second and walked through the crowd, away from the fighting pit.

Everyone's attention was riveted toward the center.

"Pin him, Guard Walker!"

"Mason's so weak. He wouldn't last a second on the surface."

The different cacophony of voices surrounded her as she pushed through the prisoners. Khalani raced through an opening, and out of nowhere, a leg appeared in front of her. Before she could react fast enough, she tripped over it, catapulting to the ground. Pain ran up her arm as she landed on her elbow.

"Get used to staying on the ground," Dana's arrogant voice sounded above her.

Not again.

Khalani quickly stood up to face her opponent, ignoring the shooting pain as she put weight on her palm. Dana had her hands planted on her hips and wore an ugly smile.

"What's your problem?" Khalani growled, about ready to explode.

Dana scoffed. "*You* are my problem. Do you think screwing the guards will grant you favor? It won't."

"What the hell are you talking about?"

Dana stepped forward, her mouth twisting cruelly. "I saw you trying to get friendly with Captain Steele in the pit your first day. You are sadly mistaken if you think he'll help your situation by getting close to him."

Friendly was not a term she would use to describe her interactions with the cold Captain. The thought of viewing a guard, especially Takeshi, in any way positive made her want to vomit.

"Then you must have watched him taser me. Getting close to Captain Steele is the *last* thing on my mind. I have no idea why you would like any guard, but there is zero competition from me. So, you can back off." She lifted her hands, a last chance for reason and peace.

"Like him?" Dana gave an ugly sneer. "You're even dumber than you look. You have no idea of the plotting and games that go on down here. Get in my way again, and I'll kill you."

Her blood boiled. There were only so many times that her life could be threatened in one day before she snapped.

"I'd tell you how I really feel about your so-called games, but I wasn't born with enough middle fingers to express myself," Khalani snarled, cutting all pretenses of civility.

Dana's mouth opened, and she quickly snapped it shut. She leaned closer to Khalani as her eyes transformed into daggers. "I would sleep with two eyes open if I were you, 317." Dana abruptly walked past her, bumping into her shoulder.

Khalani's eyes turned into a serpentine glare as Dana disappeared through the crowd. The harder she tried to keep a low profile, the more enemies she made. Everything was going horribly wrong. She scrubbed a hand through the top of her hair.

Space. Endless space. That was what she needed.

She moved away from the crowd, looking for an area where she could be momentarily alone. She wouldn't leave the pit but needed to find temporary solace for her own sanity.

Khalani turned her head to ensure she could still see the prisoners surrounding the fighting pit. Alone but not alone. It would have to be good enough for now.

Suddenly, Khalani bumped into a hard body as her head was turned. "Sorry," she mumbled, twisting herself backward.

"Where do you think you're headed?"

The familiar voice was so deep it had its own vibration. Khalani's insides dropped. She lifted her eyes, and Takeshi Steele stood in her way. His thick arms were crossed over his chest like an impenetrable wall.

"I...um," she hesitated. "I was just getting some fresh air."

"Fresh air. Underground," he repeated.

Her lips formed a grim line. "Yes. Can prisoners do that?"

"Prisoners must remain in the pit until break is over." Takeshi's chin raised in suspicion. "Venturing toward the exit is not following those orders. I'm sure you'll find suitable entertainment at the fighting ring."

He nodded, motioning her to go back the way she came.

Everything about Takeshi angered her. His voice. His face. Even his freaking hair annoyed her. Interacting with him was its own form of torture.

"The fights made me sick. Am I allowed to throw up in private, or does that require an audience too?"

"Go ahead." Takeshi gestured to the floor, calling her bluff.

Shit. Nothing was working.

"Can't I just get some space? Is that too much to ask for?" She was close to begging at this point.

His brows furrowed at her expression, but he remained in her path. "Do you usually ask questions you already know the answer to?"

"I don't know. Do you find it difficult enhancing the misery in this place, or does that just come naturally?"

Khalani's chest rose in agitated breaths. She expected—almost welcomed—a sting from his taser, but Takeshi merely raised an eyebrow, refusing the painful escape she desired.

"Are you finished?"

"Please." She made a last-ditch effort. "I won't cause any trouble."

He gave a humorless chuckle that made her want to slice him apart. "You have trouble written all over you, Kanes."

"Well, maybe you're wrong."

"I'm never wrong."

Khalani hated men. Especially the ones with muscles. They couldn't be trusted.

She lifted her hands in exacerbation, giving up on Takeshi holding any sympathy in his tiny, pea-sized heart. "Fine."

Takeshi's body froze. "What is that on your arm?"

"Don't worry about it," she muttered, turning hastily.

She hadn't moved a couple inches before he struck.

He swiftly moved forward and grasped her wrist. Her heartbeat increased at the sudden movement, and she tried to break free. But there was no match against Takeshi's firm grip. The inky depths in his eyes pulsed with savagery. The Captain focused on her forearm, the long cut on full display.

"Your doing? Where did you get a knife?" Takeshi snapped, staring at her accusingly. Her mouth opened in shock, and she tried to pull away, but he wouldn't let her move.

"Nowhere. I didn't try to kill myself," she huffed indignantly. "One of your guards did that."

"Who?" his voice deepened, chilling the already cool air.

"It doesn't even matter," she fumed. "Let me go." Khalani didn't want him to find out, didn't want to give him the satisfaction of fully believing that she was, in fact, too weak for Braderhelm.

A vein pulsed from his neck, and his jaw visibly tightened at her words. Takeshi inched closer, appearing ready to strangle her. His murderous expression hardened, but another cold-blooded voice ripped through the space.

"Well, isn't this a nice surprise?"

9

Teach me your fears
so I may become a horror of my own.

Khalani's feet held frozen, rooted to the spot. The color drained from her face. She knew that voice. The repulsive baritone belonged to the guard who assaulted her in the lower levels. A deep pressure constrained her lungs and took root in her pelvis.

Takeshi's muscles tensed alongside her, and he abruptly released her arm. Mind-numbing fear encompassed the very air around her. She slowly turned, and a sadistic smile greeted her. The bald guard stood a few feet away like a dangerous predator, his attention fixated on her.

Her skin crawled, and the hairs on her arms stood up at attention. It took everything inside not to bolt and run. His eyes promised punishment. A punishment he would enjoy. Even the way he stared at Khalani made her feel violated.

Should she run? Should she fight back or just accept her fate? Trapped. She was trapped. Stuck between two guards of Braderhelm. She couldn't fight both Takeshi Steele and the guard at the same time. A dangerous glimmer flared in his eyes, and the grim reality of her situation lay bare. There was no escape.

Her hands fisted by her side. Death would not be greeted with open arms. If this was to be her end, she would go down swinging.

"What do you need, Barron?" Takeshi's deep voice cut through the tension.

Barron's attention switched to him. He plastered on a cold smile. "Captain Steele. Always a pleasure. You *can* help me, actually. This is the new prisoner on your cell block, correct?" He gestured to Khalani, not looking away from Takeshi.

"Yes," Takeshi said impassively.

"Would you mind if I have a word alone with her?" Barron's smile grew wider. The stabbing fear intensified throughout her body, eclipsing everything else. This was it. Takeshi would hand her over to him, and she would undoubtedly suffer a fate worse than death. She imperceptibly glanced toward the exit. If she ran now, she could potentially gain a head start.

"Anything you need to say to my prisoner, you can say right here." The words brokered no room for argument.

Her head snapped to Takeshi in surprise as her muscles tightened. Would they try to kill her in public to send a message? Takeshi didn't meet her gaze. He folded his arms over his chest, focusing solely on the guard.

Barron rested a hand on a baton strapped around his waist casually, but there was nothing casual about the tone of his voice when he said,

"I'll have you know that *your* prisoner assaulted me in the lower levels. She's coming with me alone so punishment can be dealt. This involves her and me, Captain Steele. No one else."

Rapid breaths came out of Khalani's chest as Barron turned his attention to her, gesturing to come to him. She didn't move. The only way she would go with that man was kicking and screaming.

"As your Captain, it *is* my business," the words bit out in a low warning. Takeshi stood immobile. It was eerie, like the too-quiet calm before imminent carnage.

Barron's callous smile faded, and his eyes narrowed.

"When I didn't give her what she begged for, she attacked like an animal. She's a disgusting criminal who needs to be disciplined." He pointed at her accusingly, the vile hatred apparent in his expression.

Her mouth fell open as the color drained from her face. *"You liar,"* Khalani hissed, taking a step forward, but Takeshi yanked her back roughly.

Barron tsked. "What did I tell you, animals. She's a little slut like the rest of them and needs to learn a thing or two about respect. This girl could have done permanent damage to me."

She should've done more damage to him! She should've killed him when she had the chance. No doubt, Khalani had not been his first victim. She couldn't see Takeshi's face, but his hands tightened into fists at his side.

"What I find more appalling, Guard Barron," Takeshi stated, ever stoic and calm, "is that you let your guard down, and a prisoner was able to overwhelm you. I think the Warden would be more inclined to hear about a guard too weak to fend off small girls. That would mean you're unfit to handle your job."

Barron's face turned crimson, and he opened his mouth to say something, but Takeshi interrupted him.

"This is what's going to happen. You will go back to your duties and stay away from Prisoner 317. We can't risk her overwhelming you again, can we? Since she is my prisoner, I will give any necessary punishment for her actions. If you do those things, then the Warden won't find out about this," Takeshi commanded, his intense gaze unflappable.

Khalani vaguely realized that her mouth hung open. She couldn't believe her ears. Takeshi Steele was defending her.

"This fucking *bitch* attacked me." Barron's eyes flickered with revenge as he took a threatening step toward her. "For that, she should be dead. This prisoner is coming with me."

"Let me be clear." Takeshi's muscles appeared to ripple as he stepped forward, going toe to toe with him. "As your Captain, I have the final say on this. I would do well to remember that, Barron. You will stand down. Disobey me, and I'll deliver your punishment myself in the fighting pit. And trust me, you don't want that to happen."

Even Khalani shivered at the underlying menace in his threat.

With each passing word, Barron seemed to shrink where he stood, like a deflated balloon. Takeshi was unmoving. Unwavering. A mountainous force.

Awareness of the other prisoners and guards ceased. The air was so quiet she could hear the blood pumping through her chest and the veins pulsing in her neck. The knot in her throat refused to dissipate as she awaited her fate.

"Apologies…Captain," Barron bit out, his smug confidence gone. His face turned a concerning shade of red, but after shredding Khalani with another death glare, he abruptly turned around.

Neither Khalani nor Takeshi moved for a few moments as Barron stalked away in silence. When he disappeared, Khalani let out the deep breath she didn't realize she'd been holding. Her adrenaline was still kicking in full gear, her heart hammering so fast that she was confident he could hear the beats.

She glanced over at Takeshi, who unclenched his fists, stretching his fingers out by his side. The last thing she ever expected was for him to intervene.

Why did he do it?

She was unable to read Takeshi's face as he turned in her direction, his foreboding, distant complexion firmly in place.

"Is this the part where you kill me instead?" she asked.

Sometimes it was easier to say screw you instead of thank you.

Takeshi's lips pressed into a hard line as he gave her the side-eye. "Not yet." He walked past her without a word.

Khalani frowned. She didn't know what to make of Takeshi. He was her biggest adversary, but he didn't let Barron kill her on the spot. Was it a game? A way to toy with her emotions, to keep her off-balance and strike when she least expected it?

"Are you coming?"

Her face scrunched up, eyes darting over her shoulder.

Takeshi stood immobile as he studied her, his expression unreadable.

Her forehead crinkled in confusion. "Coming where?"

"To your cell. I'll allow it this once." He crossed his arms. "You've caused enough trouble for one day."

Her brows furrowed, and she opened her mouth to argue over his choice of words but thought better of it. She desperately wanted to be alone behind bars, but danger loomed.

"What if that guard tries to find me?"

"He won't." His tone was so assured and sinister that she believed him.

She rubbed her palms together, muscles coiling anxiously. She escaped one deadly predator and was in the grasp of another. Takeshi couldn't be underestimated. In many ways, he scared her more than Barron.

There was no physical match against Takeshi, and he knew it. But it was more than that. His onyx eyes were poised and calculating, like he could see through every wall she erected and every lie she strung by just staring at her.

"Decide now or stay here," he stated after she didn't move. She swallowed and stepped forward, her body making the decision for her.

His head lowered ever so slightly, but he didn't say anything. She quickly caught up beside him, working double-time to keep up with his long legs. Everyone else was in the pit, so it was just the two of them as their footsteps echoed along the dark tunnel toward Cell Block 7.

The silence between them expanded.

Khalani stared straight ahead, but Takeshi held her entire focus. She was keenly aware of his forceful presence beside her. He could crush her like a bug—an unceremonious end to an unceremonious life—but something about his steady, ruthless energy made her fingernails release their incessant digging into her palms.

She didn't feel the need to look over her shoulder, worried that someone would attack her. Because no one in Braderhelm was more dangerous than the man beside her.

"He was the one who cut your arm," Takeshi concluded, staring ahead.

"Yes." No point in hiding the obvious. She glanced sideways at him. "You know he was lying, right? I was instructed to deliver the Ordinances. I didn't randomly start attacking him."

"I wouldn't put it past you, Kanes. But I always know when one of my own is lying. I've had issues with him in the past and know of his tendencies. I believe you were defending yourself," the macabre in his voice was unnerving, and she bit her lip as they kept walking.

"So, I'm not getting punished then?"

"I never said that."

She shot him a sharp look. "What?"

"You've caused more trouble than anticipated, so I'm still deciding." He looked up in thought. "Maybe some hard labor to pack on muscle or sewage duty since you have a knack for getting in deep shit."

"Are you trying to be funny?" she snapped.

He stopped right in her path, startling her. "Careful, Kanes. You put yourself in a dangerously stupid position today, and I was forced to step in. Either exercise control or die a slow death while I watch. Got it?"

Blood rushed to her chest. "What was I supposed to do when he grabbed my throat and cut me? Was I supposed to go into his room and let him rape me? Am I to get punished for not dying?" she yelled.

"I *should* punish you for welcoming danger as if it's a long-lost friend." An untamed fire blazed beneath his eyes. "Don't go to the guards living quarters again, and don't cause any more problems. Are you capable of that?"

"Yes," she growled. He didn't need to tell her twice.

"Good. Now, I could put your mind at ease and say that I won't hurt you for what that pathetic excuse of a guard forced your hand in doing." His jaw ticked—one of his dangerous tells—and Takeshi leaned down to whisper in her ear, "But you prefer being close to death, isn't that right?"

He walked past her, leaving her alone with her mouth open, fuming. If Khalani had laser beams for eyes, pieces of Takeshi would have been splattered all over the walls by now.

They walked back to her cell in silence, and he pulled out an electric pad to open the bars. His hard mask was back in place as he started touching the screen. He was so difficult to read. He saved her from being murdered, but Takeshi certainly wasn't an ally.

He was an enigma. A dangerous one at that.

The bars opened with a buzz. Takeshi nudged his head toward her cell. "In you go, Kanes."

She walked in and turned back to him. "Why did you help me?"

He frowned. "What?"

"With the guard. Why didn't you just let him take me? That's your job, isn't it?"

His face turned icy.

"As Captain, my job is to keep everyone in line. Even the guards have boundaries. That *guard* overstepped those boundaries with his assault and attempt to potentially kill a prisoner from my block."

"That makes sense, I guess." She fumbled her hands. "You were just helping me because he disrespected your authority."

After a few moments of silence, Khalani glanced up.

Takeshi's gaze severed her like the edge of a knife. "I may be the Captain of Braderhelm, Kanes, but I am not a monster."

With that, he pressed a button on the screen, and the bars started to close with a low hum. Their eyes didn't leave one another as the metal slowly slammed home. The firm barrier represented the opposite halves of their world. She was the prisoner in a house of bars, and he held the key.

Takeshi let out a harsh breath and walked away, disappearing from her line of sight. Khalani wondered at that moment if Takeshi felt like a prisoner too. Sometimes you can hold all the power and still be trapped.

She wished she hadn't used all the space on the back of her parents' picture to write about it. Then, she suddenly remembered.

Khalani reached into her pocket and produced the pencil and sheets of paper Winnie gave her to count the guard's cells. She carefully folded the notes and put them back in her pocket. Winnie would need it. She fell to her knees and placed the blank sheet on solid ground.

She gripped the pencil, and words began to flow from her like a stream of water. Spilling and cascading. Till a whole sea of her mind poured out on paper.

I am not a singular object or definition
Infinite variations of my soul exist

The great manifestations of the world we live in
Human hearts written on a mental list

No one person will view me the same
Love comes in the same intensity as hate

Judgment from strangers, fickle as paper planes
Unable to know your story, we suffer the same fate

Clear mirrors won't display your desires
Outer shells are no reflection of the inner core

Dreams inevitably crumble as they ascend higher
Consequences turn into coveting more

This recurring reflection whispers to be free
I can see my darkened image in the hue

And then I realized, it wasn't me
What I was staring at was you

10

My truths don't speak, they bleed.

Number 65: The inability to control how much something hurts.

Khalani had a running list of things she wasn't in control of. What she ate, what she wore, what time she woke, and where she slept were all obvious. Hair growing in weird places, like her chin. That one sucked.

But the list slowly turned grittier, like the inability to control being born. Or how each morning Khalani woke up, she was 24 hours closer to death. Inescapable truths that grew heavier with each passing day.

Last night, a chilling rendering of Guard Barron forcefully grabbing her from behind and slicing her throat played on a feedback loop. The knife sliced and her blood sprayed across the stone walls. Over and over.

Takeshi was in the nightmare.

He stood quietly in the background as her life ended in a bloody slaughter. She looked to him for help, but he remained poignantly still, a grim resignation on his face.

Her mind spoke the truth.

Trusting Takeshi would equal her death. He was the Captain for a reason. Now more than ever, she needed to keep her wits about her, or her worst fears would come to fruition.

Fears.

Make that **Number 66.**

"Prisoner 317, you're assigned to the library today," George said.

Khalani's eyes widened in pleasant surprise. A whole week had passed since she'd been assigned to the library. She was worried Winnie wouldn't request her again because of what happened.

"Another thing." George studied the electric pad. "We have a small group assigned for Apollo cleanup in a week. These are the prisoners ordered to join."

Both Khalani and Serene's numbers were called.

"Stealing some decent food this time," Serene mumbled to herself and turned to Khalani. "That partly makes up for getting assigned waste duty again."

"We'll get to leave Braderhelm?" Khalani's voice raised in hope.

"Just for half a day to clean up around the city. Under armed supervision, of course. It's a way to make people believe the Council focuses on rehabilitation, not torture. And to remind everyone of the place they go if they step out of line. You ready?" Serene asked.

Leaving Braderhelm was the specific detail her mind centered on. A few weeks in prison equaled a lifetime. Walking the streets of Apollo wouldn't free her, but she'd do anything to leave these walls, if only for a few hours.

"Have fun dusting books while I clean up shit." Serene gave her a salute after they arrived at the winding stairs, making good on her promise of walking Khalani to her afternoon shift every day.

"Someone's gotta do it," she joked.

Serene gave her the finger and left.

Khalani knocked on the library door, impatiently fidgeting with the side of her uniform. No one came to the door. She banged louder, and minutes passed with no Winifred in sight.

Her eyes did a quick scan around her, and she tried the handle on the door. To her surprise, it opened. The sound of music was the first thing she registered. A strange melody radiated through the air, something completely unfamiliar to her. She frowned, walking between the bookshelves to find Winnie sitting at the desk, adorned in her purple dress.

Winnie leaned forward in concentration, pushing buttons on a strange machine. The metal was green in color and the size of a small TV. The device was old and rusted, with a single sheet of paper placed in the contraption. Next to the peculiar object lay another foreign apparatus. It was a sizeable brown box with an opaque black disk on top. A sizeable golden speaker connected to the disk, and Khalani realized the sound was coming from this machine.

It wasn't the recorded pledges each Apollo citizen had to recite as a kid, or any ordained music played at town events. A girl was singing passionately. The noise reverberated across the walls in a breathtaking hum of vibrant energy. The melody started out slow and intensified in a show of raw passion and fervor.

She stood motionless as if the beautiful women's voice cast an enchantment on her, leaving her in a dazed trance. Khalani had never heard anything so beautiful, heartbreaking, and utterly captivating. Her eyes slid to Winnie, who hummed along with the music, her back to Khalani, still pressing letters on the green machine. The song ended, and Khalani let out a breath. She didn't want the music to end.

She wanted it to extend boundlessly. Forever ingrained in the space around her. "What was that?" Khalani asked in a wistful tone.

Winnie turned in surprise and smiled, "Oh, Khalani! Glad you are here! Sorry, sorry! Winnie knows it's loud." Winnie leaned over and adjusted a knob on the music machine. "What did you say, dear?"

"What is that machine? I've never heard anything like it." The words rushed out of Khalani, her excitement palpable. She lived in Apollo long enough to *know* this was contraband.

Winnie laughed and turned fully in her chair. "You like it, don't you?" Her smile deepened.

Khalani's mouth curved up. "I love it, Winnie. I honestly don't even have words. But how…"

"Winnie got the machine from Charles. He works in the Archives and has a secret old-world artifact shop." A dreamy look appeared in Winnie's eyes, and she shook her head as if to wash away her train of thought. "After Winnie was sentenced here, she managed to have it snuck in, along with this gem."

Winnie rubbed the silver machine adoringly.

Khalani walked over to the mysterious box. "They used this before the Great Collapse?"

"Yes. After years of tinkering with it, Charles got it to work. Before the Great Collapse, they called it a record player. Back when life flourished on the surface, people recorded music on these circular disks, which would play the song back. Remarkable thing. Right now, it's playing an album of the movie Grease. By the time I got thrown in here 15 years ago, Charles was still trying to fix the old television set, so I never got to see the movie. But it's one of Winnie's favorites." Winnie rocked side to side with happiness, her energy infectious.

"You've been here 15 years, Winnie?" Khalani's eyes widened.

Winnie's gaze fluttered upward, and she started counting with her fingers. "Hmm, let's see. 1, 2, 3…Yep! 15 years. Goodness, has it been that long?" Winnie continued to stare at the ceiling like an intricate pattern resided in the cracks, one only she could see.

Would Khalani be able to survive 15 years in Braderhelm?

A part of her didn't want to last that long.

"Winnie, why were you sentenced here?"

Winnie waved her hand dismissively and returned to punching letters on the machine. "Oh, Winnie got thrown in here for having too big of an imagination. You see, my great great great great great great great grandfather." She pursed her lips, counting her fingers with each great.

"Not sure if that's correct. But right before the Great Collapse, my grandfather was a big scientist. Timothy Talbot was his name. Yes, that was it. He was brilliant. Worked on something so grand you couldn't even dream it. Something…unbelievable," Winnie trailed off, staring at the painting, which caught Khalani's eye the last time. The one with the man heading toward the strange, imposing structure.

Her eyebrows pinched together. There was something odd in Winnie's voice as she continued the story. Almost a sense of unease, a stark contrast to her usual disposition.

"What did he work on?" Khalani asked.

Winnie struck out of her stupor. "Oh, nothing. Nothing, dear. Don't even know why Winnie would say that. A tale of eons past. Winnie would take some of the books from the Archives home with her. Incredible stories. Winnie has a feeling you would like them." Winnie grinned.

Khalani sat forward as Winnie spoke, her elbows on her knees and hands clutched together, completely enraptured. "What did they say?"

"Everything you didn't know you needed to hear."

The statement resonated with how the poetry book enraptured her mind that fateful night. The intricacy and shaping of every story, as potent as the blood flowing through her veins, set her mind ablaze, and she relished the burn.

Reading was like sucking in a gulp of air after holding your breath for a lifetime. Or falling in love. Khalani had never been in love, but she imagined that that's what it felt like. An emotion that gave your soul wings.

"But," Winnie continued, "Someone else at the Archives saw Winnie taking the books and ratted her out. That's how Winnie ended up here. But the damage was already done. That's the beauty of knowledge. If it's remembered, the meaning can't be fully erased."

Khalani frowned as Winnie turned to the machine. She remembered it all. The crackling of the fire. Complete despair nearly crippling her body as the book disintegrated before her very eyes.

"What are you working on?" Khalani cleared her throat, shoving the never-ending torment away until it became a dull sensation.

"This is an old typewriter." Winnie rubbed the faded, green metal adoringly. "What they used to make books long ago."

She blinked in surprise, bending to inspect the odd apparatus.

"Writing what?"

Winnie pursed her lips together and narrowed her eyes at Khalani, as if her soul laid bare. "Can you keep a secret?"

She leaned forward. "Of course."

Winnie rubbed her palms together in anticipation. "This, dear, will be a complete history of Apollo. Our journey needs to be recorded and preserved, especially the bad parts, so we don't repeat our mistakes. When we finally return to the surface, this will be our guide," she finished proudly.

Khalani threaded a hand through her hair. "Oh, you mean if we all go up to Genesis someday?"

A fairy tale for her. This was the time to take Takeshi's advice and not even dream or lose herself in hope. No point in extra suffering over something that would never happen.

Winnie waved her hand dismissively. "No, no, silly. Not that cursed dome they call Genesis. I'm talking about the surface. Earth, with the natural, free air."

Winnie really was crazy. Khalani would rather be in Braderhelm than have her organs fried on the surface. "Winnie, I'm sorry, but they said the surface will not be livable again for another hundred, if not a thousand years. Nothing's up there anymore." She turned and slumped down in the chair. "The closest we will ever get is Genesis."

Winnie shook her head emphatically.

"You're wrong! You can't believe everything they say. The system wants to keep us down. Doesn't want us to live."

Khalani rolled her eyes to the ceiling, trying to figure out how to restore logic to the conversation. "We survive by staying down here, Winnie. The workers who built Genesis died from radiation poisoning. All of them. The destruction on the surface will linger way past our generation. We survive by staying put and waiting it out," she repeated the words ingrained in her head and every Apollo citizen's head since they were little.

Some people believed the surface was livable again years ago, but the Genesis workers proved them all wrong.

Winnie didn't yell or protest her words. Her expression changed to a look of sadness and sympathy. Why was Winnie staring at her like that? Like *Khalani* was the one who was lost?

"I'm sorry they got to you. Made you forget that surviving is not living," Winnie whispered.

Khalani frowned, opening her mouth in rebuttal but found no words. Winnie's words sank deeper into her skin. Deeper...

And deeper.

Till they consumed everything.

She was alive. The air she breathed each day attested to that fact. But the words failed to leave her mouth. Because she knew they were lies. Even before she was sentenced to Braderhelm, the best parts of Khalani's life were when she slept.

The harsh truth made her skin prickle. Her parents knew better. Taught her better. They died because they fought for the quality of other people's lives; for something bigger than themselves. And what was she doing, other than wasting away, waiting to die...

She peered up at Winnie, who studied her intensely with her purple monocle. For a woman so small, Winnie was still trying to make a difference for future generations, even in Braderhelm. By helping Winnie, no matter how far-fetched the idea, her life could have meaning too.

Khalani lifted her chin, steeling herself to a new task, a new mission. "I will help you with your book, Winnie."

"Really?" Winnie asked. She nodded.

"Oh, this is wonderful!" Winnie wrapped her in a giant hug. "From the moment Winnie saw you, she realized you were more than a pretty face."

Her lips curved up. "What can I do to help?"

Winnie rubbed her chin, looking down in thought. "Hmmm. Well, I am due for the next few pages from Charles. Have they scheduled you for a city cleanup yet?"

"They have. I go sometime next week."

Winnie's purple dress whirled around as she raced to grab papers on her desk. "These are from the Apollo Council meetings. They meet every month, and the notes are stored in the Archives. This information is vital for my book's accuracy. You can get me the next report."

Her forehead puckered. "How?

"Charles." Winnie's eyes lit up. "He's my friend who owns the old artifact workshop and works in the Archives. I'll send a message to him. During the street cleanup, he'll find you."

"How will you get a message to him, and how will he know how to find me? Won't the guard's notice?" The words came faster as her anxiety doubled.

Winnie adjusted her monocle and gave her a crooked smile. "Winnie has her ways. Messages travel farther than people can. Don't worry. He'll find you when the guards are distracted. Winnie knows you can do this."

She slowly nodded, not as confident as Winnie, but if this was how she needed to contribute, so be it. If this quirky old woman can rebel within prison, so could she. Khalani was already branded a criminal.

How hard could breaking the law one more time be?

11

You hide from devils in your sleep.
I smile at them in greeting.

Khalani closed her eyes, the barest hint of a smile etching across her face as cool air brushed her skin like a feather. Strands of loose hair whipped around her cheeks in a show of freedom.

If she squeezed her eyes hard enough, she could imagine the wind sailing her away from Braderhelm forever. Destination unknown. She just wanted to find a place where living didn't have to be so hard.

Did that exist before the Great Collapse?

The transport whizzed through the dark tunnels of Apollo. The only light emitted from magnetic lines the vehicles sailed over, the soft, green glow a welcome vision. Khalani, Serene, and several prisoners, including Dana, filled three transports as they made their way to the Apollo City Center.

A rush of energy pulsated through her as the tunnel broke, revealing the city of Apollo. It must have taken years of construction to carve out the massive cavern of space. The stone ceiling was over 100 feet tall, anchored by 20 massive pillars. Electric grids wrapped around the pillars, lighting the whole city.

Homes and businesses were built intricately into the stone walls surrounding the cavern, reaching all the way to the ceiling, with magnetic elevators for access. The nice homes were built on levels 25 and up. Khalani lived on level 2.

Used to live, she corrected herself.

Only one elevator led to Genesis, heavily protected and under constant surveillance. Anyone who ventured near the Genesis elevator without approval was shot.

The transports slowed as they made their way to the City Center. Apollo citizens milled about in long, dusty robes, heading to work or trading goods. They passed the Food Distribution Center, Khalani's old workplace. The building was diminutive, box-like with sharp, grey edges, and looked more akin to a morgue. A line of people waited outside in ragged clothes.

No one conversed. No one smiled. Not all dissimilar from the prisoners in Braderhelm.

They rolled to a stop in front of the Council Chambers, the seat of the Governor, and the Apollo Council. It was by far the most beautiful building in Apollo. Hundreds of white steps led up to the entrance. The towering structure radiated wealth, with pointy spires reaching toward the cavernous ceiling.

The building was made of pure marble and decorated with stained-glass windows, like a glorious church. A shining beacon of hope for the city. It was at those marble steps where her parents and so many others lost their lives.

"Get moving!" a guard yelled, waiting for her to exit the transport.

She tore her eyes away from the city steps and jumped onto the cobblestone road. One of the guards shoved a broom into her chest. A hand pressed Khalani's shoulder when she stumbled back, steadying her. She looked to her left, and Serene nodded, reminding her she wasn't alone.

Khalani let out a deep breath, attempting to calm herself as tension speared through her nerves. She wasn't sure how Charles, Winnie's friend, would be able to communicate with her with six guards around and in front of the Council Chambers, no less.

Was this mission dead on arrival?

"You will be divided into two groups. The first group will clean the first street level in the Work Quarters, and the other group will clean the Trading District until we complete the full circle. I better not see a speck of dirt on the roads, or you'll be beaten in the streets. Get to it," the lead guard ordered, smacking the baton to emphasize the threat.

Three guards stayed with their group, casually holding guns strapped over their bodies as they walked along the street. The buildings in the Work Quarters were drab, rusted, and dirty, a complete 180 from the Council Chambers. People walked to their respective jobs, giving them a wide berth and wary glances.

A couple of hours passed. She continued to cast subtle glances around while sweeping dirt from the cobblestone into the raggedy bin. Charles had yet to approach her, and they were losing time.

"Attention!" a guard yelled.

Khalani froze, but the guards weren't looking at her. They were staring at a man she'd never met in real life. He'd only resided in her dreams when she imagined thrusting a knife through his sternum.

The Governor of Apollo.

Alexander Huxley, the Governor of Apollo, was an imposing man in his late 50s, with short, ash-colored hair speckled with grey bits. What was striking about Alexander Huxley was how flawless he looked. She wasn't exaggerating. His face was chiseled to perfection and symmetry.

He had a strong jawline, the clearest skin, and a row of straight, white teeth, rivaling the best dentist in Genesis. The Governor wore a pristine, white robe with the symbol of Apollo—a bright sun—stitched in gold on the front. The robe, combined with his incredible features, gave him the appearance of an avenging angel, here to save his constituents.

Khalani only viewed him as an angel of death.

Alexander Huxley ruled with an iron fist and was the highest-ranking leader in Apollo. Unlike the Master Judge, the Governor of Apollo would hold his position until death. He was the one who ordered the creation of Genesis, further increasing the divide between the wealthy and common people of Apollo, and he sentenced the Braderhelm prisoners to their deaths.

More importantly, Governor Huxley was the man who ordered the guards to shoot the protesters of Genesis, murdering her parents.

Six Councilmen flanked the Governor on either side, wearing robes the color of blood. Fitting. The Apollo Councilmen were the shields, and the Governor was the hand that shoved the dagger in your back.

"Governor Huxley!" the lead guard stammered and bowed deeply. "To what do we owe this incredible honor?"

Alexander Huxley held out his hands like he was about to give a sermon. "Good evening, gentleman. I was just lecturing my Councilmen while we strolled through the unbelievable city of Apollo. Life aboveground in Genesis can get quite boring, wouldn't you say?" his voice was inky smooth as if he were discussing the weather.

The guards nodded emphatically. "Yes, of course, sir. Very boring."

Governor Huxley chuckled and tilted his head to the side. "How would you know if you've never been to Genesis?"

The lead guard blanched. "N-no, sir. So sorry, sir. I would never disagree with your opinion, sir. You have impeccable taste and are assuredly correct in all your assessments."

The guard visibly gulped, his Adam's apple bobbing up and down, as the ensuing silence seemed to last a lifetime. Alexander Huxley finally broke into uproarious laughter. The three guards and Councilmen joined him.

The disturbing interaction was like watching a real-life puppet play unfold, and the Governor held all the strings.

"We are lucky to have you, son." Governor Huxley clapped the terrified guard on the shoulder. "I'm sure you would happily be at the front line in the event of any insurgence, ready to purge Apollo of all who would see her destroyed."

The guard straightened in relief and puffed out his chest. "Absolutely, sir, you can count on me."

"Good, good." The Governor took a couple steps forward, casually dismissing the guard. "I presume these are prisoners, participating in city cleanup, yes?"

Khalani kept her eyes down on the broom, vigorously sweeping, but all her focus and attention was on the Governor. The guard's voice echoed in her ear, "Absolutely, sir. We are keeping a close eye on them."

Governor Huxley slowly approached the prisoners several feet to the left of Khalani. "Participating in city cleanups is a fantastic way to oversee rehabilitation efforts. Keeps them in line. You see, Councilmen, not all Braderhelm prisoners are completely lost to society." His silky voice made her shiver.

He loomed closer to Khalani, who clutched her broom like a lifeline and kept her eyes peeled to the ground.

"For some, rehabilitation is impossible, Governor Huxley," one Councilman bravely said.

"Like the Death-Zoner." A few Councilmen muttered among themselves as tension filled the air.

Khalani frowned, ears perking up at the whispered words. Death-Zoners were celebrities. They had the most critical job in Apollo, traveling on foot to the closest underground trade city, Hermes.

Only a chosen few were selected, the strongest mentally and physically. They traded Apollo's crops for medicine and other invaluable resources. The journey took weeks to reach Hermes on foot, not to mention being weighed down with the heavy radiation suits and packs to hold supplies.

The position held the greatest need but was also the most dangerous. They were told Apollo had the material to build only a few suits that could withstand the high radiation levels. Many Death-Zoners perished on the treacherous road, walking the earth's surface.

And they lived like kings in Genesis after they returned from Hermes every six months. She heard stories of Hermes from a Death-Zoner invited to her school graduation as a special guest.

"Hermes has it all. They have shops and bars. Even a casino!" he said after one too many drinks at the reception.

She had no idea what a 'casino' was.

"They got it right over there, I'm telling you. Keep their people happy and content while they rot underground. Slow boil." The Death-Zoner laughed and took a big swig from his drink.

Her eyes didn't stray from the broom, but the underlying threat in Alexander Huxley's voice was evident. "I could have you join the prisoners, Wyatt, and then you can tell me if rehabilitation works."

No other word came out of the Councilman's mouth.

"Besides," the angel-like tone was back, and he stepped right in front of Khalani, "Some can even be put to good use. They are not all the villainous creatures you warn your children about, isn't that right, girl?"

He was speaking directly to her. She could feel the weight of his gaze crawling on her skin, but she was afraid to peer into the eyes of her parent's killer.

"Answer your Governor, prisoner!" The crack of a baton whipped out from the guards, and her head snapped up in fear, heart racing.

The Governor held out his hand to the guard. "That's not necessary. You can help ease Councilman Wyatt's mind by affirming you aren't dangerous, right?" His icy blue eyes connected with hers, and she couldn't look away. They were cold and distant, as if no life was left in them. Probably because he had taken so many lives.

"Y-yes. Yes, sir. I am a loyal citizen of Apollo." She bowed her head, gritting her teeth the whole time. A part of her wanted to take the wooden end of the broom she still held and smash it across his head. She would only have one chance to hit him before the guards stepped in and killed her. It would almost be worth it.

Doling out a tiny bit of revenge would give her instant gratification, but she was smart enough to know it wouldn't be nearly enough. Her death wouldn't be worth a small smack to the head. No. He would need to suffer the same fate her parents did.

Alexander Huxley smiled down at her, his gaze warm and inviting, and she was again struck by his perfect beauty. "Good answer. You certainly don't look like our average prisoner. What's your name? Your real name."

"It's Khalani Kanes...sir," she added, steadying her voice.

"And what did you do to warrant being put in prison?" He tilted his head to the side, the soft smile still present.

She hesitated, sensing a trap laid beneath her feet. What if she told the Governor, and he decided her punishment was not harsh enough and sentenced her to the surface? Or this was a game, and he already knew what she was in for. The Governor may be testing Khalani to reveal the truth.

She would have to take a chance.

"Governor Huxley, any crime against Apollo should warrant a sentence in Braderhelm. One would be a fool to think someone as intelligent as you would let anything go unnoticed in your city." Khalani paused, weighing her next words.

He raised an eyebrow. "Go on."

She gave him a polite smile, time to lay it on thick.

"Dwelling on my past is pointless and a waste of your precious time. I am grateful for this opportunity to work the streets of Apollo and serve your will as Governor. My focus lies on building a greater Apollo in solidarity, strength, and spirit. Even if those efforts go unappreciated above," Khalani enunciated, letting that last part slip as she lowered her head in submission.

Her hands tightened on the broom. She wanted to scream. So loud that even those on Genesis could hear. She hated herself. Hated that she had to make this monster believe she only lived to serve him. Did her boisterous thoughts ring loud, shouting that he would never have her loyalty? Did he know that all she wanted was his gruesome death?

"My, my." Governor Huxley's smile widened. "You are definitely more honest than the average prisoner. You would've made a better council member than some currently serving, isn't that right, Wyatt?" he asked without looking away from her.

"Yes, Great Governor Huxley," Wyatt replied without hesitation.

Khalani couldn't shake the gnawing pressure in her stomach. The amount of control Alexander Huxley had over everyone, even the Councilmen he insulted, was mind-blowing and frightening.

"Well, we should be going. Much to discuss in improving these streets." Alexander Huxley suddenly grabbed her hand that wasn't holding the broom, lifted it up to his lips, and kissed the top.

She was so taken aback, her mouth opened in shock.

"It was a pleasure meeting you, Khalani Kanes. It's beneficial to know my constituents better, even unfortunate ones like yourself. I'm sure we will meet again." He smiled over her hand, finally releasing it, and turned to walk away, the Councilmen closely following behind.

Her chin trembled. Time seemed to slow down. Sounds of people talking animatedly on the streets dulled into a low thrum. Khalani was sure if she stopped her breath, she could hear the machine of life slowly throbbing in her chest.

She stopped.

Did hold her breath.

Ba bump...ba bump...ba bump...

Her heart churned. How can hearts continue beating through the many cracks, fissures, and breaks?

Anyone who says time heals all wounds hasn't had many wounds. Time masks all wounds. Time was a band-aid on a broken leg.

Meeting Alexander Huxley, hearing his silky smooth, traitorous voice. To let his lips touch her hand, those same lips that commanded his guards to murder innocent people, her parents included. She shook her head to the ceiling, blinking back tears.

How much were they expected to give when all Apollo did was take?

"Get back to work!" one of the guards yelled at her.

Khalani's gaze kept returning to the top of her hand, where Alexander Huxley kissed her. She wanted to rub her skin raw and wipe his disgusting stain from her existence.

She was more determined to help Winnie, but no one had approached her yet, and the guards started directing the prisoners toward the transports.

The message must not have been sent out.

Khalani kept her head down, still in her dark thoughts, when a loud shout sounded through the cavern.

Her mouth dropped open as a fire rapidly grew in one of the food storage buildings. People gathered and screamed for help. The guards in her group ran toward the commotion and yelled for the fire brigade.

"That will keep them occupied a few minutes."

She jumped. A middle-aged man with dark skin snuck up to her side. Speckles of grey ran through his black hair, and he stared at the fire with a slight grin.

"You did this?" she whispered in shock.

"I would have come sooner, but the Governor's arrival made the guards more perceptive than usual. Had to improvise. My name is Charles."

A huge balm of relief rushed through her. "I didn't think you were coming."

"I will always help Winnie." He reached into his jacket and handed her a few sheets of paper.

She glanced around warily. No one was looking their way or paying attention to them. Everyone's focus was on the fire. She quickly grabbed the sheets of paper and folded them into her pocket.

"Thank you," she said.

Charles nodded and gave her a solemn look. "Good luck in Braderhelm. Tell Winnie I said hi." With that, he swiftly walked away, leaving behind the fiery chaos. People sighed in relief as the fire brigade arrived and put the last flames out. She put her hand in her pocket, making sure the precious items were solidly in place. The guards walked back toward the prisoners, wiping sweat off their foreheads.

"Let's go!" the lead guard shouted angrily, waving his hands toward the transports.

The prisoners in both groups quickly moved. As she got in one of the vehicles, she noticed Dana eyeing her suspiciously. Khalani ignored the sinking feeling as they returned to Braderhelm Prison. But when she walked back to her cell, Dana stepped in front of her, arms folded against her chest.

She sighed. "What do you want, Dana?"

"I couldn't help but notice you talking to someone while the guards were focused on the fire. What did he give you?" Dana asked.

Her heart hammered in panic, but Khalani had to play it off. "Nothing to do with you." She walked around her.

"I know it was papers," Dana said. "Did he give you information about escape routes or changing of the guards?"

"No." Her brows snapped together as she turned. "There is no escaping Braderhelm. How come I know that, and you don't?"

"Not for you, there isn't."

Khalani frowned and stopped in her tracks, but Dana had already walked away.

12

*An animal dwells within, sharpening your claws
against the world.*

"This can't be real."

"Which part?" Winnie asked.

"All of it," Khalani exclaimed.

Winnie paused typing and twisted in her chair. "Why? Because it strays past your wildest imaginings?" Her eyes sparkled with amusement. "You're only beginning to understand, dear. Nothing is as beautiful, harsh, and unforgiving as the Earth."

Khalani frowned, flipping through the book Winnie gave her while she typed notes. It was titled *Natural Wonders of the World*—another object Winnie managed to sneak from the Archives.

"This. Right here." Khalani turned the book so Winnie could see. Her fingers gripped the long glossy pages tightly. "These lights in the sky. Is it magic?"

Winnie leaned forward and touched her monocle to get a closer look. She glanced up at Khalani with a quirky smile. "That's the aurora borealis. They used to call it the Northern Lights. Not magic but science. But science is so crazy that magic makes more sense sometimes."

Khalani's mouth parted open as she stared at the different hues. She gently stroked her fingers across the pages, outlining the green and blue colors as if to extend the dazzling lights past the boundaries of the page. Attempting to paint distant magic into existence.

"I never imagined something so beautiful ever existed," Khalani whispered. She continued to stare at the picture, but second by second, bitterness and contempt took root in her stomach. "But the more I learn about the Earth, Winnie, the less I want to know. We had it all back then, and now…it's all gone." Her smile faded with the knowledge that humans would never gaze upon that perfection again.

"Don't be sad," Winnie noted Khalani's forlorn gaze. "You still live on Earth, do you not? Were you carted off to space?"

"Well, no. But—"

"Then don't give up on your planet if it hasn't given up on you."

Winnie gave her a gentle nod to keep reading and turned around, continuing to type up notes.

Every day, Winnie taught her more and more about the Earth, knowledge she'd never dreamed of acquiring. A month had passed since the city street cleanup. During that time, she stuck with Serene, Derek, and Adan like glue, avoiding any encounter with Barron at all costs. The task was almost too easy, thanks to Takeshi's intervention and sustained threat.

Khalani and Takeshi hadn't spoken since that day. The only time they interacted was an occasional glance from him when she left her cell in the morning and went back to her cell at night. That was it. No words of banter or simple greetings were exchanged. She was a social pariah to him.

It was better that way.

She remained vigilant, never relaxing in Braderhelm. The only thing she looked forward to daily was conversing with Winnie while they listened to music.

By now, she had every song on the Grease album memorized.

Khalani flipped the book to a picture of the Pacific Ocean. The pool of water was like a deep blue monster that threatened to swallow her through the page. "People were crazy to ever set foot in the ocean. Too big and filled with creatures that could eat you? No, thank you." She shivered.

Winnie chuckled. "Just because something is bigger than you doesn't mean it's scary. You must hold respect for nature and her power. If Winnie could travel back in time, it would be the first place she'd visit, and then go to a movie theatre."

"And watch Grease?" A smile lit up Khalani's face, a rarity before she met Winnie. She smiled more in prison than she did out of it.

Life had a wicked sense of humor.

"My dear, they played many movies, not just Grease. Hundreds and hundreds about love, war, loss, greed, happiness…Winnie would watch *everything*."

Khalani shook her head in disbelief. "Why did Apollo stop all that? Why do they prohibit us from hearing or seeing art from the Great Collapse? Why do they lock all the artifacts in the Archives?"

Khalani remembered the Master Judge's eyes of fury but never understood why the poetry was contraband. Nothing she ever read was dangerous. The question burned in her mind, but she'd been afraid to speak the words aloud and learn the truth.

The truth might've been harder to accept.

Winnie heaved a deep sigh and turned to her. "You told Winnie that Douglas gave you the poetry, right?"

She nodded.

"Why didn't you immediately turn the book in when you knew it was from the Archives? That's the law, isn't it?"

Khalani snaked a hand through her hair. "I don't know. Perhaps I should've. But when I read the book, it felt wrong to give it up; I knew the pages would disappear and didn't want that."

"Why? What did it make you feel?" Winnie pressed.

She hung her head. "Some people might think they were just words on a paper…but it was more for me. Each page was an expression of all the hope and despair in my life, as if the author's thoughts were an extension of me. That probably sounds stupid."

Winnie emphatically shook her head. "No, no, dear. Keep going! If you have a thought, do your mind a favor and speak it, so it doesn't have to house it forever."

Khalani paused, trying to find the right words. "I don't know. It was weird. For the first time…I felt alive. Not temporarily, either. That shit stayed with me. Like the book was inspiring me to create a masterpiece myself. Even in prison."

Winnie clapped her hands together in a big Aha! "Exactly! The last thing the Apollo Councilmen want is for its citizens to become inspired and creative. They want their people to remain content. Obedient. Art has the ability to embolden and galvanize people to desire more. They can't have that."

Her forehead creased. "Why would wanting more be a bad thing? If we put more minds together, we could figure out how to build a bigger Genesis to fit everyone, not just the rich. Once we all slowly migrate to the surface again, under a bigger dome, a lot of problems will be fixed."

Winnie's expression twisted, and her eyes held a deeper pain. "And what if he doesn't want our problems to be fixed? You keep assuming he wants us to survive."

Recognition dawned on her face.

"The Governor? I know better than anyone that he is evil and only has his interests at heart. But those interests are still the safety of Apollo. They at least need our scientists, engineers, and farmers, or none of us would be able to survive. Right?" she implored, waiting expectantly for Winnie to agree.

"Right?" Khalani repeated.

Winnie stared down at her hands, fiddling with them as her mouth curved downward. Silence resonated through the room. Winnie opened her mouth to speak, but the alarm shrieked through the air, signaling the end of the afternoon shift. "You better get going, Khalani." Winnie's expression turned downcast.

"What were you gonna say, Winnie?"

"Nothing. Nothing worth mentioning." Winnie gave a dismissive wave of her hand, but a flash of grief entered her eyes. "Winnie doesn't want you to be late. Go, dear."

Khalani lingered, not wanting to end the conversation, but reluctantly headed toward the door. She turned back to wish Winnie a good day, but something stopped her. Tears streaked down Winnie's face, and her shoulders slumped over as she stared at the painting of the white-robed man.

She hesitated, nearly switching directions to console Winnie and find out what was wrong, but thought better of it. When Khalani was sad, she wanted to be alone. She slowly left, giving Winnie her space. All the way to the pit, her face screwed together in thought as she tried to figure out who the white-robed man in the painting was.

When Khalani entered the pit, the immediate clamor of shouts and cheers erupted from the fighting area. A lot more than usual. In fact, everyone in the pit seemed to be clustered in the middle, in rapt attention.

Khalani and Serene's eyes met, and they surged toward the crowd. They found Derek and Adan on the outside, straining their necks to peer into the fighting ring.

"Adan, what's going on?" Serene asked.

Adan turned to them, a wild excitement in his eyes. "It's the Death-Zoner. A guard challenged him to fight in the pit."

There was only one Death-Zoner holed up in Braderhelm, and he was already infamous.

He was sentenced to prison right after the street cleanup. The coincidence didn't fall short on Khalani. He must have been the same Death-Zoner the council members cautiously whispered about around Governor Huxley.

Serene was able to find out his name, Brock, but nothing more. No one knows the crime he committed.

She heard several theories over the last couple of weeks: trying to flee to Hermes, killing another Death-Zoner, plotting to steal all the radiation suits, and attempting to bomb Apollo were some of her favorites.

A few brave prisoners approached Brock and asked why he was sentenced to Braderhelm and about his experience on the surface. He never answered them, and after breaking a prisoner's nose for lingering too long, most people gave him a wide berth.

"Oh, I have to see this." Serene grabbed Khalani's hand and pulled her through the crowd.

Few situations exist where being short is a distinct advantage, but getting through a massive crowd is definitely one of them.

"Sorry, sorry," she kept saying as they bumped into prisoners.

Serene was less polite. "Move, people."

They finally squeezed to the front. The cheers were so loud they nearly drowned out her thoughts. In front of Khalani, Brock's beefy arms were crossed over his chest, a stone-cold expression plastered on his face, with blonde hair cropped tight to his scalp. He was not what Khalani would call handsome, but he carried himself in a way that made you fear and respect him all at once.

There wasn't an ounce of fat on him. He was pure muscle and stood well over six feet, which would've been extremely intimidating if not for his opponent.

The guard he faced was a monster of a man. The guard's chest was bare, and his shoulders looked like mountains. He couldn't even put his arms fully down to his side. That was how colossal they were. Despite Brock's immense height, the guard was several inches taller and thicker.

"The Death-Zoner's entering the pit to fight *him*? Dude must want to die," Serene mumbled.

Khalani caught sight of Takeshi standing at the opposite edge of the circle, flanked by several guards. His stormy eyes suddenly flickered to hers as if he could feel her gaze. This was the most they had stared at each other in weeks.

Her pulse quickened, but she refused to be the first to back down.

Takeshi's heated gaze narrowed with irritation, and he broke the contact, reverting his concentration to the two men before him.

Some things never change.

The Death-Zoner and mammoth guard geared to face each other, and the pit lit up bigger than the tri-centennial celebration of Apollo.

"Let's go, Brock!!" prisoners yelled.

"Rip him apart, Brock!"

"Kill him!!!"

The shouts animated into a constant roar, and Khalani put her hands over her ears to slightly mask the noise. The guard gestured to the crowd to silence them, and they strangely obeyed, all attention fixated on the two men.

"You're going to die, Death-Zoner. And I am more than happy to be your executioner." The guard pointed to Brock, his deep baritone rivaling the depth of Braderhelm.

The Death-Zoner's eyes darkened. "I've been at death's door many times. I call it home."

With that, Brock crouched and angled his body to the side, holding his fists up to his face. The giant guard smirked in response and moved forward.

He didn't bother to turn his body to the side like Brock and appear smaller. He faced him head-on and took a ginormous swing to his face. Brock effortlessly dodged the fist and stepped back, hands glued in front of his face.

There was no more room for quiet in the pit. The crowd went wild, and everyone was enthralled by the scene in front of them.

Even Khalani's heartbeat increased vigorously.

Brock danced on his feet and shuffled forward a few steps, still angled to the side. With an infuriated grunt, the guard took another shot, and Brock ducked to the left, swiftly counter-punching with his right hand, nailing the guard in the face. The guard didn't even flinch and swung with his other fist again. Brock leaned back swiftly and shuffled around the circle, facing his opponent from a different angle.

Brock's back was to Khalani, and all she could focus on was the fire and rage in the guard's eyes. The guard yelled and lunged at Brock with his whole body. Brock dived and rolled to the left. Growing impatient, the guard raged and charged at him again. Brock twisted his body and jumped with his leg spinning, his foot slamming into the guard's neck. The guard stepped back in a daze, trying to shake his head from the impact, but his legs started to wobble.

The roar of the crowd reached a crescendo when the guard tried to throw a fist but was clearly unstable from the jaw-dropping kick. Brock easily knocked away the hand and pummeled him square in the jaw. The guard dropped his hands, stumbling back, and Brock went in for the kill.

He swiftly moved behind the guard and kicked him in the back of the legs. The guard fell forward to his knees, and there was no emotion on the Death-Zoner's face as he bent forward, put his arms around the guard's head, and snapped his neck. The guard's eyes went lifeless as he slumped to the ground.

Dead.

The Death-Zoner exhaled heavily as he gazed down at the body, his eyes flickering with malice. Everyone seemed to breathe in trepidation along with him. Without another word, Brock climbed out of the fighting pit.

At his movement, an explosion of cheers reverberated across the hall like rockets.

Khalani stood frozen, staring at the dead guard's body. She'd never seen someone murdered in front of her eyes. Khalani *felt* the crack of bone like the damage was her own. It was gruesome and spell-binding, and the crowd ate it up. Even Serene beside her was slow-clapping for Brock in shock and awe.

Takeshi nodded to the two guards next to him, and they dropped down to the dead guard. Khalani shuddered at the unnatural angle of his neck as the guards dragged his lifeless body out of the pit. She felt Takeshi's gaze on her but couldn't look at him, too fixated on the violent scene.

"Any other fighters?" a prisoner yelled out.

People clapped, and the energy buzzed with excitement and adrenaline. Khalani doubted anyone wanted to enter the pit after that murderous affair, and she didn't have the stomach to endure another bloody presentation.

She finally pulled her eyes away and turned to Serene. "C'mon, let's get out of here."

Serene's face was still gleaming with exhilaration. "Damn, nothing is going to beat that. Yeah, let's go."

Khalani started to turn away, but a yell echoed back. Words that dropped a cement block in her stomach and anchored her feet to the floor.

"I challenge Prisoner 317 to a fight!"

Her whole body tensed as she slowly turned. Dana stood in the middle of the pit. Her muscular arms folded across her chest as a smug grin etched across her face. The weight of every prisoner's and guard's stare bore into her. The silence was palpable.

Khalani swallowed, her throat suddenly dry. "What is this, Dana?"

Dana shrugged. "You refuse to answer my questions, and this is what happens. In Braderhelm, you pay with blood."

Several people whistled and cheered, egging on the fight between two female prisoners. After watching Brock's brutal demonstration, the last place she wanted to be was in the pit opposite Dana. Khalani had never been in a fight, and Dana was a whole foot taller than her. She would even bet against herself.

She glanced at Takeshi, and his expression was hard as stone. She noticed him imperceptibly shake his head as if to tell her not to engage.

"I don't accept," she stated in a firm voice. Multiple people booed and called her choice words. Khalani ignored the callous chatter and stood her ground.

Dana's mouth twisted in a cruel smile, and she grabbed a small picture from her pocket that sealed a dagger in Khalani's heart. It was the picture of her parents. Her only photo of them. Every muscle in her body locked into place.

How did she get that?

Dana flipped the back of the picture over to her writings. She chuckled. "Looks like someone has been crying to sleep at night. Writing in your diary like a baby. This is sad, even for you. Your parents are better off dead, so they wouldn't see what their pathetic daughter grew up to become."

Dana held the picture in front of her and ripped the most precious item she owned into multiple pieces.

The dull roar of laughter invaded her senses as the broken image of her parents floated to the ground. She couldn't move. Could barely breathe. Her ears pounded, and all the blood rushed to her head as her body held in quiet shock. Her vision narrowed and blackened.

The shattered scraps on the floor, like puzzle pieces that could never be put back together, screamed in the hollow abyss of her mind. The emotion slowly started to churn to something deeper and chaotic. Deadlier.

Her fists were closed so tightly that her knuckles could burst out of her skin. She vaguely remembered Serene pulling on her arm. But her attention wasn't there.

She had tunnel vision. Dana was the only object of her focus, and at that moment, she wanted her dead.

Without a word, Khalani lowered herself into the fighting pit.

Khalani glanced at the broken pieces on the dirt. The last thing she cared for in the world was destroyed, and rage was another entity beside her. There was no thought. No logic. No strategy. Just an innate need to hurt.

She placed herself in the center and held her fists up. The crowd's laughter turned to violent cheering, but she blocked out the sound. Her only goal was to inflict maximum pain. Every inch of her body coiled in agony as if every painful moment in her life reenacted itself like a whip breaking skin.

Dana slowly circled her. Khalani moved the opposite way, eyes locked on her target, wanting her blood to coat the floor next to the torn pieces of her heart.

"Let's go, Dana!!"

"C'mon, Khalani!"

She shuffled closer—not as gracefully as Brock—and tried to take the first shot at Dana's face. She didn't know how to properly punch, just closed her fist tight and swung upward, yelling out. She swung so hard, putting her whole body into the hit, that she missed, and her punch only collided with air particles.

Dana shifted to the right and retaliated with a vicious right hook. Her fists connected with Khalani's head, slamming in her ear. She immediately lost focus and stumbled back. The pain didn't register. She had too much adrenaline flowing through her.

She regained her balance and rushed forward, throwing a haymaker Dana effortlessly ducked. Dana threw a counter-punch that sent Khalani spinning to the outer edge of the circle.

Blood trickled down her nose, and grey spots entered her vision. She tried to catch her breath, but the prisoners behind leaned down and pushed her back into the center. She stumbled forward and didn't see the fist slamming into her nose, knocking her flat to the ground.

The crowd roared.

"Finish her!"

"End it!"

"Get up, Khalani!!"

She could still fight. She couldn't let Dana get away with this.

Don't give up.

Don't give up.

Khalani spit out blood as she stood on shaky legs.

The crowd hollered at an ear-splitting volume, and she vaguely recognized Takeshi standing on the outside with a scary expression. She thought she saw him pointing to the ground as if telling her to stay down.

But she couldn't be too sure if he did that because the room was starting to spin. Why were three Dana's suddenly standing before her? She shook her head, trying to clear her vision. Dana held a hand before her, gesturing as if to say, 'Come at me.'

She held her fists up and pushed forward, the spectators going wild.

Dana gave an ugly smile as Khalani put her head down and charged ahead. She tried pushing Dana to the ground with her body this time. It seemed like a decent plan in her head, but Dana used Khalani's body weight against her, shoving her to the dirty floor.

She was on her hands and knees, and cool drips of blood ran down her face. The red droplets crashed to the ground—weakness leaving her body—in slow motion. The thick drops cascaded around her, like the picture of her parents.

When it cracked and tore, it was really her ripping apart.

A foot connected with her face, and she couldn't see anything anymore.

13

When you face death,
give the cold bastard my condolences.

Beep…Beep…Beep.

Like a whisper in the distance, the incessant noise vaguely grew louder. Khalani felt like someone had drilled a hole in her skull. Her chest clamped down with considerable force as if someone were actively pushing her down on a bed.

That was what she was lying on, a bed.

Her senses slowly returned. She lifted her hand and met resistance. Khalani opened her eyes, and an incandescent white light hung over her bed, nearly blinding her.

If this was heaven, she prayed God had pain meds available.

She winced, trying to sit up, but her body fell back to the bed in defeat as exhaustion overwhelmed her. Thin wires wrapped around her hands, and a sizeable needle was embedded in her vein with tape stuck across. She made a sound of pain, and someone nearby hushed her calmly.

"You're okay."

The voice sounded awfully familiar, but at the moment, she couldn't remember who it belonged to. She barely remembered her own name. The patter of steps echoed further and further away until Khalani knew she was alone.

Memories gradually returned with each passing second. The snap of a neck when Brock killed the guard, Dana ripping up the picture of her parents, and the hard kick of a boot to the head.

A door closed nearby, and Khalani tensed as more footsteps echoed in the background. Two faces appeared around the corner. Her eyes widened in shock when one of them belonged to Takeshi Steele. Frown lines marred his face, and hints of concern lay buried in his dark expression.

The other man was slightly older, with white hair and kind eyes. He wore a white robe, and in contrast to most inhabitants of Braderhelm, he gave her a warm smile. "Hi, Khalani. I'm Dr. Francis. How are you feeling?"

"Where am I?" she croaked out.

Her brows snapped together. Multiple beds like hers were lined up in a row. She appeared to be the only patient. The beds were bright white, and a mix of steel plates and instruments lay scattered throughout the room, a contrast against the dark cave walls.

"You're in the medical ward. Generally, I only treat guards but will occasionally check prisoners for signs of infectious disease. You were brought to me this morning due to your injuries. And you're lucky for it," Dr. Francis said.

Her forehead crinkled in confusion, and she tried to sit up again, but searing pain stabbed her body like she was being gutted. She groaned and fell back on the pillow.

"Would you like me to lift the bed for you, so you can see better?" Dr. Francis asked.

"Yes, please."

He pressed a button, and the bed made an audible purr as she shifted upward, half sitting, half laying down. Khalani tried to move her neck to get a better view and noticeably flinched.

"I would try not to move too much. You took quite a beating." Dr. Francis studied a monitor displaying her vital signs and typed notes on a handheld screen.

"You have several lacerations to your face and suffered a concussion, but there is no bleeding to the brain. With the concussion, you may experience more vomiting, dizziness, and a major headache over the next few days. But with proper rest and time for the nasty cuts and bruises to heal, you'll be just fine."

Khalani took time to process his words. "How long have I been out?"

"A day," Takeshi answered before the doctor could.

Khalani reeled back, shell-shocked, and just that slight movement gave her a migraine from hell. Her head throbbed like someone was whacking her skull with a sledgehammer.

"Any other pain meds you can give her?" Takeshi asked the doctor.

"She has already reached the max we're allowed to give a Braderhelm prisoner." Dr. Francis hesitated at the incensed flicker in Takeshi's eyes.

"Okay." Dr. Francis swallowed nervously. "Take these."

He handed Takeshi a bottle of white pills. "There's about ten extra in the bottle. She can take 1-2 after she eats. Don't tell anyone I gave you that," Dr. Francis told Takeshi, and he nodded solemnly.

"Understood, doctor. Thanks for your help with K—the prisoner."

Was he about to say her name? She stared pointedly at Takeshi, but he ignored her. *Now* he chooses to ignore her.

"Of course, Captain." The doctor turned back to her. "Unfortunately, I can only keep you here another couple of hours before questions arise about a prisoner being here too long." He sighed, giving her an apologetic look.

"I've already told Captain Steele you need to rest. That means no shifts and strict bed rest. Captain Steele or another prisoner will bring you your meals. In two days, I want you to come back here, and I will give the final go-ahead for you to resume your normal duties," Dr. Francis concluded.

She wasn't particularly thrilled to be stuck in her cell all day, but it could be worse. She could be dead.

"Thank you, doctor." She tried to smile but gave up when her cheek muscles hurt from the motion.

Dr. Francis nodded gently and left the room, leaving her and Takeshi. Alone.

They hadn't talked in weeks, and the awkward energy in the room was apparent. It was difficult to read his emotions because the hard mask was ever-present. Khalani wanted to shrink into the bed and fade away.

"Be honest with me." She sighed. "How bad do I look?"

"Do you want the truth?"

"No, I want you to lie. Yes, the truth."

Takeshi sat in a black chair across from the bed, stretching his long legs out in front of him. "You've looked better. A lot better. You actually look like shit," he added.

Sparing feelings wasn't part of his dazzling personality, but she actually found his honesty hilarious in that moment. A pained chuckle escaped her; it was the first time Khalani didn't detest his vexing presence.

His stern expression didn't shift, and her laughter slowly faded. "What happened after I got knocked out?"

"I allowed two of the male prisoners you frequently speak with to carry you back to your cell. This morning, you didn't wake up for your morning shift. When I checked inside your cell, I noticed you threw up several times and were in and out of consciousness." The steely shift in his gaze made her pulse quicken. "I made the decision to carry you here."

Her mouth opened in surprise. Takeshi carried her? She had no memory of that happening. Of all people, she expected him to leave her. "Why?" she whispered.

He opened his mouth and hesitated. The silence intensified like a violent current threatening to rip them apart. His eyes darted away, and Takeshi's cold voice cut through.

"It would be inconvenient for a new prisoner to die on my block. And more paperwork."

She blinked at his cruel words, and her mouth snapped shut. That's all she was. An inconvenience. But she couldn't expect any more from him. He already did more than necessary by taking her here. She should be thankful.

But why did his words hurt so much?

She cleared her throat. "Well, um, thanks anyway. I don't wanna inconvenience you further, so you don't have to stay. Not that you need my permission."

His lips set in a harsh line, and she was taken aback by the aggressiveness bleeding from him. Like he was mentally dissecting her into pieces.

"What the hell were you thinking?" He didn't raise his voice. He spoke very slowly and calmly, and somehow, that was worse.

"What?"

"Why did you agree to fight in the pit?"

Khalani swallowed hard as the memory of Dana ripping her heart away returned. "I didn't have a choice."

Takeshi leaned forward, placing his elbows on his knees. "Wrong. She baited you, and you fell for it."

Khalani breathed heavily, her emotions rising. "If you only knew what I felt when she tore that picture. What it meant to me," her voice cracked.

She did her best to keep it together, but there are only so many ways a human can bend before they break. Takeshi didn't say anything. He intensely studied her as she was on the verge of falling to pieces again.

"If someone humiliated you and obliterated the only object you had left of your family, what would you do?" she asked him.

"I would destroy them."

"Then you should know why."

She wanted Takeshi to agree with her, however stupid that notion was. She wanted someone, anyone, to *listen*.

"We are not the same." He trapped her beneath his relentless stare.

"When I enter fights, Kanes, I end them. Did you think you would win?"

Khalani hesitated. She wasn't concentrated on winning. All she wanted was to hurt Dana the same way she'd been hurt. Even if it killed her.

He saw the answer in her eyes.

"My point exactly." He leaned back. "You are careless with your life. If you didn't let emotions cloud your judgment, you wouldn't be lying here."

She stared at the opaque white covers, wishing to disappear into their depths. She couldn't look at him anymore because he was right. Takeshi saw too much. Exposed her deepest flaws as if her mind was a script.

She was careless with her life because, in her mind, it didn't matter anyway. Everything was already lost. She was close to taking matters into her own hands and ending it in Braderhelm. Many times.

But there was something that always stopped her.

A small but persistent voice. And the more she talked with Winnie, the louder it became. As if the echoes of the many who've died before her shouted their dissent in bombastic fashion. Telling her to wake up.

Wake up.

"Kanes?" Takeshi asked softly, interrupting her thoughts.

"Yeah?"

His magnetic eyes captured hers, and she was lost in a sea of black. She sensed his dark anger but felt some of it slowly dissipate. "For what it's worth, even though I think what you did was stupid, you showed courage down there."

The compliment startled her, and she straightened. "Really?"

"Yeah." He sighed. "Not necessarily weak. Just irrational, illogical, and ill-tempered."

Khalani rolled her eyes. "And you only annoy me when you're breathing, really."

The corner of his lip lifted, and she feigned shock.

"I didn't know the Captain of Braderhelm was capable of smiling."

"Looking at your face in this state has improved my sense of humor." Takeshi's grim expression returned, but for a moment, the hostility in the air eased as if a strange peace resided in their mutual disdain for one another. After a few seconds in comfortable silence, his calm demeanor dissipated. Takeshi's forehead creased as he stared at her.

What was he thinking?

"I should get going." Takeshi's expression hardened as he stood. His energy grew distant, like he was a thousand miles away instead of a couple feet.

Khalani studied him as he adjusted the weapons around his waist. It was like Captain Steele and Takeshi were two different people, one ready to inflict pain and the other a quiet mystery. But both were trained killers, able to dominate every opponent. Her eyes flared, an idea setting in.

"Can I ask you something?"

Takeshi was immediately suspicious. "What?"

"Everyone saw me lose that fight. Some people—certainly Dana— will think I'm an easy target now, right?"

He paused. "Possibly."

"I want to be prepared to face anything and not find myself back here again."

She had been tossed, flung through the air, and pummeled to submission so often that torment was her life's only consistency. She held onto the pain and clutched it to her chest till it became a part of her identity. Khalani was so messed up that she mistrusted the people who didn't hurt her. But a shift was occuring. The deep-seated anger was morphing, begging her to regain control and start fighting back instead of accepting life's cruel fate.

Takeshi's jaw tightened as he gave her a cool glare. Probably because he realized where she was heading with this. She didn't want to ask for his help—never imagined she'd be in this position—but she took a deep breath and plunged into unknown territory.

"Can you train me how to fight? At least how to defend myself?"

"No," Takeshi answered, walking away.

She tried to sit up but grimaced as her body refused. "Wait. Please..."

He paused in his steps, hands fisted at his sides.

"I would be a good student. Can you at least give me a chance?"

Takeshi let out a sharp breath and turned back to her. "I'll let the inappropriate question slide because of your concussion. You're clearly confused about our dynamics. I'm not here to save you. If you attempted something stupid against me, I would be forced to kill you."

"I wouldn't do anything stupid."

He didn't look convinced and eyed the door as if he were the one about to bolt.

"If anyone asks, this would be you ensuring your prisoner stays in line and doesn't have to waste any more prison resources or your time by going to the medical ward again."

She was pretty proud of herself for pulling that reasoning out of nowhere.

He opened his mouth to undoubtedly rebut her again, but she interrupted him, needing to strike while the iron was hot. "And if Guard Barron tries retaliating against me, I need some training to defend myself."

"He was already warned." Takeshi's jaw clenched, the virulence in his statement intensifying. "I can assure you that's not going to happen."

Khalani begged to differ. "But if he doesn't listen, he'll kill me."

"It's not my job to care."

Her mouth snapped shut. His words inflicted pain like they were laced with poison. Stupid. What she needed to learn was the art of putting her mouth over her head and swallowing it.

"Fine. I understand. Sorry I asked." Khalani tried to keep the hurt out of her voice as she folded back into the bed. She accepted her fate and waited for him to leave. But he didn't. Takeshi didn't blink or back away. He steadily focused on her as if she lay under a microscope, no indication of his inner thoughts.

If her mind was an open book, Takeshi's mind was encased in a locked vault at the bottom of the ocean. Surrounded by sharks.

"*Fine.*" Takeshi growled, squaring his chest. "This is your funeral, Kanes. Once you receive the go-ahead from the doc, we will start." He scowled, clearly unhappy with the situation.

She straightened, eyes widening in surprise, but she wouldn't pass up the opportunity. "Okay. I'll be ready."

"And what happens if you try anything stupid in training?" A torrent of violence hung in his rigid expression.

"You'll kill me. I understand," Khalani repeated, attempting to downplay her anticipation.

"For your sake, you better."

"Captain Steele?" she asked before he could leave.

"What?" Takeshi snapped, halting his steps.

"Thank you."

"Don't." He swiveled his head, the black current in his eyes deepening. "Don't say you're thankful until after I'm through with you. Only then will you mean it."

14

Courage lies in baring yourself to the universe.

Khalani stared at the ceiling of her prison cell. Cracks presented themselves in rigid disfigurations. When she squinted her eyes, the cracks moved like a chromatic swell of water. Greens. Blues. Even reds. An array of images pulled from her mind and reflected on the ceiling. A smile played on her lips.

Ah. There it is.

The aurora borealis shined on the rocky surface, cascading and effervescent, like a peaceful ocean wave blanketed her soul in serenity. Just like the book Winnie gave her, but this time, it was her own creation.

The sound of footsteps ushered by, and the image dissipated. Khalani sat up anxiously on her cell bed, waiting for a guard to pass. Characteristic blue hair appeared, and she couldn't help the pained smile on her face.

"Hey, stranger." Serene held a small plate of food with a grin.

"I didn't know you were coming," Khalani croaked out, standing on unsteady legs. A full day had passed since she left the medical ward.

Takeshi dropped her off in the cell wordlessly and hadn't come to check on her since he agreed to train her. She didn't know if that was good or bad. Knowing him, it was probably bad.

Serene's eyes widened as she looked closer at Khalani's bruised face. "Wow. Good thing you can't see yourself."

She snorted and walked to the bars. "That bad, huh?"

"Like an experiment gone wrong."

Khalani nodded to the plate. "What's that?"

"Oh." Serene squeezed it through the bars. "Bon appétit."

Khalani eyed the contents warily. She was pretty confident a worm moved in the slush. "Yum." She raised her eyebrows.

"I didn't leave you completely empty-handed. I managed to steal one." Serene pulled out a small slice of bread.

Her mouth instantly watered at the sight.

"You're shitting me!" Khalani snatched the bread and almost forgot to inhale, she chewed so fast. "Thank you," she mumbled with a full mouth. She didn't mind that the bread was stale and cold. At that moment, it was the best thing she'd ever consumed.

Serene nodded at the scars on her face. "How you holding up?"

"It hurts, but I'll be fine."

"I know, but…are you okay after what Dana did to your picture?" Serene hesitated. "I've never seen you so mad."

Khalani froze. The harrowing image of her parents ripping apart repeated in her brain. Over and over. She wanted to punch something. The cell bars. The wall. Anything with physical form. She wanted her fists to be productive. And she needed Dana on the receiving end of that productivity.

"How did she get into my cell?"

"I talked to Derek. We think it happened the day Dana got assigned to clear out the toilets." Serene's lips set in a hard line. "They gave her a temporary pass to each cell on the block."

A knot lodged in her throat. Dana must have been looking for the papers Charles gave her, but she'd already given them to Winnie. She glanced at her bed, thinking of the poetry she kept hidden underneath.

Was nothing of hers safe?

Serene read the direction of her thoughts. "It won't happen again."

"What makes you so sure?"

"I overheard Takeshi talking with Dana after Adan and Derek carried you back to your cell. It wasn't pretty," Serene said.

Khalani's brows drew together. "What do you mean?"

"He told her that if she tried pulling a stunt like that again, stealing from another prisoner's cell, he would have the Warden reassign her to surface duty. You should've seen her face Khalani, whiter than a ghost." Serene grinned.

He really said that to her?

Khalani fiddled with her fingers, lost in thought. It only made sense. Takeshi had to ensure thievery was not permitted in Braderhelm. That was the only logical explanation.

"I don't understand why she's had it out for me. She thought I was getting in her way with Captain Steele, whatever the hell that means." Her muscles tensed.

"Wow." Serene's eyebrows raised in realization. "Makes so much more sense now."

"What does?"

Serene whispered through the bars, "Dana's trying to get close to Captain Steele so he can help her escape. Some of the other prisoners have tried, and their punishments were brutal. She must think you have the same plan."

"Does she actually think that will work?" Khalani gave her an incredulous look.

"Of course not." Serene scoffed. "But prisoners here will do anything, and I mean *anything*, if they think it will help them escape."

Escape. No prisoner had ever escaped Braderhelm Prison. The meaning danced around the confines of her mind like a fleeting bird, long extinct. The alarm rang, and Serene glanced away in disappointment. "I gotta go. Try not to die before I see you again."

"Thanks, Serene. Would I be a bad person to say that I'm sad and happy you're in Braderhelm?" Her own honesty bewildered her.

Serene's eyes lightened. "If you are, then that makes me a bad person too."

Khalani wasn't fond of physical affection. She hated giving hugs like she was allergic to them, but she wished the bars would disappear. In another world, she would hug Serene for all the times she stayed when Khalani was surrounded by herself for too long. In another world, they would be free.

But the only place freedom resided in was dreams. And in death.

***

Khalani practically ran up the steps to the library after she received the go-ahead from the doctor to return to her shifts. Her knuckles rasped against the door, and she let herself in at the soft sound of music. A masculine voice, dripping in melancholy, sang over the player.

Despite her reservations, Khalani's mouth churned up. She missed this more than she realized.

Her eyes fluttered closed, and she breathed in the aroma of books and the gentle warmth of the library. Winnie sat at the rusted desk, her back facing Khalani. She was huddled over a decrepit black journal, the fragile corners of the book cracked and folded in.

How old was that thing?

Khalani squinted at the new selection of books on Winnie's desk. The titles were barely visible: The Great Gatsby, Gone With the Wind, Pride and Prejudice.

She frowned. Strange names.

"Hey, Winnie," she said.

Winnie gasped and threw the journal up in surprise.

The black object fell to the floor in a heap, and Khalani reached over. "Here, let me grab that for you."

"No!" Winnie yelled, hastily grabbing the journal. Winnie's face went pale as she clutched the book to her chest. She turned to the record player, turning down the volume. "Goodness gracious, Khalani. You almost scared the cave lights out of poor Winnie."

Khalani raised her palms warily. "I didn't mean to scare you, Winnie. I finally got assigned back here. Did George tell you why I couldn't make it?"

The rigidness in Winnie's muscles eased with each gulp of air taken. She tucked the old journal in a drawer. "Yes, my dear. George told old Winnie. Horrible thing that happened. Are you okay? Winnie can make you some tea," Winnie offered with concern in her eyes.

"I'm fine, Winnie. Promise."

Winnie's shoulder's sagged in relief. "Thank goodness. Winnie was so worried about you. She's delighted you're back. The book is going along quite well. Winnie hoped to test your ear with a few pages, see if the wording flows." Winnie gave her a warm smile.

Khalani glanced over at the drawer Winnie hastily put the journal in. The fervor of Winnie's reaction took her by surprise. She'd never even seen her move that fast before.

"Winnie, if you don't mind me asking, what were you working on when I came in?" she asked nonchalantly as Winnie pulled out the typewriter.

Winnie paused for a moment, and Khalani noticed the slight tension in her shoulders. "Don't worry about it, dear, just writing down my old collective thoughts. It would no doubt bore you." Winnie swatted the air and turned quickly to her typewriter.

She was lying.

Khalani knew it. She could tell by the slight tremble in her hand and the lower pitch of her voice. Why would she lie about a journal? Maybe it was just a diary or something, she thought, trying to explain the weird encounter away.

Khalani turned to the books on the desk. Her finger traced along the cover of one of the thick novels.

"Gone With the Wind," she repeated.

Winnie swiveled to Khalani with a gentle smile, all traces of discomfort gone. "One of Winnie's favorites. You should read it."

"Is it an instruction manual about dealing with wind on the surface?"

Winnie bent over and nearly choked with laughter as Khalani stood there awkwardly.

Was that a stupid question?

"I'm sorry, my dear, I'm sorry. It's just funny how we think books are all instruction manuals or history lessons." Winnie wiped a stray tear from her eye, still chuckling. "The story is about love and strife, based in a time long before the Great Collapse. A classic of their day."

Her brows furrowed as Winnie excitedly handed Khalani the heavy text. "But what's the purpose if it's not teaching anything?"

"Sweet girl, the purpose is about life." Winnie's hands raised in emphasis. "These books aren't meant to train or give a history lesson. They are meant to stir the mind and the soul. To immerse you in the wonders and hardships of love, the most powerful force in the universe," Winnie concluded with a smile.

"That's not the most powerful force."

Winnie tilted her head to the side, overhearing Khalani. "What did you say, dear?"

Khalani traced her fingers over the gold writing on the cover. A deep weight rumbled in her chest, forming a lump in her throat. All it took was the thought of them. Gone, like the wind.

The most powerful force wasn't love.

"It's death. That's more powerful."

Death comes for all and spares none. Death was more certain than life. Her assured demise hurtled toward her at full speed, faster than a bullet sailing through the air. Her thoughts shifted to Takeshi again. What possessed her to ask him for help if the inevitable ending was the same. She couldn't stop what was coming.

Why should she even fight?

What's the point?

Winnie clasped her hands together, staring at her white knuckles as if they held unwritten answers. The silence extended. She was the first one to break it.

"You know," Winnie said, "Winnie used to have a daughter." Khalani's head snapped up. Winnie had never mentioned a daughter.

"Her name was Sarah," Winnie's soft voice echoed through the room, and everything ceased.

Like all that existed in the world was Winnie's story.

"Winnie didn't plan for it. She would run off at night in secret with a nobleman. Because of his wealth and influence, he couldn't be seen with someone as poor as her. But Winnie didn't care. She was in love. When Winnie learned she was pregnant, she was overwhelmed with happiness and joy. But he left her without even a goodbye letter once he found out.

"Winnie cried every night. Alone. Scared. She wanted to get rid of the baby. Give it to someone else to take care of because it was the object of him leaving. But then, Sarah was born. Her feet were so small." Winnie's lips curled, and her eyes teared up.

"Winnie counted each finger and each toe, and she was in love with every one of them. Sarah was the most beautiful thing she'd ever seen. The love was instantaneous. Like Winnie's body was *made* to love her. The emotion was so intense, so overwhelming, like the devotion would swallow Winnie whole. Those few years Winnie had with Sarah were the happiest of her life."

"What happened to her?" Khalani asked anxiously.

"She got sick." Anguish bracketed the lines of her eyes. "Winnie took her to the doctor. He told her the infection was spreading to Sarah's lungs. Winnie didn't have enough money for medicine, and they sent her home. Sarah died in her arms that night," Winnie's voice broke.

Tears formed in Khalani's eyes at the sheer sadness and unfairness of it all. Winnie was someone who was made for color. For light and happiness. She wished she could bottle her pain, throw it at the wall, and destroy the hurt.

But nothing can erase that.

"I'm so sorry, Winnie," she whispered.

"Do you want to know why Winnie still smiles and keeps going?"

Khalani nodded, her chest rising with shallow breaths.

"Because the dead don't want you to die with them," Winnie stated.

"Love transcends space and time. It holds no bounds or limits. Dear girl, love is stronger than death because if you love someone, they can never truly die. Sarah lives on. In me. And your parents live on in you too."

Khalani's hands trembled, and her head bowed. She tried to contain her emotions with every ounce of strength, but the burden was too overwhelming. Her failings, torments, and regrets blanketed her frail body like an endless, daunting stone slab.

It was too much.

A sob escaped her mouth. Another. And another. Till the sounds of her cries eclipsed the room, and she nearly crumpled to the ground.

And then, strong arms wrapped around her, holding her up. "It's okay. It's okay, sweet girl," Winnie whispered continuously, rubbing her hair. Khalani sobbed into Winnie's shoulder. She gripped her tight, holding on for dear life.

If she could cry out to the heavens and tell her parents one thing, it would be that she was sorry. She was so sorry for not telling them to stay home that day. For not showing them how much she loved them. For hating them when she was left alone. For giving up, year after year. She was sorry for wanting to die.

Khalani had been alone for so long. Her youth was stolen, and every ounce of pain and suffering piled high at her feet, and no one had been there to lighten the load. No one to hear her cries. Or tell her that it wasn't her fault. Before Braderhelm, Khalani had been a walking, talking, breathing machine. Wound up to march with no direction.

No purpose or conviction.

She thought her life was over when she was sentenced to prison. But something prevented her from giving up. She didn't understand before. The pain and misfortune were worse. The agony remained. But the suffering wasn't what mattered.

She had changed.

The transformation began the moment she opened Douglas's book. Poetry introduced her to a world filled with art and rapture. The beauty of embracing the fall and defying adversity. Creating hope and wielding light when surrounded by affliction. Poetry showed her things worth fighting for, surviving for.

Her heart, so broken yet full, threatened to spill over daily with the missing pieces. Every inch of her body ached and yearned for her parent's touch, their voice. Like any moment, she'd explode in a raw spectacle of feeling. She didn't believe anything could describe the depth of those emotions.

For how can words encapsulate the universe?

Because it too is infinite.

It's the only force that can break you apart and forge you back together at the same time. The pure sentiment will have you rage at the world one moment and stand on her highest peaks with wonder and awe the next.

To love is to go on.

That is why she asked Takeshi to train her to fight.

Her impartial existence extinguished and erupted into something so much more powerful. Khalani clutched Winnie tighter as the force of her emotions burst out of her chest like a tidal wave. And Winnie never let go.

When Khalani returned to her cell that night, words flowed from her body as if they were embedded in her skin. She desired to shout them into space and expand along with it, for eternity.

Monster in me

There lay wounds in me
Open scabs, bleeding marks, decrepit lines
Possessing transparency with the weight of mountains
Pressure cascades down my spine
Like drops of wax as the candle bleeds
Did you know the monster was me?

Voices cry and tremble like the earth
Trampling hopes while honoring doubts

I became fluent in every form of fear
All my bads are timestamped and memorized
All the goods of me are blotted and erased
Did you know the monster was me?

You will never be
Good enough
Loved enough
Strong enough
Twisted phrases and malicious lies
Quickly turn to wicked truths
I strike the words of destruction
I do it to be first
I do it to be worse
Did you know the monster was me?

The might of me relinquished the throne
Defeat sank me to my knees
Shuttering my gaze for the final blow
Until I heard a distant cry
Ferocious fights raged and something kept me alive
Death knocked and I peered into his face
He balked and scattered at the sight
Did you know the monster was me?

I outlived all my worst days
Survived every lonely cold night
My eyes open for all those that are closed
The voice within my voice stirs
Shouting truths that lay in waiting
These bleeding wounds encompass a story
Of someone stronger than steel
And more fearful than death
I clench the sword of life and bellow out
You'll remember the monster was always me.

15

Layer every step forward in defiance.

Khalani stood calmly in front of her cell. Her fingertips chafing against her dirty uniform were the only display of her emotion. She'd been waiting for this day with baited anticipation all week. Her training with Takeshi would finally start.

She was ready. Her muscles coiled with restless tension as her eyes scanned the block.

Since her conversation with Winnie, she opened her eyes each morning with renewed energy. A new purpose. Apollo left her to burn and spat her out in a blaze. Crushed and beaten. But breathing.

That was a tremendous mistake because the strongest substances are forged in fire.

She was prepared to take on all enemies, barriers, and demons that stood in her way. *Living* would be the ultimate act of her rebellion. And the first obstacle was Takeshi Steele.

She'd only known Takeshi for a couple months, but it already felt like they had history. And the bad outweighed the good. He was insufferable, and she was the constant thorn in his side.

Hell, he probably polished his personal knife collection in anticipation of this day. Yet, she didn't move from her spot. Nothing would make her back down now. She waited.

And waited.

What was taking so long? She stared down both sides of the hall, but he was nowhere to be found. Did he forget? She scoffed at the idea as soon as the thought came into her head.

This was Takeshi. He didn't forget anything.

"Kanes."

The deep voice sent shivers up the back of her spine. She slowly turned and drew in a sharp breath.

The very air seemed to bend around Takeshi as he walked toward her. No, walk wasn't the right word. Takeshi marched with purpose as if the swift power of death and tenacity of man were evident in his stride alone. Each step forward was layered with quiet confidence, like he could take on a whole army and emerge the victor.

His dark eyes captured hers, and a heavy lump filled the back of her throat. "For a second there, I thought you changed your mind."

An electric current ran through her as his massive body edged closer. Takeshi's expression smoothed into an unreadable mask as he slowed to a halt. Pensive and stoic, he appeared carved out of a marble statue. The only indication of any emotion was the spark in his eyes. They narrowed and pierced hers in a challenge, daring her to run.

"You should know by now, Kanes. I don't ever back down."

His deep voice stroked against her body as he towered over her. Khalani wouldn't let him scare her off. She wasn't going anywhere.

She lifted her chin and stared back daringly.

Your move, Captain.

"Let's get this over with," he snapped, turning around and mowing down the hall.

She quickly followed, and her eyes darted around the halls for witnesses, but there wasn't a soul in sight. Everyone was in the pit. Takeshi crossed his arms and strode to the far corner of the elevator. She leaned against the opposite wall, the silence palpable as the elevator whirled down. She tugged on the bottom of her dirty garment and tried to ignore him, but with Takeshi, that task was impossible.

"So," she cleared her throat, "I noticed you've been absent the past few days."

He stared straight ahead, not acknowledging her.

"You haven't said a word since the medical ward."

Silence.

"Okay, good talk." Khalani's gaze flittered to the ceiling. The elevator was too damn small. In fact, Braderhelm wasn't big enough to fit the two of them.

"Why do you have a sudden interest in my whereabouts?" Takeshi asked.

Her teeth ground together. "I don't. I was holed up in my cell and was just surprised I didn't see you. That's all."

"Really. If I didn't know better, I'd say you missed me."

"I'd sooner miss cleaning up shit," she replied hastily. "I was worried you might back out of our deal. Nothing more."

"So eager for me to hurt you, huh?" He gave her the side-eye, and her stomach flipped.

"Wha—no. That's not what I—"

"Let's go, Kanes."

The elevator door opened to the lowest level of Braderhelm. A subtle shift flickered in his expression, but he rapidly crossed the entryway before she could decipher it.

Khalani huffed a deep breath and glanced around the dark hallway. The dim light from several torches did little to alleviate the eerie flutters in her chest.

The hairs on her arms rose, and she had the sudden urge to pee. "Where are we going?"

"You'll soon find out," he cryptically replied.

A dark metal door lay at the end of the hallway. Takeshi's biceps flexed with the weight as he opened it, and Khalani's eyes widened in shock. She walked over the threshold and stood in a church.

The ceiling was arched with murals of angels along the walls with fiery swords in their hands as they flew through puffy clouds. At the front of the room, a large wooden cross was stapled to the wall. No pews were present or people kneeling in worship. In contrast to the heavenly paintings, a sandy fighting square lay in the center of the room, similar to the layout of the pit. In the far corner lay a myriad of weights and workout machines.

Her brows knitted as she lifted her head back up to the ceiling, enraptured by the beautiful murals. Takeshi stood silently, studying her reaction as she looked around with her mouth agape.

"What is this place?" she breathlessly asked.

"This room was built when Braderhelm was first constructed. It was originally supposed to be a worship area for anyone who wanted to pray to God to help cure the earth again," his words echoed off the walls and bore into her.

"After construction was complete," he continued, "Frederick Braderhelm became the Warden and said prayer was for the weak. He decided that this space would better serve as a training area for the guards."

She frowned. "Why did he leave the cross?"

Takeshi stared up at the cross, his lips set in a hard line. "Frederick Braderhelm had a taste for manipulating in cruel ways. He wanted the guards to see it and know that because of their deeds here, heaven's gates would be forever barred to them," his voice drifted off.

She turned to him, feeling a slight twist in her chest. "Do you believe that?"

He drew a long breath and turned to her. She nearly stepped back at his harsh gaze. "Don't feel pity for me, Kanes. Every decision I've made was done consciously. If there is a God, my judgment day will come, and I'll be ready."

The words cut through the air with sharp confidence and resolve. In his all-black garments, standing in the middle of the church, Takeshi looked like a fallen angel, ready to confront any obstacle, even hell itself.

And damnit, if the look didn't suit him incredibly well.

Before she could open her mouth and say anything further, he walked over to the grey lockers against the wall. She studied the room and barely noticed the blur of clothes flying at her. She caught them in surprise and glanced at him in question.

"Your prisoner uniform isn't suitable for training. These are a pair of workout clothes from one of our female guards. She got released recently, so now, you're their new owner. I noticed that your sneakers are too big for you. Try these."

He grabbed black sneakers from the locker and tossed them to the floor. "Thanks," Khalani said, inspecting the clothing.

Black tank top and black shorts. They appeared small enough to fit. The fabric even smelled nice. A smile tugged at her lips. She could finally wear something clean. The offering was simple, but she clutched the clothing close like he handed her the world's greatest gift.

Something in her expression made Takeshi frown.

"What?"

"Nothing. I've never seen you smile like that."

The space between them felt like it extended for miles. Yet, his obsidian gaze closed the distance as if a single glance permitted Takeshi to bury himself beneath her skin. He was violent by nature, but the barest hint of warmth hung in his expression.

No. She was clearly imagining things because describing Takeshi as warm and tender was like describing the grim reaper as sweet. He was likelier to cuddle in a blanket of blades and give a baby a taser as their first toy.

Her brows furrowed as his expression swiftly closed, and he strode toward the exit. "I'll wait outside while you change. Knock when you're done," he said without looking back.

The door closed with a resounding bang that bounced off each angel soaring across the ceiling. She shrugged at Takeshi's bad mood—what else was new—and put on the workout clothes.

Khalani had lost a lot of weight, and the previous owner was clearly more blessed in the chest than she was, but the black tank fit decently. The shorts were snug around her thighs and backside, but she moved comfortably. Although tight, the shoes fit much better than her previous ones.

She did a small twirl and held her hands to her chest. This was her moment to feel normal. No matter how brief or fleeting, it mattered. She tilted her head back and soaked it in for a few more seconds. The only path left was forward. Khalani nodded with determination and walked toward the door.

Takeshi opened it instantly after one knock. He blinked at her appearance. Takeshi's expression quickly morphed as he gave her a once-over, his lips forming a grim line as his brows drew together.

Did she look that bad?

"Is something wrong?" Khalani stood there awkwardly.

The muscle in his jaw ticked, and he shut the door wordlessly.

"Let's get this over with," Takeshi interjected, brushing past her.

Of course, he wasn't going to answer her. Men like him probably come out of the womb brooding.

She frowned and followed him to the middle. Black bars wrapped around the sandy area. Khalani swung her leg over the rubber bar, less gracefully than Takeshi. She faced him in the center of the ring, chills running down her body at the enclosure.

It was even more unnerving when she lifted her gaze to the striking image of heaven's army waging war above her.

Such beauty and violence; the anthem of humanity.

"What if someone comes in?" she asked him.

Takeshi shook his head. "No guard ever comes in here at this time. They're either at the pit or doing rounds. There are no cameras in here, so we're all alone."

Khalani's pulse quickened, and she wiped her sweaty palms down her side. Again.

"We need to set ground rules first." He cracked his knuckles and straightened to his full height. "First, you want to learn from me, so you need to understand that in this arena, I am the master." His husky voice reverberated over her body, and her muscles tensed at his words.

"That means I say something, you do it. No arguments. No complaining. No giving up. You need to trust that I know your limits, and when I tell you to do something, it is for your own good. Understand?"

She let out a deep breath, accepting the risks she was taking. "Yes."

"Second," he continued, "You are not to tell anyone of these lessons. This includes your three friends. Clear?"

That was a given.

Takeshi waited until she nodded before he continued. "Finally," he took a step toward her, "If I get the barest inkling of you attempting to use any weapons or skills outside this arena against me, what happens?"

Her anxiety peaked, but she answered firmly, "You'll kill me."

Takeshi tensed and nodded. "This is your one and only reminder."

He stood there resolutely. Khalani wouldn't even try to test if he was bluffing. From the short time she had known him, she realized one thing, if Takeshi Steele made a threat, he meant it.

"I understand." Her spine straightened.

Khalani was as ready as she would ever be.

"Good. Now, attack me." Takeshi stopped right in the center of the ring. His arms hung low by his side, and his stance widened as he faced her, steadfast.

"Attack you?" Did she hear him right?

He lifted an eyebrow. "That's right. Now's your chance to attack the Captain of Braderhelm, Kanes. Or are you all talk?"

Her eyes lit up at his words. Maybe it was revenge that fueled her. Or desire of payback for every lick of pain she received in Braderhelm. She rolled her neck around, her muscles readying with energy.

Here we go.

Her fists raised in line with her chest, and she slowly inched toward Takeshi. He made no movement. Not even one muscle. His eyes followed her every motion intensely.

Even though Khalani was the one moving toward him, she felt like the prey. An energy radiated from him, a silent excitement that got her blood pumping faster. She was an arm's length distance away now.

Was she really going to do this?

Khalani glanced at his eyes, still unsure. Takeshi just lowered his head. That was all the confirmation she needed.

She pushed forward and swung a punch toward his face.

So fast, she barely caught the movement, Takeshi leaned to the side and snatched her wrist. In the next millisecond, he swung his foot toward the back of her ankle, using her weight against her. Before Khalani knew what was happening, she fell right on her back, the breath rushing out of her lungs.

That was going to leave a bruise.

Takeshi stood over her calmly, placing his hands on his hips. "Do you know how I was able to do that so easily?"

Her face flushed. "Because you're stronger than me?"

"No. You will learn that it has nothing to do with strength. On your feet," he instructed, stepping back.

Khalani ground her teeth and heaved her body to stand up. She didn't understand how his massive body could move with such fluidity while she swayed and stumbled like a drunkard. She closed her eyes to bring her mind back to center.

The next thing she knew, her feet were being swiped out from under her, and she fell forward on her face. Pain lanced through her nose, and she quickly stood up.

"What the hell was that?!" Khalani yelled. She touched her nose and winced.

Takeshi gazed at her with no remorse. "You never take your eyes off your opponent, Kanes. Again."

Her fists clenched at her sides, and she tried to draw in slow and steady breaths, but her anger continued to fester. Takeshi squared his body to face her.

Khalani moved forward, faster this time, hoping to catch him off guard. She leaned down to go for a body shot to his stomach, watching out for his legs. Takeshi swatted her palm away effortlessly and grabbed her by the hair with his other hand, turning her body so her back was flush against his chest.

She gasped in pain as he snatched her elbow and twisted her arm behind in an extremely uncomfortable position. The back of her head fell against his chest as he pulled her hair back, almost to the point of pain. She tried pulling his hand away, but he grabbed her other wrist, halting any movement. Khalani moved her leg, preparing to stomp on his foot or attempt to kick him in his groin.

"Move your feet another inch, and I will dislocate your shoulder," he rasped in her ear.

Khalani's muscles quivered, and she froze. Heat flushed through her, intensely aware of his powerful body subduing hers. She felt Takeshi's breath in her ear. The rise and fall of his chest, steady against her speedy breaths. His fingers on her elbow, holding her immobile.

The slight tug of her hair in his hand.

"You cheated," she huffed out.

"Fighting's never fair."

Khalani blew a stray piece of hair out of her face. She wanted to scream. She was beginning to think that Takeshi agreed to these training sessions just to embarrass her. A way to get back at her for all the times she gave him grief.

"Let me go," she bit out.

"Are you asking nicely?"

"Sorry, left my manners back in my cell."

He lifted her elbow an inch, and she leaned forward in pain. "Okay, okay! I'm sorry. *Please*, let me go."

Takeshi abruptly released both her arms, and her mouth opened in discomfort as she gingerly grabbed her elbow.

She glared at him in accusation. "You could've really hurt me."

"I could've." He stared back unapologetically. "But I didn't. And with the way you left your guard open, I could've also nailed you in the face, as your opponents would, no doubt. I chose a less painful option."

"How is this training me?" Her nostrils flared. "You're just knocking me around."

In a flash, he got right up in her face. "You said you wanted to learn,

Kanes. Remember when I said I was the master here?"

He waited for an answer, and she grumbled, "Yes."

"Here is your first lesson. Don't let your emotions dictate your actions."

Khalani whipped her head up in annoyance. "I'm not emotional."

He gave her one of *those* looks. "Talk back, and I'll make you crawl out of here."

She wanted to yell and tell him he was wrong. But damnit, that would only prove his point. She took a deep breath after he waited silently.

"I'm sorry. I'm listening." She gritted her teeth.

"When you get angry, you respond with erratic movements. I could've stopped you with both hands tied behind my back." Takeshi even managed to sound bored.

She let out a harsh breath and rubbed a hand through her messy hair. "So, what do I do?"

"Know your weaknesses." Takeshi slowly paced around her in a circle, a true predator.

She turned in place, not taking her eyes off him once.

"Your pride has no place in the arena." His voice echoed throughout the chamber, and she felt the deep vibrations through her very bones.

"I defeated you decisively for a purpose. To show you you're no-where near ready to win a fight. Half the battle is here." Takeshi pointed to his head. He then stepped forward and placed a finger above her chest. "Not here."

His eyes pierced hers, and she was acutely aware of the position of his finger over her heart. Her chest barely moved. Takeshi paused, feeling her erratic pulse.

"Total control of your head is necessary to counteract your obvious weaknesses. You'll likely be smaller than your opponent, so you must rely on speed rather than strength. Although," his hand moved, and she got goosebumps as his fingers slid across her collarbone and his calloused palm rested on her arm.

135

He squeezed her bicep muscles, or lack thereof, giving her a disapproving glance. "This needs work."

Khalani's eyebrows pinched together. She had muscles, just ones that were hidden from the naked eye.

And he was still touching her. They made eye contact, and he let go abruptly, turning around to leave the cage. "Now that you know you're not ready to fight, we can move on." He hopped over the barrier.

She remembered how to breathe in oxygen again and frowned. "Move on to what?"

"If you have a weakness you can control, relentlessly attack it until it becomes a strength."

Takeshi left the circle and grabbed weights off the rack on the far side of the room. Khalani tucked a couple flyaway hairs around her ears, more out of her league than she thought. Takeshi turned back when she didn't move.

"These weights aren't going to lift themselves, Kanes."

For the next hour, she lifted dumbbells over her head and worked out on several machines, sweating more than she ever had in the tunnels. Takeshi was relentless. With each increase in reps and weight, she cried out in pain, wanting to give up. But Takeshi was always right there next to her.

He wasn't the type to yell.

No. It was worse. He got under her skin.

"You could just make this easy for me and give up," he whispered.

She glared at him, but the bastard knew what he was doing because she pushed harder each time his insults scraped against her mind, living rent-free.

Khalani was completing the last few of the 50 push-ups. Her arms trembled and shook as her chest bent to the ground. Her baby hairs clung to her forehead, sweat coating her body. Takeshi lowered on his haunches, surveying her every movement. The effort to push up increased tenfold.

She stared hopelessly at the ground, wanting the torture to be over. She bent down, but her arms collapsed under her.

Khalani whimpered and tried to push up, but her arms tingled and appeared to be made of noodles. Moving was impossible.

"You're not done," Takeshi chided in a low voice.

"No, I think I'm going to lay here for a while," she said to the ground. Khalani didn't have the energy to lift her head up. It was almost comical.

"Get up, Kanes. You have two more."

"I can't," she groaned.

There was a pause and a rustle as Takeshi stood. "What a shame. You almost proved me wrong."

The words caught her off-guard, and she found the energy to turn her head. "What's that supposed to mean?"

"I knew you couldn't last a whole session with me. I can spot quitters from a mile away. You're no different."

She. Hated. Takeshi. Steele.

Khalani growled and mustered every ounce of strength she had left to bust out two more push-ups. One...come on, Khalani...two. She sighed in relief and even managed to stand on both feet.

His expression was unreadable as she hobbled toward him. "You should prepare yourself for disappointment because I'm going to prove you wrong at every turn," she panted.

"Good." His eyes lit with molten fire. "I haven't even tried making you beg yet."

His words did strange things to her body. Khalani's chest squeezed tight as his dominating energy encroached on hers.

"You better start praying now, or you'll be waiting a long time for that to happen." She lifted her chin, ignoring every flight instinct telling her not to piss him off. Because screw him. That's why.

"Do you pray often, Kanes?"

She reeled back from the bizarre question. "No."

A slight but dangerous smirk appeared on his face. "Keep pushing me, and you'll need to. If I want something," he lowered his head, an inch separating them, "only God will prevent it."

Khalani let out a deep exhale as he turned toward the exit. It was becoming harder and harder to breathe around Takeshi, like her very air was his to claim. She lifted her gaze to the ceiling, but none of the angels stared back.

As if they were telling her, *good luck with that.*

16

Leave the chips and cracks in my sculpture.
Capture my failures in all their misshapen beauty.

The next few weeks fell into a torturous routine that made Khalani question her sanity. Multiple times. Takeshi refused to further train her in fighting mechanics until her muscles grew from their infinitesimal size.

Those were his exact words.

So, he worked her. Worked her to the point where walking was synonymous with pain, and breathing was no longer a silent affair but a gasp for reprieve.

Her muscles hurt in places she didn't even know she had muscles.

Takeshi was never satisfied until she dropped to the floor like a wet rag. Only then would he show mercy and say she was done for the day. He didn't show it, but deep down, Khalani knew he enjoyed tormenting her. The bastard. And she must be crazy too because she kept returning.

Today was one of those days where her arms would fall off if someone pulled on them too hard. She failed to lift a medium-sized rock into the wheelbarrow and let out a pained groan, massaging her triceps.

C'mon, squiggly arms. Work with me here.

"Nothing screams single and lonely more than having to massage yourself." Derek grabbed the rock from her.

She rolled her eyes and wiped the sweat off her forehead. "We're in prison, Derek. Like you don't do the same?"

"Oh. I do." Derek shrugged with the tiniest grin. "In private."

Khalani's face twisted. "Gross." She grabbed lighter rocks, continuing to work. If she stopped moving, the guards would notice. She didn't need further pain.

Takeshi was the star employee in that department.

Derek cocked his head. "Captain Steele still has you on tunnel duty?"

Khalani explained her absence to Serene, Derek, and Adan by telling them Takeshi discovered her trying to steal pain meds from the medical ward. Her punishment was extra tunnel duty and lashings every day during pit break.

It was the only story that sounded believable.

She nodded, but a feeble voice sounded behind her. "Prisoner 317?"

Khalani turned, and a new guard stared down at her. He was quite young with a baby face, bald head, and eyes so light, they almost appeared yellow.

"Yes?" Her brows drew together.

The young guard straightened further. "I need you to come with me."

Her muscles froze. Did someone find out about her training sessions with Takeshi? Was she being sent to the surface? No guard had ever pulled her out of her morning shift before.

She knew what to expect with ordinary. The same battles and obstacles lived in the ordinary. Ordinary was survivable. Terror existed in the unknown. She nodded at the guard, feeling the need to swallow excessively, knowing she had no choice but to follow.

He led her away from the tunnel, and Khalani glanced back at Derek, who stared at her with wide eyes.

"Where am I going?" she asked.

The young guard didn't answer, and the silence suffocated the air around her. She didn't have time to mentally dissect her thoughts as she followed the guard down the dimly lit, chilly halls. Her stomach churned after they ascended a few levels in the elevator, and she was led to an obscure metal door. The guard gave three hard knocks.

"Come in!" a man yelled from the other side in a hoarse voice.

The guard stepped to the side. "The Warden will see you now."

Her eyes nearly popped out of their sockets. She'd never met the Warden, the leader of Braderhelm Prison, before. Shivers broke out over her body as she warily glanced at the young guard, but he refused to make eye contact. He clutched the gun to his chest and stood stiffly outside the door.

"Go on," he commanded.

Breathe. Just breathe.

She closed her eyes and opened the door. The loud creak announced her presence, and she entered an archaic room quadruple the size of her cold cell. Sparks from a fireplace flamed out as a heavyset man in a worn suit sat next to the fire.

The Warden had a black handlebar mustache and well-groomed hair slicked back with gel. He peered up from the electric pad upon her entrance.

"Ah, 317. Do come in."

Khalani took a tentative step forward and jumped as the guard slammed the door shut behind her, leaving her and the Warden alone. Khalani glanced around cautiously, trying to take stock of any weapons she could use. There were none. Not even a pen. The only furniture in the room was a black marbled desk, a golden rug splayed out in the center of the floor, and two weathered-down chairs next to the fireplace.

"It's just you and me, 317. Please, have a seat." The Warden gestured to the identical red chair across from him.

Khalani played with her fingers as she stepped closer. The Warden set the pad down, studying her closely. His elbows were perched on the armrest, and his hands steepled in front of his face as she sat down.

She picked at the fabric of her uniform as he surveyed her, wanting to make a run for it. She waited for him to speak, bracing herself for the unwelcome news. That was how Khalani mentally prepared for things, expecting the worst outcome. Life taught her nothing less.

"How has Braderhelm treated you so far?" the Warden asked after a beat of silence. Her brows furrowed at the question. His calm pleasantry made her pulse quicken, like she was being lured into a carefully set trap.

"Um, very nice, sir." Khalani swallowed.

He chuckled behind his hands and whispered, "I recommend not lying."

Sweat beaded down her forehead, and she shifted uncomfortably. She didn't relish how his sharp eyes glinted at her like he was subtly boxing her in a cage, searching for answers to unasked questions. Mountains of secrets lay hidden beneath his eyes. And she was privy to none of them.

"It could use more color." Her heart raced like she was treading over a field of thick, razor-sharp needles.

The Warden tilted his head, one hand resting over his face, partially concealing his expression. "You think Apollo is a colorful place?"

"It's all I've ever known." She wrung her fingers together.

"Your family was never rich enough to be granted a day pass to Genesis."

Khalani shook her head, teeth clenching at the mention of her family. Where was he going with this?

"Interesting." The Warden leaned back, his attention fixated on her. "Governor Huxley contacted me not long ago. He is hosting a dinner tomorrow night at his mansion in Genesis, with the council members and their families present. The Governor prefers to use prisoners as servants. I think it's because he enjoys pissing the other council members off."

Her expression remained neutral, uncaring of the Governor's plans to drink tea and savor luxuries with his minions on Genesis while everyone else suffered. The Warden studied her reaction, waiting for her to respond.

"That's...great." Her lips pursed together in a fake smile.

"I'm glad you think so." He tilted his head. "Because the Governor requested that you be one of the servants at this dinner."

Only the sound of the fire crackling filled the space. She didn't move. It was like his words entered and exited her ear but never registered. Khalani shook her head. "I'm sorry, that must be a mistake. Perhaps you have the wrong prisoner."

The Warden slowly grinned behind his hands. "I would probably think the same if I were in your shoes. But I can assure you that this is very real, and you will be on Genesis tomorrow. A few others will attend, but you are the only prisoner the Governor has ever personally selected. Now, why might that be?"

He sat up straighter in his chair, narrowing his eyes. Khalani's mouth slackened, and she was suddenly lightheaded as Alexander Huxley's face entered her vision.

She pressed a nail into her leg, hard enough to draw blood. The physical pain slowly cut through her senses, but she kept pushing into her skin. Her eyes drew to the fire, but no answers or hints of clarity were hidden within the red flames.

"I don't know." No way the Governor even remembered her name after their brief encounter. It couldn't be true. It had to be a lie.

The silence seemed to stretch an eternity. After apparently being satisfied with the truth behind her words, the Warden sighed deeply and quickly stood, walking over to a dark mahogany cabinet.

Khalani relaxed her hand and noticed a dark red indent on her thigh, glaring at her. She sat in silence. Remote. Steeling herself for the moment the rug would be torn out from under her feet. She wouldn't let herself believe that her eyes would gaze upon the gates of Genesis.

She jumped at the sound of the Warden's black boots stomping toward her. He carried two glasses in his hands, filled with dark liquid.

He extended one glass to her and nodded to take it. He sat back in his chair as she sniffed it, wary.

The Warden snorted. "I promise you I didn't poison it. Have a sip with me." He held out his glass to her in cheers. He didn't take his eyes off hers as he downed his drink.

She closed her eyes and took a small sip. The bitter liquid tasted like rubbing alcohol dipped in bleach. She coughed and sputtered, her face scrunching at the unwelcome burn.

The Warden just sat there and laughed. Prick.

"You know, that's some of the finest cognacs in Apollo. It was considered a very high-class drink before the Great Collapse."

"Some things should have died with the Collapse."

He smirked and set down his drink. "Perhaps. But I didn't invite you here to solely talk about dinner plans tomorrow, 317." The Warden's silky voice sent chills down her spine, and the walls appeared to close around her.

"Use your words wisely if the Governor asks you about your stay in Braderhelm. Several years ago, a previous Warden was promoted to a Councilman, and my political ambitions take me in the same direction. A good word or two with him will make your stay here more comfortable. If not, I can make life here a lot more painful," his voice hardened, and the malice in his sharp gaze intensified.

With each word uttered, her breath hitched, and her shoulders bent forward as if she was about to cave in on herself. The favor he asked was no favor at all. The Warden spoke with assured confidence and veracity, which only meant one thing. He was telling the truth.

Khalani nodded, unable to speak. Her muscles released all tension as if she were deflating and disappearing in the confines of the red chair.

"Wise decision, 317. I know you will not disappoint me. You leave for Genesis tomorrow." He gestured toward the door in dismissal.

For a second, she didn't move. Her skin tingled like it had fallen asleep, and a substantial weight settled in her chest. She had dreamed of Genesis since she was a little girl. Dreamed of seeing the sun…

Recognition dawned within her as his words slowly began to register.

This time tomorrow, she will step on the surface of the earth.

Khalani took control of her limbs and abruptly grabbed the glass, downing the alcohol, and not even the sharp burn woke her up.

17

Wade into my abyss so I may learn how to stay afloat.

After Khalani left the Warden's office, she didn't speak. She was a moving mass of skin and bones caught in a weightless daze, like a ghost—an endless wanderer doomed to an eternity of denial.

She repeated the conversation with the Warden over and over, failing to wrap her head around the bizarre notion of visiting Genesis. The demand was illogical. Unbelievable. Outlandish fantasies weren't supposed to escape the boundaries of imagination. But the conclusion remained the same no matter how often she reinterpreted the tense exchange, searching for the gleaming error in the Warden's speech.

She would see the sun for the first time.

Khalani thought of nothing else as she sat ramrod straight in the library, chewing her nails, staring at the same sentence in Winnie's book.

Winnie kept peeking at her with concern throughout the shift, asking multiple times if she was okay.

"I'm fine," was the only response she could muster.

She wasn't. The Governor overshadowed the anticipation of

reaching the elusive, domed city. What were Alexander Huxley's motives? Why would he single her out?

Maybe he really did know about the lies she told the Master Judge during her sentencing, and Khalani would be executed in a more public forum to set an example of her. He'd done much worse. Her parent's shining faces—ever-present in her mind—darkened and warped to blank canvases as blood pooled out of the corner of their mouths, reminding her of the Governor's treachery.

Her fear shifted. Conviction set in her mind like a slab of cement. If the Governor was going to kill her, she would do everything in her power to take the bastard to hell with her.

She rounded her block and found Takeshi waiting outside her cell.

And he looked *pissed*.

"You're late," he bit out in an irate voice, not even bothering to look at her.

"Sorry, misplaced my watch."

Riling Takeshi before training wasn't the most intelligent decision she'd ever made, but practicing self-control was the furthest thing from her mind.

"Maybe I should string you up in the pit the rest of the week, so you'll remember not to waste my time." His dark gaze swept over her.

"I might just take you up on that offer," she murmured.

Takeshi's chiseled face held more aggression than usual, marred by deep lines on his forehead. Something in her expression made him shake his head. His tongue darted out, and he licked his lips. Slowly. As if he were gathering patience with each long stroke.

"Don't tempt me today," he hissed, brushing past her shoulder.

Her blood heated, but it wasn't so much in fear anymore. Her mind was a whirlwind of emotions, and Khalani couldn't explain what she felt, even if a loaded gun was held to her forehead.

They didn't talk in the elevator.

Takeshi flexed his jaw, and every muscle in his body was taut. She cracked her neck on both sides. She then cracked each finger and her wrists.

The pressure between them was so thick you would need something much bigger than a knife to cut through. She knew better than to ask what was bothering him. Takeshi never opened up about his emotions, much less spoke of his personal life. The less they knew about each other, the better.

Khalani quickly grabbed her training clothes and changed when they entered the training room. Takeshi respectfully faced away, his hands on his hips.

She closed the locker and walked to the bench to put on gloves that protected her palms from the heavy weights. Takeshi tossed them to her after he noticed her bloody blisters a few sessions back, a kind gesture that surprised her.

"You ready?" Takeshi impatiently asked with his back to her.

"Yeah." She unwrapped the Velcro on the gloves. "Just give me a sec."

"You won't need gloves today."

Khalani raised her head in confusion as Takeshi moved toward the cage in the center. He unzipped his black vest and threw it off to the side. Underneath the vest, Takeshi wore a black tank.

Each dent of tightly packed muscle in his shoulders and striations in his exposed arms was visible. He wasn't built in a way that was gross. He was strong, formidable, and agile.

Tenacious.

And she was staring.

"Oh. I, umm." Khalani cleared her throat and glanced away, tossing the gloves aside. "Am I starting with pushups in there?"

"No. Come in here, Kanes," Takeshi commanded, gesturing her to enter the ring.

Her brows lowered, but she swung her legs over the bars, joining him in the circle. Takeshi rolled his neck and slowly stretched his arms behind his back. Khalani's gaze stopped on the v-cut stretching into his pants as his shirt lifted. A raised scar spanned from Takeshi's right shoulder to his collarbone, highlighting the ridges in his muscles, honed by years of discipline.

She kept staring and quickly glanced away when she caught his gaze. "What are we doing then?"

"I'm going to teach you basic self-defense and combat moves." Takeshi squared his shoulders.

Her eyes narrowed in disbelief. "Why? You said I was too weak to do any good. 'The roaches don't even fear me' were your exact words if I recall."

She killed a couple roaches the night he said that. But their cousins always returned as if to mock her.

Takeshi turned and held one hand to the black bar. He grabbed his foot from behind, stretching out his quads. Khalani didn't fail to notice the tight grip he had on the bar, his knuckles turning opaque white.

"I was informed today that Governor Huxley requested you to be one of his servants at the dinner tomorrow."

The air immediately thickened. She moved toward the bar and re-tied her hair in a ponytail, trying to occupy herself with anything other than this topic.

"Not like I have a choice. But hey, at least I get to see Genesis."

Takeshi swiveled around. "You need to be careful, Kanes."

"From what?" She frowned.

"Genesis is a mirage. It's more beautiful than your dreams could conjure up, but when you get up close, you'll see it's just as corrupt as Apollo. Keep your head down, don't talk, and don't trust anyone, especially the Governor." The sharp lines in his forehead deepened.

Khalani nearly expected someone to burst the door down for his comments. Slander against the Governor was punishable by death. That was how oppressive and controlling Apollo's rule became.

"I don't get it. You're the Captain of Braderhelm. Aren't you on the Governor's side?" she pressed him.

"I am on *Apollo's* side. I serve this city and its people with loyalty. It's not my place to make my opinions known on the Governor's or the Council's decisions. But you and I both know that any move against the Governor, even perceived, means your death. A smart person knows when to choose their battles. Don't do anything stupid up there," Takeshi implored, staring into her soul.

The weight of his words gripped her. Her senses heightened to the point where she nearly felt the surrounding air molecules enlarge to caress every surface of her skin.

Takeshi spoke as if he were aware of her motives and potential plans of hostility against the Governor. He saw too much.

"I don't know what you're talking about." She whirled around.

Takeshi was across the circle in a flash. He gripped her arms and turned her to face him. He leaned down, and she had nowhere to look but into his fierce gaze.

"*Don't* lie to me. I know what happened to your parents. I know what they did to you the night they died," he hissed.

His words bounced off the walls, and her breath froze as if a cold breeze rushed through the room. She felt like a bug flipped on its back, waiting to be trampled. Vulnerable. Defenseless.

How did he know that?

"Is this really necessary, sir?" The mortician asked the guard who dragged 8-year-old Khalani into the eerie room.

Bright white lights hung over the ceiling. The room was frigid. It wasn't just the temperature. It was the energy. As if all life had been sucked out of the space. Khalani's attention was fixated on the bodies lying on the silver table.

The bodies had grey plastic bags wrapped over them, but their faces were exposed.

"I suggest you not interfere, doctor, unless you want to join them?" the bulky guard asked with a rough hand wrapped around the nape of her collar.

The mortician's eyes fell on her and were filled with guilt, but he backed away and let the guard pull her closer to the bodies.

Khalani started to shake. Tears ran down her face. Through her blurred vision, she could see their faces. Her lips trembled, and her sobs became more pronounced as her chest rose up and down in panicked breaths. Khalani put her head in her hands, a breath away from keening over.

"Open your eyes," the guard said.

She shook her head and cried harder. Snot was dripping out of her nose.

"Look at them."

"I-I, c-c-caaan't," she sobbed.

Stiff fingers shoved under her face and lifted her chin. "Look at them!" the guard demanded.

Her eyes opened, and her knees nearly buckled under her. Her brain could barely comprehend what she was seeing. It was her mother and father.

Their faces held no warmth or breath of life. They were pale. So pale that their skin was almost translucent. Her father's eyes were closed, but her mother's were half-open, unseeing in the distance, with her lips slightly agape.

No. No. No.

Her mouth hung open, but her parents didn't rise from the table to hug her and tell her it was only a nightmare. They lay there stiff and silent. Dead.

Her wails filled the room, and she heard the mortician leave as if he couldn't bear the sight any longer.

"Study them well." The guard wrapped his hand around the nape of her neck. "Your parents were traitors. And these are the consequences of betraying Apollo. They got what they deserved. If you follow in their footsteps, this is what will happen to you. Do you understand?" the guard yelled, shaking her.

Khalani's whole body trembled, and she shook her head. She became hysterical and tried to lunge forward so she could hug them and lay down next to their bodies.

So she could die too.

But the guard picked her up and pulled her away.

"Noooo!!" she screamed, kicking the air, reaching for her lifeless parents. He ignored her cries and carried her further and further away.

"Mommy!!!" she wailed.

Khalani quickly blinked the memory away, trying to prevent any tears from forming. She shook her head at him. "Don't…just don't. It's not a problem for me anymore, Takeshi." The lie spilled off her tongue, ready to be forgotten.

She tried to pull away, but he wasn't having it.

"Stop it, Kanes," he snapped. "Stop *lying.*"

She lifted her gaze to the heavens, praying for one of the painted angels on the ceiling to fly down and take her away. The moment was so absurd that she started laughing and held her hands up at her side.

"What difference does it make? You said it yourself. There is no room for weakness in Braderhelm." She leveled him with a vicious glare. "Why should I open myself up to you? You hate me. Is this your way of putting my guard down, only to kick me to the ground? Are you trying to expose me to be as weak as you think I am?!" By the end, she was screaming, and her words echoed across the murals.

The more her precious guard loosened with Takeshi, the harder she tried to clutch any blanket of security against him. He was too smart. Knew her too well.

Around him, she felt cracked down the middle, exposed to the world.

Her pulse quickened as he leaned closer. His enigmatic eyes flared, and only a couple inches separated them. "I want a lot of things, Kanes. But you thinking that you're weak isn't one of them. I push you so hard because I know you can handle it."

"And what do you want?" she dared to ask.

He hesitated, gazing down at her with uncertainty. Khalani held her breath, waiting for him to cut her deep. She wanted to hear the answer. So bad that she almost didn't want him to speak. She was revealing too much. Opening her soul to a bigger world of hurt.

But time couldn't flow backward. The present was all that remained.

Without thinking, Khalani leaned closer to him, giving in to Takeshi's magnetism. He paused and huffed out a deep breath, meeting her vulnerable stare. She didn't know what he recognized beneath her expression, but in the next second, he abruptly pulled back.

"I want us to continue your training. You're too feeble right now to defeat anyone." His tone hardened into steel, and Takeshi marched toward the opposite end of the enclosed arena. The moment disappeared in a vacuum. Like it never existed in the first place.

Khalani stood in silent shock.

She didn't understand what was happening. Didn't know why at that moment, a surge of disappointment ran through her.

He was the Captain of Braderhelm.

Her sworn enemy.

And her heart was racing like she'd just run a marathon. She wanted the confusing emotions to stop. Wanted to feel normal.

Takeshi swallowed and cleared his throat. Even he seemed on edge as he didn't quite make eye contact with her either.

Good.

This was all his fault. He shouldn't have said those things. He shouldn't be nice.

She was just fine with them hating each other.

"Are you ready to fight?" He turned to her, balling his hands into fists at his side.

Oh yeah. She'd never been more ready to beat a man up.

Anger rode behind her like a fiery cape. She didn't trust herself to speak, so she raised her fists and nodded.

Beware of a woman shunned. She was more dangerous than any nuclear bomb.

18

Rain has never graced my skin, nor has lightning raised my hairs. In you, menacing storms extend their rapture.

"Okay." Takeshi squared himself to face her. "Let's slowly mo—"

"Ahhh!" She charged forward and started volleying him with punches toward his chest and head. Anywhere she could reach.

Takeshi's eyes widened at her onslaught, but he easily blocked each punch with his hand. She threw a final punch, and he snatched her wrist, karate chopping the side of her neck. The nerve endings in her neck spasmed, and she stumbled back, tingly pain running down her shoulder and arm.

She grabbed her neck and grumbled, "What did you do?"

"I hit a pressure point." He turned toward her. "Now, are you done charging me like a psycho?"

"Depends," she clipped. "Have I done any damage?"

He narrowed his eyes. "You're not going to do any damage to me, Kanes."

"Then I'm not done." She kicked out her leg and actually made contact with his shin.

Khalani didn't waste another second, kicking her other leg out at his stomach. Takeshi caught her heel, and she started to do an awkward bounce, up and down. An evil look overcame his eyes and in the next moment, he swiped her other leg, and she fell sideways on her back. Hard.

He stood over her with an unreadable expression in his eyes. "Have you always been this stubborn?"

She breathed heavily on the ground. "Maybe. Have you always been this much of an asshole?"

The corner of his mouth imperceptibly lifted, and Takeshi leaned down on the balls of his feet. "When I want to be. Do you have a problem with that, Kanes?"

"What if I did?"

"You grow when you're uncomfortable. The fact that you don't enjoy it means I'm training you well."

She lifted up on her elbows and gritted her teeth. "Just admit that you get personal satisfaction from hammering me to the ground."

His eyes glimmered, and he leaned forward in challenge. "I'd like it more if you didn't make it so easy."

She scoffed and stood up, not liking how close he was. Takeshi wasn't going to fluster her anymore. Khalani rolled her neck and held up her fists.

"Let's go again."

Takeshi abruptly moved forward. "With the way you hold a fist, you'll do more damage to yourself than me. Never hold the thumb on the inside of your fist. You'll break a bone. Instead, hold it on the outside…yeah, that's it, but tuck between your curled fingers." He touched her hand, moving her thumb in the proper position. She tried not to focus on the rough texture of his fingers as he grabbed her own.

Khalani didn't realize she was holding her breath until he let go, satisfied. Her pulse stirred with indignation and a wild stimulation, but despite the shadows rumbling through her chest, she listened hard and followed his instructions closely. Takeshi challenged Khalani in ways that made her ache in agony and blissfully breathe in exhilaration.

Every task he did, even something as simple as teaching her how to hold a fist, Takeshi did with complete focus, intensity, and concentration. Each training emphasized why he was the Captain. For him, no task was too small to give maximum effort.

"The most important thing for you to memorize is the vulnerable places of the body. That's going to be the eyes, nose, throat, knees, and groin," Takeshi's deep voice bounded throughout the room. "For today, we will focus on the easier parts."

He gestured for her to reach out her hand, and what he told her next made her face blanch. "You want me to stick my fingers in someone's eyes? No. I think I would puke first."

"If it's a life-or-death situation, Kanes, you will do what you need. To survive," he stated without remorse.

She cringed the whole time, but Takeshi did have a point. He refused to move on until he was wholly assured Khalani knew how to eviscerate someone's optical organ.

"Good." His eyes held a dangerous glint. "Turn around."

"You told me I shouldn't take my eyes off the enemy."

"Right now's the exception. Turn." He made a slow swivel motion with his finger.

She hesitated and had to fight every instinct warring inside her as she reluctantly gave him her back.

Khalani's breath quickened as she waited. Her eyes centered on the bars, but her focus was outward, using all her senses to pick up Takeshi's movement. Several moments passed, and she was about to ask him what he was doing when he attacked.

No footsteps, hard breaths, or noise indicated Takeshi's presence. He was a silent assassin.

In a single heartbeat, ripped arms enveloped her from behind. His body was solid as a rock, and she grunted loudly and heaved, trying to dislodge him. Her feet scuffled as she tried to push him back, but Takeshi was an unshakeable force.

He breathed heavily in her ear as she exerted every spec of energy, failing to loosen his dominant hold. Sweat beaded against her brow as she continued to struggle. She might as well push against a wall for all the success she was having.

"Easy there, Kanes," Takeshi whispered.

Khalani shivered at the vibration of his voice tickling her ear but kept trying to break his tenacious grip.

It was no use. After several minutes, her muscles were so exhausted Takeshi nearly held her up. She stopped fighting, and they stood still, both breathing hard. The top of her head barely reached Takeshi's shoulder, and he encircled her completely in this position.

Sweat dripped down his forearms that were wrapped around her. His alluring, musty scent trickled through her nose, and Khalani gritted her teeth. Why was she noticing details like that?

"If someone grabs you from behind like this, you first need to calm down. It will be challenging, but you must conserve your energy. Then, grasp your hands together and use your elbow to hit your assailant in the stomach as hard as possible. Your elbow is one of the strongest parts of your body. I promise you, they will let go," his voice lowered, still wrapped around her.

"Is this the part where I elbow you in the stomach?"

"Not unless you want to be restrained the rest of the week." He paused. "The kind you won't enjoy."

Goosebumps formed on the back of her neck as the deep vibrations of his voice rumbled against her skin. "No, thank you," she grumbled.

"What I thought." Takeshi sounded amused. "Now that we have that settled. Let's practice the motion."

He walked her through the technique, and when she felt more confident, he slowly loosened his grip and turned her around to face him. She lifted her chin defiantly, and he returned the heated gaze. They were the only two people in the room, but it was like they were the sole occupants of all Braderhelm. She could almost feel the tendrils of scalding energy flowing along her body.

"Last part," he slowly drawled out. "If your enemy comes at you directly from the front and overwhelms you..." He held a large hand to her throat, a few inches away.

Her gaze flickered uneasily as she swallowed deeply.

"Kanes." Takeshi brought her attention back up to him. "When we prepare, we go all the way. Tuck away your fear."

She could do this. She needed to.

Khalani exhaled and nodded, giving him the go-ahead. Takeshi didn't waste another second, and his hands closed the distance, wrapping around her throat.

She could still breathe, but her eyes widened as he held her with a firm, unrelenting grip. He frowned at the panic in her eyes, and the slightest hint of consternation flashed across his face. She suspected he might let go, but a steady resolve cemented over his expression. He started walking her back toward the lining of the bars, hands still encircling her throat.

She could do nothing but walk backward in his direction. Her back hit the edge of the cage, and he leaned over her, his eyes flickering with intensity.

"Tell me what you're feeling right now," he demanded, studying her face.

She let in a small breath. There was only one word that completely encapsulated this position.

"Powerless."

Takeshi's jaw tightened. "Yes. You feel out of control, weak. *But that isn't you.* You need to take back that control and prove that you are not to be thrown around and discarded. You, Kanes, are strong."

Her face contorted at the sincerity, depth, and earnestness of his words. Throughout their sessions, he humiliated, punished, and dragged her to the ground. Frail. Defenseless. Incapable. She thought it was his mission to prove that she was too weak. But she realized the truth was far more significant and complex than that.

He was proving to *her* that she was strong enough.

Proving that it didn't matter how many times Khalani collapsed to the ground or failed over and over. She never gave up on herself, despite those failures. And that mattered more than every waking opinion in the world.

"If you're put in this position, you drive your knee into the opponent's groin. Even if it's a girl, it will still hurt like hell, allowing you to get the upper hand. Do you understand?" Takeshi didn't break eye contact.

"I do," Khalani said, grappling with the rush of her emotions like she was climbing a steep mountain filled with jagged edges. At the peak, the power and fortitude to break every chain, physical and imperceptible, bound around her body.

Takeshi nodded and released his grip around her throat. His fingers sliding over her neck made her pulse quicken. They stared at each other in silence. She wanted to say everything and nothing at the same time. Takeshi was distant and ruthless, but every time he looked at her, their bodies froze in suspension, waiting for the other person to attack their walls or reveal the fabrics of their soul.

Takeshi's fists tightened at his side, and he opened his mouth to say something, but the alarm rang, blaring across the walls. Their time was up. They continued to stand still, unsure of what to do next.

He was the first to break the spell. "We should go, Kanes."

She frowned and slowly nodded. Khalani realized that she wasn't quite ready to return to her cell. She wanted to stay and train. Or maybe she wanted an excuse to talk to Takeshi some more. And she was too bewildered and disheveled to understand the strange sentiment.

They didn't speak all the way to her cell. When he began to shut the bars—not making eye contact with her—she wrapped her hands around them and whispered,

"Takeshi?"

He breathed a heavy sigh and lifted his head to meet her gaze. His dark eyes pierced her differently. They were more subdued as if to conceal something potent. Lethal.

"What is it, Kanes?"

"Thank you," she whispered. "For training me and believing that I could do it. You didn't want to help, but you showed up anyway. I just wanted to... I'm sorry, I—" Her hands tightened on the bars as she lost the right words.

The unspoken truth swallowed deep inside, unwilling to loosen from her tongue. Takeshi's brows pinched together, and he shook his head, staring at the ground. A few moments passed, and he finally lifted his chin.

"Kanes, you better not die tomorrow. I'll only allow it when you can beat me in a fight." The intensity in his expression stole her breath.

"I doubt that would happen anytime soon," she joked. "Possibly never."

"Exactly."

The accompanying silence spoke for them. It felt like no bars were separating them. The very air was still, and not even the cockroaches were moving. As if everyone and everything was locked in stasis.

Takeshi's dark eyes fastened around her grip on the bars, and his jaw clenched as he walked away. She hung her head like a weight of bricks descended on her neck. Takeshi continued to wedge himself beneath her skin, peeling back layers, unveiling Khalani for who she really was.

She wasn't that same little girl who begged to perish with her parents.

Khalani would stand on the earth's surface tomorrow, like her ancestors before the Great Collapse. She would face the Governor, the man who murdered those she loved most. The one who robbed her of everything that mattered. Apollo taught her well.

Justice isn't true unless it's coated in blood.

19

There lies a riot in you.
With your very first breath, you cried in protest.

The entrance into Genesis was a massive, gleaming elevator. The doors were see-through with a gold G insignia written on the glass, signaling its sole destination. Serene squeezed her hand as they drew closer to the forbidden area.

When Serene learned Khalani was requested as a servant in Genesis, she made quick work stealing a pad from an unsuspecting guard and switched her number with another prisoner. Khalani objected, but one cutting look from Serene told her that it wasn't up for negotiation. She was admittedly fortunate for her presence when they were forced to change into a tight black dress and matching high heels.

Were they going to a dinner or a brothel?

They were joined by one other male and female prisoner. The girl had pale skin, a pretty, heart-shaped face, and flowing black hair that still held a shine to it. Khalani recognized the auburn-haired boy as the prisoner being shoved around the food line her first day in Braderhelm. At least the guard gave him pants to wear.

She might as well be half-naked.

Their transports swiftly hummed to a stop before the elevator. She gulped at the number of guards standing at attention. The stone-faced men wore gold uniforms, and the leader approached their group.

"These the prisoners?" he asked.

"Yes, sir," the Braderhelm guard responded.

The Genesis guard tilted his head. "Check them."

One of the men abruptly breached her personal space and started feeling around her body for weapons. She kept her eyes forward and went rigid as rough hands patted down her whole body, including her chest and groin.

Serene made a sound of disapproval but was quickly silenced.

"All clear," the guard said, resuming his position.

"Follow me." The Genesis guard turned and walked toward the elevator. He placed his hand on a screened panel, and a lightbulb flashed green as the doors opened. Khalani and Serene exchanged a wide-eyed glance of trepidation but slowly crossed the threshold.

The Genesis guard held up his hand in salute as the doors closed. "Loyalty to Apollo."

The two Braderhelm guards saluted and shouted the words back, but Khalani and the other prisoners stayed utterly silent. The elevator jolted and began rising. She shifted her weight from side to side and rubbed her palms down her legs. The elevator climbed higher.

And higher.

They turned their heads to look out the glass. All of Apollo lay below. The pristine, white Council Chambers grew smaller, and the people walking the streets appeared as black specks. Her anxiety spiked when they were suddenly surrounded by rock, dirt, and soil. Earth.

They were almost to the surface.

Khalani's body jerked to the side when they came to a screeching halt. The back door opened with an electrical buzz. The prisoners turned in unison, and Khalani witnessed something she'd only observed in dreams.

Sunlight.

The light was overpowering. Blinding. Golden rays filtered through Khalani's fingers as she shielded her face. She peered over her shoulder and spotted Serene and the other prisoners covering their eyes as well.

Even through her dirty fingers, the sun was captivating and compelled her to move forward. Her nostrils flared. The very air tasted different. Clean. The lingering stench of the cramped underground dissipated. She didn't know air could taste...*pure.*

Her knees shook as she stepped off the elevator, and her heels sank into grass. Was that what it was called? Yes. Green grass all around them. She'd only seen pictures before.

It looked to be regularly trimmed to perfection, the blades at a consistent one-inch height. It was the purest color of green she'd ever seen, and she had a near undeniable urge to take off her shoes and feel the soft blades caress her feet.

Khalani jumped as the elevator shut its doors and slowly glided down, returning to Apollo. A metallic covering closed over the hole. Her eyes slowly adjusted to the blazing sun, and she finally found the courage to remove her shaky hand and look up.

Instead of being surrounded by a desolate wasteland, she was in an open field. An array of colorful butterflies flew around her, and she slowly turned in the beautiful meadow. Her mouth formed an O when she didn't see a dome but a massive jungle encircling them in the distance.

Luscious green trees stood tall, towering higher than she thought possible. She narrowed her eyes in disbelief when a brown creature swung through the trees.

Is that a monkey?

"How is this real?" she whispered.

"It's not," the dark-haired prisoner said, sliding beside her.

Khalani whipped her head to her. "What do you mean? Where's the dome?"

"You're staring at it." The girl pointed to the jungle. "It's like the virtual windows in Apollo. The dome is translucent and will depict any illusion that keeps the Genesis citizens content. The temperature is regulated too. The only part of the dome that's not an illusion is the sun and the rockfalls."

Khalani tilted her head up further. The sun rode high in the sky, bathing them in a bright glow. The virtual tree leaves swayed as if actual wind blew through the vines.

"They make it look so real," she said in awe.

A stunning rock waterfall extended from the dome, roaring down into a long, winding river. The water was the clearest shade of blue, and a cloud of beautiful mist floated over the air. A gorgeous, white stone bridge lay directly in front of them, built over the river. The river stretched ahead and circled a sparkling city like a moat.

The city of Genesis.

The city was far, and only tall white buildings were visible from this distance, but even from over here, it was beautiful. A torrent of emotions threatened to overcome Khalani, and tears prickled the back of her eyes.

If only her parents had lived to see this.

"Stop dawdling!" the guard with a copper beard yelled.

The guards strode toward the stone bridge, and the four of them quickly followed suit. They walked through the sun-lit, grassy meadow until they reached the river crossing. The waterfall roared next to them, and a myriad of colors appeared through the mist. She'd heard of this before.

Rainbow. Yes, that's what it was. A rainbow.

She stopped momentarily, mesmerized by the sight, when Serene grabbed her arm. "C'mon, Khalani. We have to keep going."

Khalani barely tore her eyes away. It was like being transported into a real-life fairy tale, filled with color, after living in a black-and-white world. How do you ever go back?

When they crossed the elegant bridge, a winding road made of cobblestone led to the city. The buildings in Genesis were ivory-colored, some as high as the dome, with elaborate pillars supporting their structures. As they approached the many buildings, she noticed statues of animals—gargoyles—embedded on top of the pillars.

From animal history class, she vaguely remembered the names of some of the creatures. Lions. Elephants. Horses. The whole city was a mesmerizing work of craftsmanship, designed to attract attention.

Her neck ached as she craned her head at the wondrous sights.

Genesis citizens milled about as they were escorted through the city. The woman wore a mix of metallic, silver, and white dresses, and the men wore silver, gold, or black tuxedos. Each person dressed as if they were about to enter a ball.

Everything about them was different. Even the way they *walked*.

In Apollo, everyone kept their heads down, hurrying to reach their destination and complete their work. There were rarely any smiles or greetings exchanged between strangers. Happiness was as absent as the sun.

But here, everyone smiled and lazily glided along the streets as if they had all the time in the world at their fingertips.

Khalani glanced at some of the stores lined along the street. The windows were filled with dresses, tuxedos, diamonds, furniture, elaborate cakes, and even gold bicycles. Everyone gave their group a wide berth. As if they could sense the underground on their clothing. Khalani made eye contact with two older women who held golden umbrellas in their hands as they glided past. Their faces scrunched in disgust, and they abruptly turned the opposite direction, unable to be in the same vicinity as them for a second longer.

Khalani scowled, and she had half a mind to take the umbrella from their hands and smack them across the head with it.

What kind of idiot blocks the sun anyway?

"Unbelievable, isn't it?" the dark-haired prisoner whispered next to her shoulder. "They live like kings up here while we fight for scraps underground."

She turned in surprise. Something inside Khalani tightened as the prisoner's words made her think of Takeshi.

"Someone once told me that Genesis was beautiful on the outside, but up close, it's just as empty and corrupt as Apollo. I didn't know if I believed them then, but I'm starting to now," her voice softened.

"Whoever told you that is smart. What's your name?"

"Khalani. That's Serene," she whispered, nodding at Serene, who flipped her finger at two old men who were noticeably leering at her.

The girl gave a half-smile. "I'm Fiora. That's Jack." She pointed toward the short boy, who lifted his head in greeting. "Jack had his tongue cut out shortly after he got sentenced to Braderhelm. He can't talk," Fiora explained.

Khalani inwardly shivered. She ran her tongue up the roof of her mouth as if to ensure it was still there.

The streets started to clear, and tall, metallic lampposts on the road lit up around them. Khalani lifted her gaze in wonder as the sun lowered and the sky turned multicolored, from the brightest blue to a pinkish hue, with a tint of lilac. She nearly tripped over her heels as she kept staring at the dome.

If Khalani was alone, she'd lie in the middle of the street, back against the cobblestone. She'd study the buckets of color in the night sky and simply breathe.

The guards guided them away from the imposing buildings, and they started down a long, winding gravel path. Khalani chafed her fingers down her arms as her eyes fixated on an enormous white house supported by giant pillars, and her mouth dropped open. The house was too big for any one person to live in. Or twenty.

"That's the Governor's House," Fiora whispered, answering the unspoken question. "It's a replica of an old leader's house before the Great Collapse. They called it the White House because they couldn't come up with something more clever."

"How do you know all this?" Khalani asked.

"I used to be a teacher before I got jailed in Braderhelm. Kids always asked questions about it, so I learned as much as possible. This is my third time serving on Genesis." Fiora shrugged.

Khalani had more questions forming on her tongue, but her mouth closed as they approached the entrance. Multiple security guards lined up throughout the path, assault rifles in hand. Their bodies held still like statues as their eyes followed the prisoners.

They marched up the mansion steps to an exorbitant golden door. One of the guards gave three solid knocks on the door and waited. "Follow orders, or you're dead." The final warning came before a butler opened the door.

The butler was a short man who appeared not too far off from the mandatory euthanization age. He had a shiny, bald head and was dressed in an immaculate suit. "Good evening. Governor Huxley is expecting you. Do come in." The butler opened the door wider for them.

The first thing Khalani noticed was a grand chandelier hanging over the foyer. The crystals gleamed in the light and highlighted the pure luxury of the room. The floor was made of white marble with a gold G insignia etched in the center. Two guards stood at the top of the double staircase in the background, eyeing them dangerously.

"Welcome to the Governor's House." The butler held out his hands in presentation as he turned to them. "Guards, please proceed up these stairs and talk with Captain Strauss. He is the head of security here. The four of you, please follow me to the kitchen."

The butler whirled around, quickly marching through the center of the foyer, and the prisoners hastily followed him. A painting of a woman in a black dress hung in the center of the wall, a strange smile highlighting her face. Khalani had a peculiar urge to stop and inspect it, but the butler flew to the right, and she had no choice but to follow suit.

The butler pushed open a swinging door that almost banged Khalani in the face when it kicked back. They entered a spacious kitchen filled with state-of-the-art culinary equipment and servants running around frantically. Her mouth instantly salivated at the sweet aroma of food.

"Pick up the pace, people!" the butler yelled to the kitchen staff.

The staff kicked it up to turbo speed, pulling food out of multiple ovens quickly and running toward a dozen metallic refrigerators. It was controlled chaos.

The butler turned, studying the four of them closely. "You prisoners are here to help serve tonight. Remember these rules because your life depends on them. Do not talk to any of the guests unless asked a direct question. You are to be invisible, there to help deliver drinks or food and fade into the background. If you have any questions, come and ask me, understood?"

They nodded wordlessly, and he clapped his hands together. "Good. You three, go and help Bridget with any extra food that needs to be prepared." He pointed Serene, Fiora, and Jack to a heavyset woman in a white apron, pulling a thick pie out of an oven.

The butler turned to Khalani. "You, take that tray of drinks there to the lounge area. It is the room to the left of the painting. The Governor and the guests are in there until dinner is ready. Offer the guests some champagne. When you are done, come straight back here. No talking."

With that, the butler turned with a flourish and barked more orders. Khalani took a deep breath and grabbed a silver tray with several champagne glasses filled to the brim. Her hands shook, but she carefully opened the swinging door with her back and managed to walk steadily to the lounge area. Men and women dressed impeccably in suits and gowns stood about, conversing and laughing with one another. A grand, white couch lay in the center of the lounge, a myriad of gold pillows arranged across it. The whole backside of the lounge was a veranda overlooking a beautiful garden.

She immediately spotted Governor Huxley.

His pristine, white suit was a statement in itself. He stood a foot taller than everyone and held himself like he owned the room and everyone in it. He gave a heart-stopping grin as he chatted with two women in the corner, dressed in pastel ballgowns that synched their wastes into unbelievable proportions.

Was breathing for the poor too?

A line of people indiscreetly formed behind the skinny women laughing obnoxiously loud, waiting for a chance to speak with Alexander Huxley.

Khalani lowered the plate, trying to hide her head, and entered the lounge. She approached people with the tray of drinks, avoiding the corner where the Governor stood. No one made eye contact with her as they grabbed champagne glasses and continued their conversations.

It was almost too easy to be invisible.

That was fine by Khalani. She wanted to get out of there as soon as possible. The lavishness of the party, the mansion, and the opulent guests made her uncomfortable. She couldn't place a finger on what it was, but her hair stood on end like her body knew she was in a den of hungry monsters.

She recognized one of the Councilman from the street cleanup. Wyatt, that was his name. The one who argued with Governor Huxley about the Death-Zoner. He also appeared to recognize her because he gave her an icy stare as he grabbed the last champagne glass on her plate.

"Get going," he hissed.

Khalani put her head down, only too happy to oblige. She tucked the serving platter in between her armpit as she exited the room. When Khalani reached the foyer, she took a deep breath, feeling like she had crossed a minefield.

She found herself halted in front of the alluring woman in the painting. The simpering lady gazed at Khalani as if she knew all her deepest secrets. She leaned closer, examining the odd background behind the dark-haired woman.

"Do you like the painting?" Alexander Huxley's voice drifted over her left shoulder. Her body froze, and a harsh chill shot through her body like a stray bullet. She didn't even hear him approach.

"Governor Huxley," Khalani breathed out shakily as his liquid blue eyes pierced her own. "I didn't mean to…I was on my way back to the kitchen."

The Governor's ash-colored hair was gelled back, and his perfect face curved up in a slow smile, highlighting his clear, alabaster skin and strong jawline as he stepped toward her. She fought the urge to run away with each sly step he took.

Her feet locked in place, and she met his gaze, tampering down every emotion that screamed for her to flee.

"I told you we'd meet again." Alexander Huxley was only a foot length away.

Her brows furrowed at his grin, and she clutched the empty tray with a death grip, preparing to use it as a weapon. This may be one of her only chances to hurt him. Imagining his face bleeding beneath her fists filled her body with sweet anticipation.

She glanced to the left and noticed an armed guard at the front entrance, too far for hearing distance but close enough to shoot her at the first step of aggression. Despite herself, Takeshi's warning raged in her mind.

'A smart person knows when to choose their battles.'

Her teeth clenched, and it was like Takeshi, the bane of her existence, was there, reminding her to be smart. She wanted to curse because *fuck,* she knew he was right. If Khalani attacked the Governor here, she'd be shot within a second. And she could hardly kill him with a serving plate. She needed to remain calm.

"And what an honor this meeting is." Khalani plastered on a smile while plotting a gruesome death in her mind. "But I really should be getting back."

"Not quite yet." Alexander Huxley smirked. He tilted his head as if he were studying something amusing. "I must confess that our last conversation intrigued me. I grow bored of the same tired talks with council members and incessant guests. It's unending fawning and monotonous discussions. Suffocating for someone like me.

"But there was something different in your eyes," he continued. "A need to survive. An intelligence that bypassed the emotion swimming in them. Indeed, as I grow older, I find that my body craves to find stimulation in any form," the Governor's voice flattened, and his expression turned forlorn as if he was lonely.

A lonely psychopath.

The fact that she couldn't stop staring at his angelic face made her sick.

"Is that why you requested me to be a servant? To stimulate you?" She'd rather be carved into tiny slices and served with the pork.

He blinked, the faraway look receding from his eyes. "I assure you that my intentions are completely honorable. You have nothing to fear from me. But you never answered my question about the painting." He gestured to the picture of the woman.

Khalani found it hard to concentrate as the Governor stood right next to her, shoulder to shoulder.

"It's um… it's a nice painting, Gov—"

"No." He shook his head. "You can hold the formalities for now. Indulge me. This is a place for honesty."

She honestly wanted to see him dead. But that wasn't the name of the game they were playing.

She turned fully to the painting but kept him in her peripherals. "At first glance, you think it's an old portrait of a woman who doesn't seem all that captivating. But if you study her face, it feels like she has a whole story to tell in her eyes and smile alone. She's in a strange place but holds herself in a way that indicates no fear, as if she carries secrets we'll never know of."

"Hmm, very good." He nodded. "Do you find yourself in a strange place too?"

"Yes," she whispered. And let the truth slip. "Genesis is stranger and more terrifying than Apollo."

He raised his eyebrows. "And why is that?"

She hesitated and glanced at the painting. The woman stared directly into her eyes, daring her to speak.

"They have already forgotten where they came from and are perfectly content to sit around and eat bonbons while their neighbors struggle beneath their feet. Ignorance is their sword and shield." Her forehead creased at her rising emotion. "I'm not like the woman in this painting at all. Nothing I see here is amusing."

Khalani feared she revealed too much, and at any moment, he would call the guards to arrest her for treason, but Alexander Huxley gave her an assessing look.

"Would you be shocked to know that this used to be the most famous painting in the world? They called it the Mona Lisa," the words dripped from his tongue like silk.

She tasted the name in her mouth. Mona Lisa.

"I thought Apollo kept the famous art in the Archives. For no one to view." Khalani frowned.

"And do you know why we keep it that way?"

"Because it inspires people?" she hesitantly asked, remembering Winnie's lessons.

He grinned and shook his head to himself.

"I was right. You would make a better council member than those simpletons. In many ways, the focus on art and foolish fantasies in human culture led to The Great Collapse. They weren't focused on the real problems. People were more inclined to sit at home and live in a screen versus worrying about climate change, declining resources, and mass extinction across different animal and plant lifeforms. The warning signs were all there. But they knew they wouldn't be alive when the destruction they sowed came about. They waited for someone else to fix their problems, but it never happened. And here we are." Alexander held out his hands.

The Governor turned back to the painting, seeming to glare at the mischievous woman. "Unfortunately, that plague of ignorance was never cured, as you correctly surmised. I keep this painting here as an ode to that lost generation and a reminder of my duties."

She studied him further as his voice carried away, and those eyes became lost in a different world. The way he spoke...it sounded like he agreed with her, but they were saying something completely different.

Her ire was directed toward a particular group, but his disdain was toward *everyone*. An eerie, prickling sensation centered on her insides. She opened her mouth to ask him more about his 'duties,' but the kitchen door opened.

"What has taken you so long with those dri—Governor Huxley! F-forgive me, sir. This servant knew she was supposed to come straight back here. I take full responsibility," the butler stammered and bowed low to the ground.

The Governor chuckled. "There is no need for that, Arthur. I was just having a quick chat with our prisoner here. Run along now, Miss Kanes," he whispered the last part in her ear.

Say no more.

Khalani quickly rushed away, crawling at the feel of Alexander Huxley's gaze trailing her retreating form, a sly smirk resting over his face.

20

The loudest screams are hidden in smiles.

Dinner was served outside in the garden. Cascading lights floated down a willow tree, and flowers spread across the soil. The colors of the petals were so effervescent and bright, it was difficult to believe they were real. The guests sat at a grand table, and several servants stood 10 feet back with their hands clasped. One of them nodded at her when she went over, mimicking their position, and Khalani breathed a sigh of relief.

At least she did something right.

The wives of the Councilmen seated at the table were young, not much older than Khalani, wearing garish makeup and ridiculous, frilly dresses that hugged their waists and accented their cleavage. Most of the Councilmen were middle-aged and sat proudly at their seats in shining tuxedos. The Governor was seated at the head. The undeniable leader whose charisma and confidence overshadowed every man in Genesis.

Alexander Huxley exclaimed to his party, "Thank you for this evening, ladies and gentlemen. Let us feast."

Only when Alexander Huxley put a piece of meat in his mouth did the guests immediately start digging into their food and drinking wine. Plates were piled high with turkey, pork, and ham. The smell wafted through her nose, and she licked her lips. Standing there, watching them feast as her stomach grumbled in pain, was torturous.

Khalani couldn't stop staring at the fat, cooked turkey on the grand table. She'd never eaten real meat before. Very few have. Artificial rat meat was seen as a delicacy in Apollo.

Did the cloned turkey know his purpose was to die and be eaten for tonight's feast? Or was he blissfully ignorant of his upcoming demise? Maybe that's a little sexist. It could've been a girl turkey.

"I must confess that I'm awfully excited for the 10th Anniversary Ball," the voice of a woman with an obnoxiously large, white feather in her hair interrupted her thoughts. Blonde curls cascaded around her youthful face, marred by the overapplication of pink blush and lipstick that stained her front teeth as she eagerly eyed the Governor.

"I'm sure there will be many beautiful sights to behold, Pruscilla." Alexander Huxley smoothly sipped his wine.

Pruscilla giggled, completely smitten by his good looks, despite her husband seated beside her at the table.

Khalani wanted to barf in the pot of red roses behind her.

"The preparations for the ball are coming along nicely. We might even be ready ahead of schedule."

Alexander Huxley tilted his head. "And we have the labor force according to plan, Borris?"

Councilman Borris hesitated, the confident bravado slipping, but he gave the Governor a respectful smile. "Absolutely, sir. Just as you ordered."

They continued eating, and Councilman Wyatt downed his drink, slamming the glass on the table. His wife flinched by his side.

Alexander Huxley's eyes flickered up. "Something wrong, Wyatt?"

"No, Governor," Wyatt bit out, angrily cutting his meat. An uncomfortable silence ensued, and the Governor casually leaned back in his chair.

Khalani and a few others gulped at his too-relaxed pose.

"Miss Kanes." He suddenly turned to her. "Will you please grab the wine over here and refill Wyatt's cup? He seems to be empty," Alexander remarked in an eerily calm voice.

Khalani's eyes widened as everyone turned to stare at her. She anxiously jumped to the white-clothed table holding five open wine bottles. The weight of every stare rested on her as she approached the dining table and slowly started to pour wine into Wyatt's glass.

Khalani glanced at the Governor, who concealed his expression behind his hand. A yelp made her flinch back, and Khalani realized she'd spilled some red wine on Wyatt's suit.

"I'm so sorry. Forgive me, sir," she said, completely mortified. She tried to grab a napkin and blotch out the wine. And it only spread the stain across his white shirt, making it worse.

Wyatt slammed his hands on the table and stood up.

"Governor Huxley, with all due respect, I don't think it's wise to have any more Braderhelm prisoners working as servants at the ball. Or anywhere on Genesis, for that matter. They should be disposed of. Just look at the mess this one is making." Wyatt gestured his hand toward her, staring down with absolute disgust.

Everyone at the table halted their movements. Some people held their forks midair as if they feared the slightest motion would incite an explosion. She held her breath, waiting for the punishment to come. But no one was looking at her.

Everyone was staring at the Governor.

Alexander Huxley's eyes sparked with antipathy, but he leaned back and smiled placidly, his perfect white teeth showing. It wasn't friendly. It was like watching an animal toy with its prey before it went in for the kill.

"Miss Kanes," his smooth voice echoed across the table. "My cup needs refilling too."

Khalani stiffened, ramrod straight. She concentrated on breathing in and out as she walked to the head of the table. Despite the cooler weather, a bead of sweat appeared on her forehead. The Governor held out his glass, and Khalani held both hands on the bottle as she poured, sure that her heart would explode any moment.

If she spilled anything, she might just lay on the ground and make it easy to bury her.

"Ah." Alexander took a sip of the wine. "Thank you for your assessment, Wyatt. I've been thinking more about disposable things. Some of the Braderhelm prisoners may be useful." He gestured to Khalani with a nod of his glass, and she wanted to disappear in the fabric of her silk dress.

"Most, however, are expendable." The Governor leaned forward, placing his glass down gradually. "We plan to address this in light of recent events, as you know. But in reality, this is all a means to an end. Do you know what else is disposable? *Unruly Councilman*," he hissed, hostility seeping from his mouth like venom.

As quick as the words came out, two of the Governor's personal guards approached Wyatt's chair. "Come with us, sir," they said flatly, hands resting on their guns.

Wyatt's mouth opened in disbelief, and he turned to the Governor in a flurry. "N-No. No. You can't do this. I am a Councilman of Apollo!"

Alexander Huxley took another lazy sip of his wine, like he was sitting on a faraway beach, and waved his hand in dismissal. The guards pulled Wyatt out of the seat and dragged him from the table. Wyatt's hollow yells echoed across the garden, screaming and kicking while he was carried away.

The guests sat deathly still.

Alexander Huxley was the only one who moved, grabbing another piece of meat for his plate. In the next moment, a gunshot echoed throughout the garden. And they all knew what it meant.

Khalani's mouth hung open in shock. She looked at Wyatt's wife, still seated as she held her face in her hands, muted tears running down her face. Heads bowed, and no one dared to speak. The quiet felt tangible. Physical. Like a ghost of hands wrapped around everyone's throat, stealing all breath.

The Governor cleared his throat, and Khalani whipped her head to the man who killed his Councilman without pause. "Thank you for the drink, Miss Kanes. Quite tasty," Alexander quipped with a nod of dismissal.

She couldn't nod. Her heartbeat thrashed in her chest, and she quickly stepped away to take her place next to the other servants. Khalani didn't realize the death grip she had on the wine bottle until she placed it back on the side table.

"I apologize for the unfortunate disturbance, ladies and gentlemen, but let us not spoil the festivities. Eat up," the Governor commanded.

Forks raised, and food went into mouths, but no one spoke. The women seemed to shrink in their chairs, and the other Councilmen's eyes barely left the tablecloth, their heads hung low. She couldn't tell if it was in shame, fear, or submission. Maybe it was a combination of all three, as everyone pretended nothing happened.

Any lingering hope she had that the Councilmen would come to their senses and help the people in Apollo was swiftly dashed. They dared not even stand up when one of their own was murdered.

Khalani and the other servants were soon directed back to the kitchen. Delicious trays of cookies, sweets, and cakes were prepared. Her throat clogged up, feeling more nauseous by the second.

"You two." The butler hastily gestured to Khalani and Serene. "Take the trash bags here through that door. There's a large bin outside the house where you'll deposit them. Hurry back."

They quickly obeyed, her pulse racing.

"Can you believe this?" Serene asked with a heavy breath. "The Governor's insane."

"Keep your voice down," she admonished.

Her forearms hurt as the plastic bags clunked against her leg. They quickly found the large garbage bin outside. Her face scrunched up as a putrid scent filtered from the trash container.

Serene's face contorted as well. "What the hell is that?"

Khalani lifted the top of the bin and peeked inside. The sight had her scrambling back, the container closing with a loud thud.

"What is—oh my God," Serene whispered, her expression etched in horror as she opened the bin.

It was Councilman Wyatt's dead body. Thrown inside with the garbage like a discarded carcass. Blood pooled around his mouth, and his legs were bent in a position they weren't supposed to be in.

She couldn't get the image of his eyes out of her head. They were still open. The frozen shock embedded there, infinitely capturing his last horrifying moment.

"Why would they do this?" Khalani's mouth hung open. How could someone do that to another human being?

"Because they're animals," Serene gnashed through her teeth.

The sound of footsteps and harsh laughter froze her, and Serene quickly grabbed her arm and the trash bags, pulling her behind a line of bushes. They crouched just as two men emerged around the corner and stopped before them.

"See. There's no one here, Bruce. You're hearing shit again."

Khalani held her breath as she peered through the bushes. Two guards stood a few feet away, both built like linebackers and carrying assault rifles tight to their chests.

"I could've sworn I heard someone. Maybe they saw the body," the guard with a buzz cut said, casting a wary gaze around.

The other guard with pale blue eyes shrugged but tightened his grip around the gun. "We could torture a few servants. Maybe one of them saw something."

"Nah." The guard sighed, exasperated, as Khalani and Serene shared a wide-eyed look. "Too much effort. Probably came from the party. Besides, I'm not in the mood for any more squealers tonight."

"Wyatt should've gone out like a man. Too quick and freaking bleeding everywhere. At least I had time to play with that scientist last week. What was his name? Victor?"

"Vincent, idiot. And you *still* didn't manage to break him. Kept babbling on about crop failure even after you cut off his fingers. Maybe you're losing your touch, Dom." The guard chuckled.

"Shut up." Dom scowled. "If I got my hands on that Death-Zoner they locked up, he would've begged me to end his life."

"Mhmm, sure."

Bruce glanced both ways, and his voice lowered. "Did you see the equipment they recovered?"

Khalani and Serene leaned closer, straining to hear.

"—wouldn't work. The Governor insisted we put it in his study. Don't know why. It's archaic junk."

"Whatever. Let's get back." Their footsteps grated against the gravel as they disappeared out of sight.

Serene and Khalani waited a full minute before they emerged from their hiding spot. Adrenaline pumped through her body, thicker than blood.

"Did you he—"

"Shh," Serene interrupted her. "They could come back. We need to go."

Khalani trembled. No doubt if the guards spotted them, they'd be thrown dead into the bin along with Councilman Wyatt. They busted through the house, hurrying back to the kitchen.

"Where have you two been? The guests are nearly finished with dessert." The butler's face was bright red as he charged at them.

She opened her mouth, but Serene beat her to it. "We got lost. We're heading back now to assist. I just need to use the bathroom first, sir."

"Use the servant's one down the hall."

"Someone has been in there a while. And I don't think I can hold it anymore. Wouldn't want to cause a mess in the Governor's house, sir." Serene's face twisted like she was going to throw up.

"Agh, *fine*. Talk to the guard in the lobby. Tell him I sent you, and he'll direct you to the one upstairs. You don't go anywhere else," the butler instructed.

The butler quickly ushered her outside to refill drinks. She could feel Alexander Huxley's eyes on her, but Khalani deliberately didn't make eye contact, praying he wouldn't address her the rest of the night. She positioned herself by the other servants, far from the Governor.

Her face dissolved into a sigh of relief as Serene returned to the garden and stood beside her. Serene's body language was calm and composed, but her face held something different, a quiet determination and excitement that confounded her.

"Are you okay?" Khalani whispered.

"Later. Not here." Serene stared straight ahead.

The sound of clinking glass tore her attention as the Governor stood up. "A final toast for the evening."

The guests raised their glasses, even Wyatt's wife, but her eyes were still blotched from smeared makeup.

"I would like to thank you all for joining me this wonderful night. I apologize for some of the excitement that took place." He paused, looking at each of the Councilmen.

Excitement. Is that what serial killers were calling it nowadays?

"But I am deeply humbled at your continued support for the growth of Genesis and, indeed, the growth of all Apollo. When our ancestors look down upon us, I know they'll be proud of all we have accomplished for the planet. I am excited to move forward and continue our important work and celebrate the rise of Genesis at the Anniversary Ball. Loyalty to Apollo!"

"Loyalty to Apollo!" the guests shouted into the night, and everyone downed their glass.

Khalani glared at each of them, hate filling the boundaries within her skin. If there was anything she learned that evening, it was that no matter how moral and self-righteous people thought they were, the majority would turn their backs on evil, just as long as they weren't on the receiving end of those actions.

She understood then that prison forever changed her.

Because at that moment, Khalani wished she had poisoned the wine and killed them all.

21

I've witnessed the fiercest and bloodiest of wars in the battleground of my mind.

Khalani picked at her food. The brown mixtures sloshed around her plate. They were like the mishappen contents of her plagued mind. Messy and in disarray.

The Governor's keen eyes following her closely as if she were a puzzle unraveling before him. The booming echo of a gunshot ringing across the beautiful expanse, signaling the brutal consequences for those who dare step out of line. Wyatt's body splayed like a broken ragdoll, staring into the empty space. Memories raged, and she couldn't shut them down.

The horrors housed inside often take up the most space.

"You okay, Khalani? Looking a little green." Adan's voice pierced through her calamitous thoughts.

Adan and Derek sat tensely, eyeing her with concern.

"Yeah, I'm fine," Khalani said quietly, still not touching her food.

Bile crept up her throat, and at the first swallow, she might hurl. Alexander Huxley's decrepit voice slithered across her skin again.

As if he were hovering over her shoulder, breathing in her ear.

'That plague of ignorance was never cured…reminding me of my duties.'

"Hey." Derek placed a calloused hand on her palm, breaking her concentration. "You wanna talk about it? About what happened up there?" He pointed to the ceiling.

Khalani opened her mouth and closed it, unable to find the right words. How do you describe a place that manifested your most stunning and bewitching fantasies but contained terrors far beyond imaginings? Genesis was hell, guised as heaven under a perceived dome of safety. *Lies.* All of it.

No one was safe from the Governor. Not even the Council.

"We found him." Khalani's head lowered.

"Who?"

"Wyatt. The Governor had his own Councilman murdered. And we found him in the garbage, strung about like a carcass. And not one person said a word against it," she hissed.

"Damn," Adan muttered.

"We hid while the guards joked about butchering innocent people. The guards even bragged about torturing and killing a scientist who spoke of crop failure. Obviously delusional, but they will murder anyone. They're all monsters."

Her hands fisted at the memory, wanting to take out her rage on the nearest guard. The next training session with Takeshi wouldn't be pretty.

"What did you just say?"

She turned to Derek, who gazed at her with wide eyes, his body incredibly still. "I said they killed the Councilman and threw him in the garbage."

"No, no. Not that." Derek gripped her arm firmly. "The part about the scientist. You said they tortured a scientist who spoke of crop failure. Did they say who?"

"I don't know. No, wait…I do remember the guards mentioning

the name Vincent. Why?"

Derek's face paled, and his brows were pulled so low on his forehead, like he was attempting to solve the world's most complicated math equation, only to discover that it was never meant to be solved.

"Can't be," he whispered.

"What is it?" she asked, flustered by the sheer terror on his face.

"Hey, guys! Sorry, the line was taking forever." Serene gracefully set her plate down as her eyes wandered around the room, on high alert.

"Derek." Khalani didn't take her eyes off him. "What's wrong?"

"I killed him," Derek uttered. Tears pooled at the corner of his eyes, and his hands visibly shook.

"Killed who?" Serene interrupted.

Derek scraped both hands through his scalp like he was trying to rip out the pieces of his mind. "Do you remember when I told you why I was sentenced here?"

"You worked in the Research and Resource Labs. You told me you found something…something they didn't want you to find." Her lips pursed, remembering.

Derek's mouth twisted, and his resolve broke before her very eyes. "I never wanted to tell any of you."

"Tell us what?" Adan frowned.

"It all began several months ago when I still worked in the labs," Derek began. "Several farmers reported to me something strange. Five percent of their crops died after fertilization. I should've been able to locate the cause quickly. I checked the sheets on the air pumps, soil content, green lamps…nothing. The data was normal.

"I wrote it off, assuming the crops would stabilize in the next planting. But the next month comes, and 8 percent of the crops fail. The following month…10 percent crop failure. The problem was getting worse, and we didn't know why. I quickly informed my superiors, who read the charts themselves. They told me not to worry about it, assuming those seed banks weren't grown correctly, and refused to believe it was a systematic problem. What I inferred was 'impossible' were their exact words," Derek gritted through his teeth.

"I couldn't let it go, though. I felt something was wrong. Over the next few months, I started taking water and soil samples myself. And what I found was…terrifying. Another substance was present in the irrigation pumps. I've never seen anything like it in my research, but I can only describe it as a virus eating the plants from the inside out. Each month, the virus spread through the irrigation pumps, and if the spread continued at that rate, all our crops would be dead within the year."

Khalani minutely shook her head. Impossible.

Crop failure was unthinkable in Apollo. In the 300 years they've lived underground, Apollo never had a food shortage.

Serene broke the silence. "Did you show your superiors what you found? This…virus?"

"Of course, I did," Derek uttered dejectedly. "I assumed they would immediately fix the pumps and flush out whatever that *thing* was. But they didn't. They thought I was crazy and were afraid that if word of a possible malfunction in the crops were to get out, it would incite a panic. After that meeting, I had a feeling they would soon release me. Before I got thrown in Braderhelm, I gave all my data to another colleague, hoping he would continue my work. His name was Vincent." Derek closed his eyes as if he could disappear like Khalani had always wanted to.

"What are you saying, Derek?"

Derek leveled Khalani with a brutal stare.

"What you heard the guards say…it's not a coincidence. Vincent was murdered for attempting to spread the truth about imminent crop failure. You know what that means just as much as I do. Apollo never fixed the crops. It's only a matter of time before we all starve. And prisoners will surely be the first to go."

His words sucked the air out of the room. Crushing silence persisted throughout the circle as if a ghost snatched their breaths.

"How long does everyone have?" Serene's voice cracked.

"A few months at best."

"That can't be true, Derek. You must be mistaken," Adan denied, his face turning ashen.

Derek just shook his head, unable to speak.

Khalani dug the nail of her pointy finger into her thumb like a sharp blade, focusing on the cutting pain because the walls were beginning to draw in closer, threatening to suffocate and grind away every shred of her existence.

A few months.

A few months before everyone died.

She wanted, no *needed*, to deny it. To rationalize the problem wasn't real. But a memory raced through her mind, and she drew in a sharp breath.

'We have plans to address this in light of recent events, as you know. But in reality, this is all a means to an end.'

Deep down, the horrible truth screamed through her lungs and bloodstream, weighing her down with terrible certainty.

"He knew," she whispered. "The Governor knew about this."

"No way." Adan shook his head vehemently. "I hate the guy too but no way he would let this happen."

Serene's face appeared paler than usual.

"The Governor mentioned people being expendable last night. They could be keeping this all a secret to hold back the panic. But if what you say is true, Derek, the Council must have a plan, or else they'd die too."

"Isn't it obvious?" Derek asked in a scathing voice. "They'll have enough supplies for those on Genesis. But for everyone else underground…we won't be so lucky. The guards will seal off the Genesis entrance and bring up the remaining food. We can't stop it."

Khalani shook her head inaudibly. She glanced at some prisoners casually walking around, chatting over their meal. Unaware of what would happen to them. To their families.

Did the guards know?

Her muscles froze, and a sudden coldness hit her core.

Did Takeshi know about this?

Adan slammed his fists down on the stone floor, the veins in his neck popping out. "There has to be something we can do! We have to warn people."

"Keep your voice down," Derek commanded.

"What if we get help?" Serene asked with a calculated gaze.

"Who would help us, Serene?" Derek's green eyes blazed with fury. "It's impossible to escape Braderhelm, and prisoners aren't viewed as humans. The Council would sooner see us dead."

Serene's keen eyes were set in determination. "I'm not talking about Genesis." They all whipped their heads to her, unsure if they heard correctly.

Lines formed on Khalani's forehead. "What do you mean?"

Serene glanced around apprehensively, making sure no guards or prisoners were paying attention, and reached into the baggy pant pocket of her overalls, revealing a tiny black bag.

"What is it?" Adan frowned.

She placed it on the ground. "Open it."

Adan reached inside the bag and pulled out a broken mess of wires and metal, no bigger than a handheld device. The black object was smashed in, like someone aggressively disassembled the pieces.

"It's a...walkie?" Adan's eyes narrowed as he inspected the item, concealing the jumbled material with his body.

"Not just any walkie-talkie. This belonged to a Death Zoner. And you see that tiny blue H insignia? This is from the other underground city, Hermes," Serene whispered, her face gleaming.

"Where on earth did you get this?" Adan's mouth hung open.

"I stole it from the Governor's mansion last night. The guards mentioned equipment they recovered from a Death Zoner, and I snuck into his study. Stuffed it in the oversized bra they forced us to wear, and no one noticed."

Khalani's eyes widened as the puzzle pieces came together all at once. That was why Serene disappeared at the dinner.

"If we can somehow fix this, we might be able to get in touch with

Hermes from here. Maybe *they* can send help. We have to try," Serene exclaimed.

"But wouldn't the Council already have done that? Asked them for help?" Adan's brows furrowed together as he continued to eye the object in shock.

"With the few radiation suits Apollo has, widespread evacuation is impossible. Hermes wouldn't be able to send enough food to save everyone. And Apollo would never tell another city of mass genocide," Derek bit out in a dark tone.

The silence expanded at their harsh reality.

"You used to be one of their best engineers. Can you fix it?" Serene turned to her brother, her eyes blazing with hope.

Adan carefully turned the walkie around in his hands.

"I don't know. I'll need supplies, like a wrench and a screwdriver. And a battery pack. Some guards have walkies, which are not as advanced as this one, but their battery pack should be compatible. If I get those items, I *might* be able to fix it in a few weeks. But I can't guarantee it will work."

"Give me a few days. I'll get you those supplies," Serene stated, determination set in her eyes. The bell pierced through the tense air, making them all jump.

Adan shoved the broken walkie in his overalls before any passerby could notice.

"We keep this to ourselves for now. We can't trust anyone but each other," Adan implored, and they all nodded in agreement, except for Derek.

The prisoners dispersed for their afternoon assignments, and she tried to catch up with Derek, but he raced out of there as if he didn't want to speak anymore. The truth shone in his eyes.

He'd already lost faith in anything or anyone saving them.

Khalani kept rubbing her hands together and rolling her neck back and forth as she walked through the tunnels alone.

Her muscles moved. Her heart beat. But she wasn't present. As if she were stuck on a train with no conductor.

When Khalani first set foot between the stone walls of Braderhelm, she resigned herself to a slow, cold, and lonely death. *Accepting* the cruel fate handed down to her, beckoning the end to draw nearer.

But now. Everything changed. She had…friends.

People she cared about. People who cared about her. They returned something she thought was lost in her life forever, a hope that resided even when her worst imaginings threatened to tear and rip her asunder. Proving that she was more than the bad things that had happened or the mistakes she'd made.

Life was like poetry in that way. It was never meant to be shared alone.

She agreed to not give this information to anyone, but as she walked to her cell to wait for Takeshi, a crazy part of her mind yearned to confront him. To find out if he knew the truth about the crops. His duty as Captain would be to kill them all for thievery and insubordination alone.

But what if he could help?

She shuffled nervously back and forth, waiting for Takeshi in front of her cell. Every passing second felt like an hour as war waged in her mind. The heavy sound of rugged boots barreled around the corner.

About time.

Khalani stepped forward, about to deride him for being slow, when she realized who had rounded the corner. It wasn't Takeshi.

It was Guard Barron.

Khalani's body abruptly froze, taut as a piano string, as icy-cold fear shot down her spine. His characteristic, evil smile was on full display, his bulky body nearly taking up the whole walkway.

"Well, well, look what we have here."

All at once, the hairs on her arms rose, and she slowly inched backward, not taking her bulging eyes off him. Her heart pounded like a drum in her chest.

Barron cocked his head to the side. "Going somewhere?"

His eyes flickered with malicious intent as he stepped toward her.

Without hesitation, Khalani whirled away, running in the opposite direction. She pumped her arms as fast as possible, turning at the corner.

The hard slam of boots chasing behind ignited every cell of fear in her body. Her body trembled, eyes racing the dim hallways to find someone. Anyone. But no one was in sight to save her. Everyone was down in the pit, and Takeshi was nowhere to be found.

Her lungs rasped as her feet kicked up dirt. His harsh footsteps grew louder as a deep, grunting sound bounced along the walls like a lingering curse. True panic set in.

She hastily turned at the next hallway, heading toward the pit, praying with every fabric of her being to make it in time. Metal bars flew past her vision as she barreled forward. The set of stairs leading to the pit were in sight. She was going to make it.

Suddenly, a strong arm grabbed her shoulder, slamming her into the wall. Her cheek was shoved against the rocks, scraping and cutting along the rough edges.

Khalani cried out, trying to throw her fist, and immediately, Barron's arms wrapped around her from behind. He squeezed with the full weight of his massive body, robbing her of movement.

Khalani bucked backward, trying to force him off her, but he didn't budge. Hot, heady breaths exhaled through her ear.

"That's it, you fight. I like it when they fight."

She yelled at the top of her lungs for help, and Barron wrapped a dirty hand over her mouth, cutting off her screams. He shoved her face deeper against the wall, completely overpowering her. Tears flowed freely down her face and sank into his dirty palm.

"I've been imagining this moment for quite some time now."

Barron raked his teeth along her neck, and Khalani twisted her head, fighting to get his mouth off her. He banged her forehead against the stone wall, and Khalani saw stars.

"Once I'm done enjoying my time with you, no one will find your body. Not even the Captain. It will be like you never existed."

He took his hand from her mouth and tried to unhook her overalls. She used all her weight to dislodge him, but he held fast, managing to unhook the first button.

"Stop. Please stop!" Khalani wailed.

But he ignored her pleas, roughly pulling down the top of her uniform.

Her muscles burned as she fought to no avail. A torrent of tears flowed down her face as her energy and willpower began to flag. Still reeling from her head injury, Khalani squeezed her eyes shut, utterly helpless as the guard refused to let her go.

Khalani couldn't handle it. Couldn't live within herself as this man attempted to violate her in the worst way possible.

She began to have an out-of-body experience, watching her body from above, being pushed up against the wall, shutting down, as Barron attempted to undress her.

Was this really happening?

All her training...all the effort she had put into becoming stronger and learning to defend herself. Was it for nothing?

'Tell me what you're feeling right now,' Takeshi demanded.

'Powerless.'

'Yes. You feel out of control, weak. But that isn't you. You need to take back that control and prove that you are not to be thrown around and discarded. You, Kanes, are strong.'

Khalani's eyes snapped open as Barron roughly grabbed at her naked breast.

No.

Khalani braced a foot against the stone wall and pushed back with full force against Barron's chest. His intense grip loosened, and she clasped her hands together. With all the strength left in her body, she thrust her elbow deep into his gut, yelling out in fury. Barron choked out a breath, struggling to exhale as he released his hold on her and stumbled back. Khalani immediately ran toward the stairs, but he snatched her arm, throwing her back against the wall.

Barron wrapped both hands around her throat. And started to

squeeze.

"*I'm going to enjoy killing you,*" he snarled.

Khalani's vision blackened as he crushed her windpipe. Her mind panicked when she couldn't get a single ounce of oxygen in.

In a last-ditch effort, she put her thumbs out and pushed deep into his eyeballs, her nails digging and squeezing through his pitch-black pupils.

An ear-splitting scream came out of Barron as he let go of her throat, holding his hands to his face, blood gushing out of his eye sockets. Khalani collapsed to the ground, coughing and heaving excessively. Desperately trying to chug in air.

"My eyes! You fucking bitch!" he howled.

Pools of crimson poured down his cheeks, and he squinted through his damaged orifices, attempting to spot her lying on the ground. He shakily reached for his gun and pointed it in her direction.

She braced herself for the hit, but the next moment, Barron went flying as Takeshi Steele tackled him to the ground.

Takeshi roared out in pure, unadulterated wrath as he knocked the pistol from his hand and flipped Barron over like a ragdoll. Barron threw out a fist, but Takeshi simply blocked it and struck him in the throat, causing Barron to heave.

Takeshi proceeded to punch him in the head, over and over. His expression transformed into a heated rage as he slammed his knuckles into Barron's broken, unrecognizable face. Blood splayed everywhere, but Takeshi didn't relent.

She'd never seen Takeshi like this, so overtaken with fury.

When it was clear Barron's body no longer moved, Takeshi still crouched over him like a hungry animal. He breathed out heavily, his fists clenching as if he wanted to continue the blistering assault.

Khalani silently watched him, lying on the ground as her vision faded in and out. Takeshi whipped his head to her as she made a small whimper of pain. He rushed to her side and knelt over her body. "Kanes! Can you hear me? Are you okay?"

Takeshi's ferocious expression darkened as he readjusted her top to cover her naked breast. His large hand cupped her cheek, and his shadowed eyes pierced her with such concern and hurt as if he was the one who was assaulted.

Khalani nodded and tried to sit up, but vertigo almost made her pass out, and she leaned to the left, puking her lunch out. Takeshi moved behind her, holding her body up as he pushed her hair out of her face and continuously rubbed her back.

"It's okay, it's okay. I've got you now," he consoled her.

When she started to dry-heave, Takeshi moved his arms under her body and stood effortlessly as if she weighed no more than a feather. Khalani feebly shook her head, not wanting to be a burden, and tried to circle out of his arms weakly, mumbling that she could walk.

Takeshi would have none of it.

"Be still, Kanes. Nothing in this world would make me put you down right now," he declared in a guttural voice.

His words ushered into her ear like a metronome for her mind that was putting her fast asleep. That was all she wanted to do, sleep. She felt his arms squeeze her tighter, reassuringly, his gentle and protective touch the diametric opposite of Barron's.

Her lids slowly began to close, and the last thing she remembered was Takeshi's black eyes gazing down at her with concern, tenderness, and a depth of angry passion that rivaled every story that's been written and song that has been sung.

22

*You've taken all my nothings
and fashioned them into somethings.*

The first thing Khalani registered was a damp cloth gently patting along her forehead. Her head lay on a firm pillow, perfectly placed to support her neck, and a familiar scent wafted through her nose.

She shifted her head and opened her eyes.

Takeshi was sitting right next to her, watching over her with concern as he dabbed the cloth on her head. "Sorry, I didn't mean to wake you. You were getting hot," he swiftly explained, pulling his hand away.

Khalani peeked around in confusion. She was in a dark room furnished only with a tiny black dresser, a sparse desk, and the formidable bed she was lying on. A bedside lamp illuminated warm light on Takeshi's face. He still wore his black uniform, and his hair was disheveled.

"Where am I?" she croaked out.

"I brought you to my room. The medical ward's doctor is different tonight, and he would ask too many questions. The best option was to bring you here." Takeshi cleared his throat, shifting uncomfortably.

Khalani groaned as she sat up. Takeshi scooted back, his troubled gaze never straying from her. "I think you suffered a concussion, and your neck will be bruised for the next few days. You just need rest," he added like he was reassuring himself.

After considerable effort, she straightened and rested her head against the stone wall. Khalani gave a gentle nod, ignoring the pained welt on her forehead, genuinely grateful for Takeshi's presence. If he hadn't shown up when he did...

Her teeth clenched together, wanting to bathe in scalding water and cut herself apart. Anything to rid her body and mind of Barron's callous hands brushing over her skin, like the delicate pieces of her were someone else's to claim.

Takeshi tilted his head, noticing the renewed tension in her muscles.

"And Barron?" she gritted out.

Takeshi's body went rigid, and he immediately clenched his fists, glancing away, but not before she noticed the unhinged turbulence in his expression.

"After I brought you here, I notified a couple guards. I told them Barron attacked me, and I retaliated. When we went to retrieve Barron's body and hold him accountable to the Warden, he was already dead." Takeshi pressed his lips together in a thin line, not a hint of regret in his sinister tone.

She didn't know how to respond. Takeshi repeatedly put his neck on the line for her when all she did was leave a mess of destruction in her wake.

Maybe everything was her fault.

Maybe she deserved what happened.

"I'm sorry." Khalani glanced down at her hands.

Why was she so messed up?

"Look at me."

Khalani shook her head.

"Look at me, Kanes."

Her mouth twisted, but she peered up.

Takeshi's obsidian eyes pierced hers. "*You* don't apologize for any-thing. I am the one who is sorry. I should've been there, but I was running late with drills. This is my fault. You…like this. What that worthless piece of shit did. What he tried to do. I'd kill him again if I could," he cut himself off, peering away, nearly shaking with incensed rage.

She leaned forward, daring to place a hand on his shoulder. He refused to look at her as if the guilt coursing through his body wouldn't let him.

"That's not true, Takeshi. You saved me. *You* did that. And not just at the end. When I was about to give up back there, your voice from training was what gave me the strength to fight back. I'm more grateful than you could ever know."

Khalani meant it with every ounce of her being. All those times, she hated him for being hard on her…she was such a fool.

Takeshi's forehead creased at her words, and his gaze flickered up to meet hers. He opened his mouth to speak but abruptly closed it, nodding instead. As if words weren't needed.

And for once, she understood the silence.

Takeshi pointedly glanced at the hand Khalani still held on his shoulder. "Sorry." She abruptly pulled back, blood flooding her cheeks.

"Worried I'll still kill you, Kanes?" His dark eyes glinted. "I could've so easily with you in my arms."

The way Takeshi's magnetic voice stroked her skin made her shiver. Khalani almost thought that part was a dream, his arms wrapped around hers. Because being held by Takeshi felt better than it ever had a right to. Those details should've been inconsequential, an after-thought, but her mind kept returning to that moment, like it was a centerpiece.

"You might still be considering it. Hope my body wasn't too heavy for you," she added.

"Hmm. Maybe I should take you to the doctor," Takeshi mused. "The day you're too heavy for me is the day my arms have fallen off."

Khalani's pulse quickened, and she forgot the concept of breathing for a split second. "How long was I out for?" she asked, desperate to change the subject before verbal nonsense came pouring out.

Takeshi threw the damp cloth on his desk. "Just a few hours. Lights out happened not long ago."

She nodded, and an uncomfortable silence ensued. This was surely the part where Takeshi would escort her back to her cell. And despite how crazy the thought was, Khalani found that she wasn't ready to leave.

She could explain the irrationality away by being shaken about her encounter with Barron, but deep down, in the parts of her that weren't meant to be exposed, she knew it was more than that.

Takeshi's presence comforted her. It wasn't solely due to the warm energy he carried with him. It was the way he listened, as if her voice truly mattered. It was how he commanded the area around him and beckoned her to take up space too. It was the way he gazed at her with concern, like he wanted her to be more than just okay.

Maybe she stopped hating him long ago and never truly noticed until now.

Takeshi tapped his finger on his legs as he studied her. "So, you have a couple options."

"Okay."

"I can take you back to your cell, and you can sleep there tonight. I promise no one will bother you again," he stated forebodingly.

"And the second option?" She held her breath.

Silence descended for a few moments.

"The second option is to stay here…just for the night to rest. I would give you the bed, and I can sleep on the floor," he explained with a guarded expression.

She wrung her fingers together. Takeshi's words were like physical lines of energy, prickling up the sides of her arms, lighting her on fire from the inside out. Khalani knew the answer she *wanted* to say. The answer was on the tip of her tongue, waiting to be set free.

But the words swallowed tight inside her.

If they were both no longer themselves and anxiety was another meaningless thing, the truth would burst from her mouth like the first breath of air after drowning.

But they were a living contrast, marked and bound as enemies.

And yet, at this moment, it felt like every chain constraining them receded in the background. As if they were in a bubble, separate from prison, displaced from Apollo. For this one night, he was giving her a choice, the freedom to decide what she wanted, something long stolen from her.

She glanced up at his steely eyes, hoping to find a hidden solution, but he had the perfect poker face. The only indication of his inner thoughts was the breath he seemed to hold along with her.

She should go back to her cell.

It was the logical thing to do. They'd already crossed too many boundaries to count.

But despite his rough exterior, Takeshi came to her with compassion when she needed it the most. Around him, she didn't feel like Number 317. She was a human being again, in every good and sinister meaning.

When she was near Takeshi, that's when she felt most *alive*.

Khalani readied herself. Logic could take a long walk off a short bridge. "I'll stay with you tonight."

"You sure?" Takeshi's voice went a couple octaves lower.

She didn't trust herself with words, so she just nodded.

"Alright. As I said, the bed is yours, and I'll take the floor." His brows furrowed. "I'm just going to change out of my uniform, okay?"

He waited until she nodded, and he started to untie his boots. She surveyed his every movement intensely. Barefoot, he walked over to his dresser, pulling out a pair of grey sweats and a t-shirt.

For some odd reason, it surprised her that he owned different clothing. And she realized how stupid that was. He wasn't born wearing a uniform. Takeshi reached behind his head to pull off his fitted garment.

Khalani's eyes nearly popped out of their sockets.

She'd seen him without his shirt in training, but not this close, where every tendon was visible. His back muscles shifted as he pulled a softer black t-shirt over his head. He turned, and she quickly drew her attention to the other wall as if it was the most riveting thing she'd ever seen in her life. The clanging of a belt being taken off echoed in her ears.

Don't look. Don't look.

Don't. You. Do. It.

She pinched her fingers together, trying to focus on something, *anything* else.

The disgusting food she'd have for lunch tomorrow. Yeah. That was a safe topic. The meal would definitely smell foul too. But you know what doesn't smell bad? Takeshi's white sheets. That she was currently sitting on.

That he sleeps in every night.

AGH.

After several agonizingly long seconds, the soft creak of steps returned. Khalani slowly peeked through her lids, making sure it was safe.

The sweatpants hung low on his hips, and the black shirt was oversized, but Takeshi filled it up completely. His soft black hair swept over his forehead in a rough way that made him appear more youthful, but his charcoal eyes...they burned right through.

It wasn't fair. No one should be that attractive without trying.

Takeshi's jaw tightened, and he hesitated as he spotted her sitting on his bed. The awkward tension filled the air, like they were both aware of every square inch that separated them.

He quickly reached over and grabbed the smallest white pillow on his bed, tossing it to the floor.

"You keep the covers. It can get chilly in here at night."

She bit her lip and waited, like sinking in his covers was an illegal affair. But she eventually scooted her body toward the head of the bed and pulled the warm blankets over herself. The soft sheets caressed her skin, and a contented sigh escaped her mouth.

After months of sleeping on a hard stone slab, nestling in his bed was like laying on a puffy cloud. Takeshi's eyes tightened as he stared at her and nodded, lowering his body to the ground and out of her vision.

They laid in silence. Her body was exhausted, but her mind was wide-awake, sending signals like she was sprinting a marathon.

Takeshi was sleeping on the cold, hard floor instead of his bed. Because of her. Their lives appeared to have been switched for the night, and she was unable to enjoy or feel good about the new positions. With each passing second, guilt and another heated emotion crept up her throat, preventing her eyes from closing.

After nearly a minute, she couldn't take it anymore. Khalani leaned over the bed. Takeshi was lying on his back, palms folded against his chest, and his eyes locked with hers.

"You don't have to sleep on the floor. You can sleep in your bed," she said.

Takeshi shook his head.

"I'm okay, Kanes."

"No, seriously."

She frowned, but he didn't budge.

Fine.

Grabbing the pillow, Khalani stood up. Stepping over Takeshi, she placed the pillow next to his.

Takeshi abruptly sat up, his eyebrows drawing in a tight line. "What are you doing?"

"You saved my life. I'm not sleeping on the bed while you're on the floor. If you're down here, I will be too."

Takeshi squeezed his eyes shut in exasperation, and the next moment, he heaved his body up, grabbing his pillow. He surprised Khalani by grabbing hers as well. He set both pillows back on the bed and interrupted her before she could speak.

"Don't even attempt to sleep on the floor. It will only upset me." He pulled the covers back and gestured for her to get in.

Her heart jackhammered inside her chest as she moved back under the covers. Takeshi straightened out the blankets and laid on top, keeping space between them. Even on the bed, the size of his body completely dwarfed hers. They stared at the ceiling, the quiet like a physical being hanging over them.

Khalani was hyperaware of his body next to hers. The indentation of the covers with his full weight, the sound of his soft breaths, the body heat coming off his arms, only a few inches away.

Yep, she was getting no sleep tonight.

Khalani glanced over at his virtual window on the wall. A full moon glowed in the frame, the picture so clear, you could trace every dark crater.

"Do you think the moon really looks like that on the surface?" she whispered, trying to break the tension.

Takeshi turned his head to stare at the window. He paused for a few moments. "I think on the surface, everything appears more beautiful."

The corners of her mouth turned up.

"I think so too. As much as I hate Genesis and everything it stands for, it was the most beautiful place I'd ever seen." She felt him move an arm behind his head as they continued to stare, lost in thought.

"Genesis used to be my home," his voice lowered.

Khalani whipped her head to him in shock. "You lived in Genesis? How did you end up being a guard in Braderhelm?"

Takeshi shook his head with a half-smile that didn't reflect in his eyes. "My tale isn't a happy one, Kanes."

She shifted on her side to fully face him. "Is anyone's personal story ever truly happy? We're all fucked up. Some are just better at hiding it than others."

He followed her movement with a deep frown, testing the sincerity of his words.

"I never knew my father," he started. "He left when I was born, and my mother raised me on her own, barely making enough to support herself. But she always made sure I was fed and happy, completely unaware of how little we had because her love filled the gaps.

"But she wanted to give me more, a better education, and started dating a wealthy businessman in Apollo. His name was Hector. I did like him…at first. They married right when the dome was completed, and he had enough money for all of us to live in Genesis. That's when our problems started."

Khalani lay there in a trance as his words floated through the air like a magical spell, beckoning her to only listen and be still. As if any movement would break the story's hold over her.

Over him.

"For the first couple of years in Genesis, my mom seemed happy, but slowly, her laughter faded. Every now and then, I noticed bruises on her arms. Her cheeks. I often asked about them, but she'd always say that she tripped or was too clumsy. My happiness mattered more than hers, and she never wanted me to know the truth. I was fifteen and came home from school early one day. I walked in the door and heard him screaming at her. He called me a disobedient bastard, a constant disappointment, and a pitiful excuse for a son. They didn't know I was standing in the doorway. My mother slapped him, and he punched her.

"I was frozen. My mother lay on the hard floor, and Hector didn't care. He just walked out the door. I held my mom on the ground, and we both cried in each other's arms. I couldn't speak. I was horrified and scared. But mostly, I was angry. Angry that I didn't know what was happening. Angry that Hector hurt my mother. And I was furious at myself when I didn't do anything to stop it."

The muscles in his arms tightened. "I dropped out of school the next day and enlisted in the Academy to become a guard. My mother objected, but I didn't listen. I needed to be able to protect her if he tried hurting her again. A few years passed, and there were no more bruises on my mother, at least, none I could see. I graduated the top of my class in the Academy and was selected as one of the Governor's personal guards. After my final qualifications, I came home early to share the good news. Only this time, when I walked in the door, Hector had my mother up against the wall in a chokehold."

"I didn't think. I just attacked. I used all my training to wrestle him off her. I punched him over and over again. With each hit, I visualized him hurting my mother, who would never harm a fly, and it only enraged me further. But I was too late. Her injuries were too severe, and she was already gone by the time I killed him."

A light sheen was in his eyes as he continued, "No one cared about her murder. In everyone's eyes, she was her husband's property, to do with as he saw fit. I was the one punished for murdering Hector. Because I was the best pre-guard they'd ever seen at the Academy, the Master Judge spared my life and decided I would be best put to use in Braderhelm Prison."

Khalani lay there with her mouth hung open. Takeshi had a life ripped away from him in the worst way, like Khalani's was stolen. Takeshi didn't come to Braderhelm by choice. He was sentenced here.

A prisoner without the title.

Takeshi's gaze was far away, face hard and muscles rigid. She saw herself in his eyes. Takeshi's consistently harsh demeanor made sense to her now. He pushed people away so he wouldn't get close enough to care if they got hurt. Like his mother.

"I'm sorry, Takeshi. What happened…you didn't deserve that," she whispered.

Takeshi glanced back as if he could feel the weight of her focus. He studied her like a kindred soul, both lost in their cruel, pain-filled world. "You didn't deserve to lose your parents either."

Tears formed, and she pursed her lips, trying to hold herself together. "Do you think that," she paused to swallow, choking on her words. "One day, we'll see them again? Like in heaven?"

It was the first time she ever let those words escape.

He frowned and pondered her question.

"For the longest time, I didn't believe in God. I mean, how could God do that to me? To her? But my mother believed. If there is a heaven, and anyone's there, it's her. And when I look at you…" Takeshi's chin lifted, and his heated stare halted her breath, like her oxygen was his to preserve.

"I know I shouldn't say this, but your beauty is so overwhelming sometimes that it makes me ache. It's more than physical. It's who you are, radiating from your heart. That's how I know if your parents are anything like you, they are in heaven too."

Tears fell down her face without permission. And at that moment, she didn't even care.

"It's not fair," she whispered.

"What is?" He searched her eyes.

"For you to know me better than I do."

He recognized her deepest scars. Scars she didn't show anyone else. The immense pain, anger, and regret for being powerless to stop your loved ones from being taken away resonated beneath their skin.

It didn't weaken Takeshi, though. No, he was stronger because of it, ready to take on the world fighting.

"But I'm thankful," she confessed. "Not just for trusting me with your story, but for being there for me earlier."

Takeshi's face tightened. "I was scared. I saw your body on the ground, and the first thing I thought of was my mother. I thought I failed you too."

"I know...but you didn't fail me. I'm okay," Khalani insisted, but his troubled gaze shot to the red marks on her neck.

"I even did the squishy eye finger trick you taught me," she added. "Freaking gross. You're the only one who could convince me to do that."

"I noticed. But you sound less badass when you call it the squishy eye finger trick, you know that, right?"

"Perhaps. But I just got you to admit that I'm a little badass."

Takeshi rolled his eyes, but the tension slowly eased from his firm body. "Are you trying to distract me from being upset, Kanes?"

"Yes, is it working?"

Takeshi turned on his back, face still hard, but the barest hint of a smirk appeared. "Maybe."

She laid on her back as well, smiling to herself. A gentle peace lay between them. A truce. Just for this one night. And after his story,

Khalani was compelled to share a small detail of herself that no one else knew.

"You know, I wanted to be a gardener when I was younger." She focused on the ceiling, imagining a whole array of flowers growing in the grey cracks.

"Really?" Takeshi's deep voice softened as he stared at the ceiling with her.

Could he see the art too?

"Yeah. Every other kid in my class wanted to be a scientist, a Death-Zoner, or a Councilman. Something grand. Not me, I drew myself watering flowers in Genesis."

He chuckled. "I would've thought you wanted to be the first female Governor with your stubbornness."

"I don't like to be in the spotlight. I'm more inclined to fade into the background and the shadows. I guess Braderhelm was the perfect place for me, even though there are no flowers," she joked, putting her arms over the covers and snuggling deeper.

Takeshi didn't speak for the longest time. When she started to close her eyes, the weight of exhaustion hitting her, he whispered,

"I'll find some flowers for you."

Takeshi put his arms by his side, still lying on top of the covers. Then slowly, like there was static electricity trickling up the side of her body closest to him, the pinky of his finger grazed hers.

And stayed there.

Khalani breathed out, feeling like her heart was galloping at the slightest touch. That was it. They didn't hold hands. It was the most minimal connection, but those skin cells connected to his were like electrical rods, pulsing and beaming with energy.

She didn't remember what purpose her pinky ever served before it was touched by his.

She swallowed, trying to ease her pulse. They didn't move except for their chests, rising up and down with each beat. Khalani eventually closed her eyes as the soft sound of his breathing helped calm her erratic mind.

She soon found herself down a sleepy tunnel and sank further in its depths, the side of their fingers still connected, right till she fell asleep.

23

If what we have is unknown,
no one can spell the chaos it will reign.

Khalani released a heavy breath. Her head was buried in a soft pillow, and she groaned, stretching her legs and toes out. The satisfying sound of cracks and pops echoed in her ears. For the first time, she didn't wake up with knots burning through her spine and neck.

Her fingers clutched the cool sheets closer, and Khalani slowly opened her eyes. The first thing she noticed was Takeshi's absence. She sat up, realizing her pillow had a lovely drool stain.

Swell.

What a wonderful departing gift that would have any man lining outside her cell, awaiting her tantalizing presence. She promptly flipped the pillow over to hide the evidence and glanced around the empty room.

Where was Takeshi? She never heard him leave.

Almost as if he heard her thoughts, the door opened, and Takeshi walked through in his guard uniform. He halted a few steps in, enigmatic, surprised eyes locking with hers. "You're awake."

"I just woke up," Khalani cleared her throat, rubbing a hand through her tangled strands of hair.

"Good. That's…that's good." A line appeared between his brows. "I need to escort you back to your cell before roll-call."

"Oh, right. Almost forgot I was in prison for a split second," she joked with a half-smile, flipping the sheets and awkwardly crawling out of his bed.

Takeshi didn't return it. The hard mask was back in place, and his frown deepened as he followed her movement. Khalani stretched her arms behind her back, ignoring the renewed tension in the room.

"We need to talk, Kanes."

Her brows knitted at the solemn expression on his face. "About?"

"What happened last night."

Khalani straightened, traces of exhaustion abruptly disappearing. "Are you in trouble for what happened with Guard Barron or something? Whatever it is, I'm sure we'll figure it out," she reasoned, already doing mental calculations of how best to help him.

It was the least she could do after Takeshi saved her life. And since last night…something changed between them. He wasn't her enemy anymore.

But why was he staring at her like that? Like she was the living manifestation of all his angels and demons brought to life.

"No." He brushed a rough hand through his hair. "It's not that."

"What exactly are you referring to?" She stood very still, a sizeable knot forming beneath the center of her chest. The knot grew tighter under her skin. Hotter as blood pooled away from her heart.

Takeshi shifted uncomfortably.

He opened his mouth but hesitated. War waged in his eyes, but a firm resolve planted over his face.

"You already know the answer, Kanes. I brought you here for a good reason, but us sleeping in the same bed. Me telling you things that I have no right to share with someone like you. The way you're staring at me right now. It has to stop."

She recoiled. "Someone like me?"

"Look at you, Kanes."

The invisible knife he held threatened to split her in two. And all she could do was stand immobile in her dirty overalls.

"You're a prisoner. And I'm not." His jaw clenched tighter. "You were sentenced here for a reason, and my responsibility is to keep you locked up. There is *nothing* between us. There is no 'we,' and to think otherwise is laughable."

Her muscles contracted like she was punched in the gut. The dark walls of his room were closing in around her.

Escape.

She needed to escape.

If Khalani stayed in his presence a second longer, she would explode. Every single emotion residing inside would scatter against the cold floor, staining every corner in her pathetic tendrils.

She rushed past him.

"Where are you going?" he demanded.

"Leaving. Like you wanted. And just so you know, Takeshi." Khalani whipped around, her heart forming into a block of solid ice. "The only thing laughable is you thinking that I would ever believe there was something between us. God wouldn't be so cruel."

Takeshi's eyes tightened, a surge of pain flashing across his face, but he quickly recovered.

"Glad to hear it."

She hastily left his room, a cluster of nerves swarming her fingers, face, and chest. The weight of loathing and embarrassment threatened to pull her under, like a chunk of cement was hog-tied to her heart.

"Is it this way?" She'd already started barreling down the hall, refusing to make eye contact.

"No." Takeshi soundly shut his door. "The other way."

With all the dignity she could muster, Khalani turned and started walking by his side.

The callous dismissals manifested physically between them, like magnets repelling one another as they marched toward her cell in complete silence.

Takeshi completely severed any peace or connection that rested between them. Words faded by morning. It was better that way. She was not upset.

She was just fine.

The heat of blood rushed to her face, and a pinprick of tears reached the corner of her eye. She gritted her teeth and discreetly brushed her eyes, wiping away any signs of emotion.

How could she let this happen? When did this happen?

Why did it hurt so much?

This may be the exact wake-up call that she needed. She was starting to care for the one person who locked the gates to her home. What an idiot.

He played her for a fool and won.

They made it to Cell Block 7 in record speed. With a click of his electric pad, the metal bars swished open, and she brushed past him without looking back. Khalani stared at the marked walls of her confined cell, pangs of ruin grinding the remnants of her heart down to splinters.

The bars slammed shut, and Takeshi walked away without a word or utterance of regret. She wanted to scream into the cold air. Her lips trembled, but Khalani refused to cry. Refused to let Takeshi have any more power over her.

Takeshi understood the game; it was past time for Khalani to read the rules. Pieces shift, but the board never changes. Braderhelm was no place for delusions or misguided fantasies. This was her home. Her reality.

Heartless, cold, and cruel. Just like him.

And just like her.

****

Khalani raced up the stairs to the library. Whenever Takeshi slithered through her brain, she dug her nails into her palms to raze those unwanted thoughts.

And at this point, her hands would permanently be scarred with claw marks. The memory of his deep voice cutting her down was like barbed wire chafing against her skin.

"Look at you, Kanes."

Khalani grimaced and didn't bother knocking on the library door, letting herself in. The warm aroma of books helped calm her erratic mind and reminded her of the critical task at hand. She needed to talk to Winnie about the crops and their plan to contact Hermes. She could tell Winnie. She trusted Winnie with her life.

And she'd been beginning to trust Takeshi too.

A fresh lick of pain rushed through her chest, and she shook her head. Just let it go.

Let it go, you idiot.

She brushed past the bookshelves, the characteristic hymn of soft notes breezing through the air. Khalani rounded the corner, and Winnie sat in her chair, nodding as she read a book and sang along with the music.

"Hey, Winnie." Khalani emerged from the bookshelves.

Winnie immediately swiveled around, a radiant smile completely overtaking her face. "Oh! Khalani, my sweet girl." Winnie turned the music off and rushed over to her, the purple fabric of her dress floating across the ground.

"Winnie's missed your company. But you're looking a little pale. Are you sick, dear? And what are those marks on you?" Winnie's eyes squinted as she gently touched the bruises on her neck.

"No. I'm okay, Winnie. But I have to talk to you," Khalani insisted.

She wasn't okay. She was far from okay. But those damages weren't meant to be seen or shared.

Winnie frowned but didn't protest as Khalani pulled her to sit down. Before she could talk herself out of it, Khalani proceeded to tell Winnie everything they learned about the crop failure, the Governor's cryptic speech in Genesis, and their plan to contact Hermes.

Winnie sat silently as Khalani spoke, an odd expression on her face. Surprise wasn't evident in her eyes but rather a wave of anguish and crude recognition that threatened to buckle her fragile body. She paused as Winnie's eyes glistened, tears forming a blanket over her gaze.

"Winnie, don't cry. We have a plan. I'm sure Hermes will send help if we can contact them." Khalani didn't know if she genuinely believed that, but everything was lost if they didn't try.

"It's finally happening." Winnie sobbed into her hands. "I thought it would take longer, but it's happening now." Tears flooded down Winnie's cheeks.

Her brows furrowed. "What do you mean, Winnie? You knew about this?"

"Winnie was told this might happen," Winnie's voice cracked as she stared down at the ground.

"Who? Who told you, Winnie?"

Winnie sniffled and anxiously shook her head.

Khalani *needed* answers. So, she pushed.

"Winnie, whatever it is. You can tell me. You don't have to hold whatever weight you carry yourself. I can help lighten the load, and we can figure something out together. You can trust me."

Winnie glanced up, wet pools shining down her face, and her eyes held a mystery. She bit her lip and asked hesitantly, "Do you promise Winnie can trust you, Khalani?"

The potency of the moment filled the room, and Khalani reached for Winnie's hand. "*I promise.* I would never break your trust. Winnie…my parents have been gone a long time now, and I know we aren't related, but you have become my family."

The emotional truth cascaded from her lungs without hesitation or fear. Winnie was the first person to open the dark holes within her heart and expose her to a world of color, beauty, and rapture. Winnie taught Khalani how to love again. How to live within herself.

Because if she couldn't forgive herself, then why should anyone else?

"Family," Winnie whispered to herself.

Winnie locked eyes with Khalani, a determined look over-shadowing her fear. Winnie stood and rushed to her desk. She rummaged through a cabinet and pulled out a black book. The one she never let Khalani read and always kept hidden.

"Do you remember when Winnie told you about Timothy Talbot?" Winnie asked.

Khalani frowned, vaguely remembering the name. "Only a little. You said he was your great great great grandfather or something like that?"

Winnie gave a small smile that did little to alleviate the tension on her face. "Exactly. That is Timothy Talbot." Winnie pointed to the painting of the white-robed man walking toward a strange structure. The mysterious art grabbed her attention the first day she met Winnie.

"This was painted by him before he died and passed down through the Talbots, along with his journal." Winnie clutched the book so hard her knuckles were turning white.

"He was a great scientist before we all went underground. Winnie was told to keep this secret. Sworn not to tell anyone but family, and now…that is you."

Winnie handed Khalani the black journal. A weird pressure centered over her body, like she knew everything was about to change. As if all the experiences in her life led her to this singular moment.

"What does it say?"

"The truth."

Khalani's muscles hung taut, and she opened the ancient text.

Journal of Timothy Talbot
Day 100 After Global Meltdown (AGM)

The United Nations declared a global crisis from the nuclear fallout, and humanity faces imminent extinction. We knew this would happen, but now, the whole world knows. Panic set in. Riots flutter every continent, and our select coalition of the world's top scientists must take our Project into hiding. We live at the base now, working tirelessly every day. There is no leaving, no turning back, for the fate of the human species rests in our hands.

Day 200 AGM

They killed Hunter and Brian today. They couldn't handle the isolation and wanted to return to their families and tell them about the Project. I'm trying to hold tears back as I write this. They were my college roommates at M.I.T., my best friends. And now they're gone, lost like so many people who have perished since the bombs. But I can't let myself cave to those emotions. I now lead the Project and must carry on. I will not succumb to the daunting pressure holding me down. The future is what I need to think of. The future is all that matters.

Day 365 AGM

The United Nations announced a lottery for underground cities. Because of the Project, our families will have a secure spot in the nearest underground city. I wish I could feel better about it. They tell people they will be underground for only a short time. They say the earth's surface will heal, and plant life will grow again. The air will be sustainable in no time. They lie. They have to. For the lucky that win a spot underground, they don't know radiation levels will take hundreds of years to decrease to a habitable level. Everyone alive at this point will either die from the fallout and nuclear winter, or they will live the rest of their lives underground, never to see the sun again. Life on the surface will cease to exist. Our only hope is the Project. We need to move faster.

Day 425 AGM

Saving the world is tiring business. I have started to engage with Alan. Preliminary tests look promising.

Day 460 AGM

The status of the Project looks better every day. The sequences are nearly complete, and I have presented to the

President. I should be relieved and grateful. But I feel a weight in the pit of my stomach. Some of my conversations with Alan concern me. I expressed those concerns to John, but he attempted to assuage my fears.

Day 475 AGM

We will complete the mission. There is no other alternative. John has doubts as well, but our minds won't let us go there. If our fears are correct, we are doomed.

Day 505 AGM

Alan profoundly troubles me. Some things that have been said...does he truly have our best interests at heart? At this point, I don't know anymore. I need to have one final talk with him. I pray that my instinct is wrong, but I cannot take the risk. Something must be done.

Day 531 AGM

Project Helix is complete. I never thought I would write down these words. The team celebrates in the cave, but I don't join them. They don't know what I have done.

We will join what family we have left in the underground cities of Apollo and Hermes. And now, it's the waiting game. When radiation levels decrease, Project Helix will begin its motor function, and humanity can return to the surface. Return home. This will be long after I am dead. I shall join my daughter and granddaughter in Apollo. Security closely watches me, ensuring no one spreads the truth of Project Helix. But this secret cannot die with me.

Final Journal Entry

Dear Maybell,

My sweet granddaughter. Seeing your smiles and beautiful face fills me with nothing but joy. A joy I thought I would never *feel again. You look just like your mother did when she was your age. If your mother had lived longer, she would've been so proud of you. The radiation we've been exposed to on the surface has taken a toll on all of us. Indeed, I feel my body growing weaker by the day. It's time to leave you my journal.*

I know you will have many questions, sweet girl, and I wish I had all the answers. The simple truth is that there may be some forces outside of our control that don't want to see us prosper. After my time on the Project, even I questioned whether we were worth saving. All the wars, famine, loss of life, destroying our planet...how can we be trusted again? But I look at you and see all the goodness in the world deep inside your eyes, and then I remembered. Love is worth saving. Life is worth saving. Never forget that.

I hope my fears have been misplaced, but we must prepare. There are very few in Apollo you can trust. Based on our calculations, the resources in Apollo should last for 300 years. The surface air will be breathable before then. If there comes the point where resources decline, and we still don't go to the surface, then you must find a way to leave Apollo. Find the truth about Project Helix. That is our only hope. Even if this happens long after you're gone, you must pass this knowledge down through our family.

Let them know the path starts at Prometheus.

- Your loving grandfather, Timothy Talbot

Khalani silently closed the book, a sudden coldness enveloping her like a cloak. All she could focus on was the rise and fall of her chest. Her hands trembled as she handed the journal back to Winnie.

"Do you see it now?" Winnie asked, looking deep into her eyes.

"I...I need a second."

Her breath hitched as she stood and started pacing the room. Her face tingled, and her vision grew blurry. Project Helix, Apollo, declining resources, Genesis, Prometheus…all parts of a puzzle splayed out, and she could scarcely fit the pieces together.

"The journal doesn't say anything about what Project Helix is?" Khalani asked Winnie.

Winnie shook her head. "No. But it must have been something great, something that could save us all. And if what your friend said about the crop failure is true, then Timothy was right, and we need to leave Apollo! We need to find Project Helix."

Khalani placed both palms against her face, her mind spinning. "But Timothy said the resources would last until the surface air is survivable again. The surface is filled with radiation, Winnie. What if he was wrong?"

"Winnie believes Timothy. What if Apollo's been lying to us about the surface? Don't you feel the wrongness too?"

She did feel something. Like the weight of knowledge would bury her alive. She learned so much in the past few days…it was too much. Her world was turning upside down, and she was spinning along with it. Questions shone on every corner, and no answers were in sight.

"Winnie, they showed us the dead bodies of the Genesis workers. The burns, their skin deteriorating. They died from radiation poisoning."

"What if it was all a show?!" Winnie exclaimed. "To make us believe that the surface was still too dangerous?"

Khalani heaved a sigh and moved toward Winnie, placing a gentle hand on either side of her shoulders.

"Winnie, I know you want to believe this. I know you want to believe Timothy Talbot. Let's just say you're right, and Apollo has been lying to us the whole time, and some mysterious force wants us to die. Where would we even start? He said the path starts at Prometheus, but do you know where Prometheus is? We don't even know if it's a person, a place," she trailed off, searching her face for recognition of how crazy this sounded.

Winnie's eyes blazed with hope.

"Winnie doesn't know, but don't you want to discover the truth? We can escape to the surface and figure it out together! We're family, right?"

Khalani glanced heavenward, pressure overwhelming her. She loved Winnie but could not watch her walk this path to self-destruction.

"We *are* family, Winnie. But listen to yourself. This isn't a plan. This is suicide. If escape was even possible, we'd be aimlessly wandering a barren wasteland. That's all the surface is now. We'd die in a few days. But we do have a plan. We contact Hermes, and I'm sure they will send us help. That is our smartest move right now, Winnie. Our *only* move."

Winnie's face transformed from conviction to despair. "Winnie hoped she could trust you."

"You can trust me!" she insisted. "I'm only looking out for you."

Winnie turned her head, and a stray tear ran down her face, piercing Khalani like shards of glass. "We're not meant to stay underground, Khalani. We were meant for more. Winnie knows this, but you...you don't want to leave the puppet show."

Her stomach tumbled like she was being gutted from the inside out. "Winnie," she whispered.

The afternoon alarm pierced the air. "It's time to leave." Winnie turned her back on her.

"Winnie...we can fix this."

"Not today, Khalani. Maybe not ever. Please just go," Winnie's voice broke.

Guilt and regret mounted like spires upon her chest, but too many words were spoken. And none of them could be snatched back. She slowly turned and left the library, shoulders hunched over like her body wanted to cave in and disappear. Takeshi left her a vulnerable fool. Her relationship with Winnie was crumbling before her eyes.

Khalani had never felt more isolated. Not even when her parents were murdered. And this time, it was all her own doing.

24

I clutch the misery, fear, and sadness in my palms.
I too know what it's like to be unwanted.

Silence is a mirage. From a distance, the vast emptiness appears enticing, captivating even. A safe haven for the mind to be within one's thoughts. But as soon as you draw near, the illusion washes away, and silence turns into a deafening thing.

Boisterous and maddening.

Weeks had passed, and Khalani hadn't spoken to Winnie. She was never assigned to the library, never caught a glimpse of Winnie to say she missed her and was sorry. When Winnie cried and stared at Khalani with *disappointment,* her heart crumbled from the inside out.

And Timothy Talbot never escaped her mind.

A part of her wished to forget the journal completely. To not place her hope in someone from a lost generation, a generation responsible for forcing humanity underground in the first place. Believing in nothing would be easier.

But what if Timothy Talbot was real, and he worked on a Project to return humanity to the surface?

The notion may very well be wishful thinking of a secret master plan, but her mind clutched the information like a lifeline.

Not only was she unable to visit Winnie in the library, but Takeshi's only interaction with Khalani since she spent the night in his bed was to tell her they were taking a break from training. He never gave an explanation. The warmhearted person who revealed his troubled past was gone. The dismissive Captain, who glared in her direction with vexation and ire, was all that remained.

She tried not to think about him. She really did. But her brain kept circling to the night when she lay beside his warm body. Her muscles were able to relax. Her forehead released its lines of tension. For a small moment in time, she felt safe.

But everything and nothing can change in a single breath.

He pierced through her armored heart and never patched the hole. Why was life always like that? The ones who do the most damage never think to repair it. They just leave you broken for the next person who has to deal with those twisted scars.

"You alright?" Serene eyed her with concern.

"I'm fine." Khalani raked her fingers through her hair. "Just a lot on my mind." She didn't tell the others about Timothy Talbot. Not when she couldn't determine whether his journal was truth or fantasy. For now, it was her burden of knowledge to carry alone. She could only wait and hope their plan to contact Hermes would work.

"Please tell me you have an update." Khalani peered at Adan as they walked to the far corner of the pit, away from prying ears.

Adan gave them an uneasy smile. "Do you guys want the good news or bad news first?"

"Good news first," Serene deadpanned.

"The good news is I can get the walkie to work."

Derek frowned. "And the bad news?"

Adan heaved a deep sigh and rubbed the corners of his eyes. "I can't get the walkie to work down here. Apollo is too deep for the signal to get out. The signal can only be sent on the surface. In Genesis."

With those words, a surge of disappointment and despair hung over them like a haze. "What if we wait for another dinner at the Governor's mansion?" Serene prodded, grasping for anything.

"That could take months. We'd be dead by then."

Derek shook his head bitterly, staring off into the distance like he was upset at himself for beginning to hope in the first place.

"What if there's another way?"

They snapped their heads to her.

"At the dinner, the Council said they were preparing a ball for the 10th Anniversary of Genesis. The Governor said Braderhelm prisoners were being used as servants. That's our way in," she exclaimed.

"But the 10th Anniversary of Genesis…that's only a couple weeks away," Derek argued.

"And security will be through the roof with all those guests," Serene replied tersely.

A plan was already forming in her head. "Serene can steal a pad to ensure we're on the list to serve at the ball. We sneak the walkie on Genesis, find a moment to slip away, and turn on the walkie to send out a signal."

Khalani searched Adan's face for confirmation. "It's possible," Adan hesitated. "But we need to be certain no one is around to interrupt the feed. It might take a few minutes for someone from Hermes to respond. If anyone sees us, we are dead."

"And if we don't do this, everyone is dead anyway." Khalani countered. "We don't have a choice. Are you guys in?" She stared at the three of them with fragile hope in her eyes.

Serene pursed her lips. "And miss a chance to give it to those assholes again? No way. I'm in."

Adan lifted his gaze to the ceiling. "There she goes, ready to jump into the fray without regard for her own preservation. But I don't see any other option either. Count me in."

Khalani nodded. "Derek?"

Derek lifted his head, the weight of a thousand suns dripping from his eyes.

"All my life, I only wanted to help those in Apollo. And every day I spent in Braderhelm, I thought of everyone I failed by not fixing the crops or spreading the truth. I had given up. I'm not going to miss this chance to make things right."

Khalani reached out her hand and gently squeezed his fingers. "Thank you."

"Okay," Adan said. "You all know the plan. Remember, there can't be any mess-ups because we'll only get one shot."

One shot. Only one chance to save Apollo.

All the underground city ever brought her was despair, but it took Khalani becoming a prisoner to realize she wasn't ready to give up on the people who caged her. There were bigger things worth fighting for.

Shit. She was starting to sound an awful lot like Timothy Talbot.

"We need to walk," Serene whispered, inclining her head toward a guard who was sending suspicious glances their way.

They swiftly proceeded toward the front of the fighting ring to blend in with the prisoners, the raucous crowd unaware of their impending doom. Or maybe they always knew, and ignoring the inevitable was easier.

But she was done retreating into the shadows. Done accepting things out of her control. Someone out there achieved what most thought was impossible. The underground city of Apollo was a living testament to that fact.

Impossible was just a word created to assemble boundaries.

And she was an expert at crossing those.

She cracked her neck as a bald prisoner in the crater fought a scraggly tooth man with wild black hair and fell in an unconscious heap. Khalani impatiently patted her fingers against her side, ready to contact Hermes *now*.

Time was the silent torturer.

"What's got the roach up your ass? Afraid you'll get your pathetic life handed to you in the pit again?" Dana's characteristic, snarky tone sidled up next to her.

"Go away, Dana." Khalani didn't bother giving Dana the satisfaction of her gaze.

"Or what? Gonna cry on me?"

Derek turned, noticing the commotion, and stepped in front of Khalani. "Don't you have a petri dish to crawl back to, you uncultured piece of swine?"

Dana smirked. "Look, it's her bodyguard. Because the baby can't fight battles herself."

"I'm not going to ask you to leave again," Khalani hissed through her teeth.

"Ohhh, she's mad." Dana's voice grew louder. "Maybe we'll get a ballad this time about her stupid dead mother before she kills herself and spares everyone."

Several prisoners choked on laughter.

Blood rushed to the surface of her skin. Heating her up from the inside, like a furnace about to explode.

And that's what she did.

Khalani stepped around Derek, wound her arm back, and punched Dana in the nose, feeling cartilage break beneath her knuckles. Dana stumbled back with a yell, her feet grating against the edge of the pit. Her nose instantly turned red, and her eyes began to water.

"You bi—"

Khalani pounced forward and pushed Dana over the crater's edge, throwing them both down into the pit. Gasps surrounded her as they crashed to the ground, rolling away from each other. Khalani ignored the pain in her back and lithely jumped to her feet, scraping gravel from her red arms.

Dana winced and scrambled upright with a snarl. "You're fucking dead." Dana gnashed her teeth, wiping the drops of blood dripping from her nostril.

Khalani readied her stance and raised her arms to protect her face like Takeshi taught her when Dana rushed forward and threw a wide punch toward her head. Khalani ducked to the right, barely dodging it, and quickly threw a counterpunch that collided with Dana's ear.

Dana barely reacted as she grabbed Khalani's shoulders and kneed her in the stomach. She gasped, hunching forward, unable to catch a breath.

Dana took advantage and rammed her fist into Khalani's face. Her ears rang from the hit, and her body jerked to the side as pain lanced through her head, like her brain was being rattled continuously with cymbals.

Her hair was suddenly pulled back in a tight grasp, and Dana's knee met her face. Khalani jerked backward and fell to the ground in a heap. Blood poured down her face, her vision blurring in and out.

"Finish her!" a guard roared.

"Get up!" a few prisoners yelled.

She placed weight on her hands and grunted, pushing up. The cheers of the crowd amplified. Dana narrowed her eyes and pulled out a thin knife from her pocket. The blade's edge caught the light and reflected in Khalani's wide eyes.

She didn't stop to think how Dana came to possess such a weapon. It didn't matter. In Braderhelm, no one intervenes in pit fights. She was on her own, even in death.

But Khalani wasn't the weak, hopeless girl Dana destroyed months ago. She trained for this. Learned from the best. If there was one thing she gained from Takeshi, it was how to read opponents, attacking every possible weakness.

Khalani's focus never strayed from Dana, noting how she favored her left leg and dropped her elbow when she threw a punch. Khalani licked the trail of blood that slipped past her upper lip, and Dana hesitated, suddenly unsure of the unhinged look in her eyes.

Khalani bounded forward, kicking up dirt as she stalked toward her. Dana reacted exactly as she predicted, by jabbing the knife straight toward her stomach. Khalani dodged to the right and punched Dana in the throat.

Dana dropped the knife and fell back, heaving labored breaths as a hundred gazes fell on Khalani in amazement. Dana tried to quickly compose herself and rewound her first, jumping forward in a frenzied movement. Khalani dropped her body to avoid the wild throw as it raced above her head. Quick as a flash, she twisted and rammed her elbow with brutal force into Dana's already broken nose.

A chorus of *ooh's* rang out from the crowd.

Dana clutched both hands to her face, her fingers noticeably trembling. But Khalani wasn't done. She gripped Dana's collar and punched the side of her head, and Dana's knee fell to the ground.

"Take back what you said about my mother," she rasped.

Dana shakily rose, swaying on her feet, and spat a lob of blood in her direction. "Fuck you."

Khalani punched her again.

Dana fell to both her hands and knees. Thick blood poured from her nose and splashed to the ground, reminiscent of the position Khalani was in those short months ago when she last fought Dana in the pit.

A chorus of cheers echoed around her as Dana's body started to shake. But it wasn't from crying. Chills cascaded down her spine as Dana lifted her gaze. Bright red blood ran between the cracks of her yellow teeth as she snickered.

"Didn't think you had it in you. Turns out you're just as mangled and broken as the rest of us."

Khalani's chest rose in rapid breaths. The painful vision of her parent's picture tearing apart replayed once more.

Moments may fade, but scars don't. The pain always remains.

Like a trained killer, she grabbed the knife from the ground and lowered to the tips of her feet. She placed the knife against Dana's jugular, an eerie excitement coursing through her at the sight of Dana's blood nicking the blade.

"You took away the last thing I cared about. *You* were the one that tried to ruin me like this place ruined you," the harsh whisper grated against her tongue.

"So go ahead and finish it then," Dana snarled. The volume of the crowd faded into the background. All she could hear was the sound of her heartbeat raging in her chest.

Khalani's grip tightened on the knife, ready to take the final slice. She'd been waiting for this moment for so long. To make each of her enemies pay in blood.

Her hands shook, and Khalani exhaled roughly. Hesitating. Why was she hesitating? Dana didn't deserve mercy.

But Winnie's face filled her vision. Images of the books she read, conversations they had, and the dreams she shared pierced her mind, kindling a fire that beckoned Khalani to see beyond her darkness.

People will perish. Pages can rip to shreds and burn to ruin, but Khalani's own life meant the things that mattered the most never disappeared from her, not while she remained. Winnie taught her that.

She didn't need to take anymore. What more is there to take when you already encompass the world?

A sticky weight relinquished its hold on her body, her vision. She momentarily pushed the blade deeper into her neck and had the satisfaction of watching Dana flinch.

"Look at me," Khalani commanded.

Dana's first sliver of fear was present when their eyes connected.

"I'm nothing like you. I won't ruin others to fill my empty spaces." Khalani leaned down to whisper, "And I don't need to finish what I already won."

Dana's stare turned into shocked disbelief as Khalani dropped the knife and pulled away, leaving a piece of her darkness behind.

She lifted her head, and Derek was right at the front, eyes wide in shock. Even Serene stared at her in bewilderment, a sly smirk beginning to form on her cheeks. Adan and Derek reached out their hands as Khalani walked closer, and they hoisted her up the pit.

"Didn't think you could refuse to kill someone and still look like a badass," Adan exclaimed, tussling her hair.

Khalani's lips curved, and she caught sight of the Death-Zoner standing to the side, tilting his head in curiosity. She didn't care about the curses or chorus of boos coming her way from the other prisoners for not ending the fight in death.

Khalani turned, and her muscles froze. Across the pit was someone standing there, watching the entire time.

Takeshi.

His muscular arms were crossed over his chest, staring straight at her. As if no object or force surrounded the space between them. Their eyes locked, and the weight of his gaze had her heart galloping faster.

His lips imperceptibly lifted in the slightest grin.

And in one simple gesture, he encapsulated everything that couldn't be communicated in words.

All those grueling trainings. Every time he knocked her to the ground or criticized her form, yelling at Khalani that she could give more. Every look exchanged that bled fire, tenacity, and passion.

Noises grazed across her skin, clamoring for her attention. But all she saw was Takeshi before he turned and disappeared through the crowd like a flickering shadow.

In another life, she'd forget all the horrible things he said to her. She'd race after him, asking him if he saw what happened, knowing full well he did. If he knew Khalani had the strength in her all along.

But she didn't need to ask.

Takeshi simply *understood,* just like she did, all the answers that didn't need to be questioned. The emotions racing through her were so poignant they filled the entire room.

Hell, they filled her whole twisted universe.

Because, for once…she was damn proud of herself *too.*

25

I've retreated into myself for far too long.

Pain is not something to cower from. Pain is a product of pursu-ance. When sweat falls in a puddle, tears run dry, and blood hardens into scabs, only then does the mind rest soundly at night, knowing every ounce of effort was given.

The strong don't envision pain as a barrier but rather a rocket ship propelling past the limits of the mind. Without pain, victories would be worthless.

Otherwise, everyone would win.

A loud grunt sounded from her left. Derek winced as he released his tight grip on the shovel. Blood stained the dirty wooden handle.

"You alright?" Khalani set down the heavy wheelbarrow.

"Yeah. Fresh blister popped." Derek huffed, and she glanced at his hands, bloodied and gashed, worse than usual.

"Here."

She grabbed a cloth used for wiping sweat and quickly wrapped it tight around his palms, protecting the fresh wounds.

"Thanks." Derek's mouth twisted as she tightened the cloth, but he made no protest. "I vaguely remember doing this for you when you first arrived."

She smirked, finishing the knot with a pull. "Seems like a lifetime ago." At this point, Khalani lost track of how long she'd been in Braderhelm.

"Too long," Derek whispered.

She frowned at his expression. It was the kind of tired that bled past the physical, where your will holds no more power, and your brain doesn't remember why it's pushing anymore.

"We're gonna make it through this," Khalani insisted, gently squeezing his wrist.

"How do you know?" Derek searched her eyes.

"I know because the alternative isn't an option," she emphasized.

"You two!!"

Startled, they turned their heads as a bald prison guard charged them. "Why aren't you working?"

"W-we are working, sir," Derek stammered, and the guard's face seemed to harden as he stalked over. "We were just taking a quick bre—" Derek fell to the ground as the guard brutally slashed him across the face with a baton.

"Does it sound like I wanna hear your excuses?" The guard reared his boot and kicked Derek in the stomach with crushing force.

"Stop!" she yelled as Derek folded in on himself like a fetus.

The guard whipped his head and took a menacing step toward her. "What did you just say?"

She breathed heavily as Derek struggled to rise to his knees. "If you keep hurting him, he won't be able to work. And the Warden won't be happy about that."

The guard narrowed his eyes. "What would a pathetic prisoner like you know about the Warden?"

Her mind scrambled as she tried to stand straighter. Even so, the top of her head barely came to his chest.

"I've met with the Warden several times," she lied through her teeth. "And he voiced his displeasure about the tunnels being incomplete. Hurting another able-bodied prisoner will further slow the work, and I'm sure you wouldn't want to explain the delay to him."

The guard closely studied her as he clutched the baton tighter.

Any moment, he could turn his weapon on her and use her skin and bones as a punching bag, but Khalani didn't shy away from his gaze, airing a placated confidence as her hands slightly shook.

The cruel guard's eyes swept over her body lewdly, and he grunted. "You wouldn't be the first piece of prisoner ass the Warden has taken a liking to. But I can hurt you in ways the Warden won't notice."

Before Khalani could react, he pushed a taser into her bony ribs. The voltage was high and hot electricity raced through her muscles as she collapsed to the ground, shaking uncontrollably.

The guard leaned over her, smirking sadistically.

"Talk back to me again, and I'll find other uses for that mouth. But I won't kill you. I'll kill him."

He pointed to Derek, keeping eye contact with her. She ground her teeth together, imagining taking the steel weapon from his hand and beating his ugly face in. Kicking and scratching and biting, over and over like an extinct animal. And then she'd stick the taser in every hole in his body—on max voltage.

But she withheld those dark instincts, letting the quiet resignation speak for her. The guard held her gaze with a threatening glare and eventually walked away, cursing under his breath.

After several seconds, her muscles stopped twitching, and she slowly gained control of her limbs.

"You alright?" Derek panted from the ground.

"I've had worse." Khalani hobbled over to Derek. "Are you okay?"

"No." His face contorted, a fresh scar running from the corner of his eye to his lip as she helped him to his feet. "But if it weren't for you, I probably wouldn't be moving."

She eyed him with concern as he gingerly picked up his shovel and placed rocks into the barrel, low groans escaping him.

"Don't push so hard."

He lifted his eyes but kept shoveling. "We don't have a choice, Khalani. Not in here. They'll let us rest when we die." Her brows pulled together as he clutched his ribcage and turned away to hide the pained tears in his eyes.

Contacting Hermes might not be enough.

They needed to escape Braderhelm.

Khalani passed her cell as she headed toward the pit, trying to figure out how the impossible could become possible when an untamable voice sounded behind her.

"Kanes."

The deep reverberations in the masculine tone made the hairs on her arms rise and were enough to kickstart her heart within a millisecond. Khalani slowly turned. Her pulse quickened when a familiar, shadowy gaze connected with hers.

Takeshi stood a few feet away, muscular arms crossed over his chest as his eyes roved over every inch of her, pausing on the bruises around her eye and the cuts on her lip. His gaze was physical, like fingertips caressing over each focal point.

Her hands instinctively tucked her hair behind her ears, intrinsically aware of her ragged appearance. The strands of her messy bun were frayed, sticking out in every direction. Sweat dripped down her neck. The fabric of her uniform was stained with dust and soot.

"Look at you, Kanes."

His words from that fateful morning sliced her anew. It was easier to focus on the worst of him versus the way he stared at her in the pit, or the delicate words uttered in the safety of his bedroom. Good or bad weren't apt descriptions for Takeshi. He was the warmth of the fire and the sadistic burn of the flames.

Men like him should come with a warning sign.

"What do you want?" She crossed her arms.

He took a few steps toward her. Slow. Predatory. The black uniform clung to his broad shoulders, weapons hidden except for the sharp blade clipped to his belt. His handsome face was calm and composed, but when Takeshi's scalding eyes connected to hers, the dangerous temptation of him made her muscles tingle as if preparing to run.

Or take one step closer.

"I've been thinking," he stated.

"Careful. Too much of that will hurt you."

Takeshi's eyes glinted in challenge. "Since when did either of us ever mind the pain?"

"I can punch you in the face to test the limits of that theory."

"Go ahead. But I choose the punishment if you miss."

She huffed, fully convinced that Takeshi was put on this earth just to spite her. Storming through life, breaking down walls, only to survey how she reassembled the pieces.

"Am I in your way or something?"

"Depends." He leaned closer, his large body enveloping her vision. "Barron's dead. You decisively won your fight in the pit. It would seem as if you're done with training."

"It would seem that way."

"Unless you wanted one more round against your main enemy." Takeshi subtly cocked his head to the side with that daring look, eyes locked on her every movement.

At this point, her heart was conducting a drum competition in her chest. His deep gaze searched hers, and her fingers curled as if electricity tingled down her bloodstream. Around Takeshi, she was a live wire, a ticking time bomb with his finger held over the trigger. His words sank deep into her gut, repeating like a metronome. And the way her stomach fluttered, like a naïve, stupid child, only made her want to hurt the both of them in retaliation.

"I thought you didn't want to be around me anymore. You made that perfectly clear to me in your room."

Takeshi's jaw tightened. "I know what I said and won't apologize for it."

"Glad to hear it." She turned around, giving him the same courtesy he gave her that morning.

"Wait."

Her fists tightened by her side, but she stopped, her body acting on instinct before her mind could think. She slowly faced him, and raw emotion hung from Takeshi's gaze, vulnerability shining like the moon in his window.

"The truth can't be taken back, Kanes. It had to be done. And if you think watching your face that morning didn't make me want to destroy something, you're wrong. But the idea of not having one more moment where I'm just your trainer, and you aren't my prisoner, makes me want to kill someone."

She pulled back like his words struck her. Her forehead pinched together, and her mouth hung slightly open, his voice doing weird things to her chest. What he was saying didn't make sense.

Because her heart ached the same. Maybe heart wasn't the right word. When Takeshi walked away from her that morning, she felt it in the back of her throat, in the cracks between her lips, in the heavy joints of her shoulders. All the inconsequential parts of her were brought to life around him, like her body would rather burn than be invisible.

"Takeshi, I..."

She didn't dare finish speaking.

One more syllable would destroy the remnants of her strength. Completely eradicate her control. As it was, she wasn't ready to turn away. No, Takeshi's gaze alone held her feet stapled to the ground.

He was the anchor when her resolve threatened to slip away in shrouds of dust. She bit her lip and lifted her gaze, preparing to be sliced open. Her body would accept nothing less.

Traitor.

"One last time," she agreed.

Takeshi didn't speak. His expression was focused and controlled, but his eyes flickered with a slow-burning fire. He nodded his head, sealing their pact.

She exhaled deeply as they made their way toward the training room. They walked in ponderous, deliberate steps. Slower than usual.

Like time was their enemy, more than prison ever was.

Takeshi opened the door to the gym, and it was like coming home. Home is not where the heart is. Home is the place that accepts the worst of you, the ugly crying where snot slides down your nostril, the anger when your fists clench to connect with something physical, the floors your knees fall to when life wins the prize for the biggest bitch on the planet.

The smell of sweat and pine drifted to her nose, and she inhaled deeply like it was perfume. Khalani walked past him and squeezed through the rubber bars, stretching her arms across her chest as she walked into the center.

This place was the same, but something was different. An air that had Khalani's muscles tightening and the pressure between her lungs increasing. When she turned around, and Takeshi easily strode over the bars, his body relaxed but gaze glued to her like he could see through the back of her skull, she knew the answer.

You don't have to physically be with someone to know them intimately. When someone touches your mind, kisses your memories, and licks your dreams, you become molded together. And that was the problem. Being molded to Takeshi would equate to her own destruction.

"So," She lifted her hands out to her side. "How should we do this?"

"We play a game."

She scoffed. "Since when did you ever make training a game?"

"Life is nothing but a game consisting of winners and losers," Takeshi replied in all his muscley wisdom.

"Fine." She succumbed. "What's the game?"

"It's simple." He cracked his fingers, staring down at them like he was relaxing under the sun. "A hit to the body equals a point. The first to five points wins."

Her lips twitched. She liked this game. She liked this game *a lot*. Takeshi was strong, agile, and able to end her life in a flash if he wanted, but an insane part of her enjoyed the high of battling him.

He wouldn't make this easy, though.

She'd have to play smart to win.

"Fine. But I need something from you." She faced him. "I have a sizeable knot in my back from the first shift and can't reach it."

Takeshi's gaze narrowed. "And you expect me to what...rub it out for you?"

"Thought you wanted it to be a level playing field, but if not, that's fine. I'll deal with it." Khalani shrugged and turned away.

An exasperated sigh sounded over her shoulder. "Get your ass over here, Kanes."

Khalani fought the grin tugging at her lips as she edged closer. His hooded eyes blazed intensely, and he jerked his chin for her to turn around. Takeshi's fingers brushed her shoulder as she gave him her back, kneading the skin slightly with his warm touch.

She forced herself not to groan in bliss as goosebumps raised on her collarbone.

"Where's the kn—"

She quickly pulled her arm back and elbowed him in the stomach. A loud grunt left his mouth, and she bounded forward, ready for his retaliation.

Takeshi heaved in a rough breath and slowly straightened, a menacing flicker stirring beneath his glower.

"You cheated."

"Fighting's never fair. One point for me." She couldn't help the slight upturn of her cheeks.

A nefarious expression played on his face. "You know I'm going to make you regret that."

"Maybe a cane will help you move faster. It would make me feel better about beating the elderly." Khalani readied her stance and tightened her fists. A part of her core shook at the narrowing of his eyes, but the wicked side of Khalani laughed and told her to cut deeper for all the times he made her care without giving anything in return. His tongue smacked against his teeth like a caged animal, and he launched forward without warning.

She panicked, barely managing to block a hit toward her core, but Takeshi was incredibly fast. He smacked her on both sides of her ribs with an open palm. Damnit.

Her teeth clenched together as she showered him with a barrage of punches toward the body. He effortlessly blocked each one without breaking a sweat. A sly look overshadowed his expression, and he countered her with another hit to her core, grabbed her wrist, and turned her body around so her back was flush to his chest.

Takeshi's large forearm quickly wrapped around her neck, not tight enough to where she couldn't breathe, but his other hand held her left wrist immobile by her side.

"Elderly, huh? I think you mean experienced, Kanes. I know some tricks that would make a girl like you turn crimson at the thought. Still wanna fight dirty with me?"

The heated and not-so-gentle whisper against her ear brought shivers down her arms and spun her mind into forbidden territory. Their chests rose in unison, and she fought the urge to turn around and see how riled up he was. "You wanted to play. Let's play," she retorted and stomped on his ankle.

Takashi grunted and, quick as a viper, swiped her legs out from under her and brought her down on her back, but not before she wrapped her arms around his head, bringing him down with her. They rolled on the hard ground, and she felt two more hits to her chest before she landed on top of him.

Khalani quickly captured his wrists with both her hands as she straddled him, knowing full well that he let her hold him down. Her eyes widened in triumph but paused at his vicious smirk.

"Shit." He made it to 5.

"I win," Takeshi huffed out. "Almost forgot how hard you like to make things."

Their eyes connected, and she didn't immediately move her hips from the top of his. Her nails tightened over his wrists, digging into his skin, nearly drawing blood in a cruel effort to deal him pain like he dealt her that humiliating morning in his bedroom.

But Takeshi didn't move. Didn't object. His face cemented in resolve as if he was more than capable of handling all the punishment she had to give, like he could take every inch of suffering from her and bear the weight himself.

Knots of tension appeared on her forehead. He shouldn't look at her like that. Like he would fight any battle for her, defeat any adversary that stepped in her way. Because it wasn't true. It was all a game to him.

And she was in far more danger now than at any point in prison. Because it wasn't her pride, strength, or body on the line. That annoying, fragile beast in her chest was beating up a storm just by the hint of vulnerability in his gaze, mirroring her own.

Her eyes lowered to his lips.

What would it feel like to have that part of him brushing against her body? She'd probably become undone.

"Kanes," a rough whisper escaped him.

Her eyes lifted, and a deep frown etched into his forehead. She noticed that his fists were balled against the floor, and he shook his head, wanting her to stop the trail of her gaze, but his eyes communicated so much more, as if begging her to keep going.

Her heart pumped faster, and she found herself leaning forward.

Stop while you still can. The logical part of her brain that was switched off found the on button. Khalani quickly scrambled off Takeshi, rubbing her hands down the sides of her knotted hair.

What was she thinking? What the hell was she doing? Khalani was letting herself get distracted and pulled in by Takeshi when she needed to focus on their plan to contact Hermes.

This needed to end.

"Sorry," she muttered, a warmth of blood pooling into her cheeks. "We should probably go."

Takeshi stood up to his full height. "What's wrong, Kanes?"

"Nothing." She waved her hand in dismissal. "Nothing's wrong."

"Bullshit," he raised his voice. "I know you too well. I've noticed the stress in your eyes for the past month. What is it?" His intense gaze drilled a hole right through her as he waited for an answer.

She shook her head, turning around. "No. Just drop it, Takeshi."

"Kanes!" The deep roar bounced off the angels in the ceiling, and she turned in shock. His muscles flexed in irritation. "Why do you have to be so goddamn stubborn? You can be honest with me."

All the tension, frustration, and anger were bubbling up inside her, ready to ignite and destroy everything in her path.

"You're joking, right? The king of the cold shoulder is accusing me of being stubborn? Why don't you go first? Tell me all your thoughts, Takeshi!"

His lips pressed into a hard line. "We're not talking about me."

"Oh yes, we are. This is about how you want me to be upfront with you, but you can't extend me the same courtesy."

"What are you talking about?"

She took a few steps toward him. "You know damn well what I'm talking about. Why were you kind and sweet the night I slept in your bed, and the next morning, you go back to being a cold and indifferent *asshole*. Explain that to me!"

Takeshi's inflexible gaze hardened. "Forget I asked, Kanes." He strode toward the exit. "I guess we're finally done with your training."

She let out a humorless laugh that echoed throughout the church. "Wow. Look who's scared now."

Takeshi froze as if someone shot him, and his eyes tracked her across the room.

"What did you call me?" his voice lowered.

Khalani felt a storm rising within her, and she refused to back down. "You heard me. I said you are scared."

"Watch yourself, Kanes. You're treading on thin ice," he growled.

Khalani was too far gone to stop, and she raised her chin. "Go ahead." She lifted her hands and stepped up to his large frame. "I'm not afraid of you. Hell, I might understand you better than I understand myself. You're not like Barron or the other guards here. You're the person who dropped out of school to protect your mother. You killed another guard to protect me.

"But you're also a total mystery and too damn complicated of a puzzle to even *want* to solve. Your lips say one thing, but your eyes say the complete opposite. You go from hot to cold because you are scared that I might be more than just a dirty, disgusting criminal that deserves to die in prison." Her pulse raced like she was crossing a battlefield.

Takeshi stiffened, and the air held still as if the floating dust and bodies within the paintings were paying attention to her every word.

"When I first came here, I was completely empty. If you were to scream inside my mouth, your voice would echo back at you across the empty spaces! So, you want the truth? All of it?! I can't tell you because somehow, through all this shit, I developed feelings for you. I don't know how it happened because you annoy the hell out of me and get under my skin like it's your mission in life. But that simple fact burns inside me so often, I don't even remember what it's like to not feel the pain.

"I feel so damn much that at any moment, it all comes blurting out, and I make myself look like the world's biggest idiot. So, there it is, Takeshi! I like you. And my deepest secret doesn't mean anything because you don't feel the same about me. We are worlds apart. And that's where we'll always stand."

By the end of her speech, she was panting. Takeshi's eyes widened, and he seemed to stop breathing as well. At that moment, it was like Khalani had an out-of-body experience, and she replayed every non-sensical utterance that escaped her mouth.

"Oh my God." Her eyes widened in horror. "Just forget everything I said, Takeshi. Don't worry about it."

"Kanes."

"No, seriously. I was being stupid, and it didn't mean anything," she explained in a rush. Khalani glanced at the ceiling, wishing for one of the painted angels to fly down and strike her on the spot.

"Kanes." Takeshi stepped toward her, his broad chest a few inches from her face.

"Please. Do me a favor, and let's just pretend this conversation never happened. I need to go ba—"

"Khalani!"

Her muscles froze solid. It was the first time Takeshi had ever called her by her real name. And the sound of it rolling across his tongue and lips was like liquid fire stroking through her veins.

"Yeah?"

"Shut up," he rasped. "We were never worlds apart. If we were, you wouldn't be everywhere inside of me. When I look at you, my chest feels like it's about to crack open, and all the emotions I've beaten down to submission come roaring back with a fucking vengeance." The power beneath his voice shook her.

"For every scar visible on your body, I have to prevent myself from seeking out your assailants and slashing each one of their throats to the bitter bone. I've watched you fight through every battle, despite the trials and tragedies you've faced, and it never ceases to astound me. Just staring at you right now makes me want to take you every way imaginable, and *nothing* about it is innocent."

Khalani forgot the concept of breathing. Heat rushed through every inch of her body, and her heart threatened to burst into a million pieces. His energy dominated the room, and all the barriers she futilely built against him came crashing down. Takeshi was her black hole, sucking every detail of her in until she finally stopped resisting and dove head first.

"You know I was never innocent." She lifted her head, pulse racing. "That's why you met me in prison."

His eyes blazed sinfully, and then he grabbed her by the back of the neck and kissed her.

26

You're the story I read slowly. I want to savor and memorize every word of you.

The moment Takeshi's full lips touched hers, fiery energy raced beneath her skin, kickstarting her heart and lungs. Every organ worked overtime to keep her body standing upright. Khalani gripped his shirt to steady herself but found her hands tugging Takeshi closer.

When her lips slowly moved against his, Takeshi tightened his hold, deepening the kiss even further. All the tension, frustration, and intimacy built between them spilled and overflowed like a beating wave. They were no longer in Braderhelm, no longer in Apollo. For a brief moment in time, they were the sole occupants of the earth, without fear, without thoughts of right or wrong.

Only pure abandon.

When his tongue slipped out, her heart raced into the stratosphere. Khalani stood up on her toes, wanting—no, *needing*—more. Takeshi placed his hand on her lower back, pulling her even closer—their bodies wedged together—as if they could fuse themselves into one person.

Takeshi started to walk her backward, his demanding lips glued to hers. Her back met the rubber bars, and he pulled his mouth away. She was about to protest when his tongue met her neck, right below her ear. Goosebumps raced up and down her spine as the warmth in her stomach burned hotter.

Khalani felt the scrape of Takeshi's teeth as he bit down, not deep enough to scar, but the light sting sent her pulse racing.

His tongue stroked away the pain. A deep moan escaped her lips. The tendons in her neck eased their tension, and her head fell back as Takeshi continued to lick, bite, and suck, the strong muscles of his body molding against hers.

Nothing should feel this good.

Every nerve ending in Khalani's body was alit with desire, and it felt like she would combust in his arms. Simply come apart at the seams. But Takeshi was right there to pull her back together. His tongue lowered to trail the lines of her collarbone, and her nails dug into his biceps as his hand gripped her thigh, securing her body to his.

"Captain Steele, come in," a male voice rang from Takeshi's back pocket. Khalani frowned, lifting her head, but the heated look from Takeshi halted her movement.

"We're ignoring that," Takeshi grunted, kissing his way down her chest.

His lips were gentle and melodic, but he then centered his lips over her breast and sucked her nipple hard as if the fabric wasn't even there. A whine left her throat, and her neck fell back, eyes connecting with the rising angels above her.

His hand cupped the back of her neck, holding her in place as he consumed her. Giving her a taste of heaven.

"Captain Steele."

Takeshi's other hand slid to her backside, and he pulled her even closer as if he wanted to fasten her to him and never let go.

"Captain Steele, do you read us?"

Takeshi growled against the fabric. Looking like he wanted to commit murder, he released his possessive grip, and snatched the walkie from his back pocket. "What?!" he yelled, and the person on the end of the line hesitated.

"S-sorry, sir. We know you like to work out alone at this time, but the Warden is requesting your presence in his office."

She stiffened, giving him a wide-eyed look, and Takeshi muttered a curse.

"Can't it wait?" he demanded.

"I don't think so, Captain. The Warden was very insistent we call you to meet him right now," the guard stammered.

Takeshi's brows were pulled incredibly low as he turned off the walkie. "*Fuck.*" He ran a frustrated hand through his hair. Their chests rose rapidly, reluctant to let go of one another. As if the second they did, prison would steal this moment too, destined to be forgotten and dismembered.

"You have to go?" she asked, her lips swollen.

"We both do," his tone was virulent, like he would rather bar the door shut, preventing anyone from entering. But they both knew that couldn't happen. His position wouldn't let him.

She nodded solemnly, releasing her vicelike grip on his shirt and straightening. The loss of that connection already made her chest feel like it was being punctured with knives, but Khalani didn't dare show it.

"I understand," she admitted, trying to remain impassive when all she wanted was to ask him to stay with her. Maybe nothing changed between them. But her insides were twisted and knotted together. Her lips tingled as if her body was attempting to memorize his touch.

"Khalani." Takeshi gazed deep into her eyes. "It's taking all of my self-control not to barricade this room, make you scream with pleasure, and take away every bit of torment you've endured in this place." His jaw tightened as if he were tempted to do just that.

"But you can't," she finished for him.

"Not now," Takeshi seethed. "And if you don't want this to happen again, I understand and will keep my distance. But if you do, it's not over for me. To be honest…I might never be over you." Deep lines marred his forehead as if his own admission surprised him.

Grappling with the cacophony of emotions his words revealed was like climbing a cliff without a harness. The fear of falling is constant and endless, but you keep going at the hint of freedom when you reach the top. And the fact that she was scared made the decision easier. Because the things worth seeing through require the most effort.

"It's not over for me either," she whispered, relinquishing her truth.

Takeshi released a deep sigh, leaning his forehead against hers.

For a second, a fleeting breath in a human lifetime, time slowed down for them. When his skin rested against hers, there were no titles or restrictions, no qualms or antagonist retorts. They were simply two people surrendering to the iniquities of the heart.

Takeshi's heated breath against her lips made the hairs on her arms rise, desire flooding her once more, but he pulled away. Takeshi shook his head with a chuckle, but his eyes were scorching.

"We better go now, or else my hands and tongue will be all over you, and we won't leave this room until tomorrow."

Oh no…

Not that…

Takeshi devilishly grinned at the expression on her face and grabbed her hand, pulling her to the exit. Khalani's brows rose to her hairline at the sight of their entwined hands. She wanted to say something, but cohesive sentences weren't forming, as if her brain went on vacation the moment Takeshi's lips met hers.

When they left the training room, Takeshi squeezed her hand, reluctantly letting go as they strode through the desolate halls. Silence permeated the air, his face twisting in a promise of violence as they veered closer to her cell.

"I wish I didn't have to leave you in this cell," Takeshi hissed indignantly, his jaw ticking. He was like those sleek jungle cats she had learned about in school. Swift and calculating, waiting to strike and devour.

"I'm used to it now," Khalani said. "The roaches don't bother me, nor do I bother them. Very symbiotic relationship we got going on."

Takeshi grunted and opened the bars. "We'll talk more tomorrow, okay?" His eyes were pensive but tinted with hope, a sentiment rarely seen from Takeshi.

She nodded, afraid that if she spoke, the entirety of her heart would spill over. After this day, no force, not even herself, could abnegate her feelings for Takeshi Steele. And judging by the way he clutched her in his arms and kissed her with wild unrestraint, Takeshi was unable to deny those vehement emotions either.

Takeshi's brows drew low as her bars slammed home, and they stared at each other through the barrier, remnants of their heated thoughts rippling in the space between. His expression hardened as if preparing for war before he whisked out of sight.

Maybe that's what she needed to do. Prepare for war.

If there was anything Khalani had learned in her short, tumultuous life. It was these two rules.

Every action has a consequence. And the truth always comes out. Always.

They would either be free or dead when that happened.

****

Takeshi didn't arrive to conduct the cell block count the next morning. Another guard with cold, grey eyes, twice Takeshi's age, stood in his place.

Khalani's pulse quickened, and deep lines marred her forehead. "Excuse me, sir," she whispered when the guard walked by her cell. "Where is Captain Steele?"

Her head whipped to the side, pain erupting through her cheek as the frigid guard backhanded her across the face.

"Did I say you could talk?" the guard seethed. "Next time, I cut out your pathetic tongue."

Khalani gritted her teeth and nodded in submission, the sharp pain persisting as the guard walked away. She felt Serene's gaze but couldn't look in her direction. She couldn't stare or concentrate on anything as her mind rippled through violent ends.

Did the Warden somehow find out about their kiss?

Was Takeshi released from his job?

Worse?

"Everyone to the pit!" the guards yelled.

Khalani's head lifted in surprise. They were supposed to enter the pit at the end of the day. The other prisoners glanced around in confusion, but everyone started shuffling toward the pit.

A gentle hand grasped her shoulder. "Are you alright, Khalani?" Serene asked, her bright blue eyes filled with concern.

Her lips trembled, and she shook her head, desperately trying to maintain composure. "Why are they taking us to the pit?"

"I don't know." Serene frowned. "But we better go before that guard comes back. I wonder what happened to Steele."

Khalani flinched at the mention of his name. Maybe nothing happened, and the guard was just filling in for Takeshi this morning. It could be a simple explanation. But her heart pounded frantically as every prisoner in Braderhelm made their way to the pit.

Khalani's brows pierced together when they entered the vast cavern. A raised wooden platform, about fifty feet in length and width, was placed in the center of the room over the fighting pit, and the Warden, dressed in his dusty black uniform, stood on the platform.

His piercing stare swept over the room, briefly landing on her, but he quickly glanced away. Every guard appeared to be in the pit, standing at attention around the large circle of prisoners, with black rifles held aggressively in their hands.

Every guard...except for Takeshi.

She stood on her tiptoes, hastily glancing around the room, hoping to be mistaken. A warm hand suddenly clasped hers, and she nearly leaped out of her skin.

"What do you think's going on?" Derek squeezed her hand tighter, his anxious gaze sweeping over the wooden platform.

"I don't know. But I don't like it," she whispered back.

Adan moved beside Serene, the siblings exchanging worried glances. Grumbles of confusion and anxious chatter abated from the prisoners.

"Stop talking!" One of the guards yelled, pointing the barrel of his gun at the crowd.

Everyone instantly quieted, and the Warden smacked his lips together and held out his hands in greeting.

"I'm sure you're all wondering why you're here." The Warden's calculated gaze moved between each prisoner.

"I won't delay the suspense any longer. Despite your sorrowful mistakes, you've all been given a second chance at life in Braderhelm. Some have helped with street cleanups. Others have even had the pleasure of serving the Governor himself in Genesis."

The Warden made eye contact with her, and she swallowed hard, unease seeping through her.

"The Council and Governor have decided to reward your hard work by granting half the prisoners the opportunity of serving at the Genesis Ball, celebrating the 10th Anniversary of the Great Domed City."

Whispers of shock billowed through the crowd, except the four of them. Derek squeezed her hand tighter. Their plan to sneak the walkie onto Genesis and contact Hermes was slowly taking shape.

The Warden continued, "Our Captain, Takeshi Steele, has diligently planned security measures for this event and compiled a list of…deserving prisoners."

Khalani's heart released the weight holding her immobile when Takeshi entered the pit. No one found out about their forbidden kiss. Takeshi was *alive*.

Derek hissed when her nails dug into his palm.

Her chest furiously beat as Takeshi made his way onto the wooden platform and handed the Warden a large sheet of paper. The Warden nodded to him, and Takeshi stepped down, taking his place beside the guards. His face was iron smooth—zero emotion emitting from him—

and his incredibly hard gaze stared straight ahead.

"The following prisoners will serve at the Genesis Ball."

The Warden began reading the list Takeshi handed him, yelling number after number. The austere moment nearly felt like a graduation ceremony, except there were no diplomas or congratulations, and guns were pointed at nearly every prisoner.

The Warden's loud voice permeated the air, but her focus was solely on Takeshi.

She didn't realize how much he meant to her until the dreaded voices in her mind whispered of his permanent demise. It would've been her fault. Death creeping outside her door, waiting to slash and expunge the ones she cared for the most.

And the speed at which Takeshi went from being nothing to consuming everything terrified her.

Khalani flinched when the Warden yelled her number.

The clenching sensation in her stomach didn't cease until Adan, Serene, and Derek's numbers were shortly called after. They were fortunate. The dangerous plan to contact Hermes was still feasible, reachable.

This day may turn out okay.

The Warden slowly folded the sheet, seemingly done. "If I haven't called your number, stand on the platform, and you'll be given your new assignment."

Prisoners around her grumbled but gradually shuffled forward. Fewer than half of the prisoners remained still while the rest—around 200 people—made their way onto the wooden stage, faces marked with confusion and wariness.

The Warden hopped down, and the prisoners on the stage stood shoulder to shoulder, dirty and emaciated. Khalani couldn't help but notice that most of the men and women who remained on the ground were the strongest and youngest of the prisoners.

"Wonderful," the Warden exclaimed, pulling another piece of paper from his pocket. "I shall read you this from the Great Governor Huxley."

The Warden cleared his throat. "To my Braderhelm constituents, while it is unfortunate that you all have committed various crimes for which you should be ashamed, we acknowledge the hard work put into making up for those atrocious deeds. Apollo is a parent to us all, and we must maintain that precious balance of life.

"In light of recent developments that have shifted resources, difficult decisions have been made to help preserve that balance, but we are proud to know that Braderhelm has volunteers ready to sacrifice for the greater good. Indeed, you shall be commended, and people will speak of your heroic deeds for years to come."

The hairs on her arms raised, and she glanced at Takeshi, who whipped his harsh gaze to the Warden, his Adam's apple bobbing as he swallowed.

The atmosphere was tensely still as the Warden nodded to the ten guards directly in front of the platform. In unison, they raised their rifles to the stage. The prisoner's eyes widened, mouths raised in horror, hands inching up in surrender. But it was too late.

As one unit, the ten guards pulled their triggers, and gunfire rang through the pit like an explosion.

BANG. BANG. BANG.

Bullet. After meteoric bullet.

Screams ricocheted faster than ammunition. Bodies dropped, one on top of another like rain she used to dream of as a kid. Like a crimson wave, each prisoner on stage collapsed to the floor, bodies twitching, and howls of agony raged in symphony until the next crash of bullets also killed those cries.

Khalani's mouth hung agape. Her whole body trembled like an earthquake. She couldn't speak. Think. Wales of horror emanated from the prisoners who remained standing, rough hands covering their ears to block the horrible sounds. People collapsed to their knees, shaking their heads in denial, unable to look at the bodies.

A few surviving prisoners fiendishly jumped off the stage, screaming in terror as they attempted to escape the bloodshed, but they were brutally shot down, falling face-first to the ground.

The flash of gunfire finally stopped, and no movement remained on the platform. Mountains of dead prisoners, men and women, lay over one another, their eyes still open in panic and terror. Blood pooled across the wooden stage like a crimson blanket, dripping over the edge.

"What the hell is going on?!" Brock yelled from a couple prisoners beside her and stepped forward as if to jump on the stage.

"Get back, Death-Zoner!" the guards yelled at Brock, brandishing their weapons toward him. The putrid scent of death rippled through the air, and prisoners cried and shook. Some puked bile, but no one dared move another inch.

The Warden cleared his throat, looking uncomfortable, but faced the surviving prisoners. "Unfortunately, this had to happen, but we serve the will of Governor Huxley and the city of Apollo. Afternoon shifts are canceled. Return to your cells immediately. Any hints of rebellion, and I promise, you will suffer the same fate as these prisoners."

His words bounced around the walls like a distant drum but were meaningless. When nightmares coil and weave their way into reality, the importance of life either shrinks to a pebble or pummels you down to one. Her vision narrowed, and Khalani focused on one of the dead prisoners.

The girl was hunched over on top of the pile, blood dripping from her mouth. Her head was half-shaved, her face slightly turned to the light, and Khalani recognized the piercings.

It was Dana.

Shallow breaths came in tiny heaps as if her lungs were pierced with a bullet themselves. Tears billowed over her eyes, and she swayed in her spot, vision blackening as prisoners around her slowly began to move, heartbreaking sobs echoing around the cold room.

Dana's eyes were partially opened. Khalani felt like her stare was carving right through the nerves in her skin as if to scream, isn't this what you wanted?

Khalani shut her eyes, cupping her hands to her face in a vain attempt to cut off her sight forever, but it was useless. Nothing would ever erase that image. The sheer brutality and blatant disregard for human life terrified her far more than if a gun was held to her forehead.

Why was Kalani spared while Dana—one of the strongest female prisoners in Braderhelm—was picked for death? Why was she on the list...

She suddenly froze, and her gaze snapped to Takeshi.

A vein in his neck throbbed, and fists were balled to his side as his murderous stare drilled through the Warden. But he made no move forward. No protest. No argument against the Warden's actions.

Takeshi handed the Warden the list of names, sparing her life and executing the others.

He knew this would happen.

The horror, guilt, and betrayal were like metal shards that landed on her chest and nearly brought Khalani to her knees, crushing every sentiment of hope.

She thought he was different, but in actuality, Takeshi was molded by the same violence the rest of the guards thrived on. In her stupid infatuation with him, she forgot who he really was. Her heart splintered and fractured like broken glass that spider-webbed to every corner.

Lifeless eyes bore into her soul, compounding her shame and sins. Hundreds of voices screamed in her mind that it was her fault, the loudest being her own. She should've killed the Governor when she had a chance. She should've protected her heart more.

It should've been her lying down on that stage.

"You heard the Warden," one of the guards pushed her shoulder with the butt of his gun. "Back to your cell!"

"I'll take this one from here," Takeshi's deep voice cut through. He towered next to the guard, the underlying threat apparent in his menacing gaze.

"Y-yes, Captain," the guard stammered and hastily retreated.

Khalani's chest tightened further, but she refused to look at him. Refused to break down in front of him. He didn't deserve her pain. Her anger. Her tears. He rescinded his right to those the minute he sentenced all those people to their death like animals.

She walked straight for the exit, ignoring him completely. Hard steps followed behind, and she felt Takeshi's rough gaze burrowing a hole in her back.

Fury and despair were separate entities inside her. For every prisoner who died, she wanted to bury a dagger in those responsible. She wanted it to *hurt*. She wanted the bastards to look into her eyes as she took the life out of theirs, knowing that hell was waiting for them right on the other side.

Takeshi's tender eyes flashed through her mind, and she rubbed her chest, clawing it to distract from the tears threatening to fall. She couldn't make sense of it. Why would he let this happen? Why didn't he try and stop it?

He may as well have killed her along with the rest.

Her lips quivered, the barest hint of grief escaping her, but Takeshi heard it. He gripped her elbow and pulled her off into a desolate hallway, not a soul in sight.

"Kanes."

She shook her head minutely, staring at his broad chest, wishing she could sink into the shadows. If she saw the betrayal in his eyes, that would make it real.

"Khalani," the rough whisper escaped him like her name was a forgotten prayer. He brushed his finger against her cheek, capturing an escaped tear, and she leaped back like his caress burned.

"Don't touch me," she hissed.

Takeshi's face twisted in agony. "I had no choice, Khalani."

"Stop. I don't want to hear it." She was losing control.

"If I hadn't written their names down, the Warden would have, and you could've been on that list. I *refuse* to let that happen. I was protecting you," he insisted, searching her eyes for recognition, for light. But all he saw was an empty abyss where futures die.

"I'm not the only person that deserves your protection! We all mean something to someone. That was someone's daughter, mother, husband up there on that stage." Tears flowed freely down her cheeks, the gruesome images refusing to dissipate.

Takeshi's muscles stiffened, bitterness and resignation hovering over his expression.

"Not everyone can be saved."

She ground her teeth and found the strength to stare straight into his blazing eyes, and it was like all the fiery passion in the world was bottled in those charcoal spheres.

"Why did you choose to be a guard?"

"To defend my mother and those who can't protect themselves," he answered without hesitation.

"So, will you help us fight the Governor and escape Braderhelm?"

Takeshi tensed, and his brow deepened further in consternation. The ensuing silence was all the answer she needed.

She narrowed her eyes and got right in his face.

"I think your mother would be rolling in her grave if she knew what became of you."

He visibly flinched at her words, but she kept going.

"The person who stands by is just as guilty as the one who pulls the trigger. The dead don't need your apologies or thoughts and prayers. They need action. But you're still holding on to the hope that the Governor won't allow this to happen again. He will. It might be me on the list next time, and you won't have a say in it. What will your move be then? Until you can look me in the eye and tell me that you're ready to fight back against your superiors, *against Apollo*, I have nothing to say to you," the hostile whisper escaped her.

Takeshi was shocked into silence. He was the strongest and most confident person she'd ever met, but in that moment, he never looked more unsure of himself.

She turned and walked away. Done with the conversation. Done with him. And he let her leave.

When the bars to her cell shuttered close, she roughly deposited herself on the cot and put the thin blanket in her mouth, biting all the way down. And she screamed. Screamed till her voice was hoarse and her teeth chattered. Screamed till her throat could produce no more sound.

She lifted her head to the dirty ceiling as if to ask God for help, but no one answered. She was alone. Abandoned within destruction.

Some things are better left in shatters, lest they use their strength to topple the world.

She carved a poem to remember that night.

It was a lesson.

A warning.

A vow.

Severed Dreams

When hearts no longer cope
And lungs no longer breathe
What happens to their dying hopes?

Are they whisked to the light?
Flown with shadows in the dark?
Or do they stay with those lost in sight?

Cover your eyes and hold onto that fear
These fates will be delivered in the cold
Beware the girl containing severed dreams
Her revenge is known to lacerate the soul

27

My fury extends without the presence of wind or the lash of a whip. It's silent, corrupting, and makes you bleed all the same.

Khalani's hands restlessly tapped against the scratchy black material chafing against her thigh. Her body briefly listed to the side as the Genesis elevator lifted her and the remaining prisoners toward the cavernous ceiling of Apollo. Tension hung in the air like a noose coiled around their necks. Unyielding. Relentless.

She glanced around at the other prisoners, dressed in the same promiscuous dress or black pants and matching button-down shirts, eyes wide with apprehension.

Her muscles coiled tight as the beautiful Genesis meadow came into view. The waterfall roared in the distance, and the sun shone radiantly. Each prisoner, even a handful of guards, held their mouths open in amazement at the glimmering city and expansive dome beyond.

She was no longer spellbound by the sheer beauty. Cruelness can be covered with pastel paint. Khalani saw through it all, straight to the rotten core.

On the grassy surface of Genesis, they waited for all the surviving prisoners, around 100, to be brought up.

Nearly every guard of Braderhelm was assigned to keep a strict eye on the prisoners, armed to the teeth, ready to shoot any who dared escape. Takeshi's intimidating presence stood at the front, danger lurking beneath his vigilant gaze.

Khalani placed herself as far from him as possible. Judging by the way Takeshi's jaw tightened, and his violent eyes sliced her apart, it didn't go unnoticed.

"Let's go." Takeshi's large body strode forward with assured dominance as if a boulder would even move out of his path.

The citizens of Genesis whispered and avoided the prisoners as if they were a black tidal wave ready to wash over them. Twinkling lights were hung across the street lamps and adorned on window fixtures in celebration, the domed sky a mix of pinks and purples as the sun set over the city.

The City Hall stood in the center of Genesis, a grandiose building with hundreds of ivory steps leading to its doors. She craned her neck at the colossal marble statue in front of the building. It depicted a very naked man with a chiseled body that left *nothing* to the imagination. His muscles were sculpted to perfection as he looked out over the city like a valiant conqueror. A golden sign before the jaw-dropping structure read, 'Statue of David.'

Khalani's eyes widened when they entered City Hall. An exquisite ballroom lay before them, radiating wealth and power. The interior was massive, with high, vaulted ceilings—covered in shimmering lights— and walls coated with breeds of rare flowers. Even the floor appeared layered in gold.

Hundreds of ornate tables were set up on both sides of the room, with the center area cleared for dancing. Servants rushed around the ballroom, hurriedly placing giant floral centerpieces, and smoothing out golden tablecloths. The air itself savored of sweet fragrances and ambrosial offerings, unabashedly displaying prestige and authority like they were hors d'oeuvres to relish.

Takeshi turned to address the prisoners, his face granite smooth as his lips pulled into a hard line, seemingly unimpressed with the brazen demonstration of wealth.

"All prisoners will head to the kitchen over there to receive your assignments from Arthur." He called several guards to go with the prisoners, and the rest of the guards stayed for a debrief.

Despite her fury and resentment, she couldn't help but make eye contact with him as she passed, and in that one look, layers of resentment billowed between them. She was the bitter frost and Takeshi the hostile flames, endlessly clashing and forever locked in battle.

Khalani's hands fisted at her sides, trying to lock her emotions toward Takeshi to the deepest abyss of her mind. And throwing away the key.

The kitchen was five times the size of the one in the Governor's mansion. The smell of spices and delicious foods licked the air, and her mouth watered. Audible growls of empty stomachs sounded from the prisoners around her. Arthur, the Governor's butler, entered the room in a flurry, dressed impeccably in a black tuxedo, not one hint of dullness on his shiny, bald head as his coattail trailed behind him.

"Okay, everyone!" He clapped his hands. "There's much to do and not enough time to do it! The guests will arrive in an hour, and we need plates, food, decorations, and drinks finished setting up."

He grabbed a list and called each prisoner's number to a particular station. Khalani waited for her number to be called, but Arthur folded the paper with a flourish.

"No more dawdling. Report to your stations!"

She frowned, approaching him. "Um, excuse me, sir. I didn't receive an assignment."

Arthur scrutinized her. "What's your number?"

"317. The name is Khalani Kanes. I served at the Governor's mansion not too long ago."

"Ah yes...I remember you." Arthur flipped through the paper. "I see it here. The Governor has specifically selected you to be his table's servant for the evening."

She recoiled. "Excuse me?"

"You'll serve the head table, the round one in the center. It's a tremendous honor but comes with huge responsibility. You can help set up drinks for now, but once the guests arrive, you are glued to the Governor's every need. Mess up, and it is likely your death." With that lovely parting gift, Arthur walked away, yelling at someone about burning the bread.

Khalani stood immobile, unable to close her mouth. Why was the universe constantly pulling her closer to the one man she loathed with every facet of her being?

What did he want with her?

Pressure rose like an inflated balloon inside her chest, but she couldn't let those foreboding emotions overcome her focus or let the Governor's presence distract her from the plan. Tonight, they would contact Hermes and find a way out of this hell.

The guards framed the walls like a mural, and she felt their cruel gazes scan over her body, but Takeshi was nowhere to be seen. The next hour passed at lightning speed, and before she knew it, she stood posted at the head table, waiting for the guests to enter.

An orchestra composed of only men entered the room in crisp suits. They sat in the far corner with poise and grace as they readied their instruments. A light, airy tune sounded throughout the ballroom, and her body stiffened.

A myriad of people dressed in luxurious gowns and tuxedos began to flood the ballroom. Butlers escorted guests to their seats as excited chatter and boisterous laughter filled the room. She stood in silence, anxiously awaiting the Governor's arrival. Ten minutes passed, and every seat was filled except for her table.

And then, a raucous sound of applause erupted from the guests like a tidal wave, muting all conversation as Alexander Huxley entered the ballroom.

He wore an immaculate, gold suit, hair slicked back, with an aura that exuded strength and confidence. It was easy to be drawn in by him. Even Khalani couldn't tear her eyes away from his handsome features and perfect smile that would make any sane person fall crazy in love. He was flanked by two beautiful women hanging onto his arms, beaming with awe-struck smiles.

Behind him were three Councilmen, nodding at guests as they passed by, but all attention was fixated solely on the Governor, a mix of adoration, lust, and worship in people's gazes. Her lips screwed together as he ventured closer.

Little did the guests know, he'd recently sentenced over two hundred people to their deaths. The Governor had long completed the breakdown of the people, for he did no wrong in their eyes. If it sounded bad, the denials were abundant. Even if it was true, the Governor had every right to act accordingly, they would say.

Cowards, the lot of them.

Alexander Huxley approached the table slowly, like a viper waiting to strike. "Ah, Miss Kanes. A pleasure to see you again."

She swallowed tightly and forced herself to smile. "Thank you, sir. It's an honor to serve here tonight."

The two beautiful girls, one with platinum blonde hair in a slick, yellow dress with a plunging neckline and the other in an emerald, green ballgown with gorgeous red locks curled by her breasts flanked the Governor.

"Aren't you gonna pull out the chairs for us?" the woman in the yellow dress sneered.

Her teeth clenched, but Khalani held her emotions in check, only giving a terse nod. She begrudgingly pulled out the seats for each one of the guests, but when she went behind the Governor's chair, he waved his hand in dismissal.

"I think I can pull my own chair, Miss Kanes. It's a beautiful night to celebrate, don't you think?"

Alexander's eyes flickered to her as he stood beside the table, giving her a knowing smile. The Governor was far too smart not to be aware she hated Genesis. She was convinced he liked making people answer questions they didn't want to.

He liked that sort of control.

"I'm sure it'll be a night to remember." She gulped as he shifted closer.

The Governor slowly grinned, his piercing blue gaze sending chills down her spine. "Indeed."

A ball of knots twisted in her chest as the Governor gracefully sat down, and conversation resumed in the ballroom. She could hardly breathe with him this close. "I think I'll start with a bottle of red wine for my drink. Ladies, would you like some wine or champagne?" Alexander asked with a disarming grin.

The girl with red hair licked her lips flirtatiously. "I will drink whatever you are having, Great Governor."

"The same for me." The other woman's eyes roved down the Governor as if she was mentally undressing him.

She was going to bash her own head with the bottle of wine before the night was over. Alexander chuckled, turning back to her, but she noticed the smile didn't reach his eyes. They were conspicuously blank.

"Make that two bottles of red wine. And whatever my fellow council members want." He waved his hand dismissively.

Khalani nodded and escaped as quickly as possible. The Governor's energy was like sticky glue fastening to her skin. She let out the breath her lungs were holding as she walked into the kitchen.

"We picked out a spot to send the message," Serene whispered behind her shoulder.

Khalani whirled, glancing around to make sure no one else was listening. "Where?"

"Adan found a storage room to send the signal. After food is served and they are distracted dancing, meet in here, and we'll sneak—"

"You two! Get back out there!" Arthur yelled.

Startled, Khalani kicked into overdrive mode and hastily brought the drinks to the Governor's table, trying to control her erratic breathing. The smell of artificial steak and chicken hung over the air, and she forced herself not to stare at the food as she stood a few feet from the table in silence, hunger pangs clawing her stomach. Khalani turned her head at the sound of commotion.

"You pathetic imbecile! I asked for my steak well-done!" an old woman with garish makeup and a thick, lilac dress shouted at one of the female prisoners.

"Sorry, miss. I will get another," the prisoner apologized, reaching for the food.

"I don't want your dirty hands touching my plate! Send someone else for my food. Someone competent." The wrinkled lady flicked her hand in disgust like the girl was a fly that needed to be swatted.

"*Get it yourself then,*" the girl spat out.

Two guards suddenly appeared behind the prisoner, holding a taser to her neck. The girl started seizing and fell to the ground in a heap. She was still convulsing and making low-moaning sounds as the guards dragged her away. The musicians began to play louder, and the guests switched their attention away from the tortured girl, continuing to laugh and converse with excitement as if nothing happened.

She hated all of them. Every single one.

"The planning for the ball came along nicely, Borris. You should be commended for your diligent work," one of the Councilman said as he stuffed an abnormally large piece of chicken breast in his mouth.

Borris bowed his head in appreciation. "Thank you. We worked hard to reflect the momentous occasion for our beloved city."

"It's hard to imagine life before Genesis." The red-haired lady shivered. "The fact that we used to live underground with those dirty people, the same people who protested the very construction of the great dome. It disgusts me."

The blonde nodded in agreement and waved her empty glass at Khalani. She stepped forward to fill the glass, clutching the bottle with a vice-like grip.

"If those protestors had helped build the dome, it would've at least given their pathetic lives some meaning. They got what was coming to them."

Khalani's thoughts turned murderous, and her hands visibly shook as she visualized taking the bottle and smashing it across the girl's face. She'd enjoy watching the blood spray across her hands and coat the golden floor, enough to paint a mural out of. With all the self-discipline she could muster, she refilled the girl's glass without causing bodily harm. No small feat.

"And what do you think of that assessment, Miss Kanes?" Alexander Huxley held his fingers over his mouth, obscuring his sly smile as he studied her. As if he knew of her violent imaginings and liked it.

"The opinions of a prisoner don't have meaning in Genesis, sir." She placed the wine bottle down with a loud thud.

"How cute of you to think your opinions matter anywhere." The woman in the yellow dress chortled.

"You can shut up now, Francine." The Governor's sharp tone cut Francine down to the size of a pea, and she sunk deep into her chair, her mouth open in shock.

Silence descended on the table.

The Governor's gaze never strayed from hers. "We're on the edge of our seats, waiting," he probed craftily.

Khalani swallowed. A carefully laid trap was placed before her, clearly visible, but she couldn't find a way out.

"She's clearly too stupid to speak," the redhead scoffed.

Khalani narrowed her eyes and dared to let out a single ounce of her emotion. "I think those protesters killed were worth more in their middle fingers than every person on Genesis combined." Venom dripped from her tongue with absolution.

The words said aloud felt better than she imagined they would. She mentally prepared herself for the punishment surely coming her way. Everyone's jaw dropped to the floor, except for Alexander Huxley.

He smirked as if she were his toy of amusement.

"How dare you?!" The woman's face nearly matched the color of her red hair as she turned to the Governor. "I demand that this prisoner be killed for disrespect."

"You *demand?*" the Governor asked in a dangerously low voice.

Fear overtook her expression. "N-No, forgive me. Not demand. I only humbly request. She doesn't deserve to be alive any longer for her appalling disrespect to you," she quickly explained. Francine smartly kept her mouth shut, cowering in her chair.

Alexander Huxley tapped his finger on the table, looking deep in thought. No one dared move, the discomfort thicker than the ground they stood on.

"Deserving." The Governor tasted the word off his tongue. "That's interesting. Let me ask you, Nora, what have you ever done to *deserve* living on the surface?"

Nora drew back at his cool glare and responded in a shaky voice, "My father owns many stores in Apollo. I'm a higher-class citizen."

Alexander Huxley snorted, but no humor lay in his sharp gaze. "Stupid girl. You don't deserve any respect because your kind never appreciated the land you are on and those who work to preserve it. One more word out of you tonight, and I'll send your pathetic father that lovely little tongue gift-wrapped."

Nora's face paled, eyes widening in terror.

"And you." Alexander turned to Khalani. "Your quips may amuse me but don't forget whom you serve, or I'll give you a lesson as a reminder. And I don't think you'd be as fond of my teachings as you are of others." His cryptic, icy-blue eyes narrowed.

Paranoia ruptured inside her at the Governor's choice of words. She trembled along with everyone seated at the table.

"Well then!" the Governor exclaimed, startling the group. "Enough of this serious talk! I believe it's time to get this party started." He stood and walked to the center of the ballroom.

Enthusiastic chatter slowly died down along with the music as a servant handed the Governor a microphone. Khalani backed away from the immobilized table, her skin crawling as his eerie words stayed with her.

"Hello, my beautiful subjects! I must say that you all look radiant tonight, especially you ladies." Multiple women giggled in infatuation, but Nora and Francine silently stared at the ground, expressions shuttered as if they were trapped in a nightmare.

"Many years ago, no one thought we'd be standing on this hallowed ground today. But here we are, on the surface of the earth, safely protected by the Genesis dome. Ten years have passed, and Genesis continues to be a beacon of light and hope for all Apollo." Cheers extended throughout the ballroom, and the Governor held out his hands, quieting the crowd.

"Before the Collapse, our ancestors were strife with greed, selfishness, and ignorance. Unfortunately, those qualities have not fully disappeared in our cities. As expected, of course, change does happen slowly." Alexander chuckled, and the people laughed, not realizing he insulted them.

"Nonetheless, Genesis remains a wondrous city, and this is a momentous day. I shall not bore you any longer. Let us dance tonight, for wise is the man who is grateful for each day, knowing it might be his last."

Khalani frowned, knowing with each thing the Governor said, a purpose lay behind it. A hidden motive that she was unable to explain or foresee.

His chilling gaze shifted to her, and she glanced away, her nerves crawling with apprehension. To everyone else, he was a divine savior, but she saw the truth layered under the alluring surface, down to the treacherous foundation beneath.

Chairs scraped against the floor, and the mindless chatter of the Governor's generosity and hospitality grated against her skin. Guests made their way to the dance floor, partnering up as the orchestra started a waltz. Khalani piled the plates on the now-empty table on top of one another a little too harshly as she hurried to make her way back to the kitchen. It was time to contact Hermes.

Her skin prickled as she felt someone watching her like they trailed fingers down her spine. She turned over her shoulder and did a double-take.

Takeshi Steele stood in the shadows of the wall like a silent assassin, his dark gaze boring into her. The sharp lines of his handsome face stood out, and she fought the urge to march over there and tell him to take his spying ass somewhere else.

His brows began to lower, and Takeshi's face turned scarier with each passing second. She frowned in confusion as his hand inched closer to where she knew his gun was hidden, readying himself.

For what?

"Quite an interesting night so far." The honey-smooth voice slithered behind her shoulder, and her muscles locked and coiled with tension. She slowly turned and came face-to-face with Alexander Huxley. He was significantly taller than her, and up close, he was even more captivating and bewitching. Dangerous.

"Very," she said in a clipped tone.

The corner of his mouth turned up. "You hate me, don't you, Miss Kanes?"

Her hands shook as she abruptly turned her attention to the table, arranging the plates furiously to get the hell out of there. "That's not true, Governor Huxley."

Words severe enough didn't exist in English to encompass her hate for him.

He chuckled. "You can cut the pretenses. I don't have the patience anymore for such frivolities."

"What do you want from me? To slowly torture me before you inevitably kill me?" The burning question slipped as she took a harrowing breath.

"Quite the opposite." He edged closer. "I have lived a long time, Miss Kanes. Do you know what I have constantly searched for?"

"Morality?"

His eyes imperceptibly narrowed as she turned to face him. That appeared to strike a nerve.

"Unpredictability. I long for variability in this monotonous play, and you, Khalani, provide that much more than any of these blubbering, shortsighted, and mindless constituents living on Genesis."

She flinched at the sound of her name echoing across his deceptive lips. "You shouldn't say that about your people."

"They were never my people." A darkness flickered over his expression.

Khalani drew back and froze, like she was trapped in a venomous web. He loomed over her, studying her with a predator's unwavering attention. "There are few things in common between us, Khalani. Fewer than you realize. But our hatred for this city is an analogous thread that connects us."

She didn't want to have anything in common with him.

"You're... you're wrong."

He grinned. "Ah, there it is. Denial. A consistent hallmark of emotion. Let me ask, what has Apollo done for you other than reap destruction in your life?"

Blood rushed to her face, and the hatred she bottled close began to pour out. "Destruction by *your* hand. Under your rule, my parents died, and I was sentenced to Braderhelm Prison...you took everything away from me."

"Death is but a cycle in life." Alexander flicked his hand. "You are born just to die, and that's the human curse. But it was not I that took your life or your parents. It was the people that came before you. If destruction is in the equation, peace can never be the outcome. And the people who lived on the surface fooled themselves into believing otherwise, and they selfishly destroyed their lives and every future generation. Your ancestors destroyed your life, not me. I am but a catalyst to bring about necessary change."

"And what change is that?"

His eyes flickered with antipathy as he bent to whisper in her ear, "Taking destruction out of the equation."

The harsh lines on her forehead deepened as the Governor stepped away, the perfect mask back in place. "You should get back to your duties, Miss Kanes."

She numbly nodded, grabbing the plates and walking as fast as possible toward the kitchen. She felt Takeshi's gaze on her the whole time but kept going straight. That was all she could do.

Her mind raced. Everything was somehow connected. The crop failures, Genesis, the killings, the Governor, she just didn't know how. The truth was beyond her grasp.

The kitchen was crowded with prisoners. She craned her head and finally spotted Serene, Derek, and Adan in the back corner.

"Hey." Khalani practically ran at them.

"Where the hell have you been?" Serene asked.

Adan shook his head. "Explanations later. We don't have much time."

They nodded and left out a side door in the kitchen. They moved down a dimly lit hallway, away from the ballroom, and Adan opened an inconspicuous wooden door.

"Hurry, get in."

They shuffled in, and Derek closed the door, putting them in complete darkness. Someone switched on a light, and they were in a tiny room where their heads almost touched the ceiling, and a large trashcan filled most of the space.

"The janitor's closet?" Serene sniffed her nose in disgust.

"Oh, I'm sorry, were you preferring the palace?"

"This works! Let's hurry." Khalani brushed a shaking hand through her hair.

Adan pulled out the walkie from his back pocket. He lifted the antenna and breathed heavily.

"Here we go." He pushed a button, and a light on the walkie turned green, a weird buzzing noise reverberating from the machine.

Khalani swallowed excessively and shifted back and forth in the confined space. They waited.

Two minutes.

Five minutes.

"What's taking so long?" Derek asked.

"I told you. It will take some time for the signal to reach Hermes. It's a long distance. It should be reaching them any minute, though." Adan anxiously gripped the walkie, his nerves showing through.

All of a sudden, someone knocked on the door.

They all froze in utter fear, and Khalani held a finger to her lips in silence and turned off the lamp, pitching them into darkness.

Don't open the door.

Don't open the door.

Don't open the door.

The knob slowly started to turn, and her insides twisted in panic, and they silently lowered to the ground, praying they wouldn't be noticed in the dark. The door creaked open, and a tall figure entered the room, their face hidden.

The stranger pulled down on the bulb, and light flooded the room, revealing Takeshi.

"What are you doing here?" she forcefully whispered, standing up.

He glared at the four of them, shutting the door as his giant frame filled the tight space. "I should be asking you the same question." He folded his arms over his chest, waiting for an explanation.

She racked her brain for a believable lie, but nothing could explain why they were hidden in a closet, holding a walkie-talkie with blatant fear in their eyes. The only option left was the truth.

"Apollo's in trouble, Takeshi. We're trying to save it."

"Is that so? You have approximately two seconds to explain." Takeshi glared down at her with fury, and she found the courage to continue under his disarming gaze.

"Derek used to work at the R&R Labs. The crops are dying. That's why they killed those prisoners. And it's going to keep happening until we're all dead. We're contacting Hermes for help."

The lines on his forehead deepened as he processed her words. "That can't be true. They wouldn't let the food supply be destroyed."

"They've been lying to you. I need you to trust me."

"What you're saying is impossible, Kanes. You all need to go back before someone notices your missing."

"No, Takeshi!" A weight like lead dropped in her stomach. "You have to listen to me!"

Takeshi opened his mouth to argue.

And then, a voice came through the walkie.

28

Breathe in obedience. Exhale dissent.

"Come in, Brock?"

They whirled in shock at the mysterious voice echoing from the device.

"Yes, hello?! We are reaching you from Apollo." Adan's eyes danced with excitement as he gripped the walkie-talkie.

The ensuing long pause made her muscles tighten.

"What comes alive in the shadow of the night?" the cryptic man asked.

Adan reeled back in confusion. "What?"

"What comes alive in the shadow of the night?" the masculine voice hitched lower.

"I...I don't know what you mean."

"You're not with Brock. I'm ending the line."

"No, no!" She snatched the walkie out of Adan's hands. "This is Khalani Kanes from Apollo. We need your help. The crops in Apollo are dying, and our leaders aren't doing anything to stop it. They've already started killing people. We need the city of Hermes to help us, or we're going to die," she rasped, holding the walkie close to her mouth.

A lengthy silence crept through the narrow space like a knife waiting to strike. Even Takeshi leaned forward, waiting for an answer.

"If you're not part of their government, how did you get this secure line from Brock?"

"We are being held as prisoners in Apollo, along with Brock. They confiscated all his belongings, but we managed to steal his walkie back. I'm telling you the truth. Please...you need to help us," she begged.

The mysterious man didn't respond, and her fingers shook, waiting for a glimpse...the barest thread of hope that not everything they suffered through was in vain.

"I'm sorry. Hermes can't help you," the unknown voice stated.

"Did you not hear what I just said?"

"I heard you perfectly. But if what you say is true, Hermes will not send help. Not when the same thing is happening over here."

Derek exchanged a wide-eyed glance with her. "What did you say?"

"The killing is not only in your city. Our governmental regime in Hermes has started placing our homeless and outcasts in work camps. And once you go in, there's no coming out. So, if you're looking for Hermes to send Apollo resources or manpower, you're wasting your breath."

Adan turned away in disgust, and Khalani's shoulders hunched over as if a stone mass piled on top of her. They were too late. They would lose everything.

Everything.

"But *you* might still make it," the man's voice crept through the line like oxygen.

She clutched the device tighter. "What do you mean?"

"There's a resistance group within Hermes who may be able to help you. The Death-Zoner, Brock, was one of them, and he delivered needed supplies from Apollo. If you want to survive, you must travel to Hermes."

The hard lines of Takeshi's body went rigid next to her, his energy becoming more intoxicating by the second, filling up the entire room with the weight of his presence, like a silent predator waiting to pounce. And by the looks of it, on her.

"We can't escape," she breathed into the walkie. "The radiation suits are locked away, and we wouldn't know where to go."

"If you can escape, Brock is your only way of survival. He can guide you to us, but you need to leave soon while the weather is still good. Contact me when you reach the Gateway Arch, and I will sneak you into Hermes. This is your only chance, so take it or die. Goodbye." The line shut off.

They stood in complete and utter silence, staring at each other incredulously. "Shit," someone whispered.

"Do you believe him?" Khalani asked.

Adan frowned in disbelief. "He didn't sound like he was lying."

"What are the chances of Apollo and Hermes experiencing the same crop failure?"

"Astronomically low," Derek muttered. Khalani raked her hand down her face. The prospect of them traveling to Hermes, on the surface? The sheer idea was insane.

"Give me the walkie," Takeshi demanded, holding out his hand.

She hesitated, unable to read his cool expression. Even in the face of insurmountable news, Takeshi always kept his composure, the most challenging book to read. His scorching eyes were unyielding, and she tepidly handed him the walkie.

"Are you going to report us?" she asked as he placed the device in his back pocket, fear sliding through her veins like icy cold water.

A muscle in his jaw twitched.

"Listen to me carefully. You don't mention this to anyone, understand?" He leveled each of them with a harsh glare and waited until they nodded. "There is no making plans or plotting escape until I find out more information. *Is that understood, Kanes?*"

Her lips drew together as Takeshi centered his fierce gaze on her.

He was the last person she wanted to take orders from, but they had no other choice now.

"Fine."

"Good. Now, walk out this door and don't look back," his deep voice reverberated in the enclosed space with such authority, they quickly obeyed and rushed out of the tight closet.

Takeshi's body heat crowded her space, and the memory of his tongue tracing the skin beneath her neck made her ungraciously slide out the door as fast as she could.

She smoothed her dress, trying to calm her erratic breathing, and hastily hurried back to the kitchen, afraid of her own actions if she looked back.

****

In Braderhelm, she continued to work on autopilot, there physically but gone mentally. Her mind zeroed in on what the mysterious man suggested. Escape. Leaving Apollo behind and fleeing to Hermes for refuge, traveling the deadly surface of the earth.

Her chest tightened further, not because the thought frightened her but because the idea coiled inside her heart like a wave of fresh air after drowning in coarse gravel.

Every sign pointed in the direction away from Apollo, and the subtle whisperings of her mind that begged Khalani to find the truth no longer spoke faintly. Answers lay behind the horizon, and after ceding control her entire life, she would no longer sit back and let someone else decide her ending.

"Look," Serene whispered. "There's Brock."

Khalani, Serene, Derek, and Adan hovered in the far corner of the pit. It took little convincing for them to agree that trusting or waiting for Captain Steele wasn't viable. They needed to escape Braderhelm. For themselves. For each other. Even if it meant risking death.

Luck and grace were never staples in Khalani's life. In fact, she always thought that God had it out for her. But looking at the people surrounding her, ready to sacrifice what was left of their lives for one

272

another, she'd never felt more fortunate. Khalani turned and narrowed her eyes. Brock was by himself, at the other end of the pit.

Alone.

"Let's go."

The muscles in Brock's back constricted as he did push-ups on the ground. Sweat gleamed down his bare spine. He glared at the ground with such intensity that she hesitated to interrupt him, remembering the swift death he delivered in the pit.

"Sorry to interrupt, Brock." Her voice shook. "Can we talk to you for a few minutes?"

"No," Brock growled, continuing to lower himself to the ground.

She glanced at the others warily, and Serene not-so-subtly pushed her forward. "It's really important, and I think you'll want to hear this."

"Get beat, kid."

Khalani glared at him and got down on her haunches. "You can't be more than a few years older than me, so don't call me kid. We made contact with one of your resistance members in Hermes," she whispered the last part.

Brock stopped mid-push-up and bounded to his feet. His forehead pinched together, and Brock stepped forward aggressively, the intensity in his grey eyes unsettling her. "You contacted Hermes? How?"

Brock listened intently as she explained what happened in Genesis, occasionally glancing around to see if anyone stepped close enough to overhear them. His jaw clenched when she finished, and he breathed sharply.

"I know what you're going to ask me, and the answer is no. I can't get you to Hermes." He crossed his arms over his chest.

"What do you mean?" Adan leaned in closer. "You can't get us the radiation suits?"

Brock let out a low laugh. "You have no idea what you're getting yourself into. The radiation suits aren't a problem because they aren't even a factor."

She drew back in confusion. "What the hell is that supposed to mean?"

"This information would kill you. But according to you, we'll already be dead in a year anyway." His expression hardened. "On my last supply drop heading back to Apollo, I was attacked."

"By who? Other Death-Zoners?" Derek asked.

"No. I don't know who they were, probably citizens from Hermes who managed to escape to the surface. They followed me for a few days. You can imagine my surprise when they weren't wearing radiation suits and showed no signs of radiation poisoning." Brock glared beyond them in memory.

"Are you sure? That can't be possible." Her mouth hung open.

Brock scoffed at her. "I'm sure, sweetheart. I managed to shoot them before they could overcome me. I returned to Apollo and requested a private meeting with the Governor, which he granted. I informed him of everything I saw, and the next hour, I was thrown in Braderhelm without a trial. The Governor spared my life because he didn't want to draw attention to my death, and he knew my words would be meaningless down here."

Khalani stared at the ground in shock. Everything Winnie had been telling her was true.

What if Timothy Talbot was real too?

"Are you telling us that the surface is survivable?" Derek breathed out in disbelief.

"Just now putting two and two together?" Brock scoffed.

"But that doesn't make sense. If that's true, why are we still stuck underground?"

He tilted his head. "That's the million-dollar question, isn't it?"

The tension grew thicker with the weight of his implications. Nearly suffocating the air around her. Were they forced to live underground, never to walk the earth's surface, all because of a lie? She listed to the side, feeling like she might throw up.

"But if the surface is no longer polluted with radiation, why won't you help us?" Adan interrupted.

"Have you looked around lately? They've doubled up on security. There's a secret entrance to the surface, not far from Braderhelm. It is one the Death-Zoner's use, but we'd be shot long before we made it close by. For an escape plan to even be feasible, we'd need a guard to help, and in case you haven't noticed, those are in short supply." Brock rolled his eyes. "It's over. Just accept it as I have."

Khalani wrung her hands together. The answer to their problem was on the tip of her tongue, but she was afraid to say it. Terrified of the implications.

"If we find a guard on our side, would you help us then?"

The others turned to her in surprise, and Brock raised an eyebrow. "Who?"

"That's not what I asked. Let me worry about who." Her eyes blazed with determination. "I know you hate Apollo just as much as we do. You can either stay here and rot or fight with us and escape."

"No man has ever escaped Braderhelm." Brock crossed his arms. "You stand no chance of surviving."

"Is that so?" She inched closer, and Brock's feverish eyes narrowed. "Then a woman must not have tried yet."

Brock studied her for a few moments and let out a crack of a smile. "You talk a big game when I could kill you where you stand. But I'll give you the chance to defy death. Or attempt to, rather. I will help only *if* you manage to get a guard to aid our escape. If not, you're on your own. Don't talk to me again until you have an update." Brock walked away.

Serene stared after him with her mouth agape and turned to Khalani incredulously. "You're not going to say what I think you are about to say."

"It needs to be Takeshi," she said in a clipped voice, hating the words escaping her mouth.

They argued with her.

"He is the Captain. That is suicide."

"I know he didn't turn us in, but he helped kill all those prisoners."

She held her hands up. "Trust me, I know what you guys are thinking. But he's literally the only one whom we could even ask. If he says no, we will just have to do the plan without Brock. We have to try."

They eventually conceded, and Khalani took a deep breath.

She readied herself, preparing to talk to the one person who unraveled her the most. The one who restarted her heart only to break it with his own hands.

It was time to face Takeshi.

29

Carve open my mind and witness a sea of you pouring out.

She cracked her fingers individually in the dark, hollow slabs of her cell, again. Her joints' echoing snaps and pops filtered through the space like a distorted melody of impending doom. The chalked lines on the stone wall held her attention.

Khalani wished she could have met the prisoner who once lived in this cell, who had the energy to mark their days in Braderhelm Prison, 497. She counted many times.

Did they die with their dreams stuck inside?

She didn't dare number how many hopes, beliefs, and wishes perished underground. How sad a fate, to be born out of pain, only to have the cycle of suffering continue. As if humans pass down the misery embedded from their mothers.

Hard footsteps sounded outside Khalani's cell.

Her back stiffened. Stress lines bracketed the corner of her mouth as she stood and peeked out her cell. Khalani's hands tightened around the cold bars as Takeshi came into view.

The sharp, angular lines of his cheekbones stood out as the soft locks of Takeshi's black, disheveled hair swept over his face. Not in a way that appeared messy or sloppy, but in a way that was effortless and captivating, as if his harsh beauty didn't require attention but manifested it anyway.

His long legs ate up the walkway as he strode through the halls, finishing the cell count for the night. Dressed in all black with that unrelenting fire in his gaze, he looked like hell's liberator, prepared to protect and annihilate.

"Takeshi," Khalani whispered when he passed her cell.

He immediately froze. The lines on his forehead deepened as he slowly turned to her. The guarded expression in his sharp gaze made her pulse beat faster. Memories of the kiss they shared speared her mind.

Try as she might, there was no forgetting that.

The way his lips claimed hers. The way his fingers grazed over her body with tenderness, but his inky eyes stared into her own with a promise—a warning—no longer simply the quiet, vigilant force. When Takeshi surrendered to his desires, he wouldn't just take.

He'd possess and linger over every square inch, until no doubt remained of who you belonged to.

And she'd been prepared to yield everything to him, all her doubts and fears wrapped in a jar, but he took that glass and smashed it against the wall. And judging by the intensity in his cool glare, the vulnerable parts of him scattered across the floors of this prison too.

"What?"

"Can I talk to you for a second?" Her hands grew clammy.

He stepped closer, wariness apparent in the rigid set of his frame.

"Do you mind coming in here? No one else listening," she mouthed those last words.

He hesitated but pulled out the touchpad. After a moment, the bars slid open, and he walked through. Takeshi's large frame occupied her entire cell, completely dominating the space. He crossed his arms over his chest, muscles taut with caution.

She tucked a piece of hair behind her ear as his jet-black eyes pierced hers, nerves tingling through her skin. But she didn't have time to contemplate the consequences if Takeshi said no to her request or worse.

Khalani took a steadying breath, straightening her spine and staring back at him with a fierceness that made his eyes narrow.

"We've decided to leave Apollo."

Takeshi didn't react, but a static tension was present in the air, a harrowing pressure that made her suck air in a little faster as she continued,

"We talked to Brock. They've been lying to us, Takeshi. About the radiation on the surface. The crops. Everything. But we have a plan to escape to Hermes. There is a secret entrance to the surface, not far from Braderhelm. But for us to escape, we need your help...*I* need your help, Takeshi," Khalani whispered, her heart fracturing a little at the distance in his eyes.

His gaze hardened. "You don't listen to me at all, Kanes. What do you need my help for?"

"You're the Captain. You know every guard rotation and hallway in Braderhelm. You're our best chance of survival because if we stay here, we die. And I have to believe that a small part of you still cares enough to stop that from happening."

Takeshi's forehead creased as he pondered her words. "What makes you think I won't tell the Warden about your plan? I had a hand in killing those prisoners. You already see me as a cold-blooded murderer," the ire in his tone thickened with each word, and her lips parted at the harsh bitterness in his expression, trapping her to the spot.

"Maybe I do. Nothing will excuse what happened to those prisoners, but a part of me hopes that the person who tried to save his mother, who saved me, is still there. That despite the bad choices you've made, you are still capable of doing something good. And I know it's all over now, but..." Khalani hesitated, a knot lodging itself in her chest. "But I don't want to lose another person in my life who once cared about me."

The pinch between Takeshi's brows grew tighter, and a strange flicker appeared in the black depths of his eyes. Out of all the threats and adversaries he faced, he stared down at her like she was the most dangerous.

"You've already forgotten one of the first lessons I taught you." Takeshi slowly inched forward.

Her brows drew low. "And what's that?"

"Not wasting your time hoping for things down here."

"Is that your answer then?" Her glare matched the intensity of his own.

"Depends."

"On. What?"

"Escaping Braderhelm won't be easy, even with my help. And that will seem like a cakewalk compared to traveling the surface. Dying is the most likely outcome, quicker so if Brock is lying about the radiation," Takeshi's biting tone reverberated along the stone walls.

"He's not."

"Even so, the risk is there." His head lowered. "Are you prepared to face those dangers and come out alive? Or are you merely searching for a better way to die?" Takeshi was so close she could almost taste the warm, earthy scent coming off his skin.

Khalani's eyes narrowed as the question sliced through, taking her back to that fateful afternoon in the pit all those months ago, the first time Takeshi asked if she wanted to die.

He saw the truth, even then. Surrendering to the unfairness of life by escaping in death.

Thoughts as dark and cruel as the number on her wrist.

But she resisted. She *remained.* And Khalani finally realized there are things worth bleeding for.

"You're right, Takeshi. I didn't listen to you. I should've. Not hoping would've made my life a hell of a lot easier and less fucking disappointing. But in this one thing, I finally beat you."

Khalani lifted her head, meeting his sharp gaze. "I may not be able to knock you out or shut off my emotions, but if you ask me, it takes greater strength to maintain hope when everything is crumbling around you. I haven't given up and don't intend to start now. So, what will it be? Will you help us, or am I wasting my breath?"

His expression shifted in appraisal. "And if I said no, what then?"

"I'll find another way to escape. And not even you can stop me." She lifted her chin, daring him to contradict her.

The corner of Takeshi's lip imperceptibly lifted, and a hint of depravity flashed in his hooded eyes. "I'm intrigued enough to nearly let you try." The silence lengthened. "Fortunately for you, it won't be necessary. I'll help."

She let out a deep breath, cold relief spreading despite the uncertainty in trusting Takeshi. "Tha—"

"Don't." His intense voice whipped against her. "I don't want to hear it from you. Not when you're wrong."

"About what?"

"For your own survival, Kanes, don't make the mistake of searching for the 'good' in me. You'll only end up disappointed."

He turned away as her face transformed into disbelief.

"Then why'd you change your mind?" she asked, unable to keep her mouth shut.

Takeshi stopped, the large muscles of his back facing her.

"I have my reasons. Maybe someday I'll tell you. Maybe I won't."

He walked away without a backward glance.

A torrent of emotions flooded her body, bitter scents and sharp spices coating the roof of her mouth.

"Am I just another game to you?" the pained question loosened from her tongue before she could snatch it back.

Takeshi paused, and Khalani held still, not wanting to hear the answer but dying to, all at the same time.

"Everyone's a player, Kanes. I've punished. I've killed. But I never once played with your life." Their eyes locked. "Can you say the same?"

She pursed her lips in response.

"What I thought." He stared brazenly. "I'll get you to the surface.

Alive. Any changes to that summation, and you won't like my reaction."

"I've already seen you angry at me."

"No, you haven't. You wouldn't dare to be in this cell alone with me if you had."

Takeshi's lethal tone and the way his eyes glinted made her muscles coil on instinct. Takeshi inclined his head and opened the bars, leaving her alone with a soft bang of closure.

She stared at the spot he left, their conversation replaying in her mind. Over and over. If their plan worked, she wouldn't be able to rest or relax, not with Takeshi around. He might turn into an even bigger threat in the future. She continuously rubbed her hands along her legs as an unfamiliar and terrifying emotion seeped through.

Would she be able to take the necessary actions and kill Takeshi if it ever came to that?

Khalani cursed in the confines of her cell.

Yes. Yes, she would. She would have no other choice. Because the minute you start to care for the enemy more than yourself, you've already lost.

30

Alone, I fall. Together, we rise.

Since the mass execution of prisoners, a wave of silent, solemn anger hung in the air. The festering emotions stroked against her skin, making her palms itch as she walked through the pit. Khalani's eyes danced to the spot of the bloodshed, and a disturbing chill set in her bones as if the souls of the dead lingered. Watching.

Judging the dark few who remained.

Everyone was on edge, even the guards, whose numbers had increased over the past week. They were preparing. For an uprising, maybe...or something worse. The notion didn't sit well with her, and her footsteps increased as she walked toward Brock in the far corner with Serene, Derek, and Adan in tow. They weren't happy or keen about Takeshi aiding their escape, but they agreed to move forward with the plan simply because they had no other option.

Brock stood solitary with his back leaned against the stone wall and a foot kicked back, observing the prisoners with a sharp eye as he lazily drew on a cigarette.

Who gave this man a cigarette?

"Back so soon? Come to beg after you realized no guard will help you?" Brock blew out a puff of smoke as they approached.

"No, we actually came to tell you we found one." She crossed her arms over her chest.

Brock cocked his head in confusion and threw the cigarette on the ground, stomping on it. "Who?"

"That would be me."

Khalani froze as the familiar, low rumble sounded behind her, sending a tingle of nerves down her spine.

Brock's eyebrows nearly hit his hairline as Takeshi advanced to their group, huddled in the corner. His eyes found hers, and their depth made her pulse race, like black blades slowly splitting her open. Her gaze flittered down his athletic frame to the handgun strapped to his hip, one he usually didn't wear.

Serene, Derek, and Adan stiffened as if a blanket of steel was injected into their spine. He stood close, close enough for their fingers to touch, and Khalani didn't breathe until she felt Takeshi's piercing stare lift from her. The force of his presence fastened to her like glue, vicious and unwavering, placing every inch of her body on alert.

Brock gave a low whistle as he sized Takeshi up, turning to Khalani. "You managed to get the Captain on our side? Didn't know sexual favors went that far."

"I suggest not another word," Takeshi's voice deepened. "You're needed alive for this plan to work." A promise of violence hung in his obsidian eyes, like he was seconds away from slicing Brock apart. Something told her he'd enjoy it.

"Hold on. Khalani may trust you to help, but I'm not so sure I do. What's in it for you?" Serene regarded Takeshi with a serpentine glare.

"I don't expect you to trust me. I actually advise against it." Takeshi's poignant gaze slipped to her. "But you wouldn't be standing here if I wanted you dead. And seeing as I'm you're only shot of making it out alive, that will have to be good enough for you."

The antipathy in the air weighed like chains of metal hung over their shoulders.

Serene's jaw set with boiling resentment, but she stiffly nodded.

"What's the plan?" Derek's voice trembled.

Takeshi gave him an assessing look. "In two days, a few hours before the first shift, I will disable the cameras and alarms. That's the easy part. The tunnels of Braderhelm are extremely complex, designed so that any who tried to escape would never find their way out."

"But you know the way, I gather." Serene's brows pinched together, the enmity and distrust in her expression inherent.

"Naturally," he replied in a clipped tone. "We have a measure to deploy gas in certain prisoner cells that will render them unconscious for transport. I'll turn on the vents to knock out the other prisoners in their cells. We don't want any additional noise. After manually unlocking your cells, I'll guide you to the Braderhelm Gates."

"What about the rest of the guards?"

"Most guards are asleep then, and few will be on duty. By knowing their rotations, sneaking past shouldn't be difficult. But when we get to the Braderhelm gate, two guards will be stationed there. They have a separate alarm that will bring hundreds of guards on us within minutes if activated."

They visibly gulped as Takeshi continued, "I can't physically engage them without triggering the alarm. The risk is too high. One of you will need to help me take them out. I presume you know how to use a gun and not miss." Takeshi turned to Brock, the tension in the air palpable.

"You'd be correct." The corner of Brock's lip lifted, and the hairs on her arms rose.

Takeshi nodded. "Good. Both our guns will have suppressors on to minimize the sound. We need to take them out at the same time. Once the guards are dead, I'll open the gates, and we can steal one of the transports to escape. How far is this secret entrance to the surface?"

"Not far. Less than a kilometer. It will only take a few minutes to get there by transport. A hidden elevator in the tunnel will take us up to the surface."

Takeshi was silent for a moment, studying Brock with a sharp eye. "So be it. I'll grab us supplies for the two-week journey to Hermes. I expect you all to be ready." He spoke with such calm authority and steady confidence that she was starting to believe this might work.

Brock crossed his arms, puffing his chest out. "Most of this plan relies on you, *Captain*. Hope you're ready, or we'll end up being another number in the long line of people you've killed."

A muscle ticked in Takeshi's jaw. "And you're certain the radiation suits aren't necessary?"

"Don't question me. I'm sure."

"I hope so." Sheer terror and malice leeched from Takeshi as he licked his lips. "I'll rip your intestines out and feed them to you if you're lying."

"I'd like to see you try," Brock hissed, his giant fists tightening by his side.

The amount of testosterone in the air was stifling. Both men glared at each other with a blistering fury that was sure to erupt into a full-fledged fight at any moment. And her money was on Takeshi.

"If you both are done comparing dick sizes, we can get back to the plan in hand." Khalani's lips thinned.

Takeshi kept his forceful gaze solely on Brock, the muscles in his body incredibly still, like the quiet calm before a trigger is pulled. It wasn't until she said his name that it snapped Takeshi out of this incensed fixation. He slowly inched from the Death-Zoner, turning to her with a storm brewing in his eyes that had her brows pinch together.

What was up with him?

He turned to the others, barely acknowledging her. "There'll be an inspection in three days, and the guards will be on stricter watch then. That's why we do this in two days or never. All five of you must be prepared."

"Six," Khalani interrupted.

Takeshi whipped his head to her. "What do you mean six?"

"I'm asking Winnifred to come with us," she replied in a tone that brokered no room for argument. She refused to leave Winnie behind.

"The crazy librarian?" Brock scowled.

"Why?" Takeshi seethed.

"I know you won't understand, but she is like family to me and won't be a burden. Winnie is smart. She *wants* to leave," Khalani insisted.

Brock shook his head. "The woman is old. She'll only slow us down."

Her expression hardened. "This isn't up for debate."

"Fine. But no more," Takeshi growled and turned his head toward a couple of guards walking in their direction. "No more talk of this. Be ready in two days."

Takeshi marched toward the guards and spoke with them, heading in the opposite direction of their group.

"This is really happening," Serene whispered as if only now grasping the implications of their daring plan.

In a few days, they'd either be standing on the earth's surface, breathing the free air, or be buried beneath it. No second chances.

Only potential beginnings and assured endings.

****

A frenzied anticipation built inside as she hastily ran up the stairs to the library. She hadn't spoken to Winnie since their last fight, and the knot in her chest grew with each step. She didn't bother knocking and let herself into the library.

The characteristic sound of music echoed through the room, and she inhaled deeply. The warm aroma of old books and the slight hint of rosy perfume invaded her senses, and a small smile curved her lips, like she could finally breathe again.

Khalani slowly walked past bookcases as a delicate song whispered through the air, hauntingly beautiful. She rounded the corner, and Winnie's eyes were closed, swaying as she slowly sang. Khalani took a step forward, and the wood creaked under her feet.

Winnie's eyes snapped open, and she turned to her in shock.

"What are you doing here?" Winnie's mouth held open as she quickly stood and turned off the music. The wary look in her eyes speared Khalani's heart.

"Hey." She fiddled with her hands. "It's good to see you. It's been a while."

Winnie nodded with overwhelming loneliness in her gaze.

"It has."

The uncomfortable silence grew in strength like a monster widening its jaw before snapping.

She bit her lip, the pit in her stomach expanding.

"Winnie, I came to tell you that I'm sorry. I am so, so sorry. You were right. About Apollo, the surface, the Governor. Everything. And now I'm starting to believe that Timothy Talbot might be right too."

Winnie stood silent, her expression unchanged. Winnie, the most vivacious and vibrant person she'd ever met, looked…numb. Her eyes were sunken, and Winnie's body appeared frailer since Khalani last saw her. Was she not eating?

"Winnie was waiting a long time for you to say that. But you were right. There is nothing we can do about it. We will never be able to leave." Winnie bowed her head.

"That's not true, Winnie! We have a plan. We're escaping tomorrow morning. Brock knows a secret entrance to the surface, and Captain Steele is going to help us. You are coming too."

"A plan?" she asked, lifting her head.

"Yes." Khalani smiled. "We're gonna finally make it out of here."

The tiniest flicker of hope presented in Winnie's eyes but was quickly snuffed out. She shook her head, glancing down at her palms. "There's no plan for Winnie, Khalani. Winnie is getting old. She would be a burden."

Khalani surged forward and grabbed her shoulders. "Don't you say that. Don't even think that because you could never be a burden! I have learned more through my time with you about love, art, and passion than I have my entire life. Those things are worth fighting for, just like Timothy said! You can't give up now. I love you too much to let you give up."

Tears started to form in Winnie's eyes as she glanced up with incredible warmth. "Winnie forgot what it was like to hear someone say they love her."

Nothing could have prevented Khalani from wrapping her arms around Winnie. "You know I do. I love you, Winnie."

Prison beat her body to a pulp, but her many scars only began to mend when she met Winnie. Not because she forgot the past. Healing's never that easy.

Freedom lies in forgiveness.

The little girl who lay on the floor all those years ago needed to know that it wasn't her fault. It wasn't her parent's fault for leaving. And it wasn't her fault for putting her broken pieces back together the only way she knew how.

"Winnie could never replace your mother, Khalani." Winnie cupped her face, a soft glimmer in her eyes. "But her love for you knows no bounds, just like a mother's. If Sarah had lived to be your age, Winnie would've wanted her to be just like you."

Khalani's chin trembled as the aching contents of her heart threatened to spill over. "That's why we're leaving this place, Winnie. Together. Captain Steele will get you tomorrow morning, and we'll finally be free."

"Winnie can't bring the typewriter with her, can she?"

Khalani's heart clenched. "No. But when everything is better, we'll return for your story and complete it."

"Promise?" she asked.

"I promise." They held each other for as long as they could, tears billowing for all the things they had lost and gained in Braderhelm.

No sleep would be had for Khalani that night as she wrestled in bed. She gave up after a couple hours and sat on the floor, relentless energy prickling inside, untethered and expanding with severity.

Her chest rose with a deep breath as she wrote her last poem in Braderhelm.

Songs of Surrender

These walls built to contain, whisper in my ear
The Songs of Surrender beckon me closer
Those barriers represent eternal fear
While the music tells me to be my own composer

Letting go is the hardest thing
Holding on to time as if it equates to meaning
But now I know the truth and raise my own wings
Barricades may block the physical, but they can't contain the
feelings

The sweetest lies will drown out the soul
While doubts beckon you to remain
Darling, do not wait for those bells to toll
I beg of you to rise and break the chains.

31

Don't take tomorrow with a tender hand.
Seize it with all your passion and might.

Khalani paced the confines of her chilly cell, tapping her palm incessantly against her thigh. Her fingernails were bitten down to a jagged file as she waited in the hallowed dark for hours. The prison lights would power on soon.

Where were Takeshi and the others?

Barely audible coughing sounded from the cell to her right, and Khalani's ears pricked up at the slump of a body hitting the floor. Takeshi turned on the gas. Minutes passed, and the soft patter of footsteps made her muscles constrict.

She quickly turned toward the metal bars, and Takeshi appeared like a deadly assassin in the night.

The bars quietly opened, his intimidating and larger-than-life presence speeding up her pulse as he entered her lone space. Takeshi's face was difficult to distinguish, but that characteristic deep voice hummed through the shadows.

"You ready, Kanes?"

Her chest rose in steady breaths, but her feet were rooted to the ground. Once she stepped out of those bars, there was no turning back.

"Didn't think you were coming for a second," Khalani admitted.

"As if that would stop you." The stimulating vibration of Takeshi's voice raised chills on her arms.

The silence stretched between them, and she didn't have to witness his obsidian eyes to know they burned right through. His intoxicating presence made it hard to think. Breathe. She cleared her throat and moved to leave.

"Wait." Takeshi pulled a black handgun out of his pocket. "Take this."

Her brows pierced together as he handed her the weapon. The weight and deadly feel made her palms itch and stomach coil.

"I don't need this." She handed the gun back to him, but Takeshi shook his head.

"Yes, you do. I won't let you do this light. Here is the safety. Only aim at what you intend to shoot, okay?" His tone brokered no room for argument, and Takeshi wouldn't let her leave until she nodded.

After he opened Serene's cell, Takeshi quickly led them both to the end of the hall where Derek, Adan, Brock, and Winnie were waiting. No prisoners stirred in their cells as they quietly raced through the dark.

Everyone except Takeshi and Brock slightly huddled over, sending hurried glances around, expecting a guard to shoot them at any moment. They each wore backpacks, and Brock handed Khalani and Serene loaded packs of their own. The weight dug into her back, and Brock shot a surprised look at Takeshi when he noticed the gun in her hand but said nothing.

"Let's go," Takeshi ordered.

Winnie squeezed Khalani's open hand as they followed silently behind. Just as Takeshi said, no guards were in sight, and alarms didn't blare as they ran to the elevator.

"Stay behind me," Takeshi reminded them as the elevator whirled up a few levels.

Khalani's heart threatened to pound out of her chest, and no one dared speak. Overwhelming fear filled the air as if demons tracked their very footsteps.

Once the elevator opened, Takeshi swiftly led them through a myriad of tunnels. He occasionally held his fist up and halted their advance while glancing at his watch, waiting endless minutes for a guard to pass before they continued their daring escape.

They walked through a continual maze for an eternity until they approached a small opening. In the distance, a sight she hadn't witnessed since they returned from Genesis. The Braderhelm entrance.

The gargantuan steel doors were more imposing and intimidating now than the first day she saw them. Two husky guards who looked like they could snap her back in half stood at attention with rifles resting on their shoulders. Takeshi waved his hand for them to crouch down, out of sight in the stone passage.

"See that stone pillar? I led us to this passage because it blocks most of their view. Brock and I will sneak behind the pillar and shoot the guards. Don't leave here until I give you the signal." Takeshi's rough stare flickered between them and centered on Khalani, sending nerves tingling through her spine.

Brock scooted to the front as Takeshi handed him a suppressed pistol with a harsh glint. "One wrong move, Death Zoner, and I will end you."

"Don't give me any ideas, Steele. Let's just get this over with," Brock hissed as he accepted the gun with a bitter glare.

Takeshi's jaw hardened, but he turned back to the gate. Just as Takeshi inched forward to head to the pillar, he quickly held out his fist to stop Brock as a newcomer strode toward the two guards from a different entrance.

The guards straightened as the unknown man dressed in a fine suit spoke with them.

"Who is that?" Brock whispered.

Takeshi shook his head in confusion. "It's the Warden. What's he doing here?" he muttered to himself.

Their bodies tensed as a boom sounded throughout the halls, and the Braderhelm doors slowly swung open. Khalani's face turned ashen, and her mouth gaped open as none other than Alexander Huxley walked through the gates.

"What the hell is going on?" Brock muttered furiously.

Flanked by two bodyguards, the Governor moved forward and shook hands with the Warden. After a few moments, the Warden gestured for the Governor and his guards to follow, bringing them close to their hideout. Khalani and the others pushed themselves against the wall as if they were fused together.

She closed her eyes and silently prayed with fervor and voracity for them not to be seen.

"Thank you for greeting us, Warden." The unique voice of Alexander Huxley reverberated through the cave. "I know we weren't expected until tomorrow, but with recent events, there is much we need to discuss in finding other uses for this space."

"Your assessment bodes well, Governor Huxley. I would be honored to serve as a Councilman and eliminate the traitors." The Warden chuckled.

The heavy footsteps led off through a separate hallway, the Governor's voice slowly dissipating like the scraping of dust. Khalani let out a deep breath as Takeshi continued to eye the two guards still stationed in front of the gate.

"Now." Takeshi gestured to Brock, and they snuck behind the stone pillar. They glanced at each other and nodded, aiming their guns at the guards. A second passed, and two soft zaps echoed from the guns, and both guards crashed to the floor with a loud thud.

Her eyes widened as Takeshi hurriedly waved them over.

"Move."

Like a shot out of a cannon, they ran for the open door. Khalani's legs beat under her, and she tripped over a rock and lost her footing, falling flat on her face. A strong arm quickly tugged Khalani to her feet.

"Don't stop, Kanes." Takeshi frowned, scanning over her with concern. She brushed herself off and continued forward when hard thumps sounded behind them.

They turned in horror as a guard appeared in the hallway, his eyes blaring in shock when he took in the scene before him. The young guard glanced at the two dead men on the ground and hastily shuffled a walkie out of his pocket.

"Code Red! We have an esc—"

Takeshi raised his gun and shot him in the head. The boy's eyes were still open in pure terror as he collapsed.

"Let's go!" He grabbed her arm as she picked her jaw from the floor, and they surged toward the doors. They bolted through the gates, and five transports were parked outside the entrance. Brock, Derek, Serene, and Adan were in one, and Winnie waited in the other.

"Hurry." Winnie waved them over.

Khalani and Takeshi raced forward. Takeshi got in the driver's seat, and as soon as she sat down, they raced off.

The wind beat her face as Takeshi drove the transport to its fastest limits. Her heart beat so fast, it numbed into one sound as they surged down the long, dark cave, away from Braderhelm.

A few minutes later, Brock pulled the transport to a screeching halt. Khalani had to brace a hand in front of her as Takeshi slammed on the brakes. They all jumped out, and Brock started feeling along the walls.

"Where are you?" Brock mumbled to himself.

Her anxiety was crippling as she nervously glanced in the direction of Braderhelm. If any guards heard that last message, they'd be coming down on their location any moment.

"Got it!" Brock exclaimed and flipped open a switch to reveal an electric pad. He quickly input a sequence of numbers and stood back in a flurry.

Nothing happened.

"Um, Brock, where's the secret entrance?" she asked.

Brock frowned and entered the numbers again. No movement. Not even a whisper.

"Shit!" He slammed the thing. "They must have changed the password."

Takeshi cursed as their plan began to crumble into a grave. There was no backup. Nowhere else they could escape or find refuge.

"Move out of the way!" Adan pushed Brock aside and started toying with the back of the pad, pulling wires out and connecting them.

The characteristic hum of transports shooting over magnets echoed down the ominous cave. They whipped their heads, an all-consuming fear coiling tight around their necks.

"Hurry, Adan!" Serene exclaimed.

"Just a sec." Adan frowned, laboring over the wires.

Bang!

A gunshot bounced off the walls, and they dropped to the ground, covering their heads. Lights from transports barreled at full speed, completely revealing their location. There was no cover or place to hide. A few more shots echoed past them, and Khalani heard someone cry out.

"Got it!" Adan yelled, and a small section of the wall parted, revealing an elevator.

They bounded inside, and Brock slammed the letter **S** on the dashboard. The doors finally swung close just as the transports arrived, and the ground shook beneath them as the elevator began rising.

She leaned back against the wall and breathed a huge sigh of relief.

They made it.

"Khalani," Winnie whimpered.

She turned to Winnie, who had blood pouring down her chest as she held a shaking hand to her collarbone.

Khalani's jaw dropped. Her lungs barely seemed to operate as she raced to Winnie's side. Blood continued to leak down Winnie's jumpsuit, and the coppery scent invaded the air.

"No, no, no! Winnie. J-just hang on!" Terror surged through her as if a knife tore into her stomach. This was not happening. Not to Winnie.

The elevator continued to fly up at full speed. Takeshi was immediately by her side, tying a piece of cloth from his backpack. "Where was she hit?"

"I don't know!" Khalani yelled, panicking. "Her shoulder, maybe. There's a lot of blood."

"Distract her, Kanes. This will hurt." Takeshi's searing gaze ripped into her.

Khalani's hands trembled as she placed the gun in her pocket and cupped Winnie's cheeks. "Hey, Winnie. It's me. Everything's going to be fine."

Winnie's face was pale, and her bottom lip quivered as Takeshi swiftly tied the cloth around her bloody shoulder.

"Just focus on me, Winnie. Right here." Khalani pointed toward her eyes. "That's it. I was thinking about your music. Especially Grease. Wait until we reach the surface, and we can sing like Danny Zuko." Winnie's mouth perceptibly lifted until Takeshi gave a tight tug of the knot. Her scream coincided with a shrill *bing* as the elevator doors opened.

A faraway glow illuminated their shocked faces. In front of them lay a clear, glass door. Through it, a tunnel led to an opening, pooling with the brightest light.

The surface was on the other side.

"C'mon, Winnie. Stay with me," Khalani added as sweat slid down Winnie's pale face, and she swayed on her feet. Khalani wrapped her arm around Winnie's waist as they hobbled out of the elevator. The doors closed as soon as they exited, and the elevator zoomed back down.

"We need to unlock the door," Brock said, racing over to a console against the wall as Adan rushed to help.

"See that, Winnie? We're almost there," she whispered as Winnie backed up to lean against the stone wall. Winnie's cheeks were getting paler by the second, and Khalani turned to Takeshi frantically.

"Will she be okay?" her voice shook as tears threatened to fall. Any answer other than yes was unacceptable to her.

Deep lines marred Takeshi's forehead. "I hope so, Kanes."

"We're in!" Brock exclaimed as the glass doors parted open.

Takeshi went to the other side of Winnie and helped support her weight as the others raced through the tunnel. The glass door shut soundly behind them, and Khalani and Takeshi moved as fast as they could, supporting Winnie—which wasn't fast at all—but the light from the tunnel grew brighter, and rampant energy surged her forward.

Voices shouted past the glass barrier. Khalani quickly turned her head as the Governor, the Warden, and several guards entered the cave.

"Open the door!" the Governor yelled at a guard.

"We can't, sir! The radiation will kill us!" the Warden denied.

"Move faster," Takeshi growled as they raced forward, practically carrying Winnie off the ground.

"You stupid fools! I will do it!" Alexander Huxley screamed.

The glass doors whirled open behind them, and adrenaline raged through her muscles as they surged forward. She squinted, her pulse racing as the light intensified, completely engulfing their bodies as they charged out of the tunnel onto a sandy surface. Warmth caressed her skin and enveloped them like a cloak.

Sunlight pierced her eyes, and Khalani held out her right hand, shielding her face.

"The surface," Winnie breathed out next to her in a weak voice.

Khalani slowly lifted her hand away, and her body stopped, entirely ceasing movement as if frozen in time.

A gigantic dome didn't rise over them. Earth and stone failed to cover her head. On the earth's surface, the skies were a clear, crystal blue, and the burning sun was so blinding that the rays nearly eclipsed her vision.

She glanced around in shock. They appeared to be in a flat desert with collapsed buildings and rubble scattered throughout. Weird vehicles were strung about, their metal torn and rusted. Every object lay in desolation.

Ruin never looked so beautiful.

Khalani breathed in deeply. Even the air smelled and tasted different. Free. They were free.

"Don't go any further!" Alexander Huxley's voice yelled.

They whirled, and the Governor stood before them, alone. Takeshi held onto Winnie and pulled out his gun, aiming at him.

Alexander raised his arms by his side in innocence. "I have no weapons. I come to you in peace. Why don't you all just come back, and we can sort this out? I can even grant your freedom in Braderhelm."

His lies scraped against her skin, and Khalani pulled the gun out of her pocket and took a predatory step forward. "All you do is lie. Was there ever any radiation on the surface?"

Alexander's lip lifted. "Oh, I assure you, there once was. Battles raged on the very ground you stand on. Apollo saved countless lives, and only beneath the earth can those worst instincts be controlled. As you can see, there is nothing out here, nothing but death."

"In *Apollo*, there is nothing but death. It was you, wasn't it? You're the one responsible for destroying the crops." The truth bellowed from her tongue.

The Governor raised an eyebrow.

"Perceptive. Rather...poetic, isn't it? They view me as their savior when I've been biding my time, waiting for the day to strike back."

"WHY?!" she screamed, the gun noticeably shaking. "Why would you do that?"

"You know less than you could possibly dream," Huxley stated in a bored voice as if they were talking about geological formations. "You don't see it now, but this is for everyone's benefit. All you have to do is trust me."

Khalani let out a humorless laugh. "Anyone who trusts you is either stupid or insane. You've kept us locked away to cover up your lies for decades. But that ends now. We're leaving, and we'll spread the truth about the surface and the atrocities of what you've done in Apollo," Khalani hissed, her grip on the gun tightening.

The Governor's chilling smile turned into an angry scowl. "Nothing will change what is coming. *Nothing.* You'll die with the rest of them, just like your parents."

Madness coiled inside her, threatening to strike and dismember as their faces flashed in her mind.

She was no longer empty, patched with voids. All the pain and suffering she'd endured filled her cracks and crevices, the need for violence suppressing any mercy left in her. The old her would've cowered beneath the weight of such fury, but she was no longer beholden to the rules of the underground.

On the surface of the earth, humanity's greatest victory and heaviest burden was always free will.

Khalani raised her gun and shot Alexander Huxley in the chest.

The Governor didn't move. He didn't fall to the ground. Alexander glanced down at his chest…and *smiled*.

"That wasn't very nice." He smirked as Khalani's hands shook, and her eyes nearly popped out of their sockets.

Brock moved forward and threw all his weight into a punch straight toward the Governor's head, but Alexander caught Brock's wrist as if he weighed no more than a feather. With a sinister grin, he snapped Brock's arms back like a pretzel, and Brock released a shattering scream.

Quick as a flash, Takeshi crashed into the Governor like a train, taking the both of them to the ground. Takeshi immediately seized up and smashed his fist into the Governor's face, but the Governor freed his arm and punched under Takeshi's chin. Takeshi whipped his head back, and Alexander captured the advantage, quickly flipping Takeshi and kneeling over him.

When Alexander started railing his fists into Takeshi's face, blood sprayed into the dusted sand like confetti. Pure terror cut and slashed her apart as if her own body was being butchered. She didn't think. She barreled ahead with laser focus.

"Get off him!" she ferally screamed, lunging toward the Governor.

With a snap, Alexander Huxley clutched her throat in his bare hand. His cold, blue eyes were filled with hostility as he squeezed his fingers and began crushing her windpipe. It felt like her throat was being molded to the size of a straw. Black encompassed the outer edges of her vision as she desperately heaved for an ounce of oxygen. Nothing came.

She clawed the palm gripping her like a wild, trapped animal, but the fingers only tightened their chokehold. Her movements grew slower, sluggish. A gargle escaped her lips, eyes slowly rolling to the back of her head. And Khalani knew this was the end.

No matter how hard she fought, death always returned for her.

A piercing and agonizing roar interrupted her bitter acceptance, and the deadly hand around her throat was ripped away. Khalani collapsed to the sand, choking and heaving as if her throat were filled with scorching sand. Saliva dripped from her mouth as gentle hands came around her body.

"I've got you. Just breathe," Derek's voice shook. Her blurred vision barely made him out, but Derek wasn't staring at her.

Khalani twisted her head.

Time was utterly suspended as Takeshi stood over Alexander Huxley's dead body. Quite literally dead because the Governor's head was no longer attached to his torso.

Takeshi's obsidian eyes weren't fixated on the Governor but on Khalani's hunched-over frame as he raced over, panting heavily.

"Are you alright, Kanes?" He knelt beside her, pure brutality etched on the edges of his face, the vehemence in his expression staggering.

"Yeah." She coughed, attempting to move, but Takeshi's strong arms entirely supported Khalani as she rose to wobbly feet.

"You ripped off his head," Serene whispered in alarm, staring at Takeshi with wide eyes.

"Guys," Adan voiced from afar.

Takeshi's eyes roved over Khalani, jaw tightening over each and every injury. His mouth set in a hard line as he turned to Serene.

"And I'd do it again," he declared without regret.

"You...you ripped off someone's head," Serene repeated incredulously.

"Guys!" Adan yelled. "You need to look at this."

They paused at Adan's shaken voice and walked over to where he was standing, staring at Alexander Huxley's decapacitated body. Derek helped Winnie as they slowly walked closer.

Brock stumbled over, still clutching his dislocated elbow in pain, and his mouth dropped open.

Jagged heaps of metal and wires were sticking out of the Governor's torn neck. The crackling of electricity sounded where the body still twitched. Khalani looked to where the Governor's head was on the ground. His blue, dead eyes stared straight through her, and if it weren't for Takeshi holding her up, her trembling body would've sunk to the ground.

"He's not human," Derek breathed out in shock.

"He was a machine." Adan's face paled.

No one spoke as they stared at the Governor's lifeless body. The impossible lay before them, shaking their very reality. Upending the foundations of her world. The man she hated with her entire being was never a real person, only a twisted mess of wires who controlled their entire lives.

Fiction and reality bled into one piece, and Khalani dug her nails into her palm with brutal force, as if to test whether she could still bleed, whether she was real too…

"This is crazy. This is…" Serene scraped her hands through her frazzled hair. "This is insane. Did you know about this?" She swiveled to Takeshi, her fingers noticeably shaking.

"No," Takeshi denied fervently. "If I did, I would've murdered him the first chance I got," Takeshi spoke with such voracity and loathing that Khalani believed him.

"But what does this mean?!"

"Does it matter?" Brock growled, and they turned to him in shock. "We can't go back to Apollo. You all know that. Our path to Hermes remains the same, and we only have supplies for two weeks. We have to push forward."

No one moved for a long time, but Adan slowly grabbed his bag and put a protective arm around Serene, her eyes like blank mirrors as Adan urged her forward. Khalani didn't miss the distrusting glance he sent Takeshi's way.

The others slowly gathered their stuff with shell-shocked eyes as

Derek put his arm around Winnie's waist and helped her walk.

Her friends moved as if they had no choice. In the present, nightmares lived in reality, and the truth resided in fables. And the clock could never be rewound.

"I don't understand." Khalani's stare fixated on the Governor's lone head, frayed wiring sticking out of where his neck used to be.

"I don't either. But this…*machine* prevented us from finding the truth about the surface. And we're going to find out why." Takeshi's expression darkened as his powerful stare shifted from the Governor to her. He glanced at the apparent marks on her neck, and a chilling frenzy brewed in his gaze. Takeshi opened his mouth.

"We need to go now!" Brock yelled from behind them.

Takeshi shut his mouth with a snap, shaking his head. Still, his dark eyes communicated so much more, like she was the burning sun and brisk moon, striking and far-reaching, forever destined to be apart.

Her mind grappled with the impossibility of the moment. Millions of questions swirled in her mind when all that lay before them was misery, death, and destruction. But she had no choice but to put Apollo behind and embrace the earth before her, like a poem waiting to be written.

And for every *thing* or person who stood in her way, she'd etch their poem in blood.

THE ADVENTURE CONTINUES...

US DEADLY FEW

COMING DECEMBER 5, 2024

ACKNOWLEDGMENTS

Mom—Thank you for being my number one cheerleader and cultivating my love for literature. It's because of you that I am the writer I am. Your edits throughout my book helped the story immensely. Truthfully, it would take a whole other book to list out everything you have done for me. I love you. Forever and Always.

Dad—Thank you for believing in me and always making me feel like I can accomplish anything. Your suggestions have made the story so much more exciting, and I am so grateful to have a father who cares so much. The Greatest Dad Award goes to you.

Christina—Thank you for all your critiques, even the ones where you said 'ew' and 'vomit'. Haha. Honestly, you helped shape the book to be so much grittier and intense, and I am so thankful and grateful for you. You are the best sister I could ever ask for.

Rodney—Thank you for your suggestions early on that helped my writing *mean* something more. I learned from you that every sentence should have a purpose. Our principals...our lives *matter,* and we can make a difference. You continue to show me how to push forward and not give up.

Kyle—Wow. This book is so much better because of you. Thank you for helping shape Takeshi Steele, for reading every page in my book, and for coming up with the title! I love you with all my heart and I am so excited for our many adventures to come.

Kristofer Mehaffey—Have to put the full name in there so everyone knows who designed the incredible book cover!! You are so talented; it blows my mind. Thank you for putting up with me and all my last-minute changes. I'm truly grateful for you and that my brother has great taste in friends. :)

Annie—Thank you for your support since I was little and your encouragement for me to continue reading, even the books that had eyebrow-raising romance. You inspire me endlessly and I love you so much.

Justine—Thank you for your endless encouragement and for your edits early on that helped improve the book. You are wonderful, and I am so excited for our future nights where we dance to French music, drink wine, and not have a care in the world.

Abuelo—Gracias por siempre estar ahí para mi y por tu apoyo. Te quiero muchisimo.

Tom—You made it ☺ I'm so happy you're in my life. Thank you for the support.

Thank You!

There are so many books to read in the world, and you choosing mine makes my heart shine brighter than any star I could dare hold. If you enjoyed reading Us Dark Few, please leave a review to help me continue creating and sharing stories like this. Continue to bellow out your descents, beliefs, and dreams for all to hear.

With Love,
Alexis Patton

Printed in Great Britain
by Amazon